ACROSS A MOONLIT CITY,
A PUZZLE ETCHED IN BLOOD...

With the rifle in his hands, he positioned himself at the left side of the window, braced his body against the frame and stared out.

He watched through the scope and picked his target as it moved up the approach lanes to the bridge. The big yellow Checker cab swung for the center lane. Reynolds held his breath and squeezed off the shot.

An explosion of flame blinded him as the incendiary bullet hit the trunk of the cab and blew the gas tank. The flaming cab twisted in midair, hurling fire across the width of the bridge.

Reynolds, pulling back from the window and the fiery ballet of death, thought he could hear screams from the inferno . . .

**A SPELLBINDING THRILLER OF
NERVE-SEARING SUSPENSE**

THE RANDOM FACTOR

LINDA J. LA ROSA
BARRY TANENBAUM

J

A JOVE BOOK

Printed in the United States of America

Library of Congress Catalog Card Number: 77-82764

First Jove edition published July 1979

Jove books are published by Jove Publications, Inc., 200 Madison
Avenue, New York, NY 10016

Prologue

The cab crawled in snowblind traffic up the FDR Drive. Long overdue for the scrap heap, the ancient Checker's clattering heater blew lukewarm air, and one of the wipers scraped against the cold glass of the windshield, setting Reynolds' teeth on edge.

He huddled in the back seat, ignoring the snarls of the driver.

"Nobody has any brains anymore, y' know? I mean this storm started at three o'clock, right? You'd think these stiffs would know enough to get the hell out of the city early, right? Oh no, not them . . . take their own sweet time. Serve 'em right if they don't get home till midnight."

He hit the horn, swerved to the right, and went up over the curb to get around a line of cars blocking the Fifty-ninth Street exit. "Goddamn commuters," he swore.

Reynolds said nothing. It was eight-thirty, and he had been in the cab for over twenty minutes, trying to get to Clarkson Manor from his office on Nassau Street in lower Manhattan.

The cab lurched around a double-parked truck and skidded to a stop at Park Avenue. "Goddamn truck . . . I coulda made that light," the driver protested.

"I'll get out here," Reynolds said abruptly.

"Suit yourself, buddy. That's seven-fifty."

Reynolds passed a five and three ones through the opening in the Plexiglas divider, ingoring the sarcastic "thanks a

7

lot" from the driver. Reynolds stepped out into the street, pulled his overcoat collar up, and began walking the two blocks to the Manor.

The sidewalk in front of Clarkson Manor was clear of snow, and white salt dotted the cement. One of the last of a dying breed of exclusive men's clubs in New York City, Clarkson took special care of its members.

Reynolds pulled open the double doors and stepped inside. In here, he thought, the world is shut out . . . and thank God for that.

He shrugged out of his overcoat and handed it across the split door of the checkroom. The attendant took the coat, smiled, and said, "Good evening, Mr. Reynolds. Quite a mess out there. Looks like it's going to be the worst February on record."

Reynolds nodded. "Are the others here?"

"Yes, sir. Mr. Birmingham was the last to arrive, about twenty minutes ago."

"Would you have a drink sent up, please?"

"Of course, Mr. Reynolds."

Reynolds walked toward the staircase, glancing left to the paneled bar, alive with firelight and small talk. A corridor to his right led to the library, and beyond that, the game room. The stairs curved up and down. Downstairs, Clarkson offered its members a gym, two handball courts, a sauna, and a steam room. Upstairs were the private meeting rooms, twenty in all.

Reynolds took the stairs up and let himself in to the third room on the left. At the round table in the center, Andrew Birmingham looked up from his backgammon game with Richard Lyle. "We'd given up on you," Birmingham said.

"I was ready to give up on myself," Reynolds said. "A little snow and the city becomes a disaster area." He moved behind Lyle and studied the board.

"You can have the winner," Lyle said, not turning around.

Birmingham winked at Reynolds. From the corner of the room came Ed Marcus' voice: "You missed a fine dinner, Chris."

Marcus was stretched on the sofa, eyes closed. Reynolds sat down in the chair next to him. "I had a few sandwiches at the office . . . had to get some paperwork done. If I had to face it again tomorrow, I think I'd have burned it."

Marcus laughed and opened his eyes. "What's the big deal this time?"

"Not big, just complicated. I'm trying to . . ."

A knock at the door interrupted him, and Reynolds rose to admit a waiter. "A lifesaver," Reynolds said, taking his Johnny Walker Black from the tray. "Thank you."

The waiter nodded and turned to the others. "Another round, gentlemen?"

"Sounds good to me," Marcus answered.

"Bring 'em on," Lyle ordered, hoisting his huge frame out of the chair. "Chris, you're up. Maybe you can beat the whiz kid."

The waiter left silently as Reynolds took the empty chair opposite Birmingham. "Don't feel too bad," he consoled Lyle. "He's the best at this game."

Reynolds swiftly positioned his pieces and rolled a single die onto the board. Lyle stood behind him, watching the play: Birmingham going with the odds, moving with precision; Reynolds opening up, taking chances.

The round of drinks was delivered, and Marcus shook himself off the sofa, stretched, and went to the window. He stared down at Fifty-seventh Street. "They expect five or six inches," he said.

Reynolds looked up from the board. "Which, as I said, is a major disaster."

"A major disaster," Birmingham said, sliding one of his

pieces, "is leaving a blot six away from my point." He took Reynolds' piece off the board.

"Next victim," Lyle laughed.

"I concede nothing," Reynolds said with a smile. He rolled but was blocked out. Birmingham's roll allowed him to close off his inner board.

Reynolds pushed his chair back. "I concede everything."

Birmingham looked at Marcus. "Care to try your luck?"

"Luck?" Marcus laughed. "Since when is anything you do based on luck?"

"Wait a minute," Reynolds interrupted. "Before you start another game, I've got a new one for you." He moved to a corner chair.

Marcus and Lyle joined Birmingham at the table. They settled back, facing Reynolds. "Shoot," Lyle said.

"Okay," Reynolds began. "Situation: Every morning Mr. Jones leaves his apartment on the fourteenth floor of his building, takes the elevator down to the lobby, leaves the building, and goes to work. When he returns in the evening, he crosses the lobby, gets into the elevator, pushes the button for the *tenth* floor, rides up, gets off, and takes the stairs up the remaining four floors. He does this, exactly as I've told you, four out of five nights of the week." Reynolds paused, sipped his drink, and settled back in the chair, watching their faces. "Now, the question: Why?"

"Why what?" Lyle asked.

"Why does he walk up four flights of stairs, four out of five nights?"

"Is this totally logical . . . the answer, I mean?" Marcus asked.

"Totally," Reynolds said smiling.

"Okay," Lyle began, "is he trying to avoid someone?"

"Nope"

"Does he visit someone on the tenth floor?"

"No."

"He needs the exercise," Lyle joked.

Reynolds shook his head.

"Why not five out of five times?" Birmingham wondered aloud.

"Good question," Reynolds said, "but I only give yes-or-no answers."

Birmingham frowned. "He doesn't meet anyone on the tenth floor?"

"No meetings."

"They shut electricity off and the elevator stops," Marcus laughed.

"This is a luxury apartment, not a slum," Reynolds said.

"There are no elevators in slums," Lyle said.

Reynolds laughed. *"Touché."*

"Let's get back to it," Marcus said. "We need more information. Is it important to know what Mr. Jones does for a living?"

"Not important," Reynolds said.

"Does he come home late, or early, on these nights?"

"Doesn't matter. Let's say he gets home around six."

Marcus shrugged. "Why the hell does he walk up four flights if he doesn't have to?"

Reynolds' eyes danced.

"That's just it," Birmingham said, his voice rising. "He must have to, right?"

"That's right," Reynolds agreed.

"Okay, he *has* to walk up four flights," Lyle said. "Why?"

"That's the question, remember?" Reynolds taunted.

"You just love to see us squirm," Marcus said, shaking his head.

Birmingham stared at Reynolds. "Wait a minute: That fifth time, does he take the elevator all the way up to the fourteenth floor?"

"Yes, he does."

"Then what we're looking for is, why is that fifth time different?"

"You could put it that way," Reynolds acknowledged.

"Is the day of the week important . . . when he goes all the way up?" Lyle asked.

"No."

"Wait a minute," Marcus said, snapping his fingers. "Is this guy alone in the elevator?"

"When?" Reynolds asked innocently.

"When? When? On the four nights?"

"Yes," Reynolds said, smiling.

"But he's not alone on the fifth night?" Marcus pressed.

"Right."

"Which means," Birmingham said, "that on the fifth night, when he goes all the way up, the fact that someone else is on the elevator with him is the reason he can go all the way up. . . ."

"Meaning?" Reynolds prompted.

"I haven't the vaguest idea," Marcus muttered.

"Is it the same person?" Lyle asked. "The same one every time he goes all the way to fourteen?"

"Doesn't have to be," Reynolds said. "It really doesn't matter."

"Let's get back to where we were," Birmingham said. "When someone else is in the elevator, it means he doesn't have to walk up the four flights."

"He has to walk up those other nights," Marcus added.

Reynolds smiled and studied their faces. Marcus looked as if he was in physical combat, his thin features twisting this way and that as he wrestled with the problem. Lyle sat stiffly, his face blank, fingers drumming on his knees. Birmingham stared at Reynolds, as if the answer could be read in his eyes.

Reynolds knew their minds were racing; each one gloried in solving a logic puzzle.

"Chris," Birmingham began cautiously, "is there something wrong with Mr. Jones? Is that the reason someone has to be in the elevator for him to go up to the fourteenth floor?"

"Yes," Reynolds said.

"Wait, wait, I've got it," Marcus shouted, jumping up. "He's short, he's . . ."

". . . a midget," Birmingham said flatly.

"And he can't reach the elevator buttons higher than the tenth floor," Lyle said, shaking his head in exasperation.

Reynolds finished his drink. "Nice going, Ed. It was a tough one."

"They seem so obvious when you finally get them," Marcus smiled.

Reynolds nodded. It was fascinating to watch them, to compare their styles. Birmingham calmly waiting for the flash of inspiration that would put the pieces together; Lyle plodding ahead, nailing down details, trying to build an answer; and Marcus thrashing the problem into submission. And he, himself, with the power of the answer, leading them along.

"Have you got another one?" Marcus asked, flushed with success.

Reynolds shook his head. "No, not tonight. They're hard to come by. As soon as I hear a new one, you'll know it."

"We ought to try to make one up," Lyle said.

"Very hard," Reynolds said. "I've tried a few times."

"Well, they come from somewhere," Lyle persisted. "Someone has to think them up."

"Right, and why not us?" Marcus asked.

"I'd rather play poker," Reynolds said.

"No, wait a minute," Marcus said firmly. "We can play poker any night. Let's see if we can do it."

"Ed . . ." Reynolds began.

"Let's just try, okay?"

Reynolds stood up. "Just look at this: Four middle-aged men arguing over whether or not to think up a logic puzzle."

"Why not try?" Birmingham asked. "We've even got a beginning: four middle-aged men . . ."

". . . meet once a week for dinner and cards," Marcus picked it up.

"Or backgammon," Lyle added.

"Or backgammon, or handball, or anything," Reynolds snapped.

"And these men have been friends for a long time," Marcus continued.

"And are boring each other to death," Reynolds said.

"Oh come on," Marcus said, beginning to get annoyed, "help out."

"You want help? All right, I'll help." Reynolds began to pace around the table. "Situation: Four long-time friends have dinner together every Thursday night. Afterward they play cards at their club. These are not your run-of-the-mill men, however. Oh no, not these four. At one time they were quite extraordinary." He turned to face them. "Quite extraordinary," he repeated, beginning to pace again. "But now they're reduced to logic puzzles and poker, handball . . . and, of course, the day-to-day challenges," he twisted the word sarcastically and repeated it: "challenges of their business lives. Reduced to trivial things."

"What the hell are you talking about?" Lyle asked, a deep frown creasing his features.

"He's talking about us," Birmingham said.

"All right, forget it," Marcus said. "It was a bad idea. Let's let it drop."

"Oh no, let's not let it drop," Reynolds argued. "We've brought it this far, let's carry it to the logical conclusion. You wanted a logic puzzle, right?"

"What's bothering you?" Marcus asked quietly.

Reynolds said, "I don't know. Maybe working too hard."

"Problems?" Birmingham asked.

Reynolds waved it off. "No, no problems. That's the

problem, no problems." He laughed. "The same damn routine . . ."

There was silence. Each man knew what he meant, but it wasn't something they talked about, even with each other.

"So," Reynolds said, picking it up, "there you are, your situation. Now, given what you know about these four men, the question is: What the hell should they do now?"

 for was a local, and Wickie worried about the governor of

Part I

1

He stood motionless, hidden in the shadows at the front of the alley. A stiff March wind threw scraps of paper against the concrete walls, and his breath frosted the air.

From his position he had a perfect view of the Shamrock Bar and Grill, diagonally across the street.

The stalking had taken him through the long St. Patrick's Day, from early morning when Sean McMahon cheered the marching bands downtown, to parties in bars and apartments all over Manhattan. Now it was almost over: McMahon, his wife, teen-aged son, and a dozen of his friends were wrapping up the day in the bar McMahon owned.

Suddenly the door of the tavern jerked open and the babble of voices spilled out across the street. The party was breaking up, the celebrants bidding drunken good nights as they staggered off in different directions. The street returned to silence.

Sean McMahon was still inside the Shamrock.

In the alley, Christopher Reynolds smiled. He had his man alone at three-thirty in the morning.

Soon, Reynolds thought. McMahon would be cleaning up, washing glasses, placing chairs around the tables, polishing the long bar.

Finally the lights in the tavern began to wink out, and

with the last light, Reynolds knelt and opened a black at-
taché case. Nestled in custom-cut Styrofoam pieces were
blue-black metal sections. With practiced ease, Reynolds
slipped them out one at a time, fastened them together, and
moved to the mouth of the alley with the fully assembled
.30-caliber Remington resting easily in the crook of his
arm.

McMahon was on the sidewalk, drawing the heavy iron
grating across the front of the window. He snapped a pad-
lock in place. Reynolds glanced left and right: no one but
McMahon, now moving toward him on the opposite sidewalk. Reynolds raised the rifle and picked up McMahon's
figure in the sniperscope.

"Drunk," he said softly to himself. "Drunken Irishman
. . . you won't even make it to the corner."

The rifle tracked McMahon, and thirty paces from the
end of the block, Reynolds knew it was right.

The silenced weapon made virtually no sound, and Sean
McMahon never made it to the corner.

The call came over the police radio as Deputy Chief
Carl Enders sat at his desk working on reports. Over
twenty years of police work had conditioned him to sort
from the stream of calls and codes those coming from a
patrol car in his command, the Fifth Homicide Zone. Se-
lective tuning, Enders called it. Every cop has it, that ability to pick his number, his district, out of the scramble,
letting the rest drift by like Muzak.

It was almost four-thirty in the morning when the radio
crackled, "34 Frank. Send Homicide, Forensic, and an ambulance, 193rd between Fort George and Audubon."

Thirty-four Frank was Billy (the Kid) Krieg and his
partner, Ted Mallory. Krieg had been Enders' driver for a
year before being assigned to a patrol car. And tonight he
had a homicide.

Enders pushed the reports aside, reached for the phone, and dialed the garage.

"This is Enders. Bring my car around."

He pulled on his overcoat, switched off the radio and the lights, and left the office. Blake is going to have a fit, Enders thought, as he hurried out of the building.

Officer Ron Blake brought Enders' sedan to a smooth stop in front of the building, reached across, and opened the passenger-side door. Unlike most of the brass, Enders preferred to ride up front with the driver. A policeman serving as a chauffeur annoyed him, but since he couldn't do anything about the procedure, he did the next best thing by creating an illusion of two cops out on the job.

Blake didn't care much either way. The plain fact was that Enders was driving him crazy. It was Enders' habit to work sixteen to eighteen hours at a stretch, head home for a few hours' sleep, and call for the car to take him back to the office, which wouldn't be bad if Enders kept a regular schedule. It was Blake's misfortune that the deputy chief kept varying hours.

Blake got calls at noon. Blake got calls at three in the morning. Blake got calls, period. He was ready to put in for a transfer. Or a divorce.

Billy the Kid, on the other hand, had loved it. "Some guys bitch about this duty, you know," Krieg had told Enders on the second day he drove for him. "They think it's a waste." He glanced quickly at Enders, adding, "No offense, boss."

Enders laughed. "No offense. I know what the men think of driving the brass."

"Well, you see," Krieg went on earnestly, "I feel differently about it. I figure that since I drew the assignment, I might as well get as much as I can out of this."

Enders, puzzled, asked, "What can you possibly get out of this?"

He never did get an answer from Krieg, but as the weeks

and months passed, it became obvious. Krieg questioned everything, politely, with respect, but persistently and firmly. He picked up bits and pieces of Enders' experience, satisfying his appetite for the details of procedure, the structure of the department—the "inside information," as Krieg liked to call it.

Krieg never complained about the hours, kept Enders in almost constant conversation, and at the end of the year's duty had soaked up everything the deputy chief had to offer. Krieg had also earned a lasting nickname, compliments of a fellow rookie who saw that Billy's look of baby-faced innocence masked a streak of ruthless ambition. Krieg, accused of hunting for a "guardian angel"—an upper-echelon officer who would watch out for him and, when the time was right, push him fast and far in the department—shrugged innocently, his disarming smile his only defense.

For Carl Enders, who often looked across the seat at Krieg behind the wheel and saw himself twenty-five years ago, the relationship was perfect. Divorced, with two children away at college, Enders at forty-six needed someone who needed him, for whatever reason. Tired of the desk-bound duties of a deputy chief, his once-boyish face showing puffiness and hard lines around the eyes, his sandy hair rapidly graying, Enders allowed himself to fall easily into the role of father figure. Besides, he often told himself, Billy is a smart cop and deserves a break.

Blake had eased the car around the corner of 193rd, and Enders saw the dark bulk of the Forensic van, then two squad cars, an unmarked sedan, and the ambulance clogging the far end of the street.

The familiar chaos of a crime-scene investigation took shape as Enders watched. He felt his weariness slip away and he stepped sharply from the car, clipped his badge to his coat, and walked to the sidewalk. Two ambulance attendants crouched beside a crumpled form.

"He's dead," Enders heard one of them say, and the six-man Forensic team moved in. Over their shoulders Enders saw the victim: a heavy-set man in his early fifties, sprawled on his back, arms outstretched. The right side of his dark brown overcoat had been torn away, and with it half the man's chest.

"Jesus," Enders muttered, turning. He spotted two homicide detectives hovering at the outer edge of the circle of Forensic specialists: Cross and McQuade, partners for more years than anyone remembered. Almost interchangeable, they were solid, meticulous investigators. Unimaginative bulls, Enders thought.

Cross was listening to one of the ambulance attendants, while McQuade, gracefully sidestepping a police photographer, sketched the crime scene on a clipboard pad.

One of the Forensic men was measuring with a long tape, jotting down the distances: the body from the street; the body from the wall; the body from the nearest lamppost. Two other members of the team played flashlight beams in crisscross patterns over the pavement. Across the street, the remaining Forensic investigators poked their flashlights into the dark mouth of an alley.

Enders noted it all, the shapes of investigation. He had seen it hundreds of times. When it was over—the body hustled downtown to Bellevue for autopsy, the crime scene roped off, all the possible bits of evidence picked up, bagged, and tagged—all that would remain would be a chalk outline on the sidewalk to signify that a dozen men had been there, applying their specialized talents.

Enders was following a flashlight beam as it darted around the body when he saw something. "What's that?" he called to the Forensic man, who knelt and with a pair of tweezers picked a brown leather wallet from the sidewalk where it had lain partially hidden by the victim's coat.

With a second pair of tweezers, the man spread the wallet open. Enders saw a wad of bills. He frowned, then nodded, and the wallet went into an evidence bag.

Enders motioned to Cross, who had watched the scene in silence.

"Stuffed with money," Enders said.

"We didn't figure robbery. The guys from the ambulance say our friend here was blown apart. A stick-up artist doesn't make that kind of mess."

"How do you figure the wallet, then? What's it doing on the sidewalk?"

Cross shrugged. "Maybe the guy had it in his hands when he was hit and it just dropped."

Enders shook his head. Something was wrong, but he couldn't put his finger on it. "Go over the wallet very carefully," he said. "I want to know if anything's missing."

"Like what?"

"Like I don't know what . . . that's the point."

"Okay, boss," Cross muttered sourly. Enders was making extra work. A deputy chief gets all homicide reports sooner or later, but Enders' tone implied that he wanted this one right away.

"I want to know by ten o'clock," Enders added, in case Cross didn't get the message.

Cross nodded and turned away. Enders watched the Forensic team for several moments as they picked up everything on the sidewalk within a twenty-foot radius of the body. Cigarette butts, bottle caps, bits of paper, all the gutter garbage was treated in the same way: plucked gently like jewels with the ever-present tweezers and dropped into plastic bags for analysis at the police lab.

"Got some metal fragments," one of the men said to Enders. "Might be slivers from the bullet."

"I'd like a report by ten," Enders said. The man nodded and went back to poking at the pavement.

Enders crossed the street. Cross and McQuade stood in front of the alley.

"This where the shot came from?" Enders asked.

"That's what they tell us," McQuade said, gesturing toward the Forensic van.

"About sixty yards," Enders said, shaking his head. "Must have been something big to scramble the guy that way. Did you get anything from the alley?"

"Forensic pulled a ton of shit out of there, but there's no way to pick everything up."

"We may have to," Enders said shortly. "Rope it off . . . whatever the wind doesn't take we can pick up in daylight."

Cross walked deliberately to one of the squad cars and spoke briefly to a patrolman. The officer nodded, went to the trunk of his car, and lifted out two stanchions and a heavy, braided yellow rope. The alley would be sealed off.

At the perimeter of the scene stood two uniformed officers, and Enders recognized the tall, slim figure of Billy the Kid; 34 Frank was still around.

Enders came up to them as Krieg leaned back against the fender of his car. Mallory stood straight, hands in his pockets, watching the mopping up.

"Are you responsible for this mess?" Enders asked, smiling.

"I only report what I see," Krieg answered, returning the smile. Mallory glanced at Krieg, a puzzled look on his face. Krieg caught the expression and realized that although he and Enders were friends, the deputy chief was still brass and they weren't alone.

"If you don't mind my asking, sir, what brings you out on this?"

"It was a good excuse to get away from my desk for a while. Did you see anything before you found the body?"

"Not a thing. It was a nothing night till we spotted him on the sidewalk. At first I thought he was drunk, passed out, y'know? But I couldn't rouse him . . . and then I saw blood all over the place."

25

"Witnesses?"

Mallory answered, "No, sir, not as far as we know. The ghouls were out, though." He gestured to the windows of the apartments lining the block. Lights were on and dark figures stood behind slightly parted curtains. "We had quite a crowd for a cold night, until we started taking names. Then they decided it was better to do their looking form inside."

Enders smiled. Blood brought them out onto the streets, but a policeman asking for names and addresses reminded them not to get involved. It didn't make any difference. Everybody on the block would be visited by detectives.

Enders saw the ambulance attendants lift the body, slide a plastic body-bag underneath, and begin to zip the corpse in. It was winding down. "Billy," Enders said, "stop by my office after you check in."

"Sure. Anything wrong?"

"Just want to talk."

"Okay, I'll be there."

Enders made one more tour of the area: stopping at the ambulance, where the body was being strapped in; the Forensic van, where a suitcase full of plastic evidence-bags was being clicked shut; and the unmarked homicide car, where Cross and McQuade were finishing the crime-scene sketch. At every stop Enders reminded the men that he wanted reports by ten o'clock.

He slipped back into his car. "Okay, Ron, you can drive me home."

There was no reply. Ron Blake was sound asleep.

Enders was filling a lined sheet of paper with notes, questions, and possible answers when Krieg knocked on the door of his office at nine-thirty. The reports would clear up some of the questions, but Enders kept coming back to the wallet. He had a feeling that nothing the lab or the medical

THE RANDOM FACTOR

examiner or the homicide detectives uncovered would answer that one: Why had the killer pulled the wallet? Enders was sure he, or she, had. But why?

He glanced up at the sound of the knock. "Yeah?"

Krieg, looking pale and tired, came in.

"You ID the body?" Enders asked.

Krieg nooded. "I could do without it."

"Yeah, but we couldn't. Keeps the medical examiner honest."

Krieg looked puzzled, and Enders went on: "It's not a joke, Billy. We get a dozen homicides a night, average. It's a lot to keep track of."

"I think the family was coming in as I was leaving. Middle-aged lady and a kid . . . a teen-ager."

"That's the final, positive ID. I should be getting the reports within the hour. Then we'll see what we can make of this."

"You're really working on it?"

"It's just strange enough to interest me," Enders acknowledged. "The pieces don't fit . . . yet."

"Is that what you wanted to see me about?"

"Well, partly. I really wanted to ask you if you'd like a shot at Detective Division."

Krieg's eyes widened and he started to reply. Enders held up his hand and went on. "I'll assign you to the squad to work with me on this case. It's a temporary assignment. We'll see how it goes. If you're good at it and you like it, I can make it permanent."

"I'd love it," Krieg said.

"I thought you would," Enders said, grinning. "But make sure; it's a big change for you, and remember, it's only the chance to make detective. You've got to be ready, because if you don't make it . . ."

". . . I may not get another chance."

"Think it over, Billy."

"Yes, sir, I will. And thank you."

27

Krieg let himself out of the office as Enders went back to his list.

In the hallway, Mallory lounged against the wall. "What was that all about?"

Deadpan, Krieg said, "Oh, he just wanted to know if I would consider a temporary assignment to the Detective Division."

"Huh?"

"Yeah, me, a detective."

Mallory shook his head. "Well, you found your angel."

"Found?" Krieg laughed. "Hell, I developed him."

They began walking down the hall. "You know," Mallory said ruefully, "there must be a thousand guys in uniform who'd give anything for a shot at detective . . . including me."

"I'll keep you in mind," Krieg said.

The reports started coming in at ten-thirty and Enders worked through to early afternoon without a break, checking the findings of the medical examiner, Ballistics, Forensic, and the homicide teams against his list. He crossed items off, added a note here and there, and drew heavy question marks in several places.

It didn't add up.

He thumbed the intercom, told his secretary to get him a sandwich and some coffee, and burrowed back into the reports. The more he reviewed them, the more convinced he became that there was something very strange about the death of Sean McMahon.

He wasn't the only one who thought so.

Downtown at the DA's office on Centre Street, Alexa Aikman—called "Alex" by everyone from the mailroom clerk to the police commissioner—read copies of the McMahon investigation reports, frowning as she turned the pages. Six years on the DA's staff, the last two as senior assistant district attorney and head of the Homicide Division taught more than case preparation and court expertise. Alex's job had refined to an art her ability to pick out the subtle inconsistencies in a developing case.

Carl Enders had been right about the wallet, and his demand that the contents be checked was more than routine or caprice. The DD-5 follow-up report from Homicide revealed that something was missing. Sean McMahon's wife had spotted it when she went through her husband's effects.

Alex read the DD-5 twice. The missing item made no sense at all; it made even less sense that the killer would walk across the street to get it.

She put the reports back into their forders and tucked them into her briefcase. She knew that her father would be home tonight, and this was something he might find interesting.

Noah Aikman lay stretched out on the sofa in his living room in the two-family brownstone on East Sixty-fourth Street. Sheet by sheet, the McMahon reports were dropped mechanically to the floor as he read, absorbed, and discarded the pages. Alex lounged in an easy chair at the other end of the room, near the fireplace. The New York *Times* was propped against her drawn-up knees. She winced as each report page rustled to the floor.

"You have no respect for the law, Aikman," she said, turning a page of the *Times*.

"I'm just a slob," Aikman mumbled, continuing to read.

Which was light-years from the truth; it was just easier than changing his position to place the pages on the coffee table. And for all his fastidiousness, Aikman sometimes took the easy way.

Aikman was a deceptive-looking man. He had the appearance of an athlete who, despite his fifty-eight years, had rigorously maintained his fitness. Tall—a shade over six-three—trim, and muscular, he could have been a track coach, or a once-famous basketball player now holding an executive position with a sporting goods firm. Aikman was neither, and that's where the deception came in: He did his work with his mind, always had, and being in top physical condition was part of his total discipline.

"Aikman's traveling house of horrors" was how he had once described his classes in criminology that brought overflow registration to colleges and universities across the country. He carried the deception a step farther by insisting that the photographs that adorned the jackets of the half-dozen books on criminology he'd written be taken only when he was wearing his jogging suit.

Aikman, as his daughter knew better than anyone, could be perverse.

He dropped the last page to the carpet and stretched his arms above his head. "Blown away by an unusual destiny in the cold winds of March," he said.

"My God, you're terrible," Alex said, deliberately tossing the *Times* to the floor. This is his living room, she thought, let him clean it up.

Aikman jerked himself up to a sitting position. "The wallet's bothering you . . . that missing Social Security card."

"Uh huh," Alex said. "Doesn't make any sense."

"A couple of things here don't make too much sense: For instance, the medical examiner's sure that the bullet was a dumdum."

"And," Alex said, taking off her reading glasses, "according to the homicide detectives, nobody on the block heard a sound until the sirens started and the troops arrived."

"Heavy sleepers," Aikman said sarcastically.

"A silencer."

"Maybe."

Alex groaned. He could be irritating in the devil's advocate role; sometimes impossible. "Everything points to a pro—silencer, dumdum—but McMahon's family says he didn't have an enemy in the world. His life made a great story—immigrant makes good, salt of the Irish earth, and then one morning . . ."

". . . his Social Security card turns up missing."

"Which is what's wrong with the pattern. A professional with a high-powered rifle—silenced, no less—doctored bullets to really do the job, walks across the street to steal a Social Security card from his victim's wallet. Is that a reasonable thing to do?"

"There's one possibility," Aikman said, meeting her eyes.

"Okay . . ."

"Proof. The killer wanted or needed proof."

"Nope," she said flatly, shaking her head, her soft brown hair brushing the top of her shoulders. "I don't buy it. A pro doesn't have to prove anything to himself, and if it's a contract killing, his employers will know about it."

"So you're thinking not a pro?"

"Right."

"But with the weapons and methods of a pro?"

"Right again."

Aikman leaned back and closed his eyes.

"Taking a nap?" Alex asked.

"Thinking . . . thinking."

She watched him, studying his face. Relaxed, showing no emotion, it was a kind face, a good face. It amused her that they bore little resemblance to each other: He was tall, lanky, and red-headed; she was five-six and brunette; his wide jaw and large nose contrasted with her delicate features; even the eyes were of different color—his bright blue, hers brown. She resembled her mother, but Aikman disagreed with that. The mailman," he once said.

They shared the same brownstone, Aikman downstairs in his apartment, Alex upstairs in hers. Their lives were separate, though they often touched at the edges, where his work and hers overlapped.

Aikman had raised Alex alone from the time his wife died. She was twelve years old then, and he taught her to be strong, independent, to be herself and no one's shadow, and as a result they shared not only love but also respect and friendship.

Aikman opened his eyes. "I'm sticking with proof. For whatever reason, it was necessary to the killer, and he took a big chance to get it."

"And . . . ?"

"And our killer has altered the familiar pattern. He's a pro who needs proof."

"An apprentice, right?" Alex said sarcastically.

Aikman laughed. "Everybody has to start somewhere. Speaking of which, I've got to start on my lecture notes." He nodded toward the door.

"I can take the hint, Mr. Subtle," Alex said, rising from the chair. "I just thought there might be something unusual enough to interest you. After all, it's been quite a while since you worked."

He scowled. "Try teaching a lecture hall full of would-be Sherlocks that criminology is 90 per cent perspiration and only 10 per cent genius. That's work."

"You know what I meant," Alex said firmly.

Aikman nodded. He knew; for no matter how much pleasure and satisfaction he got from writing and teaching, it was the reality of an investigation that brought him totally to life. As a young man, he'd been fascinated by crime and all its elements, for he had the rare ability to turn knowledge and theory into results. His talent was later honed by service in the OSS, and over the years he had been consultant to police chiefs and investigative agencies all over the world. He could pick and choose his cases, and he invariably chose the greatest challenges. Aikman wasn't interested in crimes that were solvable by procedure and police work. He relished the ones that would, without his intervention, remain open and unsolved.

"This is straight police work, I'm afraid," Aikman pronounced, "wallet notwithstanding."

Alex shrugged and left the apartment. Aikman heard her footsteps click up the hallway staircase.

She'd deliberately left the reports behind, but Aikman ignored the scattered papers. He wasn't going to be baited. There could be a dozen explanations, and he was content to let the police dig out the right one.

Christopher Reynolds was late that night, and Marcus was sure the move was deliberate. Keep us on edge, he thought.

It was nine o'clock before Reynolds entered the room. He said nothing, strode to the table where they sat, and flipped Sean McMahon's Social Security card to the center.

"I'll be a son-of-a-bitch," Lyle said softly.

"Take a good look," Reynolds said, "because I'm going to burn it."

Birmingham picked up the card, glanced at the name, and passed it to Marcus, who turned it in his nervous fingers for a long time before Lyle reached out, took the card, and held it over the flame of his lighter. He dropped it into a cut-glass ashtray, and they watched until it was gone.

Reynolds stood silently, his eyes flicking to each of their faces. He began quietly, starting to pace around the table, his voice a monotone.

"I picked him up two weeks ago. I checked out the area at night and there it was, waiting for me, the Shamrock Bar and Grill, of all things." He laughed. "The rest was detail: I followed him for four days, picking up his pattern, his habits."

"And St. Patrick's Day was part of your planning," Birmingham commented.

"No one ever accused me of subtlety," Reynolds said.

"You were with him all day?" Marcus broke in.

"From the morning, when he left his apartment. He ran me all over the city, but I was sure he'd end up back at that bar. The only variable was whether he'd leave alone, after everyone else. But that's what he'd done every other night: It was his habit to stay and clean up." A tight smile played at his lips as he spoke. "I had him cold."

"How did you feel?" Marcus asked.

"Control," Reynolds said quickly. "I had total control. He was a dead man the minute I picked him, but it wasn't until I stood in the alley with the rifle that I felt the power." Reynolds' monotone was gone, his voice rising and falling with his description. "Nothing could save him . . . everything was working for me: my ability, my planning, my nerve . . . and my risk. Without the risk," he said, looking at each of them in turn, "we all know it's worthless without the risk. You'll see," he said, his smile lighting his face, "you'll know what it feels like, just in case you don't remember. And believe me, remembering is not enough."

He rapped out the details: his movements after firing, the card, his route out of the area. When he was done he sat down, watching their reactions, probing their faces for a trace of doubt, searching for any gesture that would betray uncertainty. They had to believe; they had to carry it through.

Marcus was visibly nervous, his thin face pinched in concentration, his hands compulsively turning the ashtray back and forth in a semicircle on the table. Richard Lyle had a smile on his face, and his beefy hands rested flat and still on the table. He met Reynolds' eyes and nodded in appreciation. Andrew Birmingham was unreadable, his aristocratic face showing no emotion. Reynolds guessed that he might be imagining himself in that alley, but Birmingham's expression showed him nothing. Reynolds waited a few more moments and faced Marcus, the only one who might stop it. "Well," Reynolds said, "I've taken the first; do we go on?"

Marcus forced himself to look directly at Reynolds. "Yes," he said, with more determination than he felt, "we go on."

Reynolds smiled as the others nodded in agreement. "All right, let's get to it."

Twenty minutes later it was decided that Reynolds would take the second.

2

The girl on the Ninety-sixth Street sidewalk was in her mid-thirties, thin, black, and carried no identification. The squad car that found her in the early-morning hours on April 11, almost four weeks to the day of the killing of Sean McMahon, called the homicide team that put a Jane Doe tag on her ankle and consigned her to the ambulance for a trip to Bellevue.

It was Avery, the chief medical examiner, who spotted the similarities, but, as he said later, he would have had to have been blind to miss them: Fragments of a .30-caliber bullet laced the chest cavity, and Avery grimaced as he faced the bloody damage. The shot had come from behind this time, but the mangling of the dumdum was unmistakable.

He finished the autopsy and typed his report. A young detective from Third Homicide waited outside his office.

They get younger all the time, Avery thought, as he rolled the last page out of the ancient Remington. "Who's in charge of this case?" he called out.

"I am," the detective answered, coming through the doorway.

Avery stood up, shaking his head. "Not any more, son. Who's the deputy chief for your zone?"

"Peter Gregory."

"I've just put him in charge. See that he gets this right away—and I mean now." Avery handed over the report, went back to his desk, and busied himself looking up Gregory's number until the detective left the office.

We're drowning in procedure, Avery thought, dialing the number. Five homicide zones: Who can keep it all straight? Which chief? What streets? Who's in charge? Does anybody care?

Insanity. No procedure, he corrected.

Same thing, he decided.

The paperwork alone gave him writer's cramp, but he was hard put to find an alternative since they'd scrapped the precincts and instituted the zone system . . . like a fuckin' football game, Avery cursed. Five zones for a borough that housed millions in 12½ miles of concrete filing cabinets, streets, alleys, and parks, where more millions worked, played, and often died violently, and the bureaucracy sliced the pie five ways, handing the responsibility to five men, who answered to the police commissioner, who answered to the mayor, who, of course, answered to the millions.

A voice came on the line, and Avery asked for Gregory. He was promptly put on "hold."

No one in this madness knows what the other guy is doing, Avery thought, unless they pay attention to the chattering teletypes that linked the headquarters—which nobody ever had the time or inclination to do.

Avery considered himself the last line of defense. Anybody unfortunate enough to die on the streets of Manhattan ended up in the morgue—his morgue. He saw them all, parceled out the work or handled it himself, and saw all the reports that went out to the zone commanders. And if not for him and Ballistics, which saw all the evidence in shooting deaths, and the DA's office, where all homicide reports came to rest . . . well, the self-important isolation would be complete. Avery sneered at the phone.

There was a click, and Gregory's deep voice came over the line: "Gregory," the voice challenged. Avery said hello, picturing the heavy-set frame and the bulldog face. Peter Gregory had the "cop look" and could be spotted a mile away as The Man. Avery knew him well enough to see beyond that, to the keen mind behind the belligerent eyes.

"I've got something I think you ought to see," Avery said.

"Yeah?"

"Yeah," Avery answered, his voice firm. "I just finished up, and the report is on the way."

"So?"

"I think you ought to come down here."

"You want me to look at a stiff?"

"I wouldn't suggest it if I didn't think it was important," Avery said quietly.

Gregory hesitated, sighed, and said, "It had better be good." The phone clicked in Avery's ear.

Avery put a call through to Carl Enders, and halfway through the description of the wounds in the Jane Doe, Enders stopped the conversation with, "I'll be right there."

Ron Blake got another call.

Gregory pushed his way through the double doors of the autopsy room and saw Avery washing his hands at a tiny sink in the corner. Three rolling carts stood side by side in the center of the white-walled room. The smell of antiseptic lingered in the air.

Carl Enders stood by the center cart, his right hand holding a stiff white sheet away from the face of the Jane Doe. He looked away, saw Gregory, and nodded.

Gregory looked at Avery, then at Enders. "Where's the commissioner?" Gregory asked.

Avery's voice came from the corner of the room. "This concerns both of you." He dried his hands and gestured toward the cart. Gregory strode over and pulled the sheet all the way back.

"Hamburger," he muttered. Enders turned away.

Gregory started to say something, but Avery waved him off. "I already checked with Ballistics, that's how I know. It's all the same: the wounds, the bullets, the weapon. And I thought someone ought to get you two together . . . you know, the way it used to be?" He threw the sheet back over the body and, with Enders holding the door, rolled the cart out of the room and across the hall to the icebox, Avery's term for the refrigerated lockers where bodies await identification.

"Let's get out of here," Enders said to Gregory.

As they crossed the hallway, Enders thought about the constant shocks to the nervous system provided by a visit to Bellevue. One of the worst was the placement of the cafeteria: right across the hall from the morgue. On his infrequent visits, Enders never attempted anything more than coffee.

Gregory scowled into a chipped mug as Enders reeled off the facts of the Sean McMahon case.

"Okay, I buy it," he said when Enders finished. "Same guy: sniper, a madman."

"I don't know about the madman part, but it's got to be the same guy. What we need now is the link."

"So we find out what's missing from Jane's personal effects." Gregory rose, left his coffee behind, and led Enders out of the building. They got into Enders' car and drove to the Police Academy, where the Forensic lab would have whatever was on or near the body of the girl.

Along with Forensic, the Academy housed Ballistics, in addition to the countless classrooms where recruits hopefully turned into cops. The atmosphere was considerably more cheerful than Bellevue's, and the office they were led to by an obsequious lab attendant was comfortable, almost plush, with stuffed chairs, brightly polished furniture, and deep carpeting.

"They really soft-soap these kids," Gregory grumbled.

This isn't their lounge, Pete," Enders said, impatiently tapping his fingers on the table.

The attendant brought two plastic bags, one with a cheap black-plastic purse, the other a matching wallet.

Enders went for the wallet first. The plastic windows were empty; the billfold section held eighteen dollars. "Nothing . . ."

Gregory opened the purse, turned it over, and showered the contents on the table. He poked through crumpled tissues, matchbooks, a half-empty cigarette pack, a torn lottery ticket, and thirty-seven cents. Among the tissues he found a single key. "Well, she lived somewhere," he said.

"You know, you're a real joy," Enders said. "You really brighten the day."

Gregory started to smile, changed his mind, and said, "I really hate this, poking around in garbage."

Enders nodded. He was familiar with Gregory's credo: Work with your mind. If Gregory never had to leave his desk and his beloved reports, he'd be a happy man.

Enders slid the wallet across the table. "No identification, nothing. Everything could be missing from that thing and we'd never know it."

"Maybe everything is missing . . . maybe your killer ripped it all off. Who knows?"

"I'm going to know . . . I'll find out."

"You taking charge of this dismal business?" Gregory asked.

"Well, Sean McMahon is my case, and since we're dealing with the same killer. . . ."

"Okay, you can have it. I make you a present. Just keep me posted."

Enders pocketed the key, and they left the building—

Gregory to return to his office, Enders to put Billy the Kid to work.

Enders knew that the only way to break in a new man was to pair him with experience, and experience meant Graham Parker, a veteran of sixteen years in the Homicide Department. A huge black man with features resembling sixteen miles of bad road, Parker looked and acted like a heavyweight, his broad, flat nose and scars giving his face expressions of limitless power and strength. It was rumored that Parker knew about every deal in the city; in fact, what he really knew was whom to talk to.

It was inspired matching, Enders thought, unless Billy became intimidated and froze.

Billy and Graham Parker went out into the neighborhood where the Jane Doe was found. They turned up Andy Reed in three hours, and Andy Reed gave them a name: Eileen Douglas, formerly Jane Doe.

In a private office at Bellevue, Enders, Gregory, Parker, and Billy Krieg formed a semicircle around Andy Reed, who owned Andy's Place, a bar on 106th, just off Madison Avenue. Andy was white and the neighborhood black, but it took Enders only a moment to realize that Reed could handle anything. His heavily muscled frame projected pure physical strength, and his quick, precise movements and wary eyes testified to his agility and endurance. Standing next to Parker, facing Andy Reed, Enders at six feet felt tiny.

Probably keeps a sawed-off baseball bat behind the bar, Enders thought . . . if not a shotgun.

But there had been a moment, when Reed stood over the body of Eileen Douglas, when Enders saw him clench his fists, saw him take the shock and calmly make the identification.

The walk to the office had been quick and silent. Enders could feel the tension as Reed strode across the tiled floor, his fists still clenched, the knuckles going yellow-white.

Eileen Douglas' empty wallet lay on the table, inches away from Reed's now-folded hands.

"What more do you want?" he asked. "I don't know nothing else."

"And if you did, you wouldn't tell us, right?" Gregory snarled, falling into the bad-guy role in the ploy of good-guy, bad-guy assault on witnesses and suspects.

Enders flashed a warning glance and Gregory backed off. "We're trying to find out who killed her, Andy," he said softly. "That's all. We need your help."

"There's nothin' I can tell you."

"Maybe. How long did she work for you?"

"About a year."

"And in all that time," Enders asked, "you never found out anything about her?"

"She could've worked for me for ten years, it would've been the same. Look," he sighed, relaxing slightly, "some people are like that, y'know? Loners . . . the city is full of them. They drift in, drift around, maybe drift back out again. You guys know that, right?"

Graham Parker smiled. "See it all the time."

"Well, okay," Reed continued, "so it's not so hard to believe. She came in about a year ago, had a few drinks, and we got to talking. I had this band then, three guys, background shit, you know? Well, she listens for a bit and says to me, 'You need a singer,' and I say, 'What I need is customers,' and she smiles and says, 'Same thing. You get yourself a singer, a good singer, you'll have more customers than you'll know what to do with.' And then she laughs, like she knows it would work just that way."

Andy Reed shook his head, fighting for control. "Yeah, it worked all right. She was great; I mean, a really class act . . . not only the voice, but style, delivery. I know about those things, y'know."

Reed paused and Enders prompted, "Go on, what happened after that?"

"Pretty soon we'd built up the steadies, neighborhood guys who'd come in all the time . . . then we start getting floaters from out of the neighborhood. Sometimes it gets heavy, but we handle it. Never had no real trouble."

"Eileen ever mention if she'd been a singer someplace else, maybe a professional?"

"No."

"Did she ever talk about where she came from?"

Reed shook his head.

"What about her voice, Andy?" Gregory asked. "You know about singers. Was it a natural, or did it seem trained? You think she studied music somewhere?"

Andy brightened. "I don't think she studied, but her voice wasn't untrained, if you get my meaning. She'd been on a stage before, I could tell. Sometimes I would get a flash of her in some fancy club, I mean really big-time. Like I'd seen her in a place like that, backed by a class band. But I'm not sure. Maybe I just wanted to believe it."

"One more thing," Gregory said. "When she started working for you, did she fill out any forms, papers . . . like Social Security?"

Andy smirked. "Man, I don't bother with shit like that."

Parker laughed.

"Okay," Gregory said, "what about union? Did she have an AGVA card?"

"Yeah, she had her union card. Didn't matter to me. I'd've let her sing, card or no card. It was the voice, man. She had a really great voice. She did blues, mostly, and . . . you see, there really aren't any new ways of singing blues—man, it's all been done—but her way was personal, real. She meant it and the steadies understood; they wanted to hear it over and over again."

"Would you take a look at the wallet?" Enders asked gently. "Was it hers?"

"I guess," Andy said.

"Not sure?"

"I didn't see it all that much."

"There's no identification in it," Enders said. "No union card, Andy. You said she had one."

"Yeah, she had one. I saw it when she started workin'. She kept it in there." He touched the empty wallet.

Enders flashed a glance to Gregory, then continued: "Was she going straight home last night?"

"Probably . . . I don't know."

Gregory put some questions to Andy, the obvious ones about particular friends she might have had or enemies she might have made, but it became apparent that he either didn't know or wouldn't say.

As he was leaving, Reed turned to stare at Enders. After a long moment, he said, "You let me know who did it."

Enders nodded. Reed closed the door quietly behind him.

After a few moments, Enders asked Billy, "Anything in the apartment?"

"Nothing," Krieg said. "Pitiful . . . some clothes, a few books, no papers or mail or anything to ID her or tell us anything about her. Forensic is going over it now."

"And no union card," Gregory said. "I think we got what we came for." He pulled the door open. "You want some coffee, Carl?"

"Not in this building," Enders replied.

Noah Aikman found a note tacked to his office door at New York University as he returned from the afternoon lecture. "Call your daughter," it read.

Aikman's office consisted of a desk in front of the window, a few chairs, and three walls of overflowing bookcases. He made his way to the desk, cleared a space, and set his briefcase down. He popped a lozenge in his mouth and dialed Alex's number at the DA's office.

"Alexa Aikman," came the voice.

"Weary Aikman," he replied.

"Tough day?"

"Throat hurts like hell," he complained.

"Then just listen. Remember Sean McMahon and the professional killer who wasn't a professional killer? The missing Social Security card?"

"It's my throat that's faulty, not my brain," Aikman said.

"There's been another one," Alex continued, disregarding his remark. Aikman heard the dry rustle of papers through the phone as Alex rattled off the details. "Eileen Douglas, cabaret singer, killed two nights ago ten blocks from the club where she worked. Same MO, same rifle, same dumdum bullets . . . the works, Aikman."

"You sound like Jack Webb," he said, smiling.

"Been practicing."

"Have I got all the facts, ma'am?"

"Not quite. There was a cabaret card . . ."

". . . which is now among the missing, right?"

"Exactly right."

In spite of himself, Aikman felt it: another victim connected in some way with a bar, another unimportant piece of identification missing.

"Alex, why don't you . . ." he began.

". . . bring both files home tonight? I'm way ahead of you. See you at six. You cook."

"Deal," he said, hanging up the phone. He opened his briefcase and checked off pages on his lecture outline. The rest of the week's classes would undoubtedly bring more sore-throat misery, he thought.

Suddenly the activities of the sniper had become very interesting.

3

Charles Witkin was under siege in the hallway outside the mayor's office. It's the press, he thought darkly, the goddamn press. They never leave you alone for a minute. He caught himself as "there ought to be a law" started to form in his mind.

Jesus, hell of a liberal I'm turning out to be. . . .

But he was right; the press was making life hard for him. He should have expected it: The first assistant to the mayor of New York, in charge of labor negotiations, was an easy target when things got out of hand, and things were rapidly getting far out of anyone's hand. Mix a healthy dash of disgruntled sanitation workers with a volatile union and simmer over warm spring days, and you get garbage boiling over into the streets of New York and Charles Witkin running interference.

He pressed back against the wall as microphones were thrust forward and television cameras trained on him.

"C'mon, Red, just give us a statement," Larry Miles from the *Post* shouted louder than the rest.

Witkin's face took on the color of his hair. Miles should know enough to have some respect, especially with the cameras rolling.

"Negotiations are still in progress," Witkin began, keeping his voice low in the hope that he could quiet the clamor by forcing them to quiet down to hear him.

"What progress?" Stevens, from the *Daily News,* cut in.

"Now look," Witkin shot back, "they're still talking, and that's progress. And if you guys would get out of my way and off my back, I might be able to get something done."

He pushed past them, with perhaps a touch more force than was necessary. He was already twenty minutes late for a meeting in New Jersey, where he was to confer with a select committee delegated by the governor of that state on a proposed renovation of Penn Station. Witkin would handle the labor contracts for New York City's part of the job.

Shove the garbage off the street and into the station, he thought. Invite the press . . . give them all shovels. If they didn't insist on publicizing his every move before and after he made it, he might be able to accomplish something. As it was, the whole city had a jump on him, and Witkin couldn't turn a corner without running into microphones or picket lines or protesters.

A black limousine waited at the curb and Witkin sprinted for it, jumped in, and slammed the door, cutting off pursuit.

Sometimes he dreamed of being mayor of New York in ten or fifteen years. Most of the time it was nightmare enough being the mayor's right-hand man.

Witkin glanced at his watch as the limousine sped through the city to the heliport at West Thirtieth Street, where a chopper waited to take him across the Hudson. It was six-thirty, and he hadn't had dinner; he could barely remember lunch.

He was amazed to see the sidewalk in front of the heliport clear. The press is slipping, he thought; either that or they don't give a shit about Penn Station.

Witkin made his way across the lobby and punched the elevator button. When the door slid open he led three others into the car and hit the button for the roof. The elevator was a local, and Witkin worried about the governor of New Jersey and his committee cooling their heels and cursing the mayor's fair-haired boy.

By the tenth floor Witkin was alone in the elevator with the big man in the dark raincoat.

Richard Lyle was conscious of everything: the slight weight of the weapon resting under his suitjacket, the position of his target standing a step to his left, the red light flashing behind the floor numbers as the elevator glided up, the stop button on the panel.

Ten . . . eleven . . . twelve; twelve more to the roof.

Lyle knew he couldn't take his man from a distance, from the shadows, as Reynolds had. Lyle would have to face his target. It could have been at night on a deserted street; it could have been another target; it could have been a lot of things, but Witkin was an ideal choice, and Lyle decided to take him the moment he'd read about the mayor's assistant's itinerary in the morning paper. A victim as prominent as Witkin would take the spotlight away from Reynolds, and the risks would convince the others that he, like Reynolds, was in for the duration. There were risks, but Lyle knew that Reynolds was right: Without risk it was meaningless. Might as well go back to poker.

Lyle had cut the risk as much as he could. It was impossible to disguise his height and weight—at 6-4 and 210 pounds there was little he could do about that. So he worked the other way: Blend in. He wore his best business suit and lightweight raincoat and melted into the group in the lobby, slipping without undue notice into the elevator . . . just another businessman. His only concession to outright disguise was the false mustache he wore.

Sixteen . . . seventeen . . . eighteen.

Lyle reached out a gloved hand and slammed the stop button as the elevator passed eighteen. The car jerked to a stop and hung in limbo between floors. Lyle's right hand was under his jacket as he continued the motion, turning in a semicircle to face Witkin, clamping his left hand over the smaller man's mouth and bringing the right hand out. Witkin saw a flash of steel and felt a searing pain as Lyle plunged the long blade into his stomach; Witkin felt an overpowering sickness and began to sag back against the wall as Lyle turned the handle and, with all the power in his arm, ripped the blade the length of the chest.

Lyle turned Witkin's body toward the corner, pulling the blade out. Blood gushed onto the walls, but Lyle had moved away in time. There was no blood on the raincoat.

Only seconds, Lyle knew: He wiped the blade on Witkin's coat, slipped the knife under his jacket, and flipped the coat up over Witkin's back. He pulled the wallet out, opened it, and saw the card immediately: Special Police Pass, in the first plastic window in the wallet. Lyle smiled when he saw Witkin's photograph on the card.

He slid it out, dropped the wallet to the floor, and pushed the button for the twentieth floor.

The car kicked to life, slid up, and then stopped. Lyle walked out calmly, glancing up and down the corridor. There was no one in sight. He reached back and pushed the buttons for the twenty-first through the twenty-fourth floors.

This was the real risk, he knew. There could be somebody on any one of the floors above him, somebody waiting for the elevator. He had to get out of the building fast. He sprinted to the end of the hall, took the stairs down two flights, and picked up an elevator on the opposite side of the corridor. The down car was empty, and Lyle was on the street in less than a minute.

Alexa Aikman was in the kitchen brewing coffee when she heard Chuck Witkin's name on the eleven-o'clock news. She rushed into the living room and stood before the set as the off-camera voice gave a drying reading of the facts and the camera made love to the death scene: through the elevators doors, circling slowly, taking in the blood-stained walls, dropping lower to the corner, moving in tighter and tighter until in sharp focus the brown stains on the carpet filled the screen.

Witkin had been found at seven o'clock and, in time for millions of viewers to see, Police Commissioner Michael Forman was on the scene, his chunky frame partially obscured by the crush of reporters. Forman repeated over and over again that he had no statement. Behind him stood Robert Ellison, deputy chief of Fourth Homicide, patiently waiting his turn to stand in front of the microphones where he, too, would decline to give a statement.

Alex knew that Witkin's position demanded the show of brass. She had met the mayor's assistant three or four times and had seen him on television on countless occasions. He always seemed harried, always on the way to somewhere. He seemed never to arrive, simply to exist in a perpetual state of "going."

Ellison was speaking now, and Alex reflected on how well he came across on TV. From the tall, slim build to the gleaming blackness of his face, to the smooth, controlled voice, his appearance and demeanor served to obscure the fact that, at this time, he really had nothing to say.

The camera returned to the bloody carpet as the reporter droned a wrap-up. Alex, unsettled, turned the set off.

The really unsettling moment for her came the next morning as she read through the homicide report on Charles Witkin. The medical report would be in by early afternoon, she thought. She was halfway down the page of the follow-up DD-5 when she sat bolt upright in her chair and said aloud, "What the hell?"

Witkin's wallet had been found on the floor of the elevator; his police ID card was missing. His watch—an expensive Omega—his credit cards, cash, and gold ring were untouched.

Alex took a chance that Avery might have finished the autopsy and dialed his number, smiling as she heard his wheezy hello.

"Alexa Aikman, Sam."

"How're you doin'?" he asked.

"Needing information on Chuck Witkin, if you have it."

He sighed. "Just finished. You'll have the report by two."

"What can you tell me now?"

"He was stabbed . . . blade came in at an upward angle, caught him low in the stomach, lots of force behind it. The killer was right-handed and probably a lot taller than Witkin. Stronger, too . . . ripped the blade up from the stomach . . ."

"What kind of knife?" Alex interrupted.

There was a pause. She could hear Avery breathing.

"Sam?"

"Yeah, well, that's the sixty-four-dollar question. I've seen a lot of stab wounds, but this is something else. Incredible wound . . . wider, deeper than it had to be, you know what I mean? Something really big."

"Hunting knife?"

"Nope, don't think so," Avery answered. "See, the blade was triangular in shape, a lot wider at the top than at the bottom. Hunting knives don't usually come that way."

"Then what?"

"Bowie knife, maybe; it's the right shape blade, but I've never seen one long enough to do this. I think, maybe, a bayonet."

Alex frowned. "A what?"

"This isn't the Army, Alex, and I'm no authority on bayonet wounds, so I'm going to do some checking before I put it down in the report; but if you want my instant, unofficial opinion, Witkin was stabbed with a bayonet."

"How long was the blade?"

"From the wound, it had to be at least eight inches, maybe ten."

"Jesus . . ."

"Like I said, I'm going to do some checking. I'll get back to you."

"Thanks, Sam."

"Something going on?"

"Maybe. Call me soon, huh?"

Avery promised and hung up. Alex stared at the phone for a full minute before replacing the receiver in the cradle. She couldn't help thinking that the bayonet that killed Witkin might belong on the end of a high-powered sniper's rifle. "Too crazy," she told herself, but how else could anyone explain the missing ID card? She kept turning it over in her mind and finally went back to the files on McMahon and Douglas. The signatures on the pages surprised her: Carl Enders. A deputy chief filing homicide reports, she thought. Well, if he's crazy enough to do that, maybe he's crazy enough to listen to me.

She dialed his office, got him on the phone, and if she was expecting him to be skeptical, she was wrong. He listened without interruption to her recital of the Witkin details.

"Jesus," he said when she finished.

Alex laughed. "That's exactly what I said. I know this may be a little strange, but . . ."

"Can you bring that report to me, the one on Witkin?" Enders cut in.

"Sure, but . . ."

"It's a long story, but I've got both cases, McMahon and Eileen Douglas. Have you got time this afternoon to talk about this?"

"I'll make time. Your office?"

"At two o'clock."

On the way to Enders' office, Alex recalled the few times she had seen him during her years in the DA's office—always in passing, with another deputy chief; once at a Christmas party in the building. She knew him only by sight or by the sound of his voice, and now from his signature on the reports. But the fact that he hadn't been skeptical and wanted to talk was a good sign. Sometimes, when you don't know the brass personally, you can run into a stone wall.

Enders, on the other hand, knew a great deal about Alexa Aikman. He knew her father, and that provided insight into the daughter. Her reputation in the DA's office affirmed the kinship: She knew her law, did her homework, prepared solid cases, and had great presence in court.

He knew she'd graduated as one of the top three students in her law class at Yale, and guessed she was probably first. He'd read with interest all news coverage of her cases and could see, from the very beginning, she was a gifted prosecutor. Absolutely nothing escaped her in court. She could be gentle yet tenacious during questionings of witnesses and made her points with the endless faces on endless juries without ever raising her voice.

She was intelligent, beautiful, and, according to her father, had an enviable imagination, but Enders didn't doubt for a moment that what bothered her about the three homicides was rooted in fact, not fancy.

They went over the cases, quickly giving the background and comparing notes. There was little they didn't already know from reading the reports.

"McMahon and Douglas are connected," Alex said. "It's the same killer. But we don't know if they knew each other. . . ."

"We're checking on it," Enders said. "We're digging into their backgrounds."

"So their deaths could be part of a pattern . . ."

". . . or the work of a madman."

"I don't think so," Alex said.

"Good. Neither do I."

"Is it too crazy to think that the bayonet fits on the end of the rifle?"

"Not at all, especially because of the missing ID." Enders leaned back in his chair. "That's what throws me, those damn stupid cards—Social Security, union card, police ID. Useless stuff—unless it's some kind of proof."

Alex smiled. "I've thought about that."

"Have you thought that the guy with the rifle and the guy with the knife know each other?"

"No," Alex said. "I've been working on the one-and-the-same theory."

"Could be either way," Enders admitted. "But one thing's for sure: There's a connection. I don't believe those missing cards are just coincidence. And it's more than that: Look at how they were killed. It wasn't necessary to use dumdum bullets. . . ."

"Just like it wasn't necessary to rip Witkin apart. I see what you mean. It's more than killing, it's total destruction. . . ."

"Overkill," Enders said.

"That's it!" Alex said suddenly.

"That's what?"

"Overkill . . . and something Sam Avery said. Who uses sniper rifles, dumdum bullets, and bayonets?"

"The Army, the Marines," Enders said.

"Right: the military. Is there any way of checking the bullet fragments?"

"To find out if they were Army-issue bullets?"

Alex nodded, but Enders shook his head. "No way. About all we can do is run a metal test on them to find out how old the bullets were. There's no way to find out where they came from."

"It's better than nothing. Why don't we run it?"

Enders picked up the phone, dialed Ballistics, and ordered the test.

Lyle was proud of himself. Choice, imagination, and style were as important as the killing itself and, as the others passed Witkin's ID card around, he felt like a schoolboy on Show and Tell Day. Reynolds gave him an admiring smile when he saw Witkin's photograph on the card, and they all sat in rapt attention as he described the killing.

They burned the card and got down to the business of the evening. Marcus pressed a steady attack on Lyle, adding a stream of comments. Reynolds, impeded for the moment, waited for his chance. It was Birmingham who took the first opportunity.

He picked up the .45 early in the morning, almost two weeks later, left the studio apartment on East Fifty-third Street, and took a subway to Sector Thirty-eight. At five-thirty he stood in a doorway waiting for his target and wondering what he was doing there.

It had taken Birmingham four days to find his man and another four to pick the spot and the time. The night before, Birmingham had gone to the apartment to prepare. He'd taken a long time cleaning and loading the gun, fitting the silencer onto the modified barrel. He poured linseed oil on a piece of cheesecloth and worked it into the soft leather of the shoulder holster. He stared at the blue-black finish of the pistol, the words "Colt, Government Automatic, Cal. .45" cut into the barrel. Birmingham had had that gun for years and practiced with it regularly on a Long Island firing range. It was accurate to seventy-five yards; at close range it was devastating.

He poured himself a drink and tried to imagine the scene

in the morning; how he would move from the cover of the doorway, come up behind his man, and . . .

His hands were shaking. He finished the drink and paced around the apartment. Marcus had rented the sparsely furnished studio for them as a base of operations, paying six months' rent in advance with a money order. Here, locked in a closet, were the weapons and boxes of ammunition, extra clothing for all of them, and elements of disguises—from false beards and mustaches to wigs and theatrical make-up kits. The apartment was stocked with food and drink, and a cabinet in the bathroom held emergency medical supplies. There was also five thousand dollars in cash in a paper bag in the dresser. They had everything they needed for their work, and everything they might need if anything went wrong.

Nothing will go wrong, Birmingham assured himself. I've handled a lot tougher ones than this.

It was five thirty-five when he heard the footsteps. He wiped his sweaty palms against his pants and drew back into the doorway. His man came into view on the right and, suddenly, as if someone had thrown a switch, all the nervousness was gone. The tension drained from his body, and his mind focused on the target and what he had to do.

The old man walked with slow, steady steps, came abreast of Birmingham hidden in the doorway, and passed. Another step, then another, and Birmingham moved forward, checked the street in both directions, and pulled the .45 smoothly from the holster. He raised his arm and pulled the trigger. There was a slight hiss of air as the bullet caught the old man in midstride and took half his head off.

Without hesitation, Birmingham stepped to the body, pulled a wallet from an inside coat pocket, and ripped out the driver's license with one gloved hand.

He was back in the apartment twenty minutes later. He carefully removed the false beard, washed and dried his face, cleaned the gun, and replaced the missing cartridge in the clip.

Goddamn, he said to himself. He had a quick drink and left the apartment.

Graham Parker munched on a cruller and watched Billy Krieg sip his coffee. They sat in the Mayflower luncheonette on Forty-seventh Street. Parker had been working since six in the morning. It was his habit to start early, check his contacts, and meet Billy at ten o'clock at the Mayflower, Parker's unofficial "office."

"Didya hear about the asshole who shot the jeweler this morning?" Parker asked between bites.

"No," Krieg said. "I was digging into the backgrounds of Sean McMahon and that singer, Eileen Douglas."

"Uh huh," Parker smiled. "Important stuff. Anyway, guy named Loesser, Aaron Loesser, got shot on Fifty-fourth Street, real early this morning."

"How do you find these things out so fast?"

"I got the sources, man. Everybody talks to me . . . especially when it's a funny one like this."

"What's funny about it?"

"Nothing funny about Loesser getting killed. The funny part comes later, when the body's down at Bellevue. Seems Loesser had seventy thou' worth of diamonds on him when they brought him in. . . ."

"Hold it," Krieg said, gesturing at Parker. "How do you know all this?"

"Okay, one of the morgue attendants keeps me posted. I told you, I got ears everywhere . . . keeps me on top of things. Anyway," Parker said, popping the last of the cruller into his mouth, "he's got all these diamonds on him, belonged to his wife, and they're taking his clothes off and all them rocks start spilling out all over the floor! Half them doctors probably had heart attacks. Shit, can you see it? Dead body, all them diamonds . . ." He grinned and licked a cruller crumb from his finger.

"Why was he carrying the diamonds? Did you find that out?"

"Sure: His wife said he was taking them to work. . . ."

"What? Where did this guy work?"

"Cartier's," Parker said, rolling the word off his tongue. "Where else would he work?"

Krieg laughed.

"He was going to supervise the resetting of the stones in a ring and bracelet for his wife. He was their hotshot gold man, a real artist, designed the setting himself. It was the craziest thing I ever heard of . . . must be a full moon. The crazies always come out on a full moon."

"There was no moon last night," Krieg said.

Parker shrugged, amending his philosophy. "So? Nuts don't obey rules."

"Why do you keep saying crazies and nuts?" Krieg asked.

"Who else but a crazy would blow a guy's head off, leave all them diamonds, and steal a driver's license?"

"What?" Krieg banged the coffee cup on the saucer.

"The old man's driver's license was missing. When the family came in, they found it missing from his wallet . . ."

Parker was talking to himself. Krieg was on the phone, dialing Enders.

Enders knocked on the door to Alex's office, heard her say, "Come in," and found her scowling at the phone.

Beautiful, he thought to himself, appreciating the way her dress clung slightly at the waist, the cool blue gently accenting her pale skin and her shapely legs crossed at the knees.

"I've been trying to get you," Alex said, replacing the phone in its cradle.

"The Loesser killing?" Enders replied, his mind back to the files.

"I just got the report," she answered, tapping a sheet of paper on her desk.

"Billy Krieg called me an hour ago. Parker knew about it early this morning, but I never told Parker about the missing items in the other cases. Maybe I should have; it would have saved some time."

Time isn't the problem. What the hell is going on?" she said, exasperated.

"I don't know, but I've got something that may help. The metal test on the McMahon and Douglas bullet fragments puts the ammo at thirty to forty years old."

Alex whistled. "How do we trace it back?"

Enders shrugged, running his hand through his hair. "We don't—not unless an armory's been robbed, and that hasn't happened: I checked."

"Dead end?"

"Uh huh. At the end of the war, when we had to turn in all our stuff, I remember seeing barrels and barrels of ammunition, and barrels of sidearms, stacks of rifles, rooms full of it. Anybody could have walked out with anything . . . the war was over, we were going home. Who cared?"

Alex picked up the homicide report. "Carl, let's run a check on the bullet that killed Loesser."

"It's being done. I called as soon as Billy told me about the missing license. We've also got a shell casing . . . no prints, but we're running an age test on that, too. Ballistics says the slug was a .45, and those automatics toss the casing. What kills me is that the bastard didn't even take it with him. He knows it can't be traced, and he's not going to do something stupid like leave prints."

"A professional," Alex said.

"I don't think so. We've had teletypes out to every state on the other killings. Nothing, no match anywhere. Some similarities, but the details were wrong. If our sniper is a pro, some police department somewhere would have heard from him before, but nothing fits."

"So you don't think the sniper killed Loesser? You don't believe the sniper and the pistol man are one and the same?"

"No, I don't. I'm sticking with separate killers who know each other . . ."

". . . with a possible military background. Can't we check service records?"

Enders shook his head. "We're not going to find them, or him—if you're right that it's one man—on any list or in any file."

"Everybody is on file somewhere," she argued.

"Sure, but what file? What list? Where do you start?"

"Veterans," she said.

"Do you know how many veterans there are in this city? Vietnam vets alone . . ."

She cut him off. "Try another war; that ammunition is old."

"Look at me," he said quietly. "Ordinary Joe, right? Veteran, right? Almost every middle-aged man in New York is a veteran of some war. Where does that leave us?"

"Back with our theories," she sighed, leaning her elbows on the desk and cradling her chin in her hands.

"Have I given you a headache?"

"I had it when you came in."

"How about some food?"

"That's the best idea I've heard all day," Alex said, managing a smile.

4

Marcus was hot, uncomfortable, and frightened. "You're the last one," Reynolds had said, "the last one to show us his style." Marcus had shrugged, saying nothing. He knew he wasn't going to go through with it.

But Marcus couldn't work up the courage to say so, not that Thursday night and not during the days that followed, when he could have easily picked up the phone and called Reynolds.

So he went through the motions, made a game of it: first by working out in the gym at the club, pushing and testing himself as the others had done before they went out; then by locating the sector, making the surveillance, choosing his spot. He was amazed at how easy it was to prepare, but he knew he wouldn't take the final step.

Hidden behind the partition of a toilet stall in a sixty-seventh-floor men's room of the North Tower of the World Trade Center, Marcus wiped sweat from his upper lip. It was so easy, he thought. The entire floor was occupied by two Japanese import-export firms. All he had to do was wait; sooner of later he would have his man. Another minute, he thought, squeezing his owl eyes tightly shut, another minute and I'll go home. This is crazy.

He heard footsteps from the hall, and a moment later the bathroom door swung open. Marcus crouched as steps approached, clicking on the tiles, and in that instant instinct took over: He knew he would do it. He drew the wire from his pocket, stretched it full out, feeling the tension in his arms, wrapped gloved hands around the short wooden handles, and pushed the stall door open with his right shoulder.

Marcus sprang at the small figure standing at the urinal, looped the wire around the man's throat, and pulled until he could feel his fingernails through the gloves, digging into his own palms. He jerked the body back, half pulling, half carrying the man into the stall, working the wire tighter, tighter, down and out, as he had been taught.

He released the pressure, pulled the wire free, rewound it, and slipped it into the side pocket of his jacket, where he had placed a small plastic bag as a lining. There would be blood on the wire, he knew.

As he bent to search through the dead man's pockets, he watched his own hands, detached from them, carried back in time to when training, reflex, and instinct were all he needed. Effortless, he thought; I'm not even breathing hard.

His hands found an inside breast pocket and a thin green folder. Passport: perfect.

It was an oppressively hot June 5, and by five-thirty Alex trudged down Sixty-fourth Street on radar: She sidestepped people and tuned out the street noise unconsciously and automatically. The four steps of the brownstone's stoop seemed a mile high, and it was an effort to unlock the front door. Inside, she walked to Aikman's door on the main landing and knocked weakly. There was no answer. She pressed her ear against the door and heard music. She knocked harder, and the music was turned down.

"Ah," Aikman said, opening the door, "thought I heard someone knock." Then, "You look beat. Want a drink?"

She nodded and padded into the cool apartment.

"Between the air conditioner and Ella Fitzgerald it's a miracle I heard you," he said. From the kitchen came the sweet tinkle of ice cubes in a glass. "Hurry up," she groaned, slumping into a chair, "I'm melting." He raced back to the living room and handed her a frosted glass.

Lemonade . . . from scratch. "Lifesaver," she said, smacking her lips.

"Thanks," he said.

Alex kicked off her shoes and put her feet up on the coffee table. "Did Hayakimo make the morning edition?"

"Who?"

"Middle-aged Japanese importer, strangled in the Trade Center yesterday afternoon?"

"Yeah, there was an item on that. Why?"

"Because I've been on that one all day."

"Someone putting pressure on?"

"More that that: We get to add the late Osea Hayakimo to our growing list of weirdo unsolvables."

"Something's missing?" he asked, eyebrows raised slightly.

"You bet. What am I bid for a passport?"

He took the glass from her, sipped, and handed it back.

"Avery called me this morning," Alex said, taking her own sip. "As close as he can figure, Hayakimo was strangled by piano wire."

"Garotte," Aikman said.

"Huh?"

"Garotte, it's called a garotte. About two feet of piano wire with wooden handles on the ends for a grip. Cuts off the air and crushes the windpipe."

"Grisly . . . and unusual, wouldn't you say?"

"Anything else?"

"The routine calls to Immigration to find out if anyone used the passport . . . calling the airports . . ."

". . . to see if anyone booked a flight in Hayakawa's name . . ."

"Hayakimo," she corrected.

"Yeah, Hayakimo," he said, brushing it aside. "Anything other than procedure?"

"Well, Carl has a theory that there's more than one person involved." She saw a flicker in his blue eyes. "Ah," she smiled, "someone's been thinking."

"Because someone else keeps giving me daily bulletins." Aikman lit the second of his five-cigarette-per-day ration.

"Guilty," Alex said. "What have you been thinking?"

He leaned forward, resting his long arms on his knees. "I'm thinking that the garotte fits nicely . . . and I agree with Carl's theory. It's a bit much to expect one person to be proficient with three—no, four weapons. Sure, it's happened, but it's rare. A rifle, a pistol, a blade, and a wire: That's a lot to ask of anybody."

"But it could happen," she said. "Somebody could be expert with all four."

He shook his head. "It's more than that. A weapon's like a signature. Besides, if it was one man, why would he switch off? Why not just keep going with the rifle?"

"Not in a bathroom at the World Trade Center," she said.

"Then kill him on the street, late at night. No reason not to."

"We don't know that."

"All right, then, let's work with what we do know. Each murder was deliberately planned and carried out. In the heat of an argument, you might pick up a bayonet and use it, if there was one around to pick up; but the killer deliberately chose it, carried it with him to kill Witkin. He's got to know that weapon—he's used it before. It's not your everyday, run-of-the-mill blade. For someone to use it, he's got to know what he's doing. He takes a chance just carrying it, it's so damn big."

Aikman picked up Alex's glass and drained the last of the lemonade. "And the rifle . . . one shot, both times, dumdum bullets to make sure of the job . . . silencer . . .

the marks of an expert. Same for the wire. Jesus, if you don't know how to kill quickly with one of those, you're crazy to try it. The wireman is very familiar with that little tool."

"And the .45?"

"One shot to the head. An amateur would empty the whole clip at the biggest target, the chest. Not our man: One perfectly placed shot does it all."

Aikman crushed out the cigarette. "Experts . . . four different men . . . and the weapons are signatures."

"You know what you're doing?" Alex asked.

"I hope so." Aikman smiled.

"You're proving the military connection."

Aikman nodded. "I know. That's what I meant by the garrote fitting in . . . wartime assassinations . . ."

"I've seen all the movies," Alex smiled grimly. "Where does that leave us?"

"It leaves you asking Carl to check the victim's whereabouts and activities during the war."

"What war?"

"All of them. From the age spread of the victims, you'd better start with World War II and work up to Vietnam," he stood up, "but not tonight. I'll make dinner, and we can resume our tournament. I'm feeling lucky."

Alex glanced at the backgammon set on the end table. Aikman strode into the kitchen, and she heard the rattle of aluminum pots and pans. "I don't like it when you say you feel lucky," she called. "I'm already in the hole sixty-five dollars."

He poked his head around the doorframe. "I think it's very tacky of you to keep a running tally."

"I like to be aware of my losses," she said.

Aikman had dinner on the table in forty minutes, a feast of lemon sole, crisp green salad, potatoes au gratin, and dry white wine. For dessert, he brought out chocolate mousse and fresh-ground coffee. He was a master in the kitchen.

But he was better at backgammon, and by the end of the evening Alex was down ninety dollars.

If Tony Rendelli hadn't been so tired, if the June day that was ending in cool twilight hadn't been such a long one for him, he might have noticed the man following him as he walked to his car. The big man in the light brown business suit closed the gap on Leroy Street and was four steps behind as Rendelli reached to open the door of the blue Nova sedan.

Rendelli was dead in seconds, the long blade of the bayonet coming in at an angle, piercing his heart. A gloved hand went to his back pocket, removed his walllet, and slipped the driver's license from its plastic window. Then, in a sudden inspiration, the hand ripped the shield from Rendelli's tunic.

Lyle had taken on the city. He'd killed a cop.

Enders' call came as Krieg was eating dinner. "Someone killed a cop," Enders said shortly. "We're calling everybody in."

"Who was it?" Krieg asked.

"Rendelli, Sixth Precinct."

"I'll be right down," Krieg said and hung up. He hadn't known Rendelli, but it didn't matter. Cops called in after the death of a fellow officer reported to the deceased's precinct for assignment, and there wasn't an officer in the city who didn't want to get involved in the hunt for a brother's killer.

Billy the Kid was getting used to death; ironically, his nickname was becoming more and more fitting.

The precinct house was a beehive when Krieg arrived. Detectives and patrolmen from all over the city milled around, talking in whispers, waiting for instructions. They would spread out all over the area in which Rendelli had been killed. Some would start digging into Rendelli's arrest record, looking for someone with a grudge against him; his private life would be scrutinized . . . there would be thousands of questions in the search for one answer.

Krieg mingled with the detectives and began picking up bits of information. Rendelli had been on traffic duty around James J. Walker Park, where doctors and nurses had been picketing in protest against citywide cutbacks in personnel and spending. He'd been relieved and was getting into his car to go home when he was killed. Stabbed, Krieg heard an officer say.

And then the most disturbing of all: Rendelli's shield had been taken. It wasn't an official statement, but the cops knew, and the word passed through the crowd in the muster room like a cold wind.

Graham Parker appeared at Krieg's side, chewing a soft pretzel. "Enders call you?"

"Yeah," Krieg said.

"So did I, but your wife said you'd left."

"Yeah," Krieg said again.

"We've got Leroy Street," Parker said, nodding toward the door.

"Who said?"

"Me."

"You sure?"

"I'm sure. We're gonna roust some people. Let's go."

Krieg and Parker spent three hours on Leroy Street and came up with a partial description: a tall man, a brown or tan suit.

Three days later, Krieg stood at attention outside St. Patrick's Cathedral during the inspector's funeral for Rendelli. One of thousands of grim-faced, silent men, he watched the mayor, the police commissioner, the deputy commissioners, and deputy chiefs arrive and walk stiffly inside as cameras clicked and the TV videotapes recorded the event. Rows of uniformed men lined the entrance, and more stood across the street. Each wore a black band across their shields, the symbol of mourning that they would carry with them for a month.

The casket was carried out of the cathedral, and the men and women of the Sixth Precinct swung into step behind the pallbearers. Special Services, a squad of men that takes over a precinct when an officer has been slain, would be relieved after the funeral. The Sixth would go back to work, each man again reminded of his vulnerability, his mortality. Krieg stared as a long line of squad cars, their dome lights spinning in the sun, followed the hearse on its slow drive to the cemetery in Queens.

As the last car disappeared around the corner, Krieg walked with the others to the tables of coffee and sandwiches set up by the PBA—the Patrolmen's Benevolent Association—on Fifty-first Street. He sipped from a paper cup and listened to the small talk: memories of Rendelli, a joke here and there; then angry comments about the city government and the mayor's cutbacks. Finally, in outrage, the missing shield: Rendelli's identity, his membership in this special club. The shield, like his gun, was sacred property; the taking of it was akin to the taking of his life.

Krieg listened, but did not join the conversation. He felt apart from it all. He no longer wore the blue uniform, and in his plainclothes somehow didn't belong among the uniformed officers. Rendelli had been a street cop, and Krieg was no more a part of them than the commissioner. Black mourning band or not, he felt alienated from them. No one would see Krieg's black band unless he had to open his wallet and flash his shield.

Rendelli's shield was missing, and Krieg's was hidden. Krieg finished the coffee and left.

"It's gotta be military," Alex said firmly, picking at her salad. "Weapons, training, execution: Everything fits."

Enders looked at her across the small table. The lunch crowd at the Oyster Bar and Grille in the Plaza Hotel created a steady din, despite the exclusive atmosphere. Hushed conversation, tinkling silverware and crystal, a *maître d'* escorting patrons to plush leather booths as waiter after waiter took orders and set places with pewter dishes and water goblets. Music drifted across the room as musicians played in one of the old hotel's dining rooms.

"We've been through all this," he said, biting into a radish. "It's impossible to track down."

"We've got a partial on Rendelli's killer. . . . "

He shook his head and sipped water from the iced goblet. "Not enough. You've never dealt with the Pentagon, have you?"

"Not in an official capacity, no."

A waiter arrived with a serving casserole of bouillabaise. With a flourish he ladled out the portions and set the dish at the far end of the table.

Alex and Enders took the toasted French garlic bread and crumpled bits into the soup. They nodded to the waiter, who poured Enders a taste of the wine they'd ordered. Enders sampled it and nodded again. The glasses were filled, and they were alone again.

"Can you give me an estimate," Enders began, "of how many vets over six feet tall, about middle-aged, and living in New York City?"

"No," Alex said.

Enders smiled. "Without a specific time that these men served, without a specific unit, without knowing what branch of the service . . . "

"I get it," Alex said. "We don't have nearly enough."

"All we have are healthy suspicions. Four men might be connected and could have had military training at some time. Even if we were sure about the military connection, we couldn't come up with a name and a photograph; fingerprints, well, that's another story."

Alex swallowed a bit of halibut. "Terrific," she mumbled. "Did you turn up anything on the passport?"

"I've been to Immigration so many times I could collect a paycheck." He sipped his wine. "We've been working backward . . . starting with Rendelli, 'cause that's where the pressure is at the moment. All knifings going back five years, anything similar . . . "

"Like missing identification?"

"Sure."

"What about Rendelli's arrest record?"

Enders' expression turned somber, and he concentrated his gaze on the bowl of soup in front of him. "First thing we checked. There's no one near the level we're looking for . . . no one cool enough to come up to him on the street and stab him. Hell, no one with nerve enough to come up to him at all."

Alex changed the subject. "You, uh, seem to be running it all."

"I am," Enders said with a slight smile . . . "or it's running me. Everytime I plug one hole in the dike, there's another leak. There have been six killings, and I know there's a connection. It only makes sense to have one person in charge."

"Is that the logic you used on the other deputy chiefs?"

"More or less . . . but it wasn't that easy. They're looking for results, not theories. I tell them the killers know each other; they don't buy it. We go around for a while, and they finally agree to put me in charge. Unofficially, of course," Enders said, grinning. "But the irony is that I put myself back behind a desk. I got involved in this thing to get out of that damned office, to get back to real police work, and I end up a glorified secretary again. I give them information, they give me feedback; they give me information, I give them feedback; before you know it, five hours are shot."

Alex laughed.

"I don't think it's funny," Enders said with a smirk.

"Oh sure it is," Alex said, playing it out. "The problems of the higher-ups. You're just never satisfied."

"Wrong," he said. "Two things will satisfy me."

"Oh?"

"Finding the killers before I take you to dinner tonight."

"That's one . . . "

"Failing that, just taking you to dinner tonight."

"I'd like to help, but I've got to win ninety dollars back from my father."

Enders' boyish face held a puzzled expression.

"Backgammon," Alex said. "Don't ever play with him. He's a killer."

"You want to do what?" Birmingham asked.

"You heard me, take a vacation," Reynolds said. "It's the end of June; I want to get away from the city for a while. I think we should all take our normal summers, same as we always do, and pick it up in August. Besides, it'll be interesting to let the cops stew for a while."

"I think you're upset just because Dick got all the headlines," Marcus kidded.

Reynolds stared at him, his eyes narrowing slightly, a thin smile forming on his lips. "Headlines? Don't worry about headlines. It's far from over. . . . "

"I'm with Chris," Lyle said. "Stick with our normal routine. . . . "

Marcus burst out laughing. "Normal routine . . . Jesus," he said, gesturing toward the driver's license and the badge on the table, "some normal routine."

"Okay, okay, you know what I mean," Lyle said.

"Birm, what do you want to do?" Reynolds asked.

"I'll go along with you."

"Okay," Reynolds said, getting out of the chair. "First Thursday in August?"

The others nodded. Lyle struck a match, burned the license, and pocketed the badge. "The shield gets tossed into the East River," he commented.

"Tonight," Reynolds urged.

"Tonight," Lyle agreed.

5

Enders spent a bad July.

The heat came from everywhere. The deputy chiefs called constantly: Holtzman, commander of the zone in which Rendelli had been killed, was getting pressure from the commissioner and the PBA, and he passed it on to Enders; Ellison, head of Third Homicide, received the mayor's demands for Charles Witkin's killer and picked up the phone to call Enders. Even Gregory got into the act: "Just letting you know I'm still around, Carl," he said, "and I've got an open file for Eileen Douglas."

Enders was beginning to feel as harried as Ron Blake. Every time the phone rang Enders considered throwing it out the window.

He'd given up reading the papers and watching the TV news, for, as July slipped by without a major financial crisis or a crippling public-service strike, the city's reporters bore down on the headline-grabbing murders of Witkin and Rendelli. An editorial in the *Daily News* blamed the lack of results on manpower cutbacks in the Police Department. Someone told the mayor about the editorial, and he jumped on the police commissioner with both feet. The commissioner jumped on Holtzman and Ellison, and they called Enders.

Worse than the calls was the paperwork. Rewards offered by the PBA for information on Rendelli's death, by the mayor's staff for Witkin, and by Cartier's for Aaron Loesser produced a flood of greedy informants which, in turn, produced a mountain of files in Enders' office.

He began to wish that he'd gone home the night the Sean McMahon call came in.

Graham Parker was on the streets—all day, every day—meeting with every informant he had, calling in every debt that was owed to him. It had always been that when Parker put the pressure on, some stoolie somewhere would turn the man he was looking for—if that man was known on the streets. But as the weeks wore on, Parker became convinced that they were looking for amateurs; his sources were useless.

Parker turned to Rendelli's arrest record, which a dozen men had already combed. He went through the names again, even if they were long dead or imprisoned at the time of Rendelli's death; brothers, sisters, mothers, fathers, friends, cellmates: Parker checked them all. He came up with a sour stomach and tired feet.

Billy the Kid was deep into the alphabet soup. Working on his own while Parker prowled the streets, he made a list of every terrorist organization known to the New York City Police Department, from Cuban nationalists to IRA activists to whatever was left of the Symbionese Liberation Army. He spent his time with the NLF, SLA, IRA, and JDL; he went from SDA to KKK, checking the whereabouts of known members, recruiting activities talking to some of Parker's informants and a few he had "enlisted" on his own—and he came up with nothing. He became frustrated, feeling that somehow he had failed Rendelli. The work that Krieg had at first thrown himself into with a sense of purpose and optimism became a murky, endless tangle of paper that went nowhere and solved nothing.

Alex began to waver in her conviction that the killings were connected. Barely watching a play one night with

Enders, she tossed the idea around in her mind. At the end of the performance Enders guided her out of the theater and held her hand as they walked across town to Fifth Avenue.

"Nothing's happened in three weeks, Carl," she said, as they turned onto Fifth Avenue from Forty-seventh Street, "nothing."

"So that's what you've been fussing with all evening."

"Yeah, that . . . I don't know what it is, but I'm nervous. I can't explain it, and I don't know what to think anymore. I was thinking that you were right, that the killers know each other, that it's all part of some pattern; now, all of a sudden, nothing. If there was a pattern, what happened to it?"

They waited for a traffic light to turn green and then crossed Fifty-fifth Street. "You can't believe they were isolated killings, just coincidences," he said firmly.

"But it's stopped. What if it's over and done with, and there are no more missing ID's?" She turned to face him. "We're just waiting for another killing to prove the theory, aren't we?"

"Yes."

"Like ghouls," she shuddered.

They walked for another few blocks, then stopped at a bar for a drink. The subject was dropped, but Enders was sure that the theory would be proven.

Noah Aikman spent a month in Britain. He allotted two weeks for London, where he hid himself in the file room at Scotland Yard reading and researching for a planned book, and then relaxed for the rest of the time—hiking through the Scottish highlands, salmon fishing with old friends, and meeting new ones in pubs and inns.

He returned to the sweltering city on August 5 and, to his own amazement, plunged immediately into the reports that Alex had been bringing him over the months: McMahon, Douglas, Witkin—names that had echoed in his mind during those quiet morning hours in Britain.

He read the DD-5's, the original reports and, finally, the memos from Enders to Alex that covered each new piece of information, scant though it was.

He realized that they were no closer to a solution than they had been in March.

Andrew Birmingham strolled down Central Park South, passed the intersection of Sixth Avenue, and entered the park. He walked slowly along the path, his eyes fixed to his left. Through the trees he saw the line of chartered buses parked on Center Drive. He left the path, eased his way into the woods, and made his way closer to the roadway. One hundred yards from the road he stopped, squinting into the bright sunlight reflecting from the blue and silver sides of the buses.

There were hundreds of children lining the sidewalks and spilling over into the street, and for each child there was a parent, social worker, or volunteer. Birmingham probed the crowd, looking for his target.

It was going to be a scorcher; the temperature hit eighty-six by ten in the morning. With no breeze to stir the air, the stillness was suffocating.

Billy Gibbs wiped the sweat from his face, took the hands of the two small boys, and led them away from the confusion. Gibbs knew the heat wouldn't keep the crowds away from Central Park, not on this day. August 15 was One-on-one Day in New York, and the annual city-sponsored benefit for retarded children would draw thousands.

With the city handling the organization, major companies donating food, toys, games, and gymnastic equipment, and volunteers supervising the activities, the day was a twofold appeal to the public: to raise money so the children could be placed in neighborhood houses, "group homes," where live-in volunteer "parents" would provide personal attention and education; and to publicize the needs of the children to the general public.

Those needs were well known to Billy Gibbs. The New York Jets' wide receiver spent most of his off-season time working with retarded children, and for this day he had made special arrangements to personally care for Raymond and Dennis, two children from the Maplewood Hospital, Staten Island's institution for the retarded. He had arrived early, met with members of the hospital staff, and picked up the boys as they got off the bus.

Birmingham backed away from the trees, took the path that arced around Center Drive, and followed it as it paralleled the edge of the Sheep Meadow. Calm and assured, he slipped through the knots of people, keeping his eyes fixed on the tall black man who moved slowly across the meadow, holding two small boys by the hand.

Despite the heat, Birmingham moved coolly through the park. The .45 in its leather holster was strapped tightly to the small of his back beneath the uniform jacket. The silencer rested in his pocket.

It was watch and wait now. All he needed was the right moment and he would turn this day into one the city would never forget.

Gibbs guided the boys along the path leading to the Sheep Meadow. At the edge of Heckscher Playground, he stopped to pick up a Frisbee and a Nerf ball—a football-shaped piece of soft foam rubber—from a pile of toys.

The still air carried the scream of a rock band from the Wollman Rink, where a series of day-long concerts was getting under way. Singers, actors, and local and nationally known bands had volunteered their time and talent, with all receipts going to the children.

At the edge of the Sheep Meadow, where the flat land gives way to the hills and trees of the Japanese Lawn, Gibbs dashed into the shade and tossed the ball back to Raymond. It bounced off the seven-year-old's outstretched hands, but Gibbs ran, scooped it up, and guided it back to him. This time Raymond grabbed it, clutched it to his chest, and laughed. Dennis picked up the Frisbee and arched it high into the air, snagging it on an overhanging branch. Gibbs leaped up, as he had done a thousand times on the football field, and snatched the plastic disk loose. Dennis fell on it, giggling.

They climbed across rocks as they moved toward the lake near the Seventy-second Street entrance. Leaning back against a tree, Gibbs told them football stories, reducing the complexities of the contest to a simple game of tag and catch. He skipped stones into the water and showed the boys how to hold the stone so it would glance off the surface and jump across. They didn't have the co-ordination to get it right, but Gibbs saw the light in their eyes as they tried to imitate him. He put his arms around them and hugged.

From two hundred yards away, Birmingham watched. With a sense of relief he had trailed them to this spot— away from the crowds, away from the people with Instamatic cameras, away from the TV crews and their vidio and film equipment. Birmingham didn't need any cameras trained on him—he had begun to realize that wearing the uniform was a mistake. There was a volunteer Army now, and a man in military dress wasn't as invisible as he had thought.

Gibbs spoke briefly to an attendant at the rowboat rental stand and exchanged his autograph for the use of a boat. He lifted Raymond and Dennis in and pushed off from the dock, letting Dennis help him push on the oar. The ten-year-old had better co-ordination than Raymond, and Dennis pushed firmly on the oar, smiling at Billy Gibbs. Gibbs rowed out thirty feet, then let the boat drift. The boys trailed their hands in the water.

They spent an hour in the boat, Billy talking about the cities he'd played in, the Super Bowl they'd won, the children he worked with in his hometown of Atlanta. He didn't know if they understood what he was saying, but the attention he paid them brought their smiles.

They helped him tie the boat to the dock, and Billy lifted the boys effortlessly in his arms and carried them to the tar path. Tow hundred feet away was a lunch stand, and Billy ordered everything the boys pointed to, carrying a heaping plate of hot dogs and french fries to a table. He cut the hot dogs into small sections, brought them milk in paper cups, and wiped their faces when they smeared ketchup and mustard.

"Does anybody have to go to the bathroom?" Gibbs asked them. The boys shook their heads.

"Well, I do, so you wait right here for me. Finish up the milk and stay here. I don't want anybody going anywhere, okay?"

The boys nodded and picked up the paper cups.

"Okay," Gibbs said, pointing to a brick building twenty-five yards away in the trees at the edge of the path. "I'll be right in there and then I'll be right back."

Gibbs was standing at the urinal when he heard the door open and the sharp click of heels on the tile floor.

Birmingham stopped two steps inside the door, one hand reaching for the .45, the other bringing the silencer out. He twisted the black tube onto the barrel and stepped forward, away from the partition that blocked the stalls. Gibbs was walking toward the sink.

"Back up," Birmingham said quietly, raising his gun.

Gibbs couldn't believe what he was seeing. "Hey, wait a minute man," he said.

"Back up. I won't say it again."

"Okay, okay, take it easy. What do you want?"

"Take the ring off," Birmingham said, the gun rock-steady, his voice low.

"What?"

"Take the ring off your finger, put it down on the floor, and slide it over."

Birmingham had thought it out carefully. Let Reynolds take chances if he wants to; I'll play it safe. He wanted the ring before he fired. He wasn't going to go near the mess to get it.

Gibbs twisted the Super Bowl ring off his finger. He bent slowly, placed it on the floor, and with his foot tapped it gently, sending it sliding across. It stopped a foot in front of Birmingham.

Restless, Raymond wandered away from the table, leaving Dennis alone. Raymond walked toward the building where Billy had gone. He passed the door and saw, high up on the side wall, a window—and below it, the huge green dumpster where the refuse from the lunch stand was collected. He struggled to the top of the dumpster and stood on the flat metal section that covered half the bin. Leaning against the windowsill, he peered down into the room.

Birmingham knelt, his arm rigid, the gun unwavering, his eyes locked on Billy Gibbs' face. Birmingham felt in front of him, picked up the ring, and put it in his pocket. He stood.

Billy Gibbs had a split second to think: This guy's gonna kill me.

Birmingham fired twice, and Gibbs' head exploded.

Raymond stumbled back and fell from the cover into the dumpster. He lay on top of plastic garbage bags, his eyes squeezed shut.

But no matter how tightly he squeezed, he still saw the man pointing at Billy. He saw Billy's blood splatter against the wall. He saw the terrible thing on the man's shoulder.

Police Commissioner Michael Forman squinted into the glaring lights as reporters and cameramen pressed toward the podium. He knew that the best defense was an offense, so he called the press conference immediately after Gibbs' body had been discovered—after the mayor had called him, screaming in his ear—which was after the president of the New York Jets had pushed his way into the mayor's office demanding protection for the team and vengeance for Billy Gibbs.

"Gentlemen, ladies and gentlemen, please . . . " Forman called out. The room quieted, the staccato clicking of press cameras giving Forman his only competition.

"Thank you." He stared for a moment at the bouquet of microphones before him, cleared his throat, and put on his best calm, capable exterior. "I have no prepared statement. We don't have time for that. This is what we've got: Billy Gibbs, of the Jets' football team, was murdered this afternoon around three o'clock in a men's room near the Seventy-second Street lake in Central Park. He was participating in the One-on-one Day benefit. He was shot twice in the head and died instantly. An autopsy is now being conducted."

Forman swallowed and continued. "We're checking all available leads, and you can be assured that we're going to find out who killed him. We will not permit this in our city. . . . "

His voice trailed off as strobe lights from the cameras winked and the clicking built to a crescendo. This was the public Forman, giving a strong promise that all would be well again; everything would be solved; everyone would be safe.

He would not answer any questions, he told himself, and he waved off inquiries with, "There isn't anything more I can tell you." He raised his hand and quieted the crowd. "I want to issue a public appeal to anyone who was in the area of the lake and might have seen Billy Gibbs. Please come forward . . . anybody who was in the park and saw Gibbs at any time." He looked directly into the television pool camera. "Somebody saw the murderer. You probably don't know it, but you saw him. Tell us what you saw . . . please come forward." He read a special hotline phone number.

"I'd also like to announce," Forman continued, hesitating for an instant, "that the Jets' team management is offering a reward of fifty thousand dollars for any information leading to the arrest and conviction of Billy Gibbs' murderer."

That announcement was to placate the Jets' president. Forman knew there was only a chance in a thousand that the reward offer would bring anything useful. Mostly it would bring the crazies; useless leads from sick minds would double the police work.

Forman abruptly thanked the reporters and left the room. Down the hall he took the elevator to his office and found half a dozen messages, all requesting that he call the mayor.

When he did, the frustration in both men touched off an explosion. Jack Donahue complained bitterly that the press was walking all over his administration, blaming the rash of notorious murders on his cutbacks in police manpower and spending . . . and if it wasn't too little spending, it was too much: for renovations, computer systems, and new equipment. Damned if he did and double damned if he didn't. He was fed up.

Forman listened impatiently and then fought back.

"What do you want me to do? Just what the hell do you expect? I know it's bad . . . first Witkin, then that guy at Cartier's, and now, Jesus, a New York Jet! Do you think I'm asleep here or something? We're doing everything we can—which, frankly, isn't much at the moment."

Forman hung up, popped a Rolaids, and wondered how soon the mayor would appoint a new police commissioner. The hell with it, he thought. If he thinks anyone else is going to walk in here and clean up this garbage overnight, let him try it.

He got on the phone and called the deputy chiefs. They were in his office in a half hour, listening as he pleaded and then demanded. "I want results," he thundered at them.

Enders was reading the ballistics reports on Gibbs, only half listening to Forman. He stopped cold when he saw the caliber of the bullet: .45.

But the capper was the robbery report: Billy Gibbs' Super Bowl ring was missing.

After the meeting, Enders took the other deputy chiefs aside in the hallway. "The .45 again," he said quietly.

Holtzman, the overweight, balding cherub, who never in his whole career looked like a policeman, nodded. "Did Gibbs' ring have his name on it?" he asked Enders.

"Yeah, all Super Bowl rings have the name of the player, his team, and the year of the victory engraved on them. I remember hearing some halftime announcer talk about it. It's an ID, same as a Social Security card."

"Another useless item missing," Holtzman mumbled to himself.

"Any ideas, Carl?" Gregory asked, impatient.

Enders hesitated. "Yeah," he said slowly, "one—but you may not like it. I'm not even sure I like it, but I think it's the only way. I'll need the commissioner's permission—and your help."

"Whatever it is, we'll back you," Ellison said quickly.

"Don't be too sure," Enders said, with a trace of a smile.

He gave it to them quickly, and before anyone could object, led them back to Forman's office.

At seven the next morning, Enders sat exhausted on a bench in Central Park. The slight mist in the air was slowly burning off as the sun rose with the promise of yet another sweltering day. In the distance, he heard a rhythmic slapping.

He'd argued all night, gone over all the cases from memory, laid out all the similarities, and pressed his theory. He pointed out that there was precedent for what he wanted to do. He argued from logic, reason, and emotion, and when he was all talked out and they finally agreed, he wasn't sure whether it was the strength of his argument or the weariness of the others that led to his victory . . . and he didn't care.

A jogger came into view on his right, and the slapping of sneakers on the tar path grew louder. Enders raised his arm and waved, and Noah Aikman, wrapped in a green warm-up suit, slowed and stopped by the bench.

Aikman sat down, blotting the sweat from his forehead on his flannel sleeve. He turned to Enders and saw the puffy eyes and the lines of fatigue on the deputy chief's face.

"When was the last time you had any sleep?"

Enders shrugged. "Can't remember." He met Aikman's blue eyes head on. "You up for some sleepless nights?"

84

Part II

6

Enders made the phone calls to the other deputy chiefs from Aikman's study while Noah showered and changed. Enders felt rejuvenated and prowled the room, running his finger along the edge of the huge mahogany desk, pulling books from the shelves, skimming the pages, and putting them back. First editions were liberally sprinkled through the collection, which occupied two huge bookcases along the far walls of the rectangular room. Between the books stood African sculpture, porcelain, and pottery.

In back of the desk, Aikman had mounted his blackboard, and Enders smiled when he realized it was genuine black slate. He sat down behind the desk gazing at the two Lautrec sketches that hung on the opposite wall, next to the doorway. A sectional sofa in deep brown occupied the corner to his right; a wing-back wooden rocker and a black leather armchair stood in the opposite corner.

The door opened, and Aikman stuck his head in. "Coffee?"

"Thanks," Enders said and followed Aikman to the kitchen.

He can afford to live well, Enders thought, as he noted the furnishings in the apartment. His fees were as legendary as his overflow classes, and Aikman received the added bonus of collecting whatever rewards were connected with a case once he solved it. And to Enders' knowledge Aikman had never failed.

Enders felt encouraged; what he had done was unusual, but he knew he was right. There were too many dead ends, and they needed help.

Enders stood with his coffee mug in the living room as the others arrived—first Holtzman, looking remarkable refreshed after the long night in the commissioner's office.

Robert Ellison arrived shortly after Holtzman. Ellison was an old friend of Aikman's, and if he felt any hesitancy about being there he hid it with an actor's polish. The image struck Enders as particularly fitting, for as the only black deputy chief in the city's history, Ellison's appearance and demeanor were as important as his ability. He was always in the spotlight.

Peter Gregory was reserved, quiet, his bulldog face impassive. He'd argued the longest against this move, saying over and over again that it demeaned the Police Department. Enders knew that Gregory really meant that it demeaned him, personally. Gregory didn't like to accept help from anyone. He shook hands with Aikman and stood apart from the others, not joining in the small talk.

Jerry Lawrence arrived last, and might have slipped into the room without notice had the door been open. Lawrence was known around the precincts as "Joe Public," a comment on his appearance and his style. He was five-ten with dark brown hair and quiet brown eyes. He was everyone's description of an ordinary-looking guy and, coupled with his tendency to speak just above a whisper if at all, he might have gone unnoticed in the Police Department had it not been for his ability. No one underestimated him, and he took his nickname with an ease born of self-confidence. He had onced signed an official memo "J. Public," wondering if anyone would notice that.

Aikman ushered them into the study and buzzed Alex's apartment. When she arrived, Gregory wasted no time. "I was not in favor of calling you in, Noah. I want you to know that from the beginning. Nothing personal."

Aikman resisted a smile. "I can understand that. But I'm in, nonetheless, and I'll need all of you to help me if we expect to solve these killings."

"That's what you're here for, isn't it—to solve them?" Gregory asked, a trace of sarcasm in his voice.

"Why don't we get that straight from the start," Aikman said. "Just what do you expect from me?"

"A solution," Gregory said.

"From where?"

Gregory tapped his forehead. "From here."

Aikman laughed. "Forget it. I'm not a miracle worker. The solution isn't here," he pointed to his temple, "yet . . . I'm only as good as the information I get. If I get the right information, I think I can put it together. You've got to give me the materials to work with."

Enders turned to Gregory. "Pete, we went through this; let's not waste time. Nine out of ten cases can be solved by procedure and legwork. This is the tenth case; we need something more."

Gregory shrugged. "Okay, I've heard it all. . . . "

Aikman sat down on the edge of the desk, his long legs reaching the floor. "Let's go over what we've got, and then we'll get into what I need." He lit a cigarette and tossed the match into the ashtray.

"From what Carl tells me, we've got a witness to Gibbs' death, but I doubt he'll be of any use. He's retarded, and after what he saw he's in some sort of catatonic state."

"That's what the hospital says," Enders agreed. "We don't know if he saw anything, but one of the detectives measured the distance from the top of the dumpster to the window. The boy was just tall enough to see inside. But he's not talking . . . not to anyone, about anything."

"Carl," Aikman said, "fill everyone in on the soldier."

Enders flipped through his notebook. "I got this early

this morning. The grill jockey at the lunch counter . . . José Pérez . . . saw a man in uniform."

"The military connection," Alex said.

Enders nodded. "Yeah, we had it figured right. Pérez says the guy was tall, had a mustache, shiny shoes. 'Neat' was Pérez's big word. Everything about him was 'neat.' " Enders looked up from the notebook. "Twenty minutes later, he finally defined 'tall' as six feet, maybe a little more. Medium build, or medium to slim, Pérez's not too sure." Enders shrugged. "Fits almost anybody," he said, looking at Alex.

"Except for the uniform," Aikman said.

"What branch of the service?" Gregory asked.

"He thinks Army," Enders said.

"Pérez ever in the Army?" Gregory pressed.

"No," Enders admitted.

"Big fuckin' deal," Gregory said.

"He remembers a cap, a visored hat," Enders said, pretending not to have heard Gregory. "And epaulets."

"An officer," Ellison said.

"Assuming it was Army," Holtzman added.

"Yeah," Enders sighed.

"Could be Air Force," Holtzman said.

"Or Navy, for that matter," Enders said. "Pérez is either color blind or just can't remember color. We showed him photos of uniforms. . . ." his voice trailed off.

"Could be a Scoutmaster," Gregory mumbled.

"I don't get it," Alex said, shaking her head. "Why would he wear a uniform? We suspect a military connection, and now one of them confirms it. Why would he do that?"

"Ego," Aikman answered. "He's spitting in our faces."

"Or there's no military connection and the uniform came from a costume shop," Ellison suggested.

"Good point," Aikman said, "Check it out."

Ellison smiled. "Thanks a whole lot."

"A few other things we can do," Aikman continued, "is

put out a call for anyone in the park who had a camera, from snapshooters to TV crews. We've got to see every picture that was taken."

Enders nodded. "But the uniform . . ."

"Hold off on that. I wouldn't broadcast that we're looking for a particular man," Aikman said. "Most people will take a quick glance at their photographs and decide there's nothing of interest to the police. They don't know what to look for, and they don't know how to look. Make it a blanket call for pictures and we'll make the decision whether there's anything there or not. Besides, I don't want to tip the killers. We're not dealing with dummies, and I don't think they're psychotic. It's better for us that they don't know who or what we're looking for."

"What are we looking for?" Gregory asked innocently.

"Four men . . . " Aikman began.

"Hold it," Alex said. "How do you know that? How can you be sure they're all men?"

"Okay, let's go over it. We've got a partial on the man in uniform. . . . "

"But we're not sure he killed Gibbs. We only think so because he was seen in the area."

"Take it this way, then: The weapons and methods indicate men. The sniper hit twice in the early morning on deserted streets, a problem for anyone in this city, but especially so for a woman. And the weapon: No matter how the rifle was carried, it would be more noticeable on a woman. Say it was broken down and put into a suitcase . . ."

"Okay," Alex conceded. "What about the others?"

"The one with the bayonet was incredibly strong and taller than Witkin. . . . "

"Circumstantial evidence," Alex said.

"Right, but that's all we've got—and it's very often accurate information. As to the others—well, Hayakawa—

sorry, Hayakimo—was killed in the men's room." Aikman shrugged and turned his hands palms up. "What more can I say?"

"Gibbs, too," Alex admitted. "I forgot the obvious."

"Well, don't worry about it, because not much about this case is going to be obvious," Aikman said. "Something about the victims ties this all together. The seemingly random factor of selection: Why a singer? Why the mayor's assistant? Why a football player? I need everything about them. You've got to dig out every shred of information, no matter how insignificant it may seem. I need everything, because the more you bring, the better the chances of seeing why they were killed."

"Which doesn't tell us who killed them," Lawrence spoke for the first time.

"But it's the place to start. The killers are doing everything deliberately. It looks like they're stalking each victim. McMahon, for example. The sniper knew his habits— staying late, alone, to clean up. And then another deliberate move: They take identification from each victim."

"To prove that the right person was killed?" Alex asked.

"Maybe," Aikman said. "Maybe just to prove that the victim was killed by one of our killers. If they know each other—and I believe thay do—and if they're working together—and I believe that, also—then they're proving it to each other."

Gregory was getting impatient. He had thought it out and put most of it together by himself. What Aikman was giving him was useless. There was nothing new. "Where do we start?" he asked, a slight edge in his voice.

"You start with anything that can connect the victims. Clubs, churches, jury lists, backgrounds—check it all again and bring me everything."

"Military clubs?" Holtzman asked.

"Do it," Aikman said. "And put someone on plays— Broadway, off-Broadway, high school, anything—see if we can find a play currently in performance that uses military uniforms."

"Okay," Enders said, rising. "Biographies, backgrounds . . ."

". . . and Broadway," Lawrence said, standing up.

Aikman opened the door. "Weekly meetings, plan on it."

They straggled out, leaving Enders at the door. "What do you do now?" he asked Aikman.

"I start to organize what I've got, and I wait for more."

Alone in the apartment, Aikman flicked on the stereo, dialed the classical music station and, with a smile of anticipation, walked back into the study. He took a piece of chalk from the center drawer in his desk, snapped it in half, and tossed one piece on the ledge at the bottom of the blackboard. He lined four columns on the slate. Each column had a heading—"Sniper," "Wire," "Bayonet," "Pistol"—and below each heading he wrote the names of the victims, sex, age, and locations of the murders. He printed each item slowly. Handwriting for the blackboard was out, as no one else could ever read it.

When he finished he stepped back and looked it over. The only sense it made came from the neat, orderly columns he'd constructed; at least there was symmetry in that.

From the bottom drawer of his desk he removed an accordion file marked "Maps," and took out a Hagstrom of New York City. One side of the map showed the island of Manhattan, and he smoothed it out and pinned it to the corkboard section of wall beside the blackboard.

With a black felt pen he circled the exact locations of the killings, consulting the files and his notes for the particular street intersections. He numbered each in sequence of the killing and initialed them for the weapon used.

Connect the dots, he thought, smiling.

Seven people—seven people in six months; the smile

vanished from his face. This would be interesting, he knew; it would be a test, as every case was a test, and Aikman liked to pass.

It was a contest, too, pitting him against four unknown men; smart, careful, cunning, they were experts.

Aikman, too, was an expert. And he liked to win.

7

Birmingham tossed the Super Bowl ring on the table. He'd waited for this moment all day and watched the others closely, eagerly anticipating their reaction.

"I knew it," Lyle said. "The minute I heard the news bulletin I knew it was you."

"They'll go crazy on this one," Marcus grinned, shaking his head in admiration. "The police will have fits!"

Reynolds picked up the ring and read the inscription. "You outdid yourself, Birm," he smiled. "You outdid all of us."

"In all modesty," Birmingham said, "I must agree." He made a mock bow. He'd expected the praise and had spent the day playing this scene over and over in his mind. He'd topped them.

"Okay, let's hear it," Marcus urged.

Birmingham settled slowly into a chair and stretched out his legs. Throughout their dinner at Lutece he'd thought about the killing: how to describe it, how to best present it. They never spoke of anything other than business matters during dinners—Reynolds' stock manipulations or Lyle's investments for the bank he served as vice president being the most frequent topics—but this night Birmingham hadn't joined in the conversation. He ate mechanically, rehearsing his lines.

"I saw Gibbs' name in the paper two weeks ago; an article on the benefit mentioned some football and basketball players who'd be in the park . . . but the article singled Gibbs out because of his work with retarded children. I wanted him, and I knew I could take him if the circumstances were right. I needed a little luck."

"And you got it," Marcus said.

"It wasn't all luck," Birmingham said. "There were problems to be worked out. I had to figure out where to carry the gun . . . the shoulder holster wasn't any good because the jacket was too tight. . . . "

"What jacket?" Reynolds said sharply. "What were you wearing?"

"I wore my uniform," Birmingham replied, smiling.

"Why'd you do that?" Lyle asked.

"Partly ego, I'll admit, but mainly to be able to slip around the crowds. Nobody notices a soldier walking in the park—especially on a day when there are thousands of people out. I stayed out of sight until Gibbs moved off with the kids, then I followed from a distance. All I needed was to get him alone for a minute, that's all it would take. . . ."

"And that's where the luck came in," Marcus said.

Birmingham smiled. "I was about to give it up when he went into the bathroom." He reeled off the details, building up to the killing. He was reliving the scene and never noticed that he'd lost part of his audience. Reynolds had tuned him out and was staring at his cigarette, flicking the filter tip with his thumb, his eyes half closed.

" . . . so I took the ring first," Birmingham was saying. "I couldn't stand too close to him because of the chance of a ricochet off those tile walls, and I didn't want to go near him once I fired. I hit him twice. I didn't even look back to see the damage. I was out of the park in four minutes, crisscrossed the city, and doubled back to the apartment." He took the ring from the table and put it his pocket.

"Just one thing, Birm," Reynolds said, his voice just above a whisper.

"What's that?"

"Did it ever occur to you that wearing your own uniform was an incredibly stupid mistake?"

Lyle began to nod his head in agreement. Marcus fastened his eyes to Reynolds'.

"No," Birmingham said calmly, "because it wasn't. The only problem was staying away from crowds, from the people with cameras; staying far enough away from Gibbs . . ."

"Bullshit!" Reynolds exploded, slamming his fist on the table. Marcus jumped at the sudden violence.

"Don't hand me that," Reynolds snarled, "don't sit there and defend what you did. You know it was a mistake! There's a volunteer Army now. Nobody wears their goddamn uniforms anymore."

Birmingham remained calm, his flushed face the only hint of the turmoil inside. "Yeah, I know, but . . . "

Marcus cut him off. "How bad is it?" he asked Reynolds.

Reynolds sighed. "No way to tell. Even if the police have a description, we'll never know it . . . until it's too late." He got up from the table and stood directly opposite Birmingham.

"You're such a careful man, so responsible. You were always the man who took care of the details. Six hours out there in that park . . . God only knows how many people saw you, or how many will remember."

"My description could fit a thousand men, if anyone remembers," Birmingham shot back.

"He's right, Chris," Lyle said. "What have they really got if someone remembers a man in uniform?"

Reynolds turned to face Lyle. "You're missing the goddamn point! This is war! We've got to survive it." He turned back to Birmingham. "We all depend on each other not to screw up. My life is in your hands!" He was shouting, and he paced around the table to calm himself.

"We'll skip tonight and next week," he said, his voice becoming steady once again. "Give things a chance to cool off. We'll pick it up in two weeks . . . if we're not in jail."

Reynolds opened the door and left the room.

He made up his mind as he walked down East Fifty-seventh Street, dragging on a cigarette and thinking out the options.

It's not good enough, he thought.

If there's one thing his background and training had taught him, it was to depend only on himself. He wouldn't put his life in anyone else's hands.

If Birmingham's uniform comes back to betray us, he decided, I'll have a way out . . . and if the others don't make their own plans, then they deserve what they get.

By the soft light that came through the curtains, Enders traced the outline of her body, first with his eyes, then with his hand. Alex rolled toward him and put her arms around his neck. Forty-seven years old, he thought, and I feel like a teen-ager.

They had begun the evening with dinner and a vow not to discuss the case, talking instead of his life and career, until he realized, sadly, that they were synonymous.

"One day I looked around and found my children grown and my wife refusing to listen to one more "day in the life of a cop" story. It was a quiet divorce," he said, managing a smile.

"The gospel according to Wambaugh," Alex said, knowingly.

"Yeah, no more, no less . . . and nothing original, I'm afraid."

Alex took a last swallow of coffee. "C'mon, let's get out of here. This place is filling up with ghosts."

Enders paid the check and they left the restaurant. Alex took his arm and they began walking up Third Avenue.

"I didn't mean to depress you," she said, softly.

Enders stopped, turned to her, and put his hands on her shoulders. "You didn't. You couldn't." He leaned forward and kissed her.

At Sixty-fourth Street they turned west. "Did you always want to be a lawyer?" Enders asked.

"Uh huh, for as long as I can remember. My father's influence, probably. Not that he said anything . . . it was just that I found his work fascinating, and the law seemed the best way to be part of it. After my mother died . . . " She hesitated.

"How old were you?"

"Twelve. She was killed by a drunk driver." They were in front of the brownstone. "Like some coffee?" Alex asked.

Enders nodded and they went inside, up the stairs and into Alex's apartment. She brewed a fresh pot and poured two mugs of coffee.

"I see your father's influence," Enders said, noting the furnishings.

"Earth colors and lots of wood," Alex said, "the best. I can't stand modern furniture. All that glass and chrome makes me nervous."

They settled into the sofa. "I like a room that's inviting, friendly . . . no sharp edges," Alex laughed.

Enders sipped from his mug and thought of his apartment. "I don't spend too much time at home. I'm more comfortable in my office, working."

"Even as a glorified secretary?" Alex kidded.

Enders laughed. "That must have been one of my low periods. You've got to learn not to take everything I say too seriously."

They talked quietly for an hour, and when it came time for Enders to leave, he didn't.

Now, as he held her tightly in his arms, he remembered that secure yet insecure feeling he'd known as a younger man. "I think I love you," he said quietly, almost a question.

Alex opened her eyes. "God, don't say that."

Enders pulled away. "Why not?"

"I don't think my father would approve of me getting involved with a cop."

It took Enders a full second to see the laughter in her eyes. "Christ, you're impossible." He eased her onto her back and fit his body to hers. "Impossible," he said, kissing her.

The clock radio woke him to music at seven. "Make sure the door is locked," Alex murmured, turning over. Enders kissed her shoulder, rolled out of the bed, and dressed.

He walked quietly down the steps and was just passing Aikman's door on the landing when it opened suddenly and Aikman, in his green jogging suit, came out.

"Coming or going?" Aikman asked.

Enders swallowed. "Uh . . . good morning," was all he could manage.

Aikman held the front door for him, locked it, and jogged off down the street.

When Aikman returned from Central Park, he put coffee on and showered and changed. With a steaming mug in his hand, he called the Maplewood Hospital and made an appointment with Dr. Arnold Hughes, head of the hospital.

Aikman rode the ferry to Staten Island, walking the deck and outlining in his mind the questions he would ask if he could get to see Raymond. It wasn't Aikman's way to prepare questions ahead of time, but this would be different. If he got to see the boy and talk to him, he wouldn't have much time, and every question had to elicit information. He couldn't afford to waste any time, not with doctors and attendants hovering over him.

Aikman hailed a cab at the ferry dock and arrived at the

hospital twenty minutes later. Consulting his notes, he told the driver to find Building A. "I'll do the best I can, buddy. I've never been out here before, you know."

"No, I didn't know that," Aikman said patiently.

They drove onto the hospital grounds and found a directory. Building A stood apart from the hospital complex, a depressing-looking cinderblock affair, three stories high and painted pastel yellow.

Aikman paid the driver and went inside. The smell of disinfectant assaulted his nostrils, and the brightly polished tile floor threw the glare of neon lighting into his eyes. "And they expect people to get well in this place?" he muttered.

A sign indicated the administrator's office, and Aikman knocked before going in. "I'm Noah Aikman," he said to a middle-aged woman at the desk inside the door. "I have an appointment with Dr. Hughes."

"Oh yes, please have a seat," she said, indicating an uncomfortable-looking wooden bench. She picked up a phone, dialed two numbers, and mumbled something into the receiver.

A door opened at the back of the room, and a man in a blue business suit came out. "Mr. Aikman?"

Aikman got up. "That's right."

"Come in, please."

Aikman followed Hughes into the inner office, which carried on the motif of the hospital: starkly furnished, with a Formica-topped conference table, three walls of bookcases, and several chairs. Hughes, settling in behind the heavy wooden desk, was the only touch of real class in the room: graying hair, trimmed mustache, and a smooth, relaxed manner. Aikman took a seat in the easy chair facing him.

"Would you like some coffee?" Hughes asked.

"Yes, please."

Hughes picked up the phone and dialed. "Two coffees, please." He put the receiver down and looked at Aikman.

"It's quite a pleasure meeting you, Mr. Aikman, but I'm not sure what we can help you with."

"I'm interested in anything that's happened to Raymond or Dennis since the One-on-one Day in the park."

Hughes' secretary knocked on the door, came in, and placed two coffee mugs on the desk. "Thank you, Angela," Hughes said. The woman nodded and left.

"The fact is, Mr. Aikman, nothing has happened. Dennis has managed to give us some impressions of the day, but nothing the police don't already know. As for Raymond . . . well, he hasn't spoken a word."

Aikman took his coffee and sipped.

"You have to understand," Hughes went on, "that it was a terrible shock to the boy. Billy Gibbs was very, very good to him, to both of them. He'd had experience with mentally retarded children, he knew how to take care of them, and he honestly cared about them. Some people are cold, Mr. Aikman. They go through the motions, but they don't really care. Billy Gibbs cared, and the children knew it."

Aikman wasn't listening. His mind raced back to the newspapers and the publicity they'd given the One-on-one Day. Billy Gibbs' name was prominent in almost every story. Everyone knew he cared, and everyone knew he'd be in the park. Somebody had plenty of time and advance information to work it out.

Aikman snapped back to the conversation. Hughes was going on about Gibbs' devotion to the children.

" . . . we think Dennis is beginning to understand that something bad happened. He may sense that Billy is dead, but he couldn't understand 'murdered' and, frankly, we wouldn't attempt to explain it."

"What about Raymond? We think he saw Gibbs killed. Is there any way to unlock what's in his mind?"

"Not any quick way. And even if we do, someday, find out what he saw, you must remember that he doesn't percieve events as we do. He sees and understands in a sort of code, and even if he spoke to us, we might not understand what he was saying. We would have to break the code, so to speak."

Another puzzle, Aikman thought. "What about visual aids: drawings, photographs?"

"We tried that two weeks ago. Leslie gave him paper and crayons. He wouldn't touch them."

"Who's Leslie?" Aikman asked, sipping the coffee.

"Dr. Hutton. She's one of the therapists who's working with the boys."

"Psychiatrist?"

"Yes."

"I'd like to speak with her, if it's possible."

"Of course." Hughes dialed the phone and asked his secretary to find Dr. Hutton.

Aikman struggled to finish the coffee, thinking that the first thing the hospital needed was a new kitchen staff.

There was a knock at the door and Dr. Hutton came in. She was five-eight with strong, even features and light brown hair cut short. Aikman put her age at forty-five. He had the sudden thought that with tortoise-shell glasses, she would be Central Casting's first choice for lady-psychiatrist roles. As she turned toward him and he focused on her blue-gray eyes, Aikman realized that she was quite beautiful and quickly shoved the stereotype to the back of his mind.

"Dr. Hutton, this is Mr. Aikman," Hughes said. Aikman rose and shook her hand.

"How can I help you?" she asked, her voice soft.

Aikman like that. No "What is it you want?" waltzing around. She understood he was here for information, for help, and she got right to the point. He was going to like her, but she might be a tough person to argue with, or convince, if she thought she was right.

He went right to it. "I'm interested in knowing if you've made any progress with Raymond."

"We're a long way from what you'd call progress, Mr. Aikman. We first have to re-establish a trust, a bond that's been broken. We brought Billy Gibbs to him, we encouraged him to trust Billy, even to enjoy Billy's company. He left these surroundings—the only home he'd known for most of his life—and went out into the world with Billy. Then Billy leaves him . . . "

"Billy was wrong to leave him," Hughes said.

"It was a mistake," Dr. Hutton said, with anger. "He should have known better."

"Doctor," Aikman said to Leslie, "we have a strong suspicion that Raymond saw Billy Gibbs die, saw the killer."

"Who is 'we'?" she asked.

Aikman smiled. "Everybody who wants to find out who killed Billy Gibbs."

"Have you been hired by the Jets?" Leslie asked.

"No, I haven't. I'm a consultant to the Police Department," Aikman said, and quickly changed the subject. "Can you tell from Raymond's reaction whether he did see Gibbs die?"

"No . . . " Leslie said, pausing. "It's possible, of course. Personally, I'm sure he saw something, something more than Billy Gibbs going into a men's room and not coming out. The hostile reaction, his withdrawal from all of us . . . something brought it on. You have to understand—a normal seven-year-old will react badly to death, but a child like Raymond will react in a stronger way. He's expressing hostility, a feeling of betrayal, and it's all mixed in with an inability to understand what happened, to understand what he saw." She shook her head. "If he saw Billy Gibbs die, it could take years for us to reach him . . . maybe never."

She watched Aikman's face and felt sorry for him. If he was depending on Raymond for an answer, he might never find it.

"This has happened before," she went on, trying to ease the situation, "people sealing themselves off. Raymond is dealing with his pain the only way he knows how. And the only way to help is by trying to re-establish his trust. That takes time."

Aikman nodded and took two business cards from his pocket. "I'd appreciate it if you'd keep me informed. I'd like to know what the child does and what he says . . . if he says anything. Any reaction you get from him, positive or negative, could be terribly important. . . . "

Hughes frowned. "Mr. Aikman, we'd like to help, but our records, our dealings with patients are confidential. . . ."

Aikman stood up. "Dr. Hughes, I can have a court order for every file in this building within the hour. I'd prefer not to go that way, if I can avoid it."

Leslie's eyes were on Aikman. "Some consultant," she said sarcastically.

Aikman fought back a smile. "Doctor," he said, his voice softening, "I'd like this to be a friendly relationship . . . but this is a homicide investigation, and Raymond didn't just decide to go sit in a garbage dumpster. He saw something, and we need to know what it was. We're not asking you to do anything other than your normal procedure. We just want to know about his progress."

"Why?" Leslie asked.

"Because, when and if the time comes, you'll have to ask the questions for us."

"You're practically asking us to set him up and then betray him again. You want him well, cured, so you can face him with Gibbs' death all over again," Leslie said.

"No, that's not what I want. I want him to trust you again, to be well enough to talk about it. When he's ready to do that, the answers will come out if I tell you what to ask. And if he starts to talk about it—says anything, no matter how insignificant it is to you—I must know about it immediately."

Dr. Hughes shook his head. "I'm still hesitant, Mr. Aikman. I don't like to give patients' files to . . . "

"Outsiders?" Aikman asked. "All right, let's try this: Dr. Hutton, would you meet with me once a month, maybe twice if need be, and bring your notes and reports? Keep them in your possession, but give me the information . . . and your impressions, your feelings about Raymond's progress."

"That sounds like a fair compromise," Hughes admitted. "Dr. Hutton?"

"Yes, I think that would be all right. But Mr. Aikman, will you trust me to bring you all the information? Or would you be more comfortable with a subpoena?"

Aikman smiled. "I'll trust you, Doctor. I know Raymond is your main concern, but I think you'd like to help us find Billy Gibbs' killer."

Leslie stood up and shook Aikman's hand. "Maybe we'll both get what we want."

When Aikman got back to the brownstone, he changed into jeans and a T-shirt and called Graham Parker at the Mayflower Luncheonette. Parker wasn't there, but Aikman left a message.

He fussed over his notes for an hour, stared at the blackboard and the map of New York City. He was setting up a time line on the killings when Parker arrived.

"Drink?" Aikman asked, leading him into the living room.

"No, thanks. What can I do for you?"

"I need your help," Aikman said, sitting down opposite Parker on one of the chairs facing the sofa. Parker scooped a huge handful of M&M's from a glass bowl on the coffee table and popped them into his mouth as Aikman spoke.

"I want you to go to Andy Reed's bar, hang around a few nights, and find a regular, someone who was there during the hours Eileen Douglas worked. Once you find him, see if he can remember a stranger, someone who came in a week or so before the killing, somebody who hung around while Eileen was on, but who never stayed till closing."

"What are we looking for, exactly?" Parker asked.

"The stranger would be checking Eileen out, but he'd be sure to be out of the place before she left so he could follow her, pick up her routine. It probably took him a few nights . . . but I can't be sure."

"Okay, I got it, but I don't see why Andy Reed himself wouldn't be the best source."

"He'd be too busy at the bar. Besides, he was too interested in watching Eileen to notice someone else watching her."

"Okay," Parker said. He took another handful of the candies and dropped them into his side pocket.

"One more thing," Aikman said. "The guy you're looking for, the stranger, is white."

"Now, that I don't figure," Parker said.

"Military, that's the key. This guy was in the service, along with the other three, maybe thirty years back, judging from the ammunition they're using. We know the soldier who killed Gibbs is white . . . "

" . . . and thirty years ago the military wasn't real big on integrated units."

"That's it," Aikman said. "If they served together, they're all white."

"So I got another question: How does a white man fit in Andy's bar?"

"Andy fits," Aikman said. "Who else would?"

"Dunno . . . it wouldn't be easy, unless . . . "

"Unless what?"

"Only one kind of cat I can think of can make it in black joints, white joints, gay bars, the works."

"Musician," Aikman said.

Parker smiled. "I'll be talking to ya . . ." He took more M&M's and left.

Enders found Billy the Kid sitting on a chair outside his office at three in the afternoon. On the floor next to the chair was a stack of manila folders and what looked like a ream of paper in a looseleaf binder. Billy nodded and followed Enders into the office, carrying the pile of papers.

"Want some coffee?" Enders asked.

"No, no thanks." Billy set the papers down on Enders' desk. "This first batch," he said, indicating with his thumb and forefinger an inch-thick section, "is McMahon and Douglas. The rest is Witkin."

"Jesus," Enders said, shaking his head. "Some long hours, right?"

"Yeah, I guess. The hours don't bother me . . . it's just . . . "

"Something wrong?"

Billy had spent the better part of an hour rehearsing it in his mind, deciding the proper proportions of respect, courtesy, and determination to mix in his delivery. But when it came out, it was a flat, calm statement.

"I didn't go to the Police Academy to learn how to write biographies of dead people. That's not why I joined the force."

"It's part of the job," Enders said pleasantly, lighting a cigarette. "Everything you do has a purpose. Sure, paperwork is boring, but it comes with the territory. Right now we need that information."

Krieg took a deep breath. "It's not only the paperwork; it goes deeper than that. The Detective Division isn't for me. It's what everyone is supposed to want, and I thought I wanted it, but I learned something: I found out what really makes me happy."

"And that's being on patrol?" Enders asked.

"I miss it. The phone calls, the research, Parker and his snitch army: That's not what I want."

"That's only a small part of being a detective. You'll be

investigating crimes, you'll be on the scene minutes after it happens, it'll be up to you . . . "

"That's just it," Krieg said. "I don't want to be anywhere *after* it happens. I can't change anything after the fact. I can't make a difference." Krieg paused and smiled. "I sound like an idealistic horse's ass."

"I understand what you're saying," Enders said. "You want to go back to the car."

"Yeah, that's what I really want. It can be boring as hell, but that's where I belong. That's where I can do something. I don't want to come around later to clean up." He leaned forward and looked directly at Enders. "Mallory and I saved a jumper one night, six, seven months back. This guy sat on the edge of the roof of this apartment building, ready to go. We talked for an hour, and we talked him down. And we lost one, too: this girl in an apartment, sitting on the floor with a gun, holding it to her head. We talked to her through the open door, but she wouldn't say a thing. Just kept staring at us until, as calm as anything you ever saw, she squeezes the trigger. That one bothered me for a long time; I always figured that if we could have gotten her talking, we could have stopped it—but we couldn't, and we'll never know why. Sometimes you can't figure out half the shit that goes on, but you do your best. If you're lucky, you learn where you belong."

"Okay," Enders said, smiling. "I wouldn't want to be responsible for taking a good man off the street and making him miserable in plainclothes."

"You know the worst of it?" Krieg asked. "Who's gonna believe I gave up detective to go back to the car? They'll think I screwed up."

"Or they'll think you're nuts," Enders said.

Krieg stood up. "I can handle it."

"I'm sure you can. Will you finish out the week for me?"

"Sure . . . and thanks. Maybe I'd never have known what I really wanted if you hadn't given me the chance."

Parker had a bowl of peanuts and a half-empty beer glass on the table. He munched and sipped, watching the door, watching for Malcolm.

Finding the regular was easy. Andy Reed had said, "Sure, Malcolm. He's here most every night—but he won't talk to cops. . . . "

We'll see, Parker thought. It was ten-thirty and he'd been waiting for an hour, coming back to Andy's after pulling the file on Malcolm at the precinct house. Militant black, cop-hater, a string of petty-larceny charges, all dropped. Then years ago, after the assassination of Malcolm X, the change: He took the dead leader's name, organized what was left of the Panthers, and decided to clean up his own neighborhood. The clean-up began with assaults on suspected pushers, but no one ever testified against Malcolm, and his record for the past years was clean.

We'll see, Parker thought, finishing the beer.

Andy Reed gestured at him and pointed toward the door, but it wasn't likely that Parker would have missed Malcolm. Six-four, two hundred pounds, with a gleaming silver medallion showing through his open shirt under a black overcoat, unbuttoned, his hands shoved into the pockets, Malcolm came into the bar like a windstorm. He waved to Andy Reed and was about to sit down at the bar when Reed pointed to Parker.

Malcolm took his time crossing the room to where Parker sat. He smiled at the faces, waved, exchanged small talk at one table, and finally came to rest opposite Parker.

"You want to talk to me, cop?" Malcolm said, not looking at the detective.

"I've got a few questions for you," Parker said.

"Forget it, man: I don't know nothin'." Malcolm shook his head.

"Okay, fine." Parker got up, leaned over, and put his

hands flat on the table. He was inches away from Malcolm's face. "I'm not going to waste time with you, you jive fucker. I don't care if you talk to me or not. . . . I've got work to do. The only thing I'm going to remember about you is that you didn't help me with my work. Do you understand what I'm saying to you, shit-for-brains?"

Parker turned and took two steps. Malcolm called his name.

"Sit down," Malcolm said softly.

Parker sat. "I got two or three questions . . . "

"About what?"

"About Eileen Douglas and who killed her."

"Shit, you dumb cop," Malcolm said, "why didn't you say that in the first place?"

"That makes a difference, does it?"

"Yeah," Malcolm said, "it does."

"I'm looking for a man, a white man, who was in here let's say a week before she was killed . . . or maybe two, three nights before. Maybe a couple of nights. He woulda been paying pretty close attention to her . . . and he woulda left before closing. Any of that ring a bell?"

"Maybe . . . let me think." Malcolm stood up, waved Parker's empty glass in Andy's direction, and sat down again. Andy brought two beers, put them on the table, and went back to the bar.

"Why didn't you ask him?" Malcolm asked.

"Because I'm asking you," Parker said, swallowing half the beer.

"There was a guy, a fruit . . . makin' eyes at the bass player in the band. Here a couple of times. I couldn't figure why he'd leave early if he was chasin' the bassman's ass, you know?"

"Remember what he looked like?"

"Faggy, man. Loose, sashaying all over the place. Red pants, man," Malcolm laughed.

"Were you high?"

111

Malcolm started to deny it, stopped, and said, "A little
. . . a few hits just to feel good. But I know what I saw.

"I need more on the description, man."

"Yeah, I'm thinkin' . . . gray hair . . . and a fine
beard, one of them pointy-chin ones, you know? Thin mustache. He sat over there." Malcolm gestured at a table near
the bandstand on the side of the room. "Oh yeah . . . an
earring. He wore an earring."

"Only one?"

"Yeah, one."

"And no one got uptight about this guy? I mean, a white
fruitcake in this joint, and nobody does a number on him?"

"Nah, forget it, man . . . not that kind of place. Besides, man, he didn't cause no trouble . . . except maybe
for the bass player; he may have had trouble with him."

Parker drained the glass. "Thanks."

"Nothin', man, nothin'."

Parker spent a minute with Andy Reed, got the bassman's name and address, and left.

At one-thirty Aikman's phone rang.

"Aikman," he said, half awake.

"Parker. You named it: white man, hanging around the
band, three nights total; a fag."

"What's he look like?"

"Under six feet, old—maybe fifty, fifty-five—gray hair,
beard, mustache . . . and gay."

"You sure?"

"Tried to pick up the bass player."

"Talk to him?"

"Just finished. He don't remember much about the guy.
Said that so many guys try to pick him up that he can't
keep track."

"He wasn't interested?" Aikman asked.

"Nope. Lives with the drummer."

"Great," Aikman said, rolling out of bed. "Mind bringing your notes?"

"Now?"

"Uh huh."

"Okay, about fifteen minutes."

"I'll fill the candy bowl," Aikman said and hung up. He threw on a robe and padded to the study.

A mountain of files was on the desk, delivered earlier that evening by messenger from Carl Enders' office. Aikman had spent the night with the histories of McMahon, Douglas, and Witkin. Somebody in Enders' office had done a fine job, but Aikman was still mired down. Not enough, he thought, even with the information Parker had . . . just not enough to lead somewhere. Unless it was there and he didn't see it.

Aikman went to the kitchen and put coffee on. Somewhere in the back of his mind was Carl Enders saying something about sleepless nights.

8

The unsolved murder of Billy Gibbs moved slowly from the front pages to the inside sections of the New York City newspapers. Reporters who had flocked to the city immediately after the killing were called home by their editors and assigned to other, hotter stories, with out-of-town papers relying on the wire services to bring them the tepid updates. But if the case slipped from the public's attention, it intensified for the police.

The flood of photographs and miles of movie film came first. The appeal to anyone in the park with a camera brought thousands of stills, but Enders pinned his hopes on the professionals—the news and magazine photographers who were paid to bring back sharp, clear images. He was looking for one man, the soldier that the lunchstand attendant José Pérez, remembered . . . but he would settle for anyone near Billy Gibbs at any time. He wound up with too much and too little: thousands of photographs, from out-of-focus Instamatics and Polaroids to razor-sharp eight-by-ten black-and-whites, but not one pictured a soldier. Many included the unmistakable figure of Gibbs, but no uniform in sight.

Enders sat through hours of TV newsfilm, ordering the projectionist at the police lab to freeze the frame whenever Gibbs appeared, standing taller than the rest, his green-

and-white jersey a flag to focus on . . . but no soldiers. Enders drank cup after cup of coffee, chain-smoked, and had the footage run through again . . . and again.

The Jets played the first two games of the season at home and lost both, but the losses had less to do with their ability than the tension that pervaded the practice field, the locker room, and the field. It was worse on the players' days off. Secluded, always in groups of two or three or more, the team felt a real fear: Was another Jet player marked for death? And what were the police doing?

Gregory was sweating. The air conditioning had broken down, and this September day felt like mid-July. The stifling office made him fidget and squirm. He mopped his face with a damp handkerchief and half listened to the small man with the nervous eyes who sat in the wooden chair across from the desk.

"Tell me again, from the beginning," he sighed, blotting his forehead.

"I told you three times," the man said.

How come he doesn't sweat? Gregory thought. "We're a bit slow, you understand? Tell me again."

"Look," the man pleaded, "just lock me up or book me or something. I told you, I did it."

Gregory studied the thin face. About forty-five, he figured, a total washout, a nothing, a turd. Why do I have to go through this? "Once more," Gregory said, stubbornly.

"I killed Gibbs, the football player. In Central Park, you know, that day when all the kids were there. When he came in the men's room I was waiting and I shot him . . . now lock me up."

"Why?"

"Because I killed him!" the small man shrieked.

"No, no, you idiot. Why'd you kill him?"

"Oh," the man said, subsiding, "because I hate them. I hate them, all of them."

"Them?" Gregory asked. "You mean blacks?"

"Oh, no, no!" the man said, genuinely hurt. "Not black people . . . not them. No, it's those . . . heroes, you know, the big shots. Better than the rest of us, big shots. Always on TV, in the papers, big hero Billy Gibbs walking around the park, being a big deal. We pay their salaries, you know, you and me, and they go around thinking they're better than us. Well, I showed him. . . . I showed that one, for sure."

"Yeah," Gregory said wearily, "you showed him . . . and now you're showing us, right?"

"I tell you I did it, that's all. Now lock me up."

"You did nothing, you son-of-a-bitch!" Gregory snapped. "Nothing but waste my time. How many times have you confessed to crimes in this city?"

The small man was silent. He looked down at his shoes.

"We've got a file on you as thick as a goddamn phone book . . . you and a couple of hundred others. You drive me crazy, you know that?" Gregory calmed himself and added, "Yeah, you know that."

Gregory stood up and pulled his damp shirt away from his body. "Get out. If you're not out of here in one minute I'll have you in a rubber room at Bellevue until your teeth fall out."

The small man made his way out. Gregory knew he'd see him again. Poor sad *schmuck*, Gregory thought.

The chairman of the Board of the New York Jets stalked out of the mayor's office after an hour-long screamfest. He'd fired threats at the silent Jack Donahue, claiming he'd move the team out of New York if the police couldn't come up with Gibbs' killer by midseason. Donahue took it for what it was, the frustration of a helpless man. What upset Donahue was the hiking of the reward money to seventy-five thousand dollars. The crazies would have a field day, and the police would be buried in false leads.

The *Daily News* reported that the One-on-one Day would not be held in New York City the following year. Unidentified spokesmen for the event asserted that the city was not safe for such an activity and they would begin seeking another location immediately. The mayor cursed, picked up the phone, and spent an afternoon talking to each member of the Board of Directors of One-on-one, pointing out that logically the killing had nothing to do with the event. He heard himself saying, "Be reasonable," over and over again. The reply was basically the same: Catch the killer and we'll all feel better. It's easier to be reasonable if you feel better. Infantile, Donahue thought, and slammed the phone down on the last director. But he was in trouble, and he knew it. One-on-one was big publicity for the city; it made national news and bolstered the sagging image of New York as "the city with a heart." Three years' work was going down the drain.

Police Commissioner Forman issued regular statements to the press, which found their way to the back pages until they disappeared entirely.

Scheduled events for Central Park were rescheduled elsewhere, and full slates of fall concerts and New York City Opera Company performances were canceled. The park, always desolate at night, became an island of unreasonable fear even in daytime. And not one of the few strollers who ventured in used the rest rooms.

While the city dealt as best it could with the present, Aikman was deeply into the past. Sitting at the desk in his study, he surrounded himself with the nearly complete files on the victims, covering the desktop, spilling over to a card table he'd set up next to the desk. On legal pads he began to isolate bits of information, working first from memory, then by careful reading, to compile the data.

He was looking for an intersection, a common ground: Something the victims knew or saw or did at some time in their lives, in some particular place, was killing them. It was the most obvious connection, Aikman knew, and if he could find the intersection, he would find a clue to the motive.

"McMahon," he scribbled on the pad. "Shadows in the man's past. Black and Tan terrorist links, left Ireland after an Easter Sunday bombing. Heavy IRA supporter/contributor." The Dublin police had wired the information, and Aikman noted dates, places, names. He shut the folder and moved on.

"Eileen Douglas: dead end. New York booking agents have two, three possibilities, but names are wrong." Aikman searched through the follow-up reports. Enders had put a man named McQuade on it. McQuade's report stated the possibility that she had come from Alabama to Chicago to New York, using the name Rose Sanders. There was a gap of several years before she turned up at Andy Reed's—if she was Rose Sanders. Aikman asked that Enders check all the drug and alcohol clinics in Chicago and New York, to try to fill in the missing years, but McQuade hadn't found anything. Aikman frowned and shut the file. The next one was the thickest: Witkin.

Charles Witkin, the success story. New York born and raised, top third of his Harvard Law School class, went to work for a state senator in Massachusetts after graduation, served as press liaison for the senator's re-election campaign. The senator swept the race, and Witkin became known in the Democratic power circles. Introduced to the powers in New York City and met with Jack Donahue, an obscure congressman with ambition. Three years later Donahue was mayor of New York, and Witkin was a power in the administration. Aikman listed more names, dates, places. He circled one item, a throwaway: In the summer of '65, Witkin had gone to Selma, Alabama, to register voters. Alabama: That was the second time the state had come up in the files.

Aaron Loesser, the jeweler. Left Germany a step ahead of the Gestapo in '37 with a cache of diamonds and gold. Settled in New York, took a series of jobs with jewelry firms until reaching Cartier's fifteen years ago. Regular vacations in Israel, heavy contributor to the UJA, well acquainted with members of the Jewish Defense League. One son, a veterinarian, lived on Long Island with his wife and daughter. Aikman wondered if Loesser had ever been to Alabama.

Aikman stretched and opened the file on Osea Hayakimo and began making notes. Spent most of his life in Japan; born into wealth and power, family in international trade. Symbol of the new Japan, Aikman thought, heritage blended with Westernization. Called "Kimo" by associates, he traveled extensively for his firm, and was on his twentieth visit to the company's U.S. headquarters when he was killed. Aikman wondered if Hayakimo had ever heard of Alabama.

Tony Rendelli had been born and raised in Queens, and from everything Aikman had in the files, had never gone farther south than Atlantic City, New Jersey. The southern intersection, tenuous as it was, slipped away . . .

. . . and reappeared with Billy Gibbs, who'd been born in Atlanta. Football scholarship to UCLA, Rose Bowl appearance, game-winning touchdown catch, first-round draft pick of the Jets. Gibbs had a home in Atlanta and returned there during the off-season with his wife and two sons. Worked with the children at an Atlanta hospital for the retarded.

Aikman made a list on a fresh sheet of paper: Witkin, Douglas, Gibbs: the South?

He picked up the phone and called Enders. Within the

hour McQuade was on his way to LaGuardia Airport to catch a plane to Atlanta, then on to Montgomery, Alabama, with a bus connection to Selma. As long as he had resources, Aikman would use them. Maybe there was something . . .

Three days later McQuade was back, and Aikman scratched the southern connection. Nothing on Witkin or Eileen Douglas, if that was her name. Lots of stuff on Billy Gibbs in Atlanta. Aikman had cost the city close to a thousand dollars, but it had to be done. You hit the obvious first, he knew.

By the end of the week he had lists on World War II, Korea, and Vietnam, pinpointing each victim's whereabouts and activities during the time. No intersection . . . and no surprise to Aikman. It wasn't going to be that easy.

He sat staring at the map one night in his study, slicing apples and mechanically chewing the pieces.

Something, anything . . .

McMahon, the first, killed at night—almost in front of the bar he owned. Aikman closed his eyes . . . McMahon was going home, leaving his place of business. Business . . . the Social Security card; you need that to do business. If you work, you have to have a Social Security card.

Douglas . . . again, killed on the way home, after she left the place at which she worked. And her cabaret card missing . . . need that to work, Aikman thought. No—wrong, not anymore, but when she started out . . . yes, like the Social Security card, it was a necessity to work.

Shit, Aikman thought, his mind racing to Witkin . . . killed while he was on the job, his police pass missing. And you sure as hell need that to work if you're in city government, Aikman thought, smiling. It's starting to fit. He stood up and walked closer to the map.

And all three missing items were issued by government agencies.

Loesser . . . missing a driver's license. No good—not

necessary for his work; he rarely drove, didn't own a car—always rented one for weekends on Long Island or upstate. But the license was issued by a government agency, and Loesser had been killed on the way to work.

Keep it going . . . Hayakimo killed on the job. Passport . . . it fits, Aikman thought.

Rendelli made it perfect. Killed on his way home after work, driver's license—an essential for his job—taken, and the badge . . . the badge was the symbol of his work. If one thing stood for Rendelli, it was the badge. But it broke the pattern: two items taken instead of only one. Issued by government agencies, but . . . Why the badge? The license was enough. Aikman shook his head; the badge was gratuitous. I'm dealing with egos, men putting on a show for each other, he decided. The badge was a gesture to top someone else, to show off. This one broke the pattern but, if he was right, he knew that it provided an insight that could be more valuable than all the facts he'd listed. . . . It would escalate, they would compete against each other. Egos . . .

Billy Gibbs . . . again, a break in the pattern. He wasn't killed at work, going or coming : . . but the Super Bowl ring could be considered a symbol of his work, and he was wearing yet another symbol when he died: the jersey. Aikman went to the files and noted the number: 87. What connection could that have? Could it have any connection? One thing for sure: The ring wasn't given by any government or bureaucratic agency, unless you consider the Jets a bureaucracy.

He paced, frowning, thumbs hooked in the waistband of the bluejeans. Some fit, some didn't . . . putting all the victims into neat pigeonholes and presenting the police with the package neatly wrapped . . . no, not this one.

If there was a pattern—and there had to be, he was sure—this wasn't it . . . or it was just the glimpse of it.

He sat at the desk and scribbled on the pad: "Need the

following lists on victims: nationality, religion, contact (if any) with police, jury duty, any travel, clubs and organizations, hobbies, places of employment throughout life, families, friends, their occupations. Did the victims know each other, or did members of their families know each other?"

Enders would get the note in the morning and Aikman would have more to work with, but in the back of his mind was the nagging thought that the answer was already there in front of him somewhere in the pile of reports.

9

Two weeks after his outburst at the meeting, Reynolds called each of the others in the early afternoon, saying that he wouldn't be at Lutece for dinner but would join them later at the club.

Long silences and visible tension marked their meal at the restaurant, as they wondered if Reynolds was going to call it all off. But later, at the club, he came into the room smiling and said, "Sorry about dinner, but the market waits for no man." He took off his jacket and tie and sat down at the table. Lyle sat up and took his seat. Birmingham waited until Marcus settled in and then asked Reynolds, "I take it we're going on?"

Reynolds nodded. "I don't see why not. If they were on to us, we'd know by now."

"They could be waiting for one of us to make a move," Marcus suggested.

"It's possible," Reynolds agreed.

"We've just got to watch for it," Lyle said. "If any one of us senses anything out of the ordinary, anything at all, we'll drop it." He looked at each man in turn. "Okay, then, let's get going."

Birmingham passed Reynolds a small black notebook, and Reynolds checked his shorthand notes.

Twenty minutes later Marcus hit in Sector Seventeen.

"Where is it?" he asked Birmingham, who was closest to the map.

"It's Harlem," Birmingham said, twisting around in his seat and staring up at the sector.

"You sure about this, Ed?" Lyle asked.

"No," Marcus admitted, "but I've got to take it."

"There's still time to change your mind," Reynolds invited.

"No, thanks. I'd rather stop you," Marcus smiled. He got up and walked over to the map.

"Okay, if you're sure," Reynolds said, making a note in the book.

Marcus' eyes took in the sector outlined on the map. What the hell do I know about Harlem? he thought. "It's not going to be easy," he said, almost to himself.

"You may have an advantage," Reynolds pointed out.

Marcus nodded. It was the kind of work he was so good at, but that was long ago. Still . . . "I think I can get in all right. I always managed to figure a way to get close . . . but finding the target, that's going to be the hard part."

Marcus stayed in the room for a half hour after the others left. In his mind he saw himself in Paris, over thirty-five years ago . . . infiltration and assassination—a specialty; he smiled at the memory. There was one that was expecially difficult, a Panzer Division commander. He'd killed him in a bordello on the Rue de Montparnasse. Some German officers preferred young men. . . .

He got up and walked to the map. Forget it, he thought, that won't help now. This is something different. It would take time, but there were no time limits. Reynolds and the others, they were hit-and-run; they had no patience for the kind of work Marcus did so well . . . weeks, sometimes months getting close to his target.

He could still do it, he decided. What he needed now was the right victim.

Marcus spent the morning in the Forty-second Street branch of the New York Public Library, scanning microfilms of the New York *Times*. Harlem . . . urban renewal, local school board battles, politicians, crime . . . lots of crime. Pimps, pushers, junkies, prostitutes. Unemployment. Welfare. VISTA volunteers. Marcus went back a week, then two, three, checking every headline in the news sections, sports, entertainment.

Finally, an item over a month old: Jacob (Jake, Jake the Indian, Indian) Cunningham, who had more arrests than nicknames, had been busted for selling six ounces of cocaine to an undercover narcotics officer and faced the real possibility of his first conviction and the next twenty years in jail. Peppered with "reported to be," "alleged," and "supposed to have been," the article hinted that the case against Cunningham was so strong that he might make a deal rather than risk conviction. Cunningham was "reported" to have connections to the big drug operations in Harlem.

Marcus studied the grainy photograph accompanying the article. Whether Indian was a real Indian or not was hard to tell: Cunningham had thrown his hands in front of his face as the photo was taken. All Marcus could see was long, dark hair and a headband. He leaned back in the chair and turned the microfilm reader off, rubbed his eyes, and stretched.

All right, he decided: Jake Cunningham. Marcus grinned at his own pun as he thought: How?

Marcus did his best thinking on the move, a throwback to his days in France when his life often depended upon movement, from sanctuary to sanctuary until he had a plan.

Now he walked along Forty-second Street into Times Square, letting the sights and sounds assail his senses: flashing marquees, even in daylight; the blare of horns from the constant sweep of traffic; explosions of sound from arcades.

How to get close to Cunningham? The man's out on bail, Marcus thought, so he's being watched by the police. They don't want him skipping . . . probably under the eye of the mob, too. Can't just walk up to him on the street . . . have to get him alone, isolated, away from everyone, lure him out. What's the bait?

Marcus circled the block. Okay, get him to come to me. What can I offer him?

Marcus slipped into Cunningham, began thinking with Cunningham's mind. "What do I want?" he asked himself.

"I don't want to go to court, that's for sure," he answered.

And suddenly he had it. Risky . . . but that was part of the game, that's what it was all about. It could work. It would take time . . . he would have to pick the spot . . . and for that he would have to know a lot more about Harlem.

The top floor of the old red-brick building on Grand Street in lower Manhattan had been renovated into offices for the managers and salesmen for Marcus' company, Image Electronics. On the floors below, the machines that turned out the precision electronic components for video games, calculators, and automatic cameras hummed smoothly, the personnel feeding in the minute chips and circuits, packing and shipping the end products to distributors and manufacturers all over the country and throughout the world.

Marcus worked in his corner office through the next day, preparing the workload for his secretary, executive assistant, and plant foreman. To everyone he announced his plans for a three-or four-week vacation, "depending on how they're biting in the Bahamas," he said, smiling.

In his Park Avenue apartment that evening, he told his

wife about the upcoming distributors' meeting. "I'm not saying there aren't worse places to be than Grand Bahama Island, but I wish they'd given me more notice."

Helen Marcus looked up from the newspaper and nodded. She'd heard that before. With a network of distributors for his electronics, her husband's sales and marketing meetings were common; either that, or he was away for weeks with his cronies from the service. Last fall it had been almost three weeks of hunting in the Minnesota woods.

"How long will it take?" she asked him.

"Probably not more than three, four days. But I'm not against staying on for a week or two and getting in some fishing . . . make a vacation out of it. How about flying down and joining me?" Marcus was taking a chance, but a small one. Helen had an unreasonable fear of the water and loathed boats.

Terminal sunburn and seasickness? No, thanks."

Marcus laughed. "How about Paris, Rome, and Athens . . . lots of shopping, swank hotels, and the best restaurants?"

"Now, *that* you can talk me into. When?"

"Spring . . . say, April or early May. It's a promise."

"It's a deal," she smiled, and went back to the paper. Marcus went into the bedroom to pack.

With Lyle's warning echoing in his ears, Marcus switched cabs three times, crossed and recrossed streets, and doubled back before going to the apartment on Fifty-third Street the next morning. He left his suitcases, changed into corduroy pants, old loafers, a sport shirt, and plaid hunting jacket. Outside, he hailed a cab and rode downtown to St. Marks's Place and Third Avenue.

With twenty dollars taken from the apartment, Marcus walked the streets of the Bowery, making his purchases in the Salvation Army thrift shop and a discount store. He stopped in a liquor store and bought a bottle of cheap wine. With his packages he rode a cab back to the apartment.

He piled everything in a corner, poured three quarters of the wine into the sink, kicked off his shoes, and stretched out on the bed with a paperback thriller.

Three days for the stubble to grow on his face . . .

The phone in the study rang, and Aikman took it from the desk and carried it to the window. "Aikman," he said, staring out at the street. The trees lining the sidewalk were shedding their leaves, and the passersby kicked through, scattering the bright colors.

"Hi," Leslie Hutton's voice came throught the line.

"Hi," Aikman answered.

"Nothing but bad news, I'm afraid," she said.

"Raymond died?" It slipped out before he had time to think.

There was a sharp intake of breath.

"I'm sorry," he said quickly. "Been working too hard."

"Getting anywhere?" Leslies's question was perfunctory.

"I'm getting out of the house. How about meeting me for dinner? I can apologize properly, and you can tell me your news. Besides, my day can use a little brightening."

Leslie hesitated. "Ive got to tell you that I've had more romantic invitations to dinner . . . "

"But none more sincere," Aikman said.

Leslie laughed. "All right, where?"

"If you like Italian food, meet me at Orsini's, on . . . "

"I know the place," she said.

"About an hour?"

"Fine."

Aikman was at a corner table when Leslie came in. The *maître d'* led her to the table and held her chair.

"Excellent veal piccata," Aikman said.

Leslie nodded, and Aikman signaled for the waiter. They ordered without a menu and waited until the wine was served before talking. "What's the bad news?" Aikman finally asked.

"Raymond's having nightmares."

"Does he say anything?"

She shook her head. "Mostly screams, moans . . . he tosses, flings his arms out. When he wakes up, he refuses any contact. I stayed at the hospital one night and saw it myself. He doesn't speak, just cries out. Afterward, he's completely withdrawn."

"What are you going to do?"

Leslie paused as the waiter brought the food. Aikman refilled the wine glasses, and when the waiter left, she continued.

"We're not getting anywhere with the therapy, and I'm afraid if this keeps up much longer we may never break through to him. I've requested a leave of absence, and I'm going to take Raymond to live at my apartment."

"Change of surroundings," Aikman said.

Leslie nodded. "It may help . . . a quieter atmosphere, seeing one person all the time. It may make a difference."

"For how long?"

"I don't know. I'd like to say, 'for as long as it takes,' but that's not realistic. I'll have to see how he reacts."

"What do Raymond's parents say? Have they been able to get near him?"

"They haven't even tried," Leslie said, with a trace of anger. "They shipped him off to the hospital when he was two years old. They've got other children, healthy children, and they don't want to be bothered."

"I guess it might work," Aikman said, "getting all your attention, learning to trust you . . . "

"It's a last-ditch effort," Leslie admitted. "We don't know what else to try."

Aikman frowned. He didn't like "last-ditch efforts." A problem must yield to logic . . .

"Something wrong?" Leslie asked.

"No, just thinking about how similar our work is . . . in this case, at least."

"Similar?"

"We're both trying to break through barriers, mental blocks. Raymond has locked himself away from you, inside himself; the man I'm looking for is locked away by a process, a selection I can't penetrate. There are logical ways through both barriers; at least I hope there are."

"I don't know if I understand," Leslie said.

"I'm not sure I do, either," he smiled. "But the key to both problems is in Raymond's head. And we're both used to success. We don't like to fail; our egos won't permit it."

"Ego is a dangerous thing for a psychiatrist," Leslie said. "Up to a point it's a necessary force; it motivates us to help our patients. But beyond motivation you can't do the work for yourself, you've got to do it for the patient."

"And that's where we're different," Aikman said.

"Noah," she said, "I'm not going to push Raymond. I know how important this is to you, but let's get that straight."

Aikman held up his hands. "I wasn't suggesting . . . "

"The hell you weren't," Leslie smiled. "You're some operator, but not with me. I want you to solve your problem, but I'm not going to risk pushing a little boy over the edge to help you."

Aikman nodded. He wasn't going to get Leslie Hutton to do anything she didn't want to do. Raymond was out of the picture, unless she managed to reach him on her own terms.

Oh well, Aikman sighed. "Dessert?" he asked.

Leslie looked at him curiously. "What's going on in that mind of yours?"

Aikman smiled innocently. "Nothing more than the problem at hand: spumoni or strawberry zabaglione?"

At nine o'clock on the evening of the third day, Marcus left the apartment, his metamorphosis complete. He wore heavy, grimy workboots, no socks, a thin, ragged shirt, frayed gray pants, and a long overcoat that had once been light green but was now stained and smeared almost black. His hair was disheveled and his face splotched and raw from constant scratching at the beginnings of his beard. In his pocket was the bottle of wine, a penknife, and five dollars in crumpled singles and change. In the thick hollowed-out heel of the left boot was the wire.

Haunched over, walking slowly as if against a stiff wind, Marcus made his way downtown.

If he was going to play the role convincingly, he would learn it downtown before going up to Harlem to find Jake Cunningham.

Below Third Street, Second Avenue widens as it empties onto Houston, and on the corner in a small park the bums sleep in the early-morning sunlight, awakening to beg change from the area residents and the few Hell's Angels who live in the building off the corner of Third Street and Second Avenue. The Angels sometimes dropped a nickel or dime into their palms, and sometimes kicked them in the shins with their motorcycle boots.

Marcus got up stiffly from the stone and board bench where he'd slept. The nights were cold, and his bones ached. He edged along the sidewalk, blocking the passage of anyone coming his way, his hand outstretched, repeating the litany, "Nickel, hey, jus' a nickel, you can spare it, huh?" When someone would hand him a coin, he would mumble, "God bless you," and pocket the money.

He had been there four days, sleeping with the other winos on the benches or in doorways, joining the lines at the Salvation Army Center up the block for free soup, coffee and, once, a shower. He spent his money on cheap wine, most of which he poured out in dark alleys, splashing just enough on the front of his coat and his face. He watched the others carefully, picking up and practicing the mannerisms and speech patterns.

At night he would dart into the street whenever a car stopped for the light at Houston and Second Avenue. He would scuttle to the driver's side and wipe the windshield with a filthy rag, dash to the front of the car and rub at the headlights, and then, with the exaggerated dignity he'd seen the others assume, walk back to the driver and hold out his hand. "Nice 'n' clean, sir . . . yessir, only cost you a nickel," he would say, keeping his eyes on his shoes. Sometimes the window rolled down and Marcus would have a nickel or a dime. Most of the time the drivers stared straight ahead and sped off as the light changed to green.

Marcus' face was grimy, his hair matted and tangled. He'd found an old leather cap in a garbage can on Tenth Street and jammed it down over his ears. He'd lost eight pounds, and he smelled.

On the morning of the fifth day he woke up in a doorway, clutching an empty bottle in his hand. He rose unsteadily, shivered, and pulled the coat tight around his body.

He smiled to himself. He was ready for Harlem and Jake Cunningham.

He rode the subway uptown, curled on one of the metal benches, moaning and talking to himself. Passengers getting on and off circled around him and stood a distance away. He jerked himself up and lurched against the doors as the subway flashed through a tunnel and began to slow for the 125th Street stop. Marcus stumbled through the doors as they slid open.

He came up into daylight blinking, holding his hand over his eyes to shield them from the bright glare of the October day. He stood at the top of the subway stairs until pushed aside by the exiting crowd. He sagged against a building and scanned the street.

From his pocket he took a paper bag and unscrewed the cap on a fifth of Southern Comfort. As he put it to his lips, a tall, thin black man in a long suede coat and a wide-brimmed black hat studded with silver, kicked at him from behind. "White piece of shit," the man cursed. "Get your ass outta here." Marcus pressed against the wall, protected the bottle with his hands, and slid away.

He wouldn't last long up here. He had to find Cunningham and pick the spot.

He kept moving throughout the day, begging for change . . . stopping once to slump against a tree in a small park, finish the bottle, and look around, sizing up the area. Everywhere he looked he saw the same faces: tight smiles from pimps in feathered hats and bell-bottom trousers as they nodded to each other, cruised the streets, or tended to their stables; children, most of them dressed in worn, clean clothing, playing amid the squalor of the tenements; young men out of work, sitting on stoops drinking beer or gliding from bar to bar along Lexington. He watched the patrol cars cruise the neighborhood, the cops glancing from side to side, taking it all in.

He got up and walked past the bars, the Legal Aid office, the VISTA storefront, the alleys. On 128th Street he stopped in front of a theater and studied the posters. Three black actors, all ex-football players, carrying submachine guns. "Held Over! Third Big Week!" a fading banner proclaimed. Kill Whitey movies, Marcus thought . . . very popular up here. Continuous showings every two hours from ten in the morning, he noted.

"What you doin', old man?" a voice behind him said.

Marcus turned slowly to face three teen-agers wearing baseball warm-up jackets and sporting huge Afros. The leader, who had spoken to him, shoved him against the wall.

"Do your beggin' downtown, motherfucker," he spat.

"You give the neighborhood a bad name, scumbag," another one said.

The third boy prodded Marcus' feet with his toe. Marcus moved to his left, nodding his head. "Go on, get outta here," the leader said. "We see you again, we bust your stupid head." Marcus kept moving, his eyes wide in fear until he turned the corner.

Jesus, he swore under his breath. He'd come close to kicking out at the leader. Cripple the bastard! Marcus cursed. He shook off the anger and kept walking.

As the daylight faded, Marcus began to note the bars, stopping and peering through windows into each dimly lit room. He went up and down the streets, covered six blocks in two hours. At eight-thirty he stood in front of the Soul Sister off Lexington, as the raw edge of rhythm and blues music seeped into the street. Pressed against the glass, Marcus saw a tall man with long black hair standing at the end of the bar talking to the bartender . . . high boots and faded jeans and a short bluejean jacket. Marcus couldn't tell for sure, but there might have been a headband encircling the man's hair.

Marcus' eyes focused on everyone in the bar. They were all black, and he stayed where he was, watching. The tall man stood at an alcove behind the bar and picked up a phone. For the next half hour he made calls, then nodded to the bartender and moved toward the door. Marcus sprinted across the street and concealed himself in a doorway. As the man came out of the Soul Sister, Marcus saw his face in the light of a streetlamp.

Jake Cunningham, headband and all.

Marcus slept in the park that night, drifting in and out of dreams, wakening to every sound. He pressed close to the base of a tree, hiding his face and hands. Throughout the park other winos tossed and moaned in fitful sleep.

In the morning he bought a pretzel from a corner vendor and at ten o'clock walked into the Soul Sister, positioning himself across from the alcove. He pulled a dollar bill from his overcoat pocket.

The bartender, a heavy black man with silver hair, came over. "Ain't you got no sense left, rummy? What you doin' here?"

"I need a drink," Marcus said.

"Go buy a bottle and get your self on the subway, man. You ain't welcome here."

The bartender began to walk away, and Marcus leaned over the bar and grabbed at his hand. "Please—I'll do it. . . . I will. Jus' gimme a drink for now."

The bartender eyed the dollar bill in Marcus' hand, took it, and shoved it into the pocket of his apron. He poured a shot of rye and placed it in front of Marcus, who tossed it down.

"I'm goin', I'm goin'," Marcus said, walking slowly to the door.

Fixed in his mind was the number on the alcove phone.

The white villains died like flies as the black superheroes tossed grenades, dynamite sticks, and gas canisters. They raked a building with submachine-gun fire, dropped their fleeing enemies with karate kicks, and cut their throats with long-bladed knives. The audience cheered and shouted

135

as cars blew up and tumbled in burning heaps over cliffs and bridges.

Marcus sat in the back row of the balcony, his eyes fixed on the screen. He'd sat through the film three times—almost six hours straight. The film was nearly two hours long, but it was the last fifteen minutes that concerned Marcus. They began the movie on the hour, every other hour. His timing would have to be right.

He made the call at five in the afternoon on the following day, after sitting through the film three more times and finding a phone booth that met his needs. It was in an all-night drugstore on 118th Street, and it was a real booth with a door, not just a phone out in the open.

"Yeah, Soul Sister," came a voice.

"I want to leave a message for the Indian."

"Yeah?"

"Yeah. You tell him to call this number at nine tonight." Marcus read off the number of the phone in front of him.

"Who're you, man?" the voice asked.

"Never mind that—you tell him to call."

"He don't call nobody he don't know."

"He'll call me if he wants to keep walking around."

"What's that mean?" the voice asked suspiciously.

"You just give him the message. You got the number?"

"Yeah, I got it."

Marcus hung up.

At five after nine, the phone in the booth rang, and Marcus picked it up after the first ring.

"You're five minutes late, asshole."

"Who is this?" Indian's voice was deep, and he talked slowly, deliberately.

"My name isn't important. You wouldn't know it, that's for sure," Marcus laughed harshly.

"What's the joke, man?"

"Look, Cunningham, I don't have time to waltz you around . . . just shut your mouth and listen. I know what you're facing, and I know you're going away for a long time. You got no way out, except for me." Marcus paused.

"I'm listenin'," Cunningham said.

"There's only one way to beat it, Jake, and it'll cost you. Twenty thousand's the price, and don't give me no shit about not having it, 'cause I know otherwise. You get the money together and call me back tomorrow night, same time, same number."

"Wait a minute, man," Cunningham said. "Just what are you gonna do for me and my twenty thousand?"

"I'm going to see to it that six ounces of very fine cocaine disappears from the police property clerk's office."

There was a pause. Marcus could hear Cunningham breathing, and in the background the rock music blared.

"How can you do that?" Cunningham asked.

"Never mind how . . . get the money and call me. You're going to court in two days, sucker. There ain't much time." Marcus hung up.

He spent the next day in the theater, not so much to study the film but to stay off the streets. Part of him was afraid he'd be hurt; the other part was frightened of his own temper. Either way, he was too close to risk walking around.

Cunningham's call came at five to nine.

"You made up your mind?" Marcus asked.

"I got to know who you are. How do I know I ain't bein' set up?"

"Try to understand this, Jake. Nobody cares about setting you up. You're already set. The DA's going to sweat you; they'll get a deal or they'll send you up for twenty, minimum. I don't know what your bosses will do; if they wanted you dead, you'd be dead. I guess they figure you ain't gonna talk, that you're gonna be a good little boy and clam up and do your time. If you don't, Jake, they'll find you and they'll kill you. You know it. But I got a way that solves all your problems."

"Who are you, man?" Cunningham asked.

Marcus took a breath. Here goes . . . he whispered into the phone, "Don't you get it, sucker? I'm the cop that set up the bust. You sold me the shit, you asshole."

After a long silence, Marcus continued. "Here's how it works, Jake. You bring ten thousand in cash where I tell you to bring it. You get there when I tell you to get there. When I walk in you'll know me. I'll be wearing the same kind of clothes . . . not exactly the same, you got that? I don't want the cops watchin' you to spot me. But you'll know it's me, Jake. You remember my face?"

"I remember."

"So when you see me, you'll know. You hand over the ten, and I take care of the rest. With the evidence gone, there's no case. You'll walk, Jake, free and clear. Then we meet at the same spot, same time, a day after you walk out of the courtroom. It may take a week, two . . . maybe more, before they find the stuff missing, but exactly one day after the case is dropped, you meet me with the second half of the payment. If you screw up, I'll find you . . . believe it."

"How do I know . . . "

"I'm tired of talking, Jake. If you're too stupid to see that it's the only way to go, then I'm hanging up. What'll it be?" Marcus shut his eyes and waited for the response.

"Where do I meet you?"

Marcus filled it in.

Cunningham put down the phone and signaled the bartender. The black man drew a beer and placed it in front of him.

A crooked cop, Cunningham thought . . . those bastards! But it was a way out. . . . Didn't stuff disappear from the property office all the time?

It could be a shakedown, Cunningham decided. He'd have to get there early, check the place out, and if anyone other than that stinkin' narc showed up for the money, he'd be sorry he was ever born.

That night in the park, Marcus twisted the heel of his left boot and pulled the wire out of the hollowed-out section. He slept with his hand in his pocket, gripping the weapon.

Marcus couldn't stand the smell. He lay on his stomach between the wall of the theater and the last row of seats in the balcony. The floor was caked with grime, and the odor nauseated him. He'd been there for two hours.

Sounds from the screen filled the theater, and he could tell from the dialogue and the sound effects what the scene was. He had over an hour to go until the climax of the film. He'd told Cunningham to be there by seven-thirty, but he was sure that Indian would come early.

There were few people in the theater, and none in the balcony. He heard footsteps, then lost them in the din of the soundtrack. He looked at his watch: almost seven. He pressed against the floor and brought the wire out of his pocket.

To his left, the seat on the aisle sagged with the weight as someone sat down. Marcus rolled slightly to his right and glanced up. He saw the long, black hair. He was back in Paris. . . .

139

Cunningham watched the stairway. The first glance would tell him if the voice at the other end of the phone had been that of the narc. In his back pocket was a switchblade and, if it wasn't the narc . . .

Marcus listened to the soundtrack and stared at his watch. Sweat formed on his forehead and upper lip; he put the wire down on the floor and pressed his palms against his sides.

After an eternity he heard the first burst of gunfire from the screen and the cheers of the audience. Someone shouted, "Kill the motherfuckers, kill 'em!" More gunfire, then a grenade . . . curses from the screen, shouts from the audience. The sound of a car, then another. Marcus picked up the wire, gripped the stubby handles, and tensed.

A burst of gunfire, and he sprang up.

Jake Cunningham died with the sounds of the exploding automobiles in his ears. Marcus pushed the body forward until it slipped off the seat and fell to the floor between the rows. He snatched the headband from Cunningham's brow.

In ten minutes Marcus was on a downtown subway, curled up on a seat, mumbling to himself, playing out the role to the end.

10

John Harmon knew something was wrong the minute he walked into Courtroom B at the Criminal Courts Building. It was eight-thirty and the trial was scheduled to begin at nine, but Harmon had been in court often enough to know that the attorneys, both defense and prosecution, and the accused—in this case, Jacob (Jake the Indian) Cunningham—would be there early, milling around outside the room.

But on this morning he saw no familiar face—and he had covered the drug story for close to two years, sending periodic reports and features to the New York *Times*; long enough to recognize Cunningham's attorney and the prosecutor.

At nine o'clock the judge called '*The People* v. *Warner,* and Harmon bolted from the courtroom. In the lobby of the building he asked a uniformed officer what happened to the Cunningham case, and was directed to the court clerk's office.

A secretary gave him the news: The police had found Cunningham's body in a Harlem theater. Harmon ran for a phone.

"Twenty-eighth Precinct, Sergeant Walsh."

"This is John Harmon, remember me, the Cunningham case?"

"Sure, sure . . . hey, ain't that something about the Indian?"

"I just heard. Let me talk to Glenn," Harmon said.

"Hang on . . . "

Harmon listened as the phone clicked and popped through its connections. Inspector Harold Glenn had been the driving force behind the investigation; he'd singled out Cunningham and planted a narcotics officer in Harlem to make a buy. It had taken close to two years from inception to today, when Cunningham was due in court. Now it was washed out.

"Glenn speaking." The deep voice was tired.

"Harmon, Inspector. I'm downtown at the court . . . "

"Oh yeah, I forgot about you . . . "

Glenn and Harmon had worked closely on the case and gotten along fine, a situation that doesn't often exist between policeman and reporter. Maybe it was because both men pinned great hopes on the case: It would earn Glenn a promotion and lead Harmon to a permanent spot on the *Times*—at least that was the way it was *supposed* to work.

"What happened?"

"Somebody iced him . . . last night. We had a tail on him the whole time, and it went down under our noses."

"How?"

"Not for publication, okay? Okay . . . he goes into a movie, early, about seven, and he don't come out. About eleven the boys call for backup and go in. They found him wedged between the rows in the back of the balcony."

"Jesus . . . "

"I guess we shoulda figured it, but the Indian was a hardnose . . . it didn't figure that he would worry the big boys. If he was going to deal he woulda kept quiet about it until he was off the streets. You can never figure it . . . "

"How was he killed?"

"Strangled. The ME says it went fast, hardly any struggle."

"Witnesses?"

"Don't know yet. Look, Harmon, you're a good guy, but do me a favor and stop playing boy reporter for a while. It's not even my case anymore," Glenn said, his voice sagging.

"What do you mean?"

"Lawrence has taken it over. Called me a few minutes ago. He wants all the files, reports, everything."

"Lawrence? Deputy Chief Lawrence?"

"Gerald J. himself. Now I gotta get the stuff together; he's coming up here for it."

"Yeah, okay," Harmon said. "Thanks."

"Sure," Glenn said, and hung up. Harmon dashed from the courthouse and hailed a cab. On the drive up to 113th Street he kept wondering why the deputy chief of homicide was taking over a narcotics case.

The cab pulled up in front of the Twenty-eighth Precinct and Harmon saw a black sedan with a uniformed officer behind the wheel double-parked in the street. He paid the cabbie and sprinted inside the building.

Sergeant Gus Walsh looked up from the desk as Harmon walked in. The reporter gestured toward the stairs with a questioning look on his face. Walsh nodded, and Harmon took a seat next to the stairway.

In five minutes Harmon heard a door slam and footsteps come across the corridor above. He stood by the stairs as Lawrence, carrying two large manila envelopes, walked down.

"Excuse me, sir, I'm John Harmon, New York *Times*. I was reporting on the Cunningham case and wondered . . ."

"There'll be a press conference at three this afternoon, my office," Lawrence said, brushing past Harmon and leaving the building.

Oh no, Harmon thought, you're not going to get away that easily. He followed Lawrence through the doors and, as the deputy chief got in the back of the sedan, Harmon ran to the corner and flagged a cab. "You see that car?" Harmon said, pointing to the sedan making its way down the street. "Follow it."

"You're kiddin'," the driver said.

"Yeah, I'm kidding. Now, follow it." The driver shrugged and dropped the flag.

The deputy chief's car wound through the streets moving downtown, turned onto Sixty-fourth Street, and pulled up in front of a brownstone. Lawrence got out and went inside.

Harmon ordered the driver to stop at the corner. "No more cops 'n' robbers?" the driver asked sadly. Harmon gave him a five-dollar bill. "I'll let you know," he said, and got out.

He walked down the street, trying his best to look casual. As he came abreast of the brownstone, he stepped close to the building and looked up at the hand-lettered names beneath the doorbells:

N. Aikman. A. Aikman.

Harmon kept walking to the end of the block, crossed the street, and walked back, finally stopping diagonally across from the house. He ran his hand through his unruly blond hair and leaned back against an iron railing. Aikman: What the hell was going on?

Harmon knew Aikman by reputation and experience. Hanging around precinct houses, he'd heard the name and became interested enough to sign up for one of Aikman's classes at NYU. That was over two years ago, but Harmon remembered enough of Aikman's teachings. This was a classic example: a situation that appears to make no obvious sense. First, a deputy chief of homicide takes over a narcotics case, then he takes all the files on that case and goes to see Noah Aikman. Why would Aikman be involved in the murder of an uptown dealer? Cunningham was small potatoes; true, he was a wedge—a place to start for the police to crack the Harlem traffic; but Aikman? Doesn't make sense.

You don't send a howitzer out after a mosquito . . . unless there's more going on here than anyone is telling . . . or is likely to tell.

The afternoon news conference should be interesting, Harmon decided.

By the time Reynolds reached the Fifty-third Street apartment, he'd changed his mind. He'd taken his lunch hour and gone uptown to take Birmingham's uniform out of the apartment and destroy it, but now, as he stood and stared at it in the closet, he knew the damage had already been done. Actually, the apartment was the safest place for the uniform. Any number of things could go wrong trying to destroy it and, after all, if the police found the apartment, the uniform would be the least of their problems. The weapons would hang them. He left the building and walked toward Fifth Avenue.

The mid-October day was cool with a taste of the coming winter in the breeze that swirled the skirts of the women on the avenue. Reynolds reviewed his plans. He'd been busy since the night Birmingham had revealed his little ego trip in the park; money had been eased out of the country; new identities set up . . . soon Reynolds would have passports, checking accounts, drivers' licenses in new names. He'd rented a studio apartment near his office, bought new clothes, and kept cash and his new papers there. Three apartments, he thought, smiling: his own, the operations center, and the escape.

He was sure the others had no inkling of what he was doing—another good reason not to destroy the uniform, he realized. It would clue them to his intentions; at the very least it would create tension among them—and tension led to mistakes.

He still needed one more thing: a car. Several garages in the area of his office would suffice to store it; they even had provisions for starting it once a week to make sure the battery remained fully charged. Something fast, maneuverable in city traffic. Not a sports car . . . a compact, six-cylinder lightweight—maybe used.

Reynolds had to balance three separate lives; his business had to remain constant—he had to stay the amiable, energetic, clever stockbroker. He couldn't deviate from patterns built up over the years. And he had to be the same man on Thursday nights. And finally, he had to tune his senses to detect the signal, the indicator that would tell him that the police were close . . . that the enemy had detected them. He didn't know what it would be: something, anything out of place, a stranger, a phone call . . . anything. He would have to know it when it came . . . if it came.

A tough balancing act, Reynolds thought. Then he smiled . . . he would enjoy it.

Harmon had gone straight to the New York *Times'* building after Lawrence came out of Aikman's house, some forty minutes after entering. Borrowing a desk and a typewriter, Harmon constructed a sidebar piece to the main news story on Cunningham's murder, reviewing the buildup of the case, and concluding with the obvious fact that Cunningham's death destroyed two years of hard police work. He held back any mention of Lawrence or Aikman.

He arrived at Lawrence's headquarters at two-thirty and was directed to the conference room, where the technicians were completing final sound checks for the taping.

Harmon compared notes with the other reporters, getting more information than he gave. Witnesses: none. Motive: unknown, but not unsuspected. Undercover cops were all over Harlem, digging. Every police informant in the area was getting a visit . . . sometimes two and three.

Lawrence led a long line of police into the conference room and stood at the podium. Harmon recognized Glenn and a few of the plainclothes officers of the precinct. Glenn looked uncomfortable, and he sweated under the hot lights. Harmon pushed forward.

Lawrence began with an explanation of his presence. "This is still a narcotics case, but its importance dictates a homicide investigation. Cunningham was a central figure in a major narcotics investigation, and there is every reason to believe that his murder is directly connected to that case." The bland statement went on, relating the facts: The body was found by the stakeout patrol, no witnesses as yet. . . . Lawrence finished and said, "If there are any questions . . ."

"Sir," Harmon said sharply, waving his hand, "I'd like to know why you took all the files in the Cunningham case to Noah Aikman's house this morning."

Lawrence began to say something. "How did . . . ?" He caught himself, shook his head, and said, "I didn't take anything to Mr. Aikman's house. I stopped by to see him on a completely different matter." Lawrence turned away from Harmon's stare and raised his arm to point at a reporter across the room.

"But sir," Harmon pressed, "isn't it true that Noah Aikman has a reputation for working on extremely difficult cases? Important cases? Is there, perhaps, more to the Cunningham investigation than you've told us?"

Lawrence stared at Harmon. "I've already told you, it was a completely different matter." He swung away and pointed to a TV reporter. "Yes?"

Harmon didn't listen to the question or the answer. He began to edge toward the door. He'd shaken Lawrence . . . he'd hit a nerve.

Something was going on.

Reynolds was stretched out in bed watching a movie on Channel 9 when the phone rang.

"Chris . . . Dick. Did you see the news?"

Reynolds sat up. "No. Why?"

"There was a killing in Harlem last night. Drug pusher named Cunningham—known as 'Indian.' "

"Strangled?"

"That's right," Lyle said.

"So he pulled it off. Incredible."

"That's not why I called," Lyle said.

"Problem?" Reynolds asked.

"I'm not sure. They ran a tape of a press conference the cops had this afternoon. A reporter asked the big honcho if he had taken the Cunningham files to Noah Aikman."

"Aikman? What did the cop say?"

"He said he went to see Aikman, sure, but about something else. Not the Cunningham case. But he was upset, Chris. . . . When this guy mentioned Aikman, the cop wasn't ready for it. You know who Aikman is, don't you?"

"I know."

"Do you think Ed made a mistake?"

"What else did the cop say?"

"The usual junk," Lyle said. "No leads, no witnesses . . ."

"We have to wait till Ed calls us," Reynolds said.

"I don't know, Chris . . . "

"Look, if they had anything, anything at all that would bring them to us, they wouldn't need Aikman . . . and if Aikman's involved, he can't work miracles. There's no way he can put it together."

"I'll feel better when we hear from Ed," Lyle said stubbornly.

"Yeah," Reynolds said, "I will, too." He hung up and prowled the apartment. If the police have Maucus, there's no way out. But if they don't . . . in three more days his excape plan would be ready. Then it wouldn't matter what the police had.

Harmon paced his apartment: from the window to the sofa, right-angle turn to the wall, turn, back across the floor . . . again and again. He'd dropped the bomb at the press conference and he'd hit: Lawrence lost his cool—only for a second, but he lost it.

Harmon reached back into his memory, to Aikman's class. . . . If you don't have all the facts to fill in the gap between what you do know, you make the jump from Fact A to Fact G, fitting and discarding every possibility until you discover the combination that builds the bridge.

Fact A: Jake Cunningham had been killed, and a deputy chief of homicide had taken the files to Noah Aikman.

Fact G: Noah Aikman didn't work on cases like the murder of Jake Cunningham.

But Aikman was working on it. Harmon was sure of that. Lawrence had given himself away and lied his way out of it.

The jump: Cunningham's killing had far-reaching implications in itself . . . or it was part of something much bigger.

He began to build the bridge. There had been another strangulation death earlier in the year, still unsolved. A big wheel in international trade . . . Harmon remembered the police investigation. Two strangulations . . . international trade . . . dope . . . smuggling . . . from the Orient? Maybe . . . if not, what else? He couldn't see anything else.

And what if? So they were connected . . . say the Oriental and the Indian were part of the big traffic. It doesn't explain Aikman's presence, not when there were bigger cases the police were still wrestling with. Shockers . . . cases still open. Billy Gibbs and—What's his name?—the mayor's assistant . . . headline stories. Why have Noah Aikman work on the deaths of an oriental businessman and a slimy pusher when the city was screaming for the killers of Gibbs and the mayor's man? If Aikman wanted tough cases, big problems—why not those? It didn't make sense, and it didn't build the bridge—but it was a start.

Forget the cops, Harmon thought. After that stunt at the press conference, he wasn't going to get anything from them, not even from Glenn.

He'd stick with Aikman.

"You don't understand," Aikman said wearily. He sat in the study, holding the phone a half inch from his ear. The calls had started in the afternoon, as soon as the press conference broke up, and now—at midnight—they were still coming. To each reporter, commentator, and city editor, he played the same tune:

"Jerry Lawrence and I had an appointment to discuss the structure of the investigative units of the Manhattan homicide departments. You see, this summer I was in Britain, at Scotland Yard, researching for a new book. Basically, I'm looking for definite conclusions on the question of the precinct system's effectiveness versus the newly installed homicide-zone method, and because Scotland Yard discontinued the zones in favor of the precincts, and Manhattan took the opposite tack, it's an incredible opportunity to trace the efficacy . . . "

"All right, Professor, I'll read the book," the reporter's voice cut in.

"Oh yes, I hope you will," Aikman said.

"Professor, are you jerking me off?"

"Now, just a minute," Aikman thundered. "I've spent a great deal of time trying to explain to you . . . "

"Okay, okay, I'm sorry . . . it's late and I'm getting nowhere . . . "

"Then I'll make it easy for you: I don't know anything about the Cunningham case."

"Thanks, Professor . . . I had a feeling that's what you were saying. Good night."

Aikman gently put down the phone. "Trace the efficacy?" he said aloud, shaking his head. "Good God."

Enders wiped his mouth and dropped the napkin on the table. "Great," he said to Janice Krieg.

"Glad you liked it," she smiled and began clearing away the dishes.

"C'mon, Billy," Enders said, getting up and taking his plate to the sink. "Janice worked hard; the least we can do is help clean up."

Billy the Kid leaned back in the chair and patted his stomach. "I'd say we worked hard, too." He stood, piled up the dishes, and took them to the counter. "Besides, I do this every night."

"I don't believe it," Enders said.

"He does, Carl, honest," Janice Krieg said.

"But don't let it get around," Billy whispered to Enders.

Janice ran some hot water. "Okay, you've done your duty, officer, now retire to the living room." She gave Billy a wink and smiled. Janice was short, with deep blue eyes and black hair. When Enders first met her, his impression was, very Irish—pug nose, freckles, and a warm, friendly smile.

Krieg returned the wink and led Enders into the living room. It was small but comfortably furnished, and Billy settled on the couch, put his feet up on the coffee table, and sighed. "Brandy?" he asked Enders.

"Okay, but you stay put. I'll get it."

Krieg pointed to a section of the wall unit opposite the sofa and Enders swung the door down, revealing a row of bottles and glasses. He found the brandy and poured.

"How's it going?" Krieg asked.

Enders handed him a glass and sat down in the armchair. "It's going," he shrugged.

"That bad?"

"Yeah," Enders nodded. "It's a circle: We go 'round and 'round, looking for a break."

"I've been talking to Parker," Billy said. "He calls about once or twice a week. Last thing he told me was that you'd checked all the victims and were pretty sure they didn't know each other."

"Right . . . we got that much, anyway. Nobody knew anyone else. Their families, friends—same thing: No personal connection at all. We've been working on the military angle—checking clubs, veterans' groups . . . so far, nothing. The VFW posts and American Legion halls all have guys who meet regularly and know each other very well, but they were set up for specific units or branches of the service. We came up with some possibles, but all of them can account for their whereabouts during the killings."

"Dead ends," Krieg said, finishing the brandy.

"That's about it. Uniform rentals, plays, even cleaners . . ."

"Looking for the uniform?"

"Yeah, on the off chance our soldier friend was dumb enough to have it cleaned after his day in the park. Needless to say . . . "

"He's too smart for that, Carl," said Krieg.

"I'm sure he is, but you've got to check everything."

"Parker tells me Aikman's involved," Krieg said quietly.

"Yeah, but we don't want it getting around," Enders cautioned.

Krieg laughed. "Then I'd suggest you tell Chief Lawrence to stop calling press conferences."

"Yeah, or start looking over his shoulder for hot-shot reporters," Enders said, shaking his head. "I think we managed to put a lid on it, though. Aikman's been denying it,

Lawrence won't say anything. If anyone says 'Aikman' to me, I say 'Aikman who?' "

"I've been doing some heavy reading," Krieg said, pointing to a stack of books on a narrow desk in the corner of the room. Enders squinted. He made out Aikman's name on the spine of three of the books. "Aikman who?" Enders said, with his best puzzled book.

Krieg laughed and Enders got up and went to the desk. "Heavy, indeed," he said. "You should have stayed on, Billy. You understand this, you would have been a good detective."

"Oh I'm interested, sure," Krieg said. "It makes great reading, but I'm happy in the car. I wasn't comfortable being a detective."

"Don't get too comfortable, Billy. That's when it gets dangerous . . . " Enders said.

"I'm not falling asleep, don't worry," Krieg said, smiling.

"I'm glad it worked out," Enders said.

"And thanks . . . " Krieg began.

"Forget it," Enders said.

"No, not for that . . . for Mallory. He got a transfer, and I drew him again. I was sure you had something to do with that."

"Don't let it get around," Enders whispered.

Janice Krieg came into the room , drying her hands on a towel. "Coffee?"

"Only if you'll join us," said Enders.

"Done," she said, and went back to the kitchen. In a few minutes she was back with a tray of coffee mugs, cream, sugar, and slices of chocolate cake. She sat next to Billy on the sofa and said to Enders, "How's the case going, Carl?"

"Oh God," Enders said as Billy failed to stifle his laughter.

Aikman worked through the night on the Cunningham reports, filling in the spaces next to Indian's name on the blackboard, reading through seemingly endless pages of police files on Cunningham's activities.

The headband broke all the patterns.

Inspector Harold Glenn had noted that Cunningham's habitual trademark, a tooled leather headband, was not found on or near the body when Indian was discovered in the theater. Glenn's sharp, Aikman thought, as he searched the files for photographs of Cunningham. Sure enough: Every picture showed the band.

So the wireman got his identification, Aikman conceded. But unlike the other missing items, the headband had no connection with Cunningham's work. Work . . . Aikman smiled . . . nice way to put it. And the band certainly hadn't been issued by a government agency . . . Bureau of Indian Affairs? I'm getting punchy, Aikman thought.

He walked around the apartment thinking about the money: ten thousand dollars in twenties and fifties in three envelopes jammed into Cunningham's wide leather belt, concealed by a denim shirt and jacket. What the hell was he doing in a stinking theater with all that money? Not making a buy, not with an indictment hanging over him, Aikman reasoned. Then what? A payoff, a bribe? He didn't go to that theater to watch the movie, that's for sure. Okay, he was meeting someone and he was going to hand over ten thousand dollars. Someone lured him to the theater, baited him with something Indian was willing to pay for. What was the bait? Got to get Parker working in Harlem . . . find out what deals Cunningham was involved in.

In the meantime . . . he flipped through a card file and found the number for Warren A. Fletcher, five-star general of the Army and one of the joint chiefs of staff. He'll love this, Aikman thought with a grin: It was two-thirty in the morning. He dialed the area code for Arlington, Virginia, and then the number. Three rings, four . . .

"Fletcher, here," drawled a heavy southern accent, the voice crisp and alert.

"Fletch, this is Aikman. Sorry to wake you up . . . "

"It's okay. You got a problem?"

"Yeah, and I need some help," Aikman said. "This is going to take a while. How about getting some coffee and calling me back?"

"That serious?"

"I'm afraid so," Aikman admitted.

"Ten minutes," Fletcher said, and hung up.

Aikman went to the kitchen to wait and brew himself a cup of coffee. Standing by the stove, he remembered all the late hours he and Fletch shared in Switzerland during World War II, the planning sessions until four and five in the morning. Recruited by General William "Wild Bill" Donovan himself, Aikman had joined the newly created OSS staff, entering neutral Switzerland weeks before the borders were shut by the Axis powers.

Fletcher, then a fresh-faced major out of West Point, joined them at the last moment, the borders closing behind him. Fletch felt as most West Pointers and snidely referred to the OSS as "Donovan's Dragoons." But a part of him respected the duty, the danger, and relished the intrigue. He seemed to like the twenty-five-year-old lanky red-headed kid with the wry sense of humor and had heard talk about the brilliant imagination and ability this Aikman possessed.

Their first official meeting in the offices of the planning staff brought a smile to Aikman's face as he sipped his coffee.

"We've got a problem," Fletcher said, "and I understand you're supposed to solve it."

Aikman nodded.

The network in Switzerland was infiltrating—via operatives—the Nazi high command, co-ordinating the escape of Jews from Germany and seeking out German nationals disillusioned with Hitler. The problem was how to get the information out of Germany without endangering the agents and at the same time set up a false trail.

Aikman had spent the better part of two weeks thinking like the enemy, reviewing lists of agents and who they dealt with, drawing personality profiles and studying both ground and aerial maps. He'd come prepared to this meeting and outlined his solution.

At its basic level, this was a logic problem, and Aikman devised a series of short-term strikes using subterfuge and distraction. In order to protect the agent leaking the information, another individual must be set up as the guilty party, he reasoned, but it could only work for a short time. When the supposed "leak" was picked up, they had to move to another command post or base of operations, and repeat the process. This kept the Nazis continuously looking for the leak and never plugging it.

Aikman also outlined routes for the information to leave Germany, and once in Switzerland, be disseminated to the proper groups. Some were incredibly simple; others, involved, complicated, seemingly haphazard. At the end of Aikman's twenty-minute explanation, Fletcher not only liked "the kid," but respected him as well.

Fletcher's call came precisely ten minutes later, and Aikman gave him the whole story. Fletcher listened without interrupting, and when Aikman finished Fletcher said, "I'd read some things in the paper—Gibbs, especially—but I had no idea . . . "

"No one has any idea," Aikman said. "The duputy chiefs, the commissioner, a few others. We can't let it get out."

"I can see why," Fletcher said. "What can I do, Noah?"

"We're looking for four men. They're in your files somewhere."

"Just like that, huh?"

"Just like that," Aikman said.

"You're sure they're Army?"

"That's the only way it fits. The weapons, the tactics . . ."

"Damn," Fletcher growled. "This isn't going to do the Army any good. Four psychos with military backgrounds . . . we'll all look like shit."

"I know," Aikman said, "but it's worse than that: I don't believe they're psychos. The killings are too well planned; they may be sociopaths, but they're not psychotics."

"What can you give me?" Fletcher asked.

"Not a hell of a lot. Can you start with weapons? These guys are experts."

"We can try," Fletcher said, making notes on a sheet of paper. "I think the sniper would be the best place to start. From the way you've described the killings, he sounds like a specialist. And anyone that good must've come out of sniper school. Maybe this guy's got a medical or psychological discharge, a Section 8. Any guess on age?"

"The partials we've got put him anywhere from forty to fifty-five, but he could be using makeup."

"You're not even sure which war they fought in, right?"

"World War I is out," Aikman offered.

"Big help," Fletcher said sarcastically. "Okay—forty to fifty-five, sniper school—not much to work with."

"Figure the others for the same age bracket," Aikman said.

Fletcher underlined the numbers "40" and "55" on the sheet of paper. "This is going to be damn near impossible, Noah. They're in the files somewhere—everything is on microfilm at Fort Benjamin Harris out in Kansas—but without knowing the war, the unit, or where they were assigned . . ."

"I don't call you with the easy ones, Fletch," Aikman admitted. "What about the descriptions? I can send them all down."

"Forget it," Fletcher said. "Service records don't carry photographs. Fingerprints, sure; medical histories, identifying marks . . . all that, but no pictures."

"Terrific," Aikman groaned.

"It would be a long shot anyway," Fletcher said. "The best way to go is the weapons. The garotte wasn't all that common; let's take a shot and start with World War II and sniper school."

"I hate to ask this, but . . . "

"You want to know how long it well take, right?"

"Can you guess?"

"Months," Fletcher said, "at least months . . . even if we get lucky."

"Get lucky, Fletch," Aikman said. "It's pretty tight up here."

"You're on the spot?"

Aikman grinned. "It's where I want to be."

"I'll keep in touch, Noah, and if you get anything at all that might help us, call me."

Aikman thanked him and hung up. He turned and faced the blackboard. Months: How many more names would be up there?

After breakfast, Marcus went back to his room, changed into a bathing suit, slipped on a pair of sandals, and grabbed a towel. He took the elevator to the lobby, stopped to buy a pair of sunglasses at the hotel's gift shop, and padded out to the pool. It was a bright warm day, and vacationers splashed in the blue water and dove from high and low boards. Marcus found an empty *chaise longue* at the corner of the pool and stretched out. He scanned the pool area, welcoming the warmth of the sun. A waiter in a white jacket stopped by his side, and Marcus ordered a drink and a newspaper. "And bring a telephone, please," he added. Drinking at eleven in the morning, Marcus thought. Well, why not? He'd earned it.

The waiter placed a tall gin and tonic on the table beside Marcus and plugged a blue Princess Touch-Tone into an outlet at the table's base. Marcus dialed the long-distance operator and gave his name, room number, and the number in New York. He sipped as the phone clicked and rang.

"Marketing Consultations, good morning."

"Christoper Reynolds, please."

"May I say who's calling?"

"Ed Marcus, of Image Electronics." Marcus waited until Reynolds' voice came over the line.

"Ed, where are you?" Reynolds asked evenly.

"Right now? I'm poolside at the Fontainebleau," Marcus said, rolling the name off his tongue.

"Miami Beach?" Reynolds asked.

My God, Marcus thought, I actually surprised him! "The very same. Chris, this is the life . . . "

"Everything all right?" Reynolds interrupted.

"Couldn't be better. Just wanted you to know that I'll be here till next week. Let's get together on Thursday."

"Fine," Reynolds said, choosing his words with great care. "I'm looking forward to discussing our business venture."

"So am I," Marcus said. "I'll see you then." He hung up, finished his drink, and signaled the waiter. "Another, please," he said, holding up the empty glass.

I actually caught him off guard, Marcus said to himself, staring at the high board as a tall, blond girl in a white bikini stepped to the edge. As she knifed cleanly into the water, Marcus closed his eyes and let the sun soak his body.

They're dying to ask, Marcus thought, a smug smile crossing his tanned face as he watched the others at the table. They can't figure out how I did it, he decided.

Marcus had arrived early and nursed a Bourbon and branch water until he saw Reynolds come through the door. Marcus had lifted the glass in salute.

"You certainly look fit," Reynolds said as he sat down.

"Never better," Marcus said, grinning.

"Florida agrees with you," Reynolds said.

"You might say that," Marcus teased.

When the others arrived they exchanged questioning glances but, true to their practice, talked about everything but Marcus' activities. Reynolds had told Birmingham and Lyle that Marcus had called from Florida . . . but that was all he could tell them.

Toward the end of the meal, Marcus began to notice that they were hurrying. The normal leisurely pace gave way to a certain impatience, and Marcus was sure something was bothering them when Reynolds passed up his after-dinner brandy and called for the check.

At eight-thirty they walked into Clarkson Manor, ordered drinks sent up to the room, and went upstairs. Reynolds led them into the room, shut the door behind them, and took his place at the table. "Something wrong, Chris?" Marcus asked him.

"You tell us," Reynolds said, lighting a cigarette.

"There were no problems, if that's what's worrying you," Marcus said. "Everything worked fine, just as I planned it."

"Ed," Lyle broke in, "there was a press conference while you were in Florida . . . the police were making a big show out of Cunningham's murder . . . "

Marcus laughed. "I'm sorry I missed it."

"Well, I'm sorry, too," Lyle said, "because a reporter suggested that the police had brought Noah Aikman in on the case."

"The cop denied it," Birmingham added, "but the denial was, well, a little weak."

Marcus had a chance to think it over as the waiter knocked at the door and brought their drinks in. When he left, Marcus took a long swallow. "Aikman on the case," he said slowly. "He's got a reputation for the bizarre, all right. But the cop denied it?"

"Yeah," Birmingham said, without conviction.

"Maybe Aikman was working on the Cunningham drug bust?" Marcus asked.

"I doubt it," Reynolds said. "That's not his kind of case . . ."

"But *we* are, is that what you're saying?" Marcus asked.

"I'm not saying anything," Reynolds answered. "Besides, we have nothing to be concerned about, do we?" He looked straight at Marcus, his face without expression.

"Nothing went wrong," Marcus said. "My work doesn't have neon signs around it." He glanced at Birmingham, who stared down at the table. "I'll let you decide," Marcus continued. "Let me tell you how it went, and you be the judges. Fair enough?" He looked at each man in turn.

As Marcus began to trace his movements and explain his plan, any thoughts of Aikman or the police slipped from their minds. In meticulous detail, Marcus created the atmosphere, the sights, sounds, and smells of Harlem; the Soul Sister, the theater, the drugstore phone booth . . . he piled scene upon scene like a master storyteller until, as he neared the end, he held the other men in the grasp of the story, as an old fisherman would hold children with tales of pirates and buried treasure.

When he had finished, Lyle was the first to speak. "You took a few chances."

Reynolds laughed. "The master of understatement strikes again."

"In a way he's right, though," Marcus admitted. "A white bum in Harlem—it was risky . . . and I wasn't sure I could hang around long enough to find Cunningham. But once I found him, I was certain he'd take the bait. That was his mentality; he had to believe in the crooked cop looking for a payoff. He had no reason to expect to be killed . . . he was totally off guard."

"You could've had problems in the balcony," Lyle said.

"But I didn't," Marcus said shortly. "And if there'd been other people up there, I'd have tried another night. I could have lured him back there—he had a lot to gain. But I'll admit that if I'd had to bail out a second time, I'd have been in trouble."

"Would you still have taken him?" Reynolds asked.

"I think so . . . I'd have had to. There weren't any other possibilities, no other target. But I got him. I worked it out, and I got him."

Birmingham was staring at the table again, shaking his head. "What's wrong?" Marcus asked.

"Nothing," Birmingham replied. "I was just thinking." He paused. "You really put yourself on the line for this one."

"I'm telling you, there wasn't that much risk," Marcus insisted.

"No, I don't mean that," Birmingham said. "You went to such an extreme . . . living up there, taking the abuse . . ."

"That's what this is all about, Birm," Marcus smiled. "I'd have gone to any extreme. It was the greatest challenge I've faced in over thirty years."

"We may be facing a greater one," Reynolds said quietly.

"Aikman?" Lyle asked.

"Yeah," Reynolds said. "He's a brilliant man, and he goes for the tough ones, the strange cases. I saw him once, at one of his lectures." Reynolds leaned back in the chair. "So?"

"So, he was damned good. He was talking about criminal investigation, but that was just a catch-all. He covered everything from the rules of evidence to the psychology of interrogation in a half hour. Mostly he talked about how he works, the way he thinks."

"So?" Lyle repeated.

"So, he's very, very clever."

"Do you think he can figure it out?" Birmingham asked.

Marcus cut in: "That doesn't matter. So what if he figures it out? There's no way he can find us."

"There may be no way the police can find us," Reynolds amended, "not with their methods. Aikman's a different story."

"Bullshit," Lyle said.

Reynolds shook his head. "The worst thing you can do is underestimate the enemy."

"In the first place," Lyle said, "he may not be working on Cunningham, and even if he is, what makes you think he'll connect that killing to the others?"

"That's his specialty, Dick, making connections."

"Even so," Marcus said, "we've got nothing to worry about."

"Worry?" Reynolds smiled. "No, we don't have to worry. But when you're faced with someone who thinks the way Aikman does, who can use logic and imagination against you, it's something to think about."

"So I'll think about it," Lyle said shortly.

"I think you're giving him too much credit, Chris," Marcus said. "Nobody could figure it out."

"Maybe," Reynolds conceded. "But Aikman's a specialist in just this kind of thing. He couldn't resist the challenge . . . "

"So you *do* think he's working on it?" Birmingham asked, trying to pin Reynolds down.

"Yeah, I'd say so," Reynolds acknowledged.

"But he's got nothing to work with," Lyle argued, raising his voice. "There's no way he could put it together, no way he could find us. He can't manufacture the evidence. Nothing points to us, nothing at all; I don't care how clever Aikman is."

"Are you trying to convince us or yourself?" Reynolds asked mildly. Lyle flushed, but before he could say anything, Reynolds went on. "All I'm saying is that it's something to consider. All right? There's no reason to panic just because the enemy adds another weapon to his arsenal; but there's plenty of reason to take greater care. We can't give him anything . . . we can't make any more mistakes."

Reynolds' eyes flashed to Birmingham, who said nothing.

"We win no matter what they throw at us," Marcus said. "Let's get to it."

Reynolds held a strong position, and after ten minutes he opened up. He saw the immediate possibility and, at the same time, projected beyond it. "What would you think of this?" he asked, spreading his long fingers over the areas.

"I don't understand," Lyle said.

"It's easy," Reynolds replied, "watch." He pointed again. "This one buys me the other. I'll take them both at the same time, if it's all right with you."

"The same night?" Lyle asked.

Reynolds nodded.

"In order," Marcus said.

"Of course," Reynolds said. "I'm just asking for a slight liberty; I don't want to change the rules."

"It's all right with me," Marcus shrugged. "I think you're making it hard on yourself . . . "

"Look who's talking," Lyle laughed.

"I can work it out," Reynolds assured them . . . but, he thought to himself, let's see if Aikman can.

The first thing to do, Reynolds decided, walking back to his apartment, was make sure they were clear.

He couldn't get Birmingham's uniform out of his mind.

True, Marcus had made a hit since Birmingham's day in the park: He'd gone into Harlem, taken his man, and slipped away. But now it was his own neck, not Marcus', and the uniform—that ghost in the shadows—could still bring them all down. It was possible that the police were on to Birmingham; it was possible that they were all being watched.

First he'd make sure he was clear . . .

In his office the next morning, Reynolds set the *Wall Street Journal* aside and called his secretary in.

"Shut the door, please," he said quietly, motioning for her to sit in the chair at the side of the desk. "I've recently become involved in a highly sensitive negotiation, a very important transaction for a new client. It is vitally important that my role in these negotiations be kept confidential. Have there been any inquiries about my business dealings . . . or me personally?"

"No, sir," she said.

"Has anyone called and not left a name or number?"

"No, nothing like that at all."

"Good," Reynolds said. "Just keep your eyes open for anything unusual, especially anyone who seems to be probing for information." He saw the questioning look in her eyes and smiled warmly. "The client represents a foreign government, and should anything leak out about his, or that government's intentions, before the deal is final . . . well, it could cause considerable embarrassment for all parties."

"I see," she said.

Reynolds wondered if she saw anything at all. She was devoted to him and meticulous in her work, but she lacked imagination. His explanation would satisfy her. He dictated some letters, made a few phone calls, and left the office at two o'clock for lunch, telling his secretary he'd be gone for the day.

He wandered uptown, pausing several times to look in

shop windows and check luncheonette menus and store dis-
plays, always gazing at the reflection in the glass to see if a
man or woman lingered nearby, if any faces kept popping
up as he walked. He ate in a small coffee shop, sitting in a
booth toward the back, studying the passersby and the customers.

He rode a subway uptown after lunch, letting the actor
in him come out, appearing bored and tired as he read the
subway posters and placards, absently gazing around the
car for something to look at, all the time memorizing faces.

As he approached his apartment building, he stopped on
the corner and scanned the street, looking for parked cars,
delivery vans, or utility trucks. A United Parcel truck was
parked opposite the entrance to his building, and Reynolds
circled the block three times until the truck pulled away.

He went up to his apartment and watched from the window as a sedan with two women pulled into the spot va-
cated by the truck. Suburban shoppers, he thought. So far,
so good.

Reynolds spent the weekend in a one-sided hide-and-seek
game, leaving his apartment to shop, to eat, to stroll aim-
lessly through the streets. On Saturday night he saw a
movie. By Monday morning he was certain that no one
was following him, and he left his apartment after seven. It
was time to check on Birmingham.

He walked through the chill morning to the building on
Central Park South and took a position diagonally across
from the entrance. There were a few cars parked along the
street, sparse traffic passing through the neighborhood. He
saw Birmingham come out at eight o'clock and turn up the
block. Reynolds didn't move as the tall figure turned the
corner. Reynolds waited for five minutes, and when no one
followed Birmingham, Reynolds caught a subway to his office.

Reynolds repeated the procedure at noon, waiting in
front of the office building where Birmingham's insurance

agency occupied a suite of rooms on the fifteenth floor. When Birmingham came out, Reynolds watched for the "watchers," anyone getting out of a parked car, anyone leaning against a building, anyone who had been standing and suddenly started to move. There were a few possibilities, but no one "followed" Birmingham for more than two blocks.

It went on for three days until Reynolds was satisfied. He could go ahead with the double hit.

11

"Billy, I don't want to hear it anymore," Mallory said, beginning to get annoyed. "Jesus, I never saw a cop happy to blow Detective Division. Turn the heat down, the car's too warm."

"I didn't blow it," Krieg protested, "I passed it up, traded it in for you."

"Swell, so do me a favor and turn the heat down." Krieg slid the lever on the heater and flicked the fan to "low." Mallory turned a corner, and his eyes followed the headlights as they probed the deserted street.

"You know your problem, Ted?" Krieg asked.

"What's my problem?"

"You've gone sour on the job."

"Sure, sure," Mallory grunted.

"It's true: You're just a sour old man with a lousy attitude."

Mallory slowed the car and turned slightly in the seat. "*My* attitude? Jesus, what about *your* attitude? All I hear from you is how lucky you are to be back in the car. You're fucked up, that's what's the matter with you. If Enders offered me Detective, you'd never see this boy again, that's for shit sure. And even if I couldn't hack it, I wouldn't run out in the middle of an investigation . . . "

Krieg, looking to his left beyond Mallory's shoulder, saw

a man running out of Inwood Hill Park. "What the hell . . ." Mallory turned and moved the car toward the curb, rolling down the window. "What's the problem?" he called.

The man ran toward the car, his breath labored, his steps unsteady. As he leaned on the door, Krieg saw that the right lens of his glasses was cracked and there were flecks of blook in the dark hair of his beard and mustache. "My friend . . . in the park . . . two muggers attacked us."

Mallory shut the engine and Krieg called dispatch, reporting his position and a mugging in progress. Mallory was out of the car. "You've got to show us: Don't be afraid, just show us where it happened."

"I shouldn't have left him," the man wheezed.

"You did the right thing," Krieg said, coming around the front of the car. "We'll follow you. Go ahead." The man nodded and led them into the park.

Stripped of their leaves, the trees and bushes cast skeletonlike shadows as Krieg and Mallory swept their flashlight beams in waist-high patterns across the path. Standing next to the frightened man, Krieg came to a split in the path. "Which way?" he asked, "Mr. . . . ?"

"Fuller, Steve Fuller. I'm not sure, I . . . "

"Take it easy . . . relax," Krieg said. "Think: Which side of the park were you on?"

Fuller glanced to his left and pointed. "That way . . . I came out that way." He darted ahead of Krieg.

"I hope he knows where he's going," Mallory said, starting after Fuller. Krieg pulled his club from his belt. The path bent and twisted, and Krieg lost sight of Fuller as the man turned a corner. "Hey, slow down!" Krieg called. As the path straightened, he flashed the light off to the left and right. He couldn't see Fuller.

"Maybe he cut through there," Mallory said, pointing with his light to a parallel strip of blacktop through a cluster of bare trees. "I'll try it, you go along here." Krieg moved on, deeper into the park, losing sight of Mallory as the paths separated. There was no moon and, except for the narrow band of light from his flash, Krieg might have been walking through a tunnel. Ahead, to his right, he saw the flicker of Mallory's light, growing fainter with every passing moment.

"Fuller!" Krieg called out, standing perfectly still and listening for any sound. "Fuller!" he called again, louder. "Shit," Krieg muttered, "where the hell does he think he's going?"

Krieg walked slowly, playing the flashlight back and forth in ever-increasing arcs, bouncing the beam off rocks and trees and thin scrub bushes. From his right he heard a sound and stopped. His breath was a frozen explosion on the air. "Ted!" he called. There was no trace of Mallory's light. Krieg began walking to his right, leaving the blacktop and cutting across the frozen ground. "Ted!" he called again, staring into the darkness on both sides of the thin flashlight beam, watching for Mallory's answering light, or a reflection, or anything. . . . Krieg felt a trickle of sweat slide down his back. *"Ted!"* he shouted. Nothing . . . Mallory was gone . . . Fuller was gone.

Krieg dropped his club from his right hand and pulled his gun. It was a trap. His thumb moved to click off the flashlight, but he was a fraction of a second too late. The dumdum bullet shot out of the darkness of the park.

At nine-thirty, Enders came back to his office with a mug of coffee. He sipped and stared at the papers on his desk, suddenly whirling around to the radio on the table behind him. From the chatter he'd heard something: 34 Frank, no response. What was that location?

He dialed for his car, threw on an overcoat, and picked up two uniformed officers as he dashed out of the building: "Two cops need help; Inwood Hill Park. Follow me."

THE RANDOM FACTOR

The transmissions came over the car radio as Ron Blake drove up the West Side Highway to the tip of Enders' zone. The siren moved the traffic aside as Blake, at Enders' urging, pushed the car to sixty, then seventy. They pulled up next to 34 Frank, the car empty, its radio still calling. There were three other patrol cars around the unit. Enders saw McQuade get out of a sedan near the curb and call three officers to his side. They were starting a search; 34 Frank had been silent for nearly half an hour.

Enders went numb; the cold, he told himself, and set his jaw. The searchlights on the cars began to sweep the park, and blue-coated men were moving in tight patterns along the paths, fanning out six abreast with powerful five-cell flashlights lighting the way ahead of them.

Enders got out of the car. "I'm going in," he said to Blake. "You stay with the car, pull it up close to the sidewalk, and get your headlights in there." Blake turned the car, and Enders followed the uniformed men into the park. Some of them had their guns drawn, and they heard McQuade shouting orders. Ten men to cover the two-mile-wide park, Enders thought. We need more. . . .

He heard Krieg and Mallory's names shouted at regular intervals. The men had split up: five off to the right, five to the left. Enders stood at the intersection of the paths. From his right he heard a shout and moved forward. There was a circle of light ahead and voices, louder than before: "Mallory . . . he's hurt. . . . " Enders ran to the light, leaving the path to cut across a sloping rise. Below him, on the path, the men kneeled over Mallory.

"He's alive," McQuade said, as Enders ran up. "Somebody bashed him in the head, knocked him out, but he's alive."

"Billy . . . ?" Enders asked.

"Nothing yet," McQuade said, shaking his head. "Get an ambulance!" McQuade called to the officers. "Don't move him—get a stretcher in here!"

Enders and McQuade doubled back along the path as three of the men moved ahead, leaving one man with Mallory. "They may have split up," McQuade said. "Krieg may have taken the other side." They came to the intersection, turned sharply to their right, and started up the blacktop. In the distance Enders saw pinpoints of light, and suddenly there was a shout. "Oh Jesus! Jesus Christ! He's over here!" McQuade began to run.

Five officers stood several paces back from Billy Krieg's body. McQuade took a quick look and turned to face Enders, who was running toward him. "Don't," McQuade said, standing in front of him.

"Let me see," Enders said, pushing, but McQuade held his ground.

"You don't want to see it. Somebody blew half his head off."

Enders slumped back and leaned against a tree. He watched as if in a dream as the support units arrived, searching the area for evidence . . . . as the ambulance crew carried the stretcher with the faceless body back to the street. He fell into step behind McQuade as the stretcher led the procession. Enders was walking in quicksand, every sound an echo reverberating in his brain . . . it was hard to breathe.

Thirty-four Frank stood like a tombstone: lights turned off, doors locked, the radio finally silent. Enders stood by the car as the stretcher was loaded into the ambulance.

"Mallory's gonna be okay . . . we just got the word," McQuade said softly, appearing at Enders' side. Enders nodded.

"You gonna be okay?" McQuade said.

"Yeah . . . I'll be okay. . . . " As McQuade walked away, Enders took a step closer to 34 Frank, his eyes on the front seat. In the darkness he made out a pair of gloves on the passenger side. Billy's hands must have been cold. Enders began to cry.

Reynolds drew the curtains from the window and looked out at the bridge. Incredible view, he thought.

It had to be this building . . . he'd known that from the first night when he'd checked the area. Any apartment on the West Side—eight, ten, twelve floors up; the corner was best.

He heard footsteps in the hallway and froze. Couldn't be her . . . but his hands gripped the rifle and he began to turn toward the door. The footsteps passed and faded. The girl who rented this apartment was downtown, Reynolds was sure. It had taken almost two weeks to pick up on her habits, and on this Tuesday night she'd met her lover after work and would spend hours with him.

Reynolds put the rifle down and pushed at the window; the frame gave slightly but wouldn't open. He ran his fingers along the edges of the wood where the frame met the track . . . paint. The window had been painted shut. He struggled, strained against the frame without result. With the heels of his gloved hands he rapped sharply upward and heard the crack as the thin line of paint broke and the window moved with a clatter. He froze again, holding his breath, then eased the window up the rest of the way.

With the rifle in his hands, he positioned himself at the left side of the window, braced his body against the frame, and stared out. Below and to the west, the George Washington Bridge was alive with light and traffic. The scope brought the city side of the bridge into close focus. He slipped the incendiary bullet from his pocket, ejected the magazine from the rifle, and placed the bullet in the first position, reloading the other shells behind it.

He watched through the scope for five minutes, until his

eyes and his senses were tuned to the speed of the traffic, and picked his target as it moved up the approach lanes onto the bridge. The big yellow Checker cab swung for the center lane and slowed as tail lights glowed ahead of it. Traffic closed in behind and Reynolds tracked for another five seconds, held his breath, and squeezed off the shot.

An explosion of flame filled the eyepiece of the scope and blinded him as the incendiary bullet hit the trunk of the cab and blew the gas tank. A rush of sound screamed across the distance to the window where he stood. The flaming cab twisted in midair and slammed into two cars in the left lane, hurling fire across the width of the bridge. Cars on both sides of the bridge were burning, and thick black smoke boiled up from the roadway. The flames licked up and around the arching supports of the bridge, and on the upper roadway drivers faced a wall of fire, jammed on their brakes, and jumped from their cars.

In a chain reaction, like a mat of firecrackers, the gas tanks began to explode. Reynolds, pulling back from the window and the fiery ballet of death, thought he could hear screams from the inferno.

Enders leaned against his car, oblivious to the cold, unaware that his coat was open, deaf to the chatter on the radio or the conversation around him.

"Boss, did you hear what I said?" McQuade repeated.

Enders turned to face him. "What?"

"The Geroge Washington Bridge is on fire."

"That's impossible. What're you talking about?"

"An accident, some collision or something . . . cars are burning on both levels of the bridge."

"So what the hell do you want me to do about it?" he snapped. "You expect me to run over there with a fire hose? Call the Fire Department."

"But the traffic . . . we need men to handle . . . "

"I don't give two shits about the traffic! The Port Authority's responsible for the bridge—let them handle it. If you're so interested in traffic, McQuade, I'll put you on traffic for the next twenty years!"

Enders turned away and shouted for Blake, who was standing with a group of patrolmen at the entrance to the park. Blake got into the car as Enders automatically reached for the front-door handle. He stopped and opened the rear door instead.

"Where to?" Blake asked him.

Enders' voice from the back seat was barely controlled. "Staten Island . . . Krieg's house."

Reynolds stepped out of the subway at Forty-second Street and Times Square and hailed a cab. "Holland Tunnel," he told the driver.

"Oh great," the man whined. "I was goin' off duty . . . I don't want to drive to Jersey . . . " Reynolds pushed a fifty through the opening in the Plexiglas divider. "That's the tip," he said. The driver curmpled the bill into his jacket pocket and pushed the flag down.

"You gonna set up house keeping in the tunnel, or you got an address?"

"How's Twenty-second and Marly, Jersey City?"

"You got it," the driver said . . . "and you handle the tolls."

Reynolds nodded and lit a cigarette. For the first time that evening, he relaxed. Baiting the cops had been just like the jungle—drawing them into his territory, splitting them, taking his man out. He inhaled deeply, smiling. In the middle of winter to feel the sweat of a jungle thousands of miles away and thirty years removed. Incredible!

He'd rested at the apartment for an hour, cleaned the rifle, and picked up the supplies he would need for the rest of the night. He'd left the trophies in a dresser drawer—the cop's shield and something extra, just to raise a few eyebrows—the wedding ring.

He crushed the cigarette out as the cab sped through the tunnel. The time for relaxing was over. In a lot of ways, what he had to do next would be the toughest job of the night. He paid the driver when the cab pulled up to Marly Avenue, adding an additional twenty. He got out, waited until the cab pulled away, and then walked four blocks and hailed another taxi.

"Fort Lee," he said as he got in. "Georgetown Avenue and Ninety-first Street."

"You got to pay my return trip," the black driver said.

"I know all about it," Reynolds answered, passing a twenty over the seat. This was the best way, he knew. The George Washington Bridge would be impassable for at least a day, maybe more. Use the cabs and the tunnel, slip through like a commuter. . . .

When the driver let him off, Reynolds walked for three blocks until he was sure the cab was gone. From his overcoat pocket he took the false mustache he'd taken from the makeup kit at the apartment and pressed it into place. Next, a pair of horn-rimmed glasses and finally a small notebook and an oversize card sealed in plastic. Walking slowly, he approached the huge fenced-in yard from the west side and moved toward the gate. A line of towtrucks was backed up at the entrance, and a man in a greasy leather jacket was gesturing to the driver of the lead truck. Behind the trucks, three flat-bed semitrailers carried the twisted and charred remains of several cars.

At the back of the yard, a winch and hoist lifted the wrecks of more cars off two other flat-beds and sent the metal skeletons crashing to the ground. The Fort Lee impound yard was filling up, thanks to a disaster on the George Washington Bridge . . . and one of those burned-out cars was the Checker.

Reynolds eased up to the gate, pinning the plastic card

to his overcoat. A towtruck drove through the gate, and Reynolds walked up to the man in the leather jacket, his notebook in his hand. "Mitch Henderson, New York *Times*," he said, taking a pencil out of the overcoat pocket and tapping at the plastic card. The man squinted at him and shrugged. "I don't have much time," the man said, waving another truck toward the gate.

"Just take a second. What's your name?"

"You gonna use it in your story?" the man asked, drawing closer to Reynolds.

"Sure, if I get a story," Reynolds smiled. "What the hell happened, anyway?"

"Don't you know?"

"Look, all I know is that the city editor on the night desk calls and tells me to get over here. I live in Jersey, you know, so I guess they figured I'd be the one to cover this end. He said a car blew up on the bridge. . . ."

"Yeah, well, that's what they tell me," the man said. "Name's Brooks, Jackson Brooks . . . not Jack, Jackson."

"Got it," Reynolds said, scribbling on the pad. "How long has this been going on?" he asked, pointing to the line of trucks.

"Over two hours; we got about twenty cars in here already."

"Hear anything from the drivers of the towtrucks?"

"Bits and pieces: A cab blew up, started the fire and, before you knew it, there were twenty, thirty cars involved. The fire's still going; got the super pumper down in the water tryin' to put it out. You know, you ought to check with the drivers back there before they go out again." Brooks gestured toward the back of the yard where the winch was lifting the wrecks off the trucks.

"Yeah, good idea. Is the cab, the one that blew up, is that back there?"

"Yeah, we got it in the first load . . . it's over by the

fence. Figured we'd keep it separated, in case the cops want to go over it."

"You must have seen cars go up before: What could cause it?"

"Oh hell, lots of things," Brooks said, scratching his head. "Most common's a leak in the gas line. Hot engine, gas leak, boom!" He flung his arms up into the air.

"Yeah," Reynolds said, writing. "Guess I'll talk to the drivers now. You don't mind if I prowl around the yard for a while?"

"No, go ahead . . . and remember . . . "

"Jackson, not Jack," Reynolds said. Brooks smiled and waved another truck up.

Reynolds made his way through the yard toward the rear, where the winch groaned as it lifted and swung the cars toward a pile of scrap. Reynolds got in close, pretended to scribble some notes, and moved off, toward the back fence. Crumpled in a corner were the remains of the taxi. He'd timed it right—in the midst of the confusion, before the police suspected anything more than a bad accident from an explosion; and he'd played the part to perfection.

The cab resembled a child's Erector Set that had been crushed and twisted by huge hands and blackened by fire. Only the front end could be said to resemble a car, and as Reynolds searched the hood area he could feel the heat from the metal. There it was, eighteen inches from the smashed windshield, toward the right side of the hood; the blackened medallion, riveted to the metal. He pulled a wide-bladed screwdriver from his overcoat, forced it underneath the edge of the metal medallion, and twisted, prying the disk from the hood. He grabbed it and slid it into the overcoat pocket.

He slipped out of the yard as Brooks was directing a driver through the gates, crossed the street, and walked four blocks and turned the next corner. Toward the darkened end of the next block he removed the overcoat, then his jacket. His eyes searched the next block and saw the alley. He ducked in, kicked off his shoes, and pulled his pants off. Underneath he wore an old pair of Levi's, and the wind cut through the thin fabric of the jeans as he exchanged the horn-rimmed glasses for a pair of wire frames, pulled off the mustache and stuffed it, along with the glasses, into the overcoat pocket. He took off his tie and shirt, revealing a black T-shirt.

Reynolds reversed the overcoat. Instead of a lining, the coat carried a flat, khaki knapsack and a short ski jacket sewn into it; both had been hidden by the bulk of the coat. He ripped them out, rolled the overcoat, jacket, shirt, and pants, and jammed them into the pack. He stuffed the tie in, pulled the flap over the top of the knapsack, and tied it shut. He got into the ski jacket, zipped it up, and slipped on the black loafers. Hoisting the pack, Reynolds left the alley. In his back pocket was a black corduroy cap, which he pushed down over his head. He pulled a crumpled cigarette from the ski jacket, lit it, and turned the corner.

It was cold and he shivered as the wind picked up and pushed at his back. He had about a half hour of walking until he hit the highway where he'd thumb a ride to Jersey City, and then to the Port Authority Bus Terminal in New York.

His stride was different, his mannerisms totally unlike his own, or Fuller's, or Henderson's. He was a new person, a different role. Deep inside the knapsack was the last trophy of the evening: the Checker's medallion.

Reynolds had pulled off the toughest part of the night's work.

Carl Enders would always remember it as the worst night of his life.

As Blake drove away from Inwood Hill Park, Enders

changed his mind about Staten Island and told Blake to take him to Bellevue. Enders went in alone, made his way down to the autopsy room and ordered Avery, the chief medical examiner, to take the prints from Krieg's hand. Enders made a phone call and waited while a uniformed officer brought Krieg's file, and the comparison was made. Avery followed the officer out of the autopsy room and took Enders aside.

"I've seen that before," he said quietly, "that kind of damage: high-powered rifle and a dumdum bullet. We won't know for certain until Ballistics tests the fragments, but . . . "

Enders turned away from him, totally numb, disoriented. He walked out of the hospital and got in his car. "You can take me to Staten Island now," he told Blake.

During the long ride he tried to think of what to say to Janice Krieg, then realized that he would have to say nothing. His appearance at her home at midnight, on an evening when Billy was on patrol, would tell her.

Blake pulled the car up to the curb in front of the two-story white frame house on the deserted street and got out. He opened the door for Enders and said, "Let me go with you." Enders glanced up at his face for a moment and then nodded. They walked slowly up the driveway, across the lawn, and knocked on the front door.

The porch light came on and the door opened the length of the security chain. Janice Krieg, in a white terrycloth bathrobe, squinted through the opening. "Carl . . . ?"

"Can I come in, Janice?"

The door closed and he heard the chain slide off, but Janice didn't open the door. Enders pushed it gently and walked in. She stood with her back to him, ten feet away.

He held her in his arms, her sobs gradually stopping as she leaned against him. "How did it happen?" she asked, her voice calm and flat.

Enders took a deep breath. "The sniper shot him—the

case we were working on . . . " The full impact hit him then. It wasn't until he spoke the word "sniper" that he fully understood what had taken place in Inwood Hill Park. His anger increased, but he controlled himself and let her go, watching as she walked steadily to the couch and sat down. "Why?" she asked Enders.

"We don't know."

Blake moved past Enders and went into the kitchen. In the silence they heard the phone dial spin and then Blake's voice: whispered, short sentences, then the solid chunk of the receiver in the cradle. The sounds seemed to come from far away.

Blake came back into the living room and stood by Enders. "The PBA will be sending some people over," he said quietly.

Janice looked up. "I don't need anybody . . . I'm all right."

Enders nodded. "I know, but they want to come."

"There's nothing they can do to help me, Carl," she insisted.

"I know that . . . "

The PBA was always prepared for nights like this one. They would contact the wives of police officers who lived on Staten Island, and the women would come and keep a vigil with the widow. Enders knew it wouldn't do any good, but at least Janice wouldn't be alone.

"Can I get you anything?" Enders asked her.

"No, nothing . . . if you want some coffee . . . "

Enders went into the kitchen and found the coffee pot and a pound can of Savarin. He didn't want the coffee, but he couldn't stand the living room's terrible silence. He poured three cups, set them on a tray, and carried them to the table at the end of the sofa.

"You didn't get him, did you?" Janice asked him, staring at the floor.

"No," Enders said.

She nodded. "I don't know why I asked that. It doesn't make any difference . . . "

The doorbell rang and, with a sense of relief, Enders admitted the three silent women who stood on the porch. He followed them into the living room. "I've got to go now," he said to Janice.

"Do you want me to come down in the morning to identify Billy?" she asked him, rushing the words, as if to deny their meaning.

"I took care of it," Enders answered. Janice nodded and with steady hands picked up the coffee cup.

Enders found Peter Gregory slumped in a chair as he opened the door to his office. Gregory cradled a Styrofoam cup in his lap and held it out to Enders as the deputy chief crossed in front of him and leaned against the edge of the desk.

"I heard about Krieg," Gregory said. "Avery phoned. Ballistics confirmed his suspicion. It was the same rifle. The fragments match. Anything you want done?"

"Go out and bring back the sniper," Enders said flatly.

"Yeah," Gregory nodded, withdrawing the coffee and sipping at the tepid liquid. "You sure you don't want some of this?"

Enders shook his head.

"The Aikman family's been trying to reach you," Gregory sighed. "Two messages from Alex, two from Noah."

"The great man himself," Enders sneered.

"If you're gonna feel sorry for yourself and throw bullshit at me, I'd rather be home in bed," Gregory said with a trace of anger. Enders' phone rang as he started to answer Gregory. He grabbed the receiver. "Yeah, Enders . . ."

"Carl, this is Max, at the Ballistics Lab . . . "

"Yeah, what've you got?"

"We got a shell, .30 caliber. It matches up with the one from the McMahon killing. I've been staring at it for an hour, wondering why a .30 should stick in my memory. Finally put it together . . . "

"I don't understand . . . "

"I was there when they found Krieg's body. It had to be the sniper with the dumdums. Avery thought as much, and someone from your office confirmed it."

"Carl, I'm not talking about Krieg. I'm talking about the bridge."

Enders sat up straight in the chair. "What about it?"

"One of your detectives took a call from a woman who lives in a building overlooking the bridge. She says her apartment was broken into, the window forced open. She found a shell casing on the floor. Don't you talk to your detectives?"

"Not tonight," Enders said. "Hold on a minute . . . " He looked at Gregory. "Pete, take this on the extension." Gregory hauled himself out of the chair and, with a puzzled look on his face, went outside to the secretary's desk and lifted the phone.

"Max, Pete Gregory's on the line. Repeat what you just told me." Maxwell went through it again, and Enders heard Gregory swear under his breath. "Thanks for letting me know, Max," said Enders as he hung up.

Gregory stood in the doorway, lines of anger creasing his face. "I don't believe it."

"I don't either," Enders said, "but I'm going to check it out. Do me a favor: Find out what happened on the bridge . . . check with the Fire Department, the traffic boys, the Port Authority. Find out if a shot caused the fire and those smashups. And call Aikman; fill him in."

"Where are you going?"

"To find the detective who took that call from the woman in the apartment, and then I'm going to take a look for myself."

"Do you think . . . ?" Gregory started to say.

"Jesus, Pete, I don't know what to think. I don't even remember how to think anymore. Leave that to Aikman, okay?"

Enders gave the young woman in the apartment a rough time.

"And you came home and found a cartridge case on the floor?" he snarled. "Just like that?"

"Yes, just like that," Andrea Linde answered coolly. She was a fashion model for one of the top agencies in the city, and she faced Enders' anger without losing her poise or confidence. "And the curtains had been disturbed and the window opened," she added.

"Was it open when you came in?"

"No, but there were chips of paint on the sill and on the carpet. I told all this to the detective who was here earlier."

"Yeah, I'm sure you did. Did you tell him where you were tonight while your apartment was broken into?"

She leaned forward on the sofa and tapped long fingernails on the glass-topped coffee table. "I really don't think that's any of your business."

"Jesus," Enders said, exasperated. "This is beautiful. Do you see what's going on out there?" He pointed toward the window. "Go ahead, take a look."

"I saw it," she said evenly.

Enders walked to the window and stared out. Needles of red and white light flashed from patrol cars and ambulances, cutting into the thick cloud of black smoke that hung over the bridge. Con Edison emergency trucks were pulled up to the bridge supports, their ladders disappearing into the smoke cloud. There seemed to be a thousand men in black, blue, and white helmets scurrying over the surface.

"*That's* my business," Enders said, turning back toward the sofa. "Who was here tonight?"

"How would I know?" Andrea Linde asked. She stood up and walked toward Enders. She was close to five-nine, slim and graceful in the manner of her profession, with sharp features and casually tossed blond hair. "If it makes any difference to you, I was downtown with a photographer friend. We had dinner and spent the rest of the time at his studio. He's doing a portfolio for me."

"Uh huh," Enders nodded. "You see him regularly?"

"Yes, twice a week, as a matter of fact. Why?"

"On the same nights?" Enders asked, ignoring her question.

"Yes, Tuesdays and Thursdays."

Enders smiled to himself.

"You didn't answer me," Andrea said.

"When you see this photographer, how long do you stay with him?"

"Not until you tell me why you want to know," she said, folding her thin arms across her chest.

"Okay," Enders said calmly. "The man who used your apartment—used, Ms. Linde—didn't casually decide to break in. He had to be sure you wouldn't come home while he was here. He had to be aware of your . . . habits."

"You mean someone's been following me?"

Enders nodded. "He wouldn't break into an apartment if he wasn't sure the owner was out. He wouldn't take the chance . . . he plans well in advance . . . "

"You know who he is?" she asked.

"No," he said, "we know *about* him, but . . . " Enders stopped. He was talking too much. "I want you to come down to my office this morning. Ask for Detective McQuade. I want you to give him everything . . . what you've done for the past three weeks, where you've been, people you've seen—and bring your friend the photographer."

"All right," she said.

"Around ten o'clock," Enders said. "And start thinking about it now . . . make some notes."

"This is important to you, isn't it? You think the man who was here was responsible for what happened on the bridge?" Enders nodded. "Then I can see why you were upset," she said.

Enders was tempted to say, "You don't know the half of it," but he resisted, mumbling "Good night" instead, and leaving the apartment.

When Enders got into the car, Blake said, "Chief Gregory's been trying to reach you, boss. He wants you to meet him at the impound yard."

"Did he say why?"

"No, just that we should get down there."

Covering four square city blocks, the impound yard on Twenty-ninth Street and Tenth Avenue resembled a huge parking lot except for the police guard at the gate and the concrete blockhouse at the far end, where the police maintain a fully equipped garage with lifts, hoists, automotive tools, and equipment. Here the vehicles involved with crime or criminals, suspected or proven, come to rest and are sometimes methodically torn apart in the search for evidence.

Enders rolled down the window and flashed his badge at the guard, and Blake rolled the sedan through the gates. Peter Gregory stood inside the guard's shack talking on the telephone and peering out the grimy window. He hung up when he saw Enders' car and came outside.

"What's going on?" Enders asked.

"We're waiting for a taxi," Gregory said.

It took two hours for the flat-bed truck to bring the burned-out cab from Fort Lee. Enders and Gregory sat on uncomfortable wooden chairs in the guard's shack and drank bitter coffee.

"I talked to the witnesses," Gregory said, "and some of

the victims at the hospital, the ones who could talk at all. They're all telling the same story: This cab blew up, all of a sudden, out of nowhere. No smoke, no fire, no tire blow-out . . . just an explosion and then fire. One guy was three cars back and got thrown out of his car. The weirdest thing," Gregory shook his head. "He was banged up pretty good, but it saved his life. He beat the fire—got away before *his* car blew up. He said there was no warning, no nothing—like a bomb going off."

Enders frowned.

"It might have been a bomb," Gregory said. He took a sip of coffee and shrugged. "There's no way of telling."

"Forget it," Enders said. "It was no bomb, not with that shell in the apartment."

"Yeah, well, I figured we gotta have that cab, or what's left of it."

"Did you call Aikman?" Enders asked, refilling the coffee cup and mumbling, "I don't know why I drink this shit."

"I gave him all of it," Gregory said. "He'd heard about Krieg. You know who called him?" Enders shook his head.

"Parker," Gregory said.

"He liked Billy," Enders whispered. "What did Aikman say?"

"Nothing about Krieg, but when I told him about the bridge and that woman's apartment, he was really thrown. He wanted me to call the hospitals and the morgue, find out if any of the victims had gunshot wounds."

"And . . . ?"

"Not as far as we can tell. Some of the bodies were in pretty bad shape, though."

"How many dead?"

"Thirty-nine so far, but some of the others aren't going to make it."

"What did Aikman say to that?"

"He kept saying, 'It doesn't fit, it doesn't fit.' "

"What doesn't fit?" Enders asked wearily.

"He didn't say," Gregory shrugged.

"Oh Christ," Enders moaned. "We go around and around and get nowhere."

They sat silently until the huge flat-bed truck eased to a stop at the gate. Roped to the truck body was the blackened remains of the taxi. "Call Forensic," Enders told Gregory and went outside to watch the unloading.

With a winch and hoist, they lifted the skeleton of the cab, drove the truck out from under, and set the wreckage gently on the ground near the front gate. "They're on the way," Gregory said, coming up behind Enders. Together they circled the wreck.

The rear end of the cab was gone, the trunk and back window blown out, the wheels misshapen lumps of metal. The stiff black springs of the rear seat twisted crazily in the air. From the driver's seat forward, the cab was still recognizable as a car. The odor of burned rubber oozed from the tangle of metal.

"Maybe the gas tank blew," Gregory suggested.

"Something toward the back." Enders said. "Whatever happened, it happened there. Could a bullet do that?"

"An incendiary bullet, sure. Explodes on contact. The gas tank goes a split second later."

"And thirty-nine people die," Enders said. He heard the sound of a horn and turned to see the black Forensic van at the gate. As the guard swung the steel fence open, Enders walked to the van.

"Go over every goddamn inch," he told the driver, pointing to the taxi. "I want to know why that thing blew up. I don't care what you have to do or how long it takes. You're gonna live here until you find me a reason, you got it?"

"Yes, sir, we'll find out," the driver answered, momentarily frightened by Enders' intensity.

THE RANDOM FACTOR

Weak sunlight was fighting the slate-gray sky as Enders and Gregory left the yard.

By the time Enders got back to his office, a thin, wet snow had begun to fall. Aikman stood at the window, staring out. The smell of stale cigarette smoke was heavy in the overheated room. Exhausted, Enders fell into his chair and rubbed at his eyes.

"What did you find out?" Aikman asked.

Enders filled him in: the witnesses, survivors, the taxi, the Forensic crew at the impound yard . . .

"But none of the victims show a gunshot wound?" Aikman asked.

"No."

"Then that's it," Aikman pronounced.

"What's it?" Enders asked.

"Our boy with the rifle. First he kills that cop . . . "

"Billy Krieg!" Enders shot back. "He has a name, you know." Either Aikman was too caught up in his thinking to notice the anger in Enders' voice, or he just ignored it.

" . . . and then he fired on the cab."

"Doesn't fit, does it?" Enders asked sarcastically.

"Nothing fits," Aikman said shortly. He lit another cigarette and stared out the window. "What was he after? What did he take?"

"He took Billy's shield," Enders said softly. "And his wedding ring. The bastard . . . "

"No, I don't mean that," Aikman said, turning to face Enders. "What did he take from the cab?"

"What the hell are you talking about?"

"No gunshot wound on any of the people who died on the bridge, that's what I'm talking about. Jesus, don't you see it?"

"No, Professor, I don't see anything."

"It breaks the pattern. He's always stalked his victims— like McMahon, like Krieg. All of a sudden he shoots into a

189

crowd from a distance, at a bunch of cars on the George Washington Bridge . . . no, wrong . . . at one *particular* car, that taxi."

"Patterns, Jesus," Enders snapped. "You keep talking about patterns. It's all nonsense, don't you see that? Tonight proves it. If you're right and he shot at the taxi, what kind of pattern is that? He's a psycho. They're all psychos. You're looking for intricate patterns and we're up against psychos."

"There's a logic to it, Carl, I know it. We just haven't seen the pattern yet," Aikman insisted.

"Goddamn it!" Enders shouted, "Can't I get through to you? Stop giving me this crap. People are dying and you're playing with puzzles!"

As Enders had said "people are dying," Aikman's eyes slid away from the deputy chief's face and stared out the window, focused on a point far away. "That's been the problem all along," he said softly.

"What?" Enders demanded.

"They're not killing people, Carl," Aikman said, his voice picking up, his words rushing together. "The cab proves it . . . Jesus, that's what I couldn't see! They're killing . . . elements. Elements, in a pattern we don't see."

"That's crazy," Enders muttered.

Aikman's voice thundered, "Listen to me! I've finally got something to work with, and you damn well better listen."

Enders was too stunned to reply. No one had ever spoken to him in that tone since his days as a rookie.

"The people they're killing represent something, that's what I mean," Aikman went on. "That's why I couldn't find the intersection, the common factor: I was looking for the wrong things. There *is* no intersection, damn it. No common factor in the victims' lives . . . it has nothing to do with them as people. They're dying because they *stand* for something."

"What does the cab stand for?" Enders asked, impatiently.

"I don't know yet, but it proves that I'm right. It's a victim, but it's not a person. It filled a requirement . . . they *all* filled requirements. Jesus, I was so far off."

"And now you're closer?" Enders asked, skeptically.

"Now I've got the angle on it," Aikman said with satisfaction. "I've got to reduce the people to elements, to the things they represented to the killers." He leaned against the wall and smiled. "Our friend with the rifle made a mistake tonight, Carl. He gave me more than he intended to, more than he should have."

"That's what you get from Billy Krieg's death, huh?" Enders hissed. "That's what it means?"

Now Aikman was impatient. "Krieg's death has nothing to do with this. The *cab* is the key: Don't you see it? Krieg was a repetition, the second policeman to die, and that's important, but the cab . . . the *cab* is going to hang them."

Enders set his jaw and stared at Aikman's face. "You're really incredible. People don't mean shit to you, do they? You 'reduce them' to elements," he spat at Aikman. "You should have been with me last night when I stood in Janice Krieg's living room. You should have seen her face."

Aikman ground his cigarette out in the ashtray. What's the matter with him, he thought, can't he see that we're finally getting somewhere?

Enders stood up, put his hands flat on the desk, and with the anger building in his voice, said, "You don't care. You never cared about the people in this whole fucking thing. From the start it was just a puzzle, a problem for you to solve . . . nothing human about it. Who do you think worked up those biographies for you? Who do you think sweated out the research and sat on his butt for days compiling it so you could make your brilliant deductions? Billy Krieg did it all. He hated it, but he did it. And it didn't help him one damn bit, did it? You didn't save him from the bad guys, did you?" Enders slapped his hand on the desk, demanding an answer.

"No," Aikman said slowly, "I didn't. Did you expect me to?"

"I expected you to have some human feelings!" Enders shouted.

"Then you expected too much," Aikman said flatly.

"Yeah," Enders said, "I did. I should've known you'd never change. Why should this case be any different for you? Maybe your way's the best. . . . It's safer not to care."

"You need a rest, Carl," Aikman said.

It was too much for Enders to take. "Don't tell me what I need!" he screamed.

Aikman sat down in the chair. "I'm sorry, Carl," he said softly. "When I get caught up in a case, I lose sight of everything else. I know what you're feeling. . . ."

Enders forced a laugh. "Sure, sure you do." He sat down and rubbed his eyes. "Okay, we're both tired, we're worn out. Let's let it go at that."

"Carl," Aikman said quietly, "I need your help now . . . more than ever."

"Where do we start?"

"We need two things right away: What did he take from the cab? Once we find that, we've got to know when he took it."

Enders, despite his weariness and anger, understood what Aikman was saying. "You're right; that would prove it. If something's missing from the cab . . . " They left the office and rode down to the impound yard.

It was Enders who spotted it. The paint was burned off the front end of the cab and the grill smashed; the fenders torn off and the hood crumpled . . . but as he studied the gutted hulk, it came to him. "Noah . . . " Aikman, his head thrust through the empty frame at the passenger side of the cab, said, "What is it?"

"There is something missing: the cab's medallion. Look." Aikman cursed and came around to the front. On a flat section of the hood, close to the windshield, a broken rivet and scratches in the metal were evident. "Jesus," Aikman swore under his breath. He ran his fingers over the area, feeling the rough grooves where a tool of some kind had dug into the hood.

"All right," Enders said, "when did he get it?"

"You'd know better than I."

"Not on the bridge . . . and not here. Maybe in transit to the Fort Lee yard, or at the yard."

Within the hour they were in a Police Department helicopter, swinging over the Hudson toward Fort Lee. Jackson Brooks was at his home near the impound yard, they'd found out. It was his day off. The chopper put down in the parking lot behind the Fort Lee Police Headquarters building. A car was waiting for Enders and Aikman.

Brooks lived in a rundown apartment house, and they trudged up five flights of creaking wooden stairs to a metal-sheathed door, bristling with locks. One by one, bolts slid back and hasps opened in answer to their knock and the word, "Police."

"Yeah, what is it?" Brooks said, staring sleepy-eyed at Enders' impassive face.

"We'd like to ask you a few questions," he said.

"About what?"

"About last night."

"Yeah, okay," Brooks mumbled and let them in.

Enders cleared the newspapers off the sofa and he and Aikman sat down in the small, dingy living room. From a back room, a high, thin voice questioned, "What is it, Jack?"

"Nothin', go back to sleep," Brooks shouted. To Enders

he said, "My wife works nights, too. You know, I ain't been to bed yet. Jesus, kept me at the yard till nine o'clock. Me and the day man were both logging in the wrecks. Never saw anything like it."

"That's what we want to talk to you about," Enders said. "Do you remember the cab they brought in, from the bridge fire?"

"Yeah, sure, all the drivers were talking about it." Brooks perched on the edge of a soiled green chair, scratching at his stomach.

"Did you see it come in?" Enders continued.

"Yeah, it was one of the first ones. We set it all the way in the back. There were a lot of them on the way—they told me that—so I started stacking from the back, you know?"

"Did you see it unloaded?" Aikman asked.

"No, I just waved 'em in, made sure the trucks could make the turns inside the fence. We got a crew to handle the unloading."

"Mr. Brooks, this is important," Aikman said. "Other than your crew, did anyone go near the cab? Anybody at all?"

Brooks smiled at Aikman. "Oh, you mean that reporter. . . . Hey, did I make the morning paper? Is that why you're here?"

"Tell us about the reporter," Enders prompted.

Brooks' face dropped. "You mean I'm not in the paper?"

"The reporter," Enders said firmly.

"Yeah, well, he showed up about two hours after the action started. We had lots of heaps piled up and he was asking about what the drivers were saying about the mess on the bridge. I thought it was weird that he would come to the yard—all the action being on the bridge—but he said the paper called him and sent him over to do a story on the yard . . . and on me. He took my name an' everything."

"Did he see the cab?" Aikman cut in.

"I guess so. He said he wanted to look around and I said, 'Sure, go ahead.' I was pretty busy and, like I said, the cab was way in the back. . . . "

"Did you see him leave the yard?" Enders asked.

"Come to think of it, no," Brooks screwed his face up into a frown. "But I was real busy. . . ."

"We'd like a description," Enders said.

"Was this guy a phony?" Brooks asked.

"We're not sure yet," Enders answered. "A description would help."

"About five-eight or -nine, dark glasses . . ."

"Sunglasses?" Aikman said in surprise.

"No, no . . . the frames . . . black or dark brown."

"And?" Enders said.

"And nothing . . . ordinary-looking guy. Kept scribbling in a pad. Had a mustache, dark . . . I didn't really see him, you know? I mean, he was standing there, but the trucks were coming in, and I was pretty busy . . . . "

"What sort of face?" Enders asked. "Thin? Round? How old?"

"Ordinary-looking guy . . . I thought he looked a little old to be running around like a kid reporter, but I guess the paper knew who to send, right?"

Enders ignored the question. "How old?"

"In his fifties," Brooks said. "Well, late forties . . . around there."

"He went to the back of the yard to see the cab?" Aikman asked.

"Oh yeah . . . well, he started off that way, but I had a lot to do, so I didn't see . . . I mean, I couldn't say for sure."

"You must've been pretty busy," Enders mumbled.

"What?" Brooks said.

"What paper did he say he was with?" Enders asked.

"*Times*, New York *Times*, . . . he looked classy enough

for that," Brooks laughed. Then the smile faded and he shook his head. "A phony, huh? Not a reporter?"

"Mr. Brooks," Aikman said, "did he give you a name or show some identification?"

"Yeah, sure, he had one of them plastic cards on his coat . . . with a picture on it."

"Did you get a close look?" Aikman asked.

"I saw the picture . . . "

"But you don't know if it was a press card? It could have been anything with a picture on it, right?" Aikman insisted.

"Yeah, I guess so," Brooks admitted. "But he gave me his name. Henderson . . . Michael, no, Mitchell . . . that's it. Mitch Henderson."

"Son-of-a-bitch," Aikman swore and smacked his thigh.

"What's wrong with him?" Brooks asked Enders, watching as Aikman got up from the couch.

"I can't believe the nerve of that guy," Aikman muttered as he paced back and forth.

"What is it?" Enders asked.

"Henderson," Aikman repeated.

"Mr. Brooks," Enders asked, turning away from Aikman, who leaned against the sofa still shaking his head, "how come you remember this guy's name and practically nothing else about him?"

" 'Cause he said he was gonna put my name in the papers," Brooks said. "You don't forget the name of a guy who's gonna do that, do you?"

"No, I guess not," Enders sighed and stood up. "Thanks . . . we'll probably be back with a police artist. We'd like you to look at some slides . . . pictures . . . and try to pick out the characteristics of the guy's face for composite."

"Like on TV?" Brooks smiled.

"Like on TV," Enders said.

Aikman walked behind Enders to the police car. As the

driver pulled away from Brooks' house, Enders turned and asked Aikman, "Will you tell me what's going on?"

"They're throwing it right in my face, Carl," Aikman answered, a grudging smile on his face. "Ten years ago, I had a case in Bridgeport, Connecticut. Arson . . . gave me a helluva time. The torch's name was Mitch Henderson."

Enders frowned. "You don't think the arsonist is one of the guys we're looking for?"

Aikman shook his head. "He's not a killer . . . setting fires was his business. But the sniper knows about that case. It got a lot of publicity, and I used it in one of my books. I still bring it into lectures and speeches." Aikman forced a grim smile. "They know I'm involved, Carl. Jerry Lawrence's denial didn't fool them. And they're letting me know that they don't care."

"Did you expect them to be afraid of you?" Enders asked sharply. But Aikman ignored the question and stared out the window.

Alex was about to hang up when the receiver clicked and Enders' voice, muffled and groggy, said, "Yeah, Enders . . ."

"I'm sorry, Carl, I didn't know you were sleeping."

Enders sat up on the bed, tilting the phone to look at his watch. It had stopped at six. "What time is it?" he asked her, rubbing his eyes with the back of his hand. "Eight o'clock," she said.

"I must've dozed off." He reached up and switched on the lamp on the night table.

"You want to go back to sleep?"

"No, I wanted to go back to the office. I'm glad you called."

"Why don't you come over here for a while? Let it go for one night," she said.

"I'm not even good company for myself," he sighed.

"Do you want to talk about it?"

"No, not now."

"Call me," she said, "and if you change your mind, I'll be home all night."

"Thanks," he said, "I'll be okay . . . "

"I know that," she said softly.

Enders smiled and hung up the phone.

Alex worked on a summation until ten o'clock and then went downstairs to Aikman's apartment, letting herself in with her key. The apartment was dark, and she made her way slowly to the living room and flicked on the ceiling light. The door to Aikman's study was closed and she could hear the rustle of paper and the scrape of chalk on the blackboard.

She made coffee in the kitchen, carried a mug to the door, and knocked. "Coffee truck's here," she called out. Aikman opened the door and stuck his hand out. She pressed the mug into his palm; he gripped the mug and started to close the door. "I guess this means you don't want to talk, right?" she asked.

Aikman grunted, "Come on in."

The room was a confusion of papers: They covered his desk and chair and carpeted the hardwood floor, and a stack of fat manila envelopes and files appeared to be growing up the wall.

"Don't say it," Aikman warned, sipping the coffee.

"Say what?"

"What you were about to say."

"Oh, you mean, 'This place looks like the Collier brothers lived here.' "

"Yeah," he muttered, "don't say that."

"Don't worry, I won't," she answered. "Mind if I sit down?"

"Be my guest," he said.

She frowned at the sheets and piles of paper covering the leather chair. "Forget it. How about a break?" Without waiting for an answer, she walked back into the living room. Aikman turned out the lights in the study and followed.

"I never thought I'd say this, but there's too much to work with," he sighed, easing himself into an armchair.

"That's not what you mean," Alex said, stretching full length on the sofa. "You just haven't hit the right combination."

"I'm pulling all the elements out . . . anything the victims could've stood for . . . it's endless."

"What've you tried?" she asked.

"I started with letters of the alphabet . . . "

"You think they're working their way through the alphabet?" she asked skeptically.

"It's possible."

"It's crazy," she said, waving it off.

"Goddamn," Aikman said with a trace of anger. "I'm sick of hearing that. It only *seems* crazy because we don't know the pattern."

"Why're you getting angry?" Alex asked innocently.

"The alphabet," Aikman said stubbornly. "C for cab, F for football player . . . "

"And two P's for policemen," she said.

"Yeah, so I eliminated that idea," he said.

"I can't wait to hear what you tried next," she smiled.

"The initial letters of the victims' names. What if they stand for something?"

"An anagram?"

"Maybe," he said, "but I couldn't make any sense out of it."

"What else?" she asked, suddenly interested in the process.

THE RANDOM FACTOR

"Location," Aikman answered. "Let's say the victims meant nothing; they just happened to be in a certain area." He paused and lit a cigarette. "George Washington Bridge and Fort George Avenue are two locations . . . "

"Two Georges," Alex said brightly.

"Central Park," Aikman added.

"George, George, Central," she repeated. "Sounds like police calls."

"Inwood Hill Park," he said, watching her think.

"In-wood," Alex said, dividing the word clearly. She sat up and faced her father. "Where's it going?"

"Don't know yet," he shrugged. "I'm still working with that line of thought, putting the names of places together: chronologically by killing, alphabetically, geographically . . ."

"It could be anything," she said. "But even if you find the patterns, it won't tell you why they were killed."

"Sure it will. Don't you see that once I find out what the victims stood for, I'll know how the killers chose them."

"No, I meant it won't give you the motive," she said. "It won't tell you why our four friends are slaughtering people."

Aikman leaned forward in the chair, placing his elbows on his knees. "Alex," he said quietly, "I've got the motive."

She did a double take. "Huh?"

"It wasn't all that difficult. Once I realized that the victims represented something other than who they were as people, I knew that none of the common motives could apply: Killing for profit, revenge, fear—they all went out the window."

"And what were you left with?" she asked, leaning forward expectantly.

"They're doing it for fun."

"*What?*"

"For the thrill or the challenge: That's the only possibility." He stood up and began to walk back and forth across the room. "It all fits. The identification they take from the victims: It's proof that they did it, and each one is proving it to the others. Knowing how and when to kill each victim—which says they're stalking them, following them, isolating each one. It's a contest of some kind. There must be some sort of guideline, some pattern, something the victims represent . . . and when I find that key, I'll know how they're choosing who to kill."

Alex shook her head. "I don't know . . . "

Aikman ignored the comment and went on, talking almost to himself. "That key won't tell us who they are, but at least I'll know how they're doing it."

"Did you tell Carl about this?" Alex asked.

"No," Aikman said.

"Don't you think you should?"

"He's not in any mood to listen," Aikman answered.

"You can really be blind sometimes, y' know?" she said, slightly irritated. "Billy's death isn't easy for him to take, to deal with. You have to understand."

"I understand," Aikman said, waving it off, wondering if he did. "He wants someone to blame, to scream at, someone other than the sniper and his three friends. Can you imagine how he'd feel if I told him that Billy Krieg died because he was part of a pattern in a series of thrill killings?"

"Do you really believe that's it?" Alex asked him slowly.

"Yes, that's it: It's probably not that simple, but that's basically all it could be. They're doing it because they want to."

"Are you going to tell Carl?"

Aikman shook his head. "No. I'm not going to tell anyone until I know the pattern." He stood up and drained the last of the coffee. Alex took the cup from his hand, and Aikman went back into the study.

As the light in Aikman's living room went out, John Harmon stamped his feet, partly in frustration and partly to keep his circulation going. It was a freezing night, and the doorway across from Aikman's apartment offered little shelter from the wind. Harmon was cold, tired, and hungry.

Aikman had run him all over town for the past two days: to Enders' office early in the morning; to the police impound yard on Twenty-ninth Street; to the helicopter pad uptown, where Harmon watched helplessly as Aikman got away from him. He picked him up two hours later as the chopper set down. Harmon would have given a lot to know where they went, but his attempts at getting information from the officers at the pad were met with stony silence. No one was impressed with Harmon's press card and the "story" he was researching on the Police Department's airborne force.

He camped across from Aikman's house that night until midnight, showing up early in the morning to see Aikman coming out of the building, walking away from him. The rest of the day had been a furtive chase, following cabs to the library, Enders' office, and the impound yard again, where Aikman and Enders stood in the cold with five men who scrambled in and out of a black van and worked over a burned-out car.

Finally, back to the brownstone. It was almost eleven o'clock, and Harmon succumbed to the need to think in the warm comfort of his own apartment.

"We never said the victims had to be human," Reynolds said simply, smiling at the expressions of the others. Marcus looked shell-shocked, Lyle impressed, and Birmingham angry. "He's right," Lyle said, grinning at Reynolds.

"That's a technicality and you know it," Birmingham

snarled. "We gave you a liberty, and you took advantage of it. We all took our chances, we went after *people*."

"You don't think I took a chance?" Reynolds asked in amazement.

"Not the way we did," Birmingham said.

"Oh, and because I didn't follow you, I'm guilty of taking advantage? Of cheating?" Reynolds said, beginning to get angry at Birmingham's attitude.

"I didn't say that," Birmingham replied, backing off.

"Well, let me tell you what kind of chances I took," Reynolds said evenly. "Except for the few moments in the apartment when I fired the shot at the taxi, I was on display all night, moving all over the city, facing and talking to people. I played four separate roles, four distinct parts in the drama," he said with emphasis. Lyle snickered.

Reynolds went on, shifting his glance to each of the men at the table. "The mugging victim: You don't call that taking a chance? And the commuter, rushing out of the city . . . and the reporter, perhaps my best role," he smiled at Birmingham. "And then the aging hippie. I think I more than made up for choosing one nonhuman target. What I did was harder, riskier . . . "

" . . . and certainly more spectacular," Lyle said.

"My fan club," Reynolds laughed.

"Your daring inspires us," Birmingham sneered.

Reynolds picked up the cab's medallion from the table and handed it to Birmingham. "That's inspiration, Birm . . . the cab's identity. Every fleet taxi in the city has to have one, and it's as good as a driver's license or a Social Security card. I doubt you'd have had the imagination to pick the target or figure out the identification." He snatched the medallion out of Birmingham's hand and placed it in his briefcase, which lay open on the table. He picked up the shield and ring from the table, tossed them in, and shut and locked the case.

"How did you know the medallion would be intact?" Birmingham asked him, fighting back his anger.

"Because I plan, Birm. I work out every detail. I took a good look at one of those things beforehand. They're riveted on. I was more concerned with getting it off the hood than I was with it blowing off in the explosion."

"Any trouble at the junkyard in Jersey?" Marcus asked.

"None at all," Reynolds said smoothly. "I showed the moron at the gate this card." He took a white card sealed in plastic from his pocket and gave it to Marcus. An oversize business card, it bore a black-and-white photograph of Reynolds wearing a beard and horn-rimmed glasses, the name "Mitchell Henderson," and the familiar banner of the New York *Times*. Marcus looked up at Reynolds and handed the card to Lyle "Very impressive,' Lyle said

"I cut the *Times* logo from their ad in the classified pages and had the picture taken in one of those four-for-a-quarter booths in Grand Central. The rest was just an IBM typewriter and a few scrawled signatures. The idiot at the yard was so excited about being interviewed that he never took a close look. Simple psychology: I gave him a name, a phony press card, and the magic words 'New York *Times*,' and he bought it."

Reynolds set his briefcase on the floor and eased into his chair. "And," he said with a wide grin, "I gave Noah Aikman something to play with, too."

"You did what?" Birmingham asked.

"The name of the reporter," Reynolds said easily. "Mitch Henderson was an arsonist whom Aikman put away years ago. It's a big case: Aikman talks about it in his lectures. So if Aikman's working against us, and the police can add two and two, and if that yard man has any memory at all, we've given Aikman the word: We know he's around and we don't give a damn."

"You idiot!" Marcus screamed, his eyes wide and his mouth trembling with anger. "What the hell do you think you're doing? *We* haven't done anything . . . *you're* doing it all! And after all your sanctimonious bullshit about being responsible for each other's lives. You stupid fool."

"Take it easy, Ed," Lyle said. "We don't know if Aikman's working with the cops."

"He sure as hell is now!" Marcus roared. "He saw to that," pointing to Reynolds who sat very still, his eyes half closed.

"Wait a minute, damn it," Birmingham cut in, looking at Reynolds. "Why should the police talk to the yard man, anyway? How could they connect you with the cab? There's no way they could find out that you fired the shot . . ."

"I left them a clue," Reynolds said.

Marcus pounded his fist on the table. "Wonderful! This gets better all the time! He's running the whole damn show!" He pushed his chair back from the table and stood up. "I can't stand any more. What did you do, leave your signature?"

Reynolds laughed. "In a way, I did: I left the shell."

"The shell," Marcus repeated tonelessly.

"In the apartment, after I shot the cab: I left the casing on the floor."

"I'm finished," Marcus said. "I've had it. As far as I'm concerned, it's all over." He grabbed his drink, swallowed what was left in the glass, and turned toward the door.

"All right," Reynolds said calmly, "if that's what you want."

Marcus whirled around. "I have no choice—you saw to that! Wasn't it enough for you without involving Aikman, for Chrissake?"

"No," Reynolds said evenly, "it wasn't enough. This is a contest of wills, Ed—of strength and cunning and experience. The police haven't got a prayer; we've proved that already. If you want to win over an opponent who's no match for you, fine, but that's not for me. If Aikman's the best there is—and he may or may not be—if he's the best they can use against us, and he certainly is that, then I want to take him on. That's what this is all about, right?" He glared at Marcus. Softening his tone, he added, "Ed, you took on the Occupation Army of France, didn't you?"

"Don't give me that shit," Marcus said, "it's not the same."

"But it should be, shouldn't it?"

Marcus didn't answer.

"I think it is already," Birmingham said, "without Aikman."

"Well, Aikman's in it now," Reynolds said. "The decision is yours, all of you If you want to quit, okay, we quit: It's over." He pointed to Marcus, who stood with his back to the door. "But let me tell you something: I've got the edge. I know you, all of you, and I don't believe that you could walk away from here tonight and forget it . . . just let it end like this. You've got to see it through. That's the kind of men you are."

"Jesus, you're incredible. Do you con yourself the same way you con us?" Marcus asked him.

"Cut it out, Ed," Lyle said. "He's right. I don't want to stop."

"Of course you don't," Reynolds said. "If you wanted to stop because of Aikman, you wouldn't be the kind of man who started this in the first place."

"You were the one who started it," Marcus said. "It was your idea . . . "

" . . . and we all loved it," Lyle added. "Didn't we?"

"You're just as crazy as he is," Marcus said.

Birmingham turned to Marcus. "It's up to you, Ed. I don't like what he did, but not for your reason. I don't care about Aikman. But," he said, turning to Reynolds, "you should have let us know what you were going to do. You didn't have to take it upon yourself to go this far without us knowing."

"Yeah," Reynolds muttered, "just like you consulted us before wearing your uniform in the park . . ."

Birmingham flushed and started to say something. Lyle put his hand on his arm. "Hold it, both of you. If we tear each other apart, we're finished, one way or another. What one of us did or didn't do isn't important now." He motioned for Marcus to sit down. "It's up to you, Ed."

Marcus walked to the table and sat down, staring at his hands spread flat in front of him. "All right," he said finally, "I'm not afraid of Aikman."

"No one said you were," Reynolds offered.

"Let's cut the crap and get on with it," Marcus shot back.

"No, not like that," Reynolds said. "If that's your attitude, then we stop. Nobody is forcing you, and I don't want this rushed. You'll get sloppy, you'll make mistakes."

"Oh no I won't," Marcis said, imitating one of Reynolds' best grins. "I'll be as ruthless as you are, Chris."

"That's not possible," Birmingham laughed.

Marcus smiled, breaking the tension. Throughout the rest of the evening he was cool and cautious, planning far ahead and keeping Reynolds at bay. There were no outbursts, but they were all relieved when, at eleven-thirty, Birmingham pushed back his chair and suggested they call it a night.

Reynolds took a cab to lower Manhattan, got out at Centre Street, and made his way through the narrow streets to the walkway of the Brooklyn Bridge. Headlights reflected off the steel surface as cars crossed in both directions.

Running his hand along the railing, he walked to the center of the bridge, stopped, knelt, and took the trophies out of his briefcase. Without hesitation, he tossed the medallion over the side. He studied the shield for a moment, turning it over in his hands, his lean fingers tracing at the raised detail on the emblem and the outline of the number at the bottom: 1744. The identity of a man, he thought. Smiling at the irony, he hurled it out as if it was a stone to skip across the plate-glass surface of a lake.

Then, finally, the ring—a plain gold band, engraved— names he couldn't read in the dim light. He tried to put it on, but it stopped at the knuckle. The cop had thin fingers, Reynolds thought. He stared at the ring for a long time and then shifted his gaze to a point downriver. He'd taken it on impulse, wanting to outdo Lyle. Now he wished that he hadn't touched it.

He thought that he'd buried his memories with his wife, but the sudden sadness brought back the pain, and Reynolds pulled the fing from his finger and threw it down into the water.

He tried to force his thoughts away, but he couldn't do it, and he stood at the railing of the bridge as the images of the long dying flashed before his eyes . . . from the moment the doctor had said "cancer" and the wit and gentleness went out of their lives, to the long cobalt treatments that failed, to the final medication that kept her in a dreamlike state until the end.

From the back of his mind, from somewhere in the past when he was a different person, he dredged the phrases:

No longer mourn for me when I am dead,
Give warning to the world that I am fled
From this vile world, with vilest worms to dwell.

Shakespeare . . . Reynolds the college freshman at Princeton, memorizing the lines. It was a different person, he said to himself. " 'I am fled from this vile world,' " he repeated.

"And I am not," he said, turning and walking off the bridge.

12

The morning of November 18 brought a preview of the winter to come. Aikman rolled out of bed at eight o'clock, parted the curtains, and stared sleepily at the bleak landscape of East Sixty-fourth Street. The night's snow had turned to rain, and the sky was an unbroken sheet of gray clouds.

He showered and dressed and was turning slices of french toast in a cast-iron pan when the kitchen phone rang. "Aikman," he said, wedging the phone between his cheek and shoulder as he pulled the pan away from the stove and with a wide spatula eased the slices onto a plate.

"Good morning, Professor. This is Mayor Donahue."

"Morning," Aikman said, sliding the pan back on the stove.

"I'd like to talk to you," Donahue said. "Can you drop by my office around three this afternoon?"

"Certainly. I'll be there." Donahue thanked him and hung up. Aikman dialed Enders' office. "Carl, I just got a call from Donahue. He wants to talk to me this afternoon."

"Terrific," Enders bitched. "Everybody wants to get into the act."

Aikman smiled. "I think I can handle it. How much do you think he ought to know?"

He's probably got most of it figured out already," Enders

said, adding, "He's a good man . . . I think he'll go along with us."

Aikman thought, What choice does he have? "I'll call you later," he told Enders.

"Yeah, or he'll call me, or the commissioner will call me . . ."

"Stay by the phone," Aikman laughed. He hung up, ate his breakfast, and took a mug of coffee and a fresh pack of cigarettes to the study, where he slumped in his chair, sipped, smoked, and stared at the blackboard.

The spaciousness of the mayor's office surprised him. The huge room held plush velvet chairs, a brocade lemon-yellow couch, a mammoth mahogany desk and conference table, antique gold-leaf lamps, and four push-button telephone consoles at strategic points throughout the room. A wall unit opposite the desk housed four television sets. The bureaucracy on display, Aikman thought wryly.

He sat in a black leather captain's chair and faced tall, austere Jack Donahue across the length of the conference table. The mayor dispensed with the formalities and got to the point as soon as Aikman sat down. "Ever since Jerry Lawrence fumbled that reporter's question at the press conference, I've been doing a little research," the mayor said slowly, measuring his words and tapping a pile of papers on the table in front of him. "I didn't realize you were such a good friend to Enders and Lawrence and Holtzman and Gregory and Ellison." Aikman began to smile as the mayor ticked off the names.

"I've got the dates, too," Donahue added. "The deputy chiefs have been spending a lot of time at your apartment." Aikman nodded. "And," Donahue went on, "there are a few cases here," glancing at the sheets of paper, "Billy Gibbs . . . Red Witkin . . . this man Cunningham . . ."

He pushed the papers away and looked up at Aikman. "What do you have to do with all this?"

"The deputy chiefs have been consulting with me on those cases," Aikman said. "It may be a bit unusual, but not without precedent . . ."

"I'm aware of the precedents," Donahue interrupted. "I'm also aware that you get results. Look, I'm not objecting to any arrangement you have with the deputy chiefs or the commissioner. What I do object to is being kept in the dark." He paused, then said, "I want to know what's going on."

It took Aikman forty minutes to fill in the background and bring the mayor up to date on what was being done. Aikman stopped short of explaining the elements theory. Donahue interrupted several times to ask questions, and once—when Aikman told him about the shot fired at the cab on the George Washington Bridge—Donahue cut him off with a wave of his hand, muttering, "It's not possible."

Aikman frowned. "It's more than possible. It happened."

"But that sniper slaughtered over thirty people," Donahue said, his face pale. "Why in God's name . . ."

Because he likes it, Aikman thought.

"All right," Donahue said when Aikman finished. "I'm going to ask Carl Enders to keep me informed, personally, of all developments. I want to know exactly what's going on at every step. And I may want to talk to you again."

Aikman nodded. "It's important to us that as few people as possible know the implications of the killings. If the press got hold of this . . ."

"I know," Donahue smiled. "I'm a politician, and I've had a lot of experience at keeping things quiet."

"We may need your help. It may come down to needing a lot of manpower," Aikman said.

Donahue nodded. "I'll do what I can," he said, thinking of the police personnel cutbacks he'd been forced to order.

As Aikman got up to leave, Donahue stopped him. "Professor, are you close to finding them?"

I wish I knew," Aikman replied.

Enders sat quietly in Alex's living room, slowly sipping from a glass of scotch and soda. He'd been there for over an hour, brooding in the dim light of a single lamp. Alex worked in the dining room, reading case reports. She heard him stir, listened as his footsteps approached, and looked up as he took a seat across from her. The lines in his forehead were deeper, and the boyish features of his face seemed at odds with the cold grayness of his skin. When he spoke, it was in halting tones, deliberately soft and restrained. It made Alex nervous.

"How'ya doin'?" she asked lightly, touching his hand.

He shrugged. "I'm doin' . . ."

She reached across the table and took one of his cigarettes from the pack in his shirt pocket.

"I thought I'd found something," he said quietly, almost talking to himself. "Something in the case: Billy had discovered the first body, and he'd done the research on the victims for your father. He put in some off-duty time on Rendelli's murder. I thought he might have stumbled onto something. Maybe he was checking it out on his own, maybe he wasn't even aware that he knew it. I put Parker on it; he spent two days going over Billy's life with a magnifying glass."

"And?" Alex prompted softly.

"Nothing . . . dead end."

"What about his partner, Mallory? Maybe Billy said something to him?"

"He was grilled like a suspect," Enders answered. "Parker talked to him in the hospital, and we had a team of detectives work with him to reconstruct the conversations he'd had with Billy. A big nothing; coincidence, I guess."

"Did you return Billy's file to my father?"

"Yeah," Enders sighed. "I dropped it off before coming up here—for whatever good it'll do."

"I gather you and my father are on speaking terms again," she smiled.

"I suppose." He looked up and forced a grin. "We have a . . . personality conflict?"

Alex laughed. "That's as good a way as any to put it, I guess."

He reached across the table, took her cigarette from the ashtray, and inhaled deeply. "It's a rotten job," he mumbled. "I ought to get out . . ."

"Is that what you really want to do?" she asked.

"I don't know," he said, shaking his head. "Sometimes I wonder what I'm doing . . . everybody forgets about *schmucks* like me, the desk jockeys. If a cop shoots someone in the line of duty, he's taken off the street, given a desk job for a month or so. The department knows what a shooting—a death—can do to a man. But guys like me— shit, they expect us to live with it, because all we do is read about it in the reports we push around. I'm not supposed to feel anything or be affected, because I wasn't there. I didn't pull a trigger or see a body." He crushed out the cigarette. "I've never killed anyone, not in twenty-five years on the force. I fired my gun on duty maybe five, six times."

"They expect you to have feelings, Carl," Alex said.

"That's not it," he said stubbornly. "Feelings I can handle. I shouldn't have become a friend. I should have stayed in the back seat, separate, isolated."

"No," she said. "You couldn't do that. It's not in your personality."

Enders remembered what he had said to her father, how it was safer not to care about people. "It's still a rotten job," he mumbled.

Alex stood up. "You know what rotten is? Rotten is going on like this all night."

"I'm sorry," he said, grinning for a second, then turning his eyes back to the table. "I shouldn't burden you with my problems . . ."

"Yeah, right," she said sarcastically, "you should be the big, strong, *macho* cop and keep it all inside. I'd really respect that."

Enders got up and walked behind her, wrapped his arms around her, and kissed her hair. She turned to him and smiled. "How about getting some dinner or something?"

Enders hugged her. ". . . or something," he said.

The Sunday night news was always the worst, Reynolds had observed. Invariably the faceless TV reporters droned disaster upon disaster without a break: Ten drown in flash flood; head-on collision kills five; man falls or is pushed; fire leaves sixteen homeless; hurricane sweeps South Florida . . . on and on, one on top of another. As bad as the news is on any given night, Sunday tops them all. The "weekend horrors," Reynolds called it.

He listened to the voice from the television set with only half his attention while he sat on the sofa in his apartment scanning the business section of the *Times*, until the final report of the half-hour news show. He looked up as a live pickup from Central Park filled the screen, and the on-camera reporter began talking about a murder.

The body of Aldo D'Angelo had been found in the parking lot near the Tavern-on-the-Green Restaurant. Apparently strangled to death, D'Angelo had been last seen leaving the restaurant after the annual dinner/dance of Local 618 of the Construction Workers Union.

Reynolds knew it was Marcus' work. Two weeks ago Marcus had drawn a hit in the Central Park sector, and this had to be the result. He's made a mistake, Reynolds thought. The sector was right, but the victim bore no connection to the target Marcus was supposed to get. A construction worker? Reynolds frowned. What the hell was Marcus thinking about? How could he have made a mistake like that?

Unless, Reynolds decided, Marcus knew something that he didn't . . . unless there was a connection he didn't see. And that intrigued him even more.

Aikman learned about the D'Angelo killing in the early-morning hours on Monday, and spent the rest of the day with the preliminary reports. He placed the name, location, and weapon on the blackboard, listed the time of death, D'Angelo's age and address on a sheet of yellow paper, and searched for an element that would match up with the other victims. At four o'clock he gave it up.

He paced the room, stepping on files and folders, his anger growing. It's slipping away, he thought to himself . . . the inspiration, the elements . . . there's nowhere to go with it. He kept returning to the blackboard, the map, his lists. The challenge that had been thrown at him by the sniper galled him as he struggled to see the connection that kept eluding him. "All right," he said aloud, "if they want a fight, they've got it." He rolled the typewriter table to the desk and pounded out the answer to the challenge.

Half an hour later, he walked in on Peter Gregory as the deputy chief was rummaging through file cabinets in his office. "What d'ya need?" Gregory asked, not turning around.

"A literary opinion," Aikman replied.

"What?" Gregory said, finally facing Aikman, who thrust a sheet of paper toward him. Gregory sat on the edge of his desk and read.

Aikman had written a news release for the Police Department to hand out to the papers. It said that the police were looking for a possible witness to the killing of Jake Cunningham, a man named Mitch Henderson, who was reported to have been in the area at the time of the murder. The release urged Henderson to come forward as a material witness.

"And," Aikman said, as Gregory looked up from the typewritten page, "I want Jerry Lawrence to call a press conference and say the same thing."

"You're stumped, right?" Gregory said.

"Temporarily," Aikman replied.

"Sure," Gregory said.

Aikman's eyes narrowed slightly as he placed his hands on his hips. "Look, what do you want me to do? Wave a magic wand and deliver these creeps to you in a gift-wrapped box?"

"Gee, can you do that?" Gregory asked, wide-eyed.

"I give up," Aikman muttered with a smile.

"What will this do?" Gregory asked seriously, holding up the release.

"I want to push them," Aikman answered, "apply some pressure . . ."

"You think they'll make a mistake?"

"Maybe."

"Or maybe they'll turn tail and run?"

Aikman smiled. "Bugger off, as they say in Britain," he said pleasantly.

Gregory chuckled. "I'm glad you still have a sense of humor, Noah."

"I try," Aikman said. "Will you do it?"

"Sure, why not? It's a chance. . . . I'll talk to Jerry right away."

"See if you can get it on TV tonight," Aikman nooded.

"You sure you want Lawrence to do this?" Gregory asked.

"It's his zone, and our friends will get the message if they see him. Just make sure he doesn't take any questions from the reporters or elaborate on the release."

"Okay," Gregory said. "Anything else we can do?"

"Well, I'm going to try one more thing, but I'll need the FBI for that."

"What've you got in mind?" Gregory asked.

"I'm going to use their computers . . . feed in all the elements, all the facts about the victims."

"Still looking for that common denominator?"

"Yes, and this is one case where a machine is better suited to the job than the human mind. There are so many things the victims could have represented that I can't possibly correlate them. We'll program the computer and let it do the work."

"Why the FBI? Why not our computers?"

"Their resources are better . . . and they can clear the time a lot quicker. I want to get started right away. Besides, they've been getting reports on the cases since McMahon was killed and his Social Security card taken. Let's let them do some work for us for a change."

"Go easy," Gregory cautioned. "We don't get along too well with them."

"I get along fine," Aikman smiled. "I'm not in any competition with them."

"Egos in law enforcement are pains in the ass," Gregory said.

"I can't believe you said that," Aikman said in amazement. "You, of all people . . . who resented bringing me in on the case because he thought the police could handle it."

"Yeah, well, you're overlooking the fact that you haven't gotten any farther than we have," Gregory pointed out.

"Only for the moment," Aikman answered, "only for the moment. It's all there, Pete, and I *will* put it together."

"If I don't beat you to it," Gregory smiled. "I've been working on another angle."

Aikman's eyebrows raised slightly. "Which is?"

Gregory lit a cigarette. "It's nothing I can really do anything about—yet. I've been thinking about these guys, doing a few mind puzzles: who they are, for example, what they do when they're not out murdering people. All the times vary: They've killed on weekends and weekdays, day and night, all over the city. They can come and go as they please. Incredible freedom of movement."

"And you're wondering what they do the rest of the time? What sort of lives they lead?"

How do they account for their time when they're out after someone?" Gregory asked, and then answered his own question. "They don't *have* to account, that's just it. Their jobs, families, friends . . . they've got to be in high positions to have that much control and freedom. Maybe they have no families, or spend so much time away that no one gets suspicious. To keep this going as long as they have, they've got to have that freedom."

"Executives," Aikman offered.

"Yeah, something like that," Gregory said. "I don't know what good it does now, but if you get a likely suspect, we'll know right away if he fits into the life-style."

"*When* I get a likely suspect," Aikman corrected, smiling. He pointed to the release on Gregory's desk. "See you in the papers," he said, and left the office.

Marcus was relegated to second billing. From the moment they got to their room in the club on the following Thursday night, the topic was Aikman and the Mitch Henderson item in the papers. Marcus knew there was no point in getting angry . . . the damage was done. Aikman's acceptance of the challenge should have been expected— and it was exactly what Reynolds wanted.

But there was a surprise reaction. Marcus watched in bitter amusement as the normally placid Birmingham squared off with Reynolds. "I've taken a lot of abuse from you, Chris," he said, his usually mellow voice an even, menacing tone. "All because of that day in Central Park. You were right: I made a mistake, but nothing came of it. But you're going too far: You're turning this into a personal fight with Aikman, and that's not the purpose of what we're doing."

"Anything that increases the challenge is the purpose," Reynolds grinned.

"You're so full of shit," Birmingham said. "Anything that boosts your ego is the purpose. We're not competition enough for you, right? Not enough of a challenge?"

"Aikman is a different kind of challenge," Reynolds replied calmly, "a new dimension. Don't you see that?"

"No," Birmingham said. "All I see is that you're inviting trouble."

"I don't understand," Reynolds said. "Why are you so upset? We went through this last time."

"But he's taken you up on it, Chris," Birmingham said. "Don't you understand? He deliberately went to the papers with that story about Henderson. He had it planted. And the press conference . . . he's accepting your challenge. Why the hell should we be put into the position of standing by while you and Aikman fight your own personal war? That's not what we wanted to do."

Reynolds shook his head. "Why should it make any difference to you? Sure, Aikman's a big brain, and he's looking for us. That puts an edge on it, don't you see? Best of all, I've given him nothing to work with. A shell casing and a name from one of his past cases: big deal! Those are really heavy-duty clues, Birm. He's going to walk right in here and grab me, right?"

Lyle and Marcus exchanged glances but said nothing. Birmingham looked at each one in silent appeal, found no support, and said weakly, "There was no need to bring him in on it, that's all I'm saying."

"And I'm saying it makes everything we're doing much more significant to all of us. Just accept it; I know what I'm doing."

"You don't run the show, goddamn it!" Birmingham shouted.

"You don't think so?" Reynolds shot back. "Who thought it up? Who planned it? It suited you then; it suited all of us. I'm not apologizing for anything. It was my creation."

"And what are we? Excess baggage in your fantasy?" Birmingham demanded.

"It's no fantasy," Reynolds said. "You're in it all the way, you agreed to it, you wanted to do it."

"I'm getting sick of this arguing," Lyle interrupted.

"Then I'll settle it," Reynolds replied. "I asked Ed last time; now it's your turn," he said to Birmingham. "If you're so worried, pull out, end it. But this is the last time I'm going to talk about this. Make a decision and stick to it."

"Look, Birm," Lyle said, "he's right. You're going off half-cocked over nothing. So the big honcho's on the case: So what? Every cop in the city has been looking for us for months, and that never bothered you. You laughed at them, didn't you?"

"Why should Aikman be any different?" Reynolds added. "The big brain is going to fall on his face."

"Jesus," Birmingham said, "don't you see what you're doing? Your ego against Aikman. It's your attitude I can't stand!"

"Sue me," Reynolds snapped.

"This is getting us nowhere," Lyle said. "I want to get on with what we're here for."

"I don't like being manipulated," Birmingham said coldly.

"I never meant to manipulate anyone," Reynolds insisted. "I simply thought that I knew all of you well enough to be certain that you'd relish the added challenge. Maybe

I was wrong . . ." He stared at Birmingham. "What do you want to do?"

"I want you to stop thinking of this as a one-man operation," Birmingham said quietly.

"All right," Reynolds condeded, realizing that Birmingham might welcome the challenge of Aikman, but would never admit it if he felt he was being maneuvered or slighted.

"So let's get going," Lyle said. "Ed?" he turned to Marcus, who slouched in his chair.

"Oh, are you ready for me now?" Marcus asked.

"What's the matter?" Lyle asked.

"Nothing," Marcus said. "I'm just another piece of excess baggage around here, right? Nobody's interested in what I did. My accomplishment takes a back seat when it comes to deciding whether Chris is as brilliant as Noah Aikman: That's the real question, isn't it?"

"Another prima donna," Reynolds sighed.

"And you head the list," Marcus answered.

Reynolds ignored the comment and smiled at Marcus. "You shouldn't complain. Your victim didn't fit . . . made a mistake, huh?"

"Really?" Marcus said. "And who decided that?"

"Come on," Reynolds insisted. "I heard the report on TV. You messed up. What were going for, anyway, location? Tavern-on-the-Green?"

"No, big shot," Marcus said. "You're wrong. I made a perfect choice. You just can't see it."

"Neither can I," Birmingham admitted.

"Okay, explain," Lyle urged.

"You really can't figure it out, can you?" Marcus teased Reynolds.

Reynolds looked thoughtful, trying to work out how Marcus' target could possibly fit the requirement. Finally Reynolds shrugged and said, "You got me. If you say it was right, I believe you, but I don't see it."

"Fantastic," Marcus said, grinning wickedly at Reynolds. "The great man is stumped."

"C'mon," Lyle sighed, "let's have it."

"Not so fast," Marcus said. "I'm enjoying this." He leaned back in his chair and picked up his drink. "You see, D'Angelo was a perfect choice; not terribly obvious, I admit, but perfect. It was easy enough to get into that dinner at the restaurant, and easy enough to pick up D'Angelo—he was alone and very drunk. By the time he got to the parking lot, I think he'd forgotten where he was. Good thing he didn't get a chance to drive." Marcus laughed at his own joke, put his glass down, and loosened his tie.

"Make yourself comfortable, Ed," Lyle offered.

Marcus paid no attention. He opened the top button of his shirt. "Hot, isn't it?" he asked, running his index finger around the inside of the shirt collar.

"What the hell are you doing?" Birmingham demanded.

"Haven't you figured it out yet, Chris?" Marcus said to Reynolds, who had been staring at him since he'd started to talk.

Suddenly Reynolds jumped to his feet. "Incredible," he said, "absolutely inspired, Ed, that's what it is, inspired." He'd walked over and smacked Marcus on the back.

"Will you tell me what's going on?" Lyle asked.

"He just told you, Dick," Reynolds said. "You have to be bright enough to see it."

"Then call me stupid because I don't see . . ." Lyle stopped in midsentence. "Oh Jesus, of course . . . what a great idea."

"I give up," Birmingham muttered. "I don't get it."

"Sure you do," Marcus laughed. "Look." His index finger flipped the points of his shirt collar. "The collar . . ."

The realization came to Birmingham slowly, and when he understood what Marcus had done, he grumbled, "Knew it all the time."

"You've got to admit: It's a very nice touch," Marcus grinned.

"It's better than that," Reynolds said. "It's proof that we have nothing to worry about. With minds like ours, Noah Aikman doesn't have a prayer."

Aikman puffed on his cigarette, oblivious to the smoke trailing up around his face. He glared at the stacks of three-by-five index cards on his desk and wondered how long it would take.

The study had undergone a transformation: Papers, files, looseleaf binders, and manila envelopes were gone, consigned to a storage closet that ran the length of the wall behind Aikman's desk. A single sheet of paper remained on the desk.

Alex brought a pot of coffee in from the kitchen and set it down on the typewriter table, cleared to hold the coffee, a huge glass ashtray, and a carton of cigarettes.

"How many is that?" Alex asked.

"What?" Aikman looked up, drawn from his thoughts by her voice.

"How many are you smoking?"

He shrugged. "Lost count."

"Over a pack," she muttered, dumping the ashtray's collection of butts into the wastebasket. "Two years' work down down the drain. You must be a wonder on the jogging path."

Aikman ignored her and continued to stare at the blackboard. "What are you trying to see up there, anyway?" Alex asked.

"Who knows? I can't read the scribbles anymore."

"I've got news for you: No one can." She gave a quick look at the hieroglyphics on the slate. "Got a Rosetta stone handy?"

"Did you come here to audition your new act or to help me?" he asked.

"Both," she answered.

"Okay," Aikman said, picking up the sheet of paper from the desk. "These are the general categories." He handed the paper to her. "Up there," he said, gesturing toward the board, "are the names in chronological order of their deaths. And in the closet, so we won't trip all over them, are the files. We'll pull 'em out as we get to them."

"Got it chief," she said. "Any idea how long . . . ?"

"Don't even ask," he grumbled. "I've got five thousand cards here"—he nudged the pile on the desk—"and a box of twenty thousand more cards in the closet. One fact per card. How fast can you write?"

"Not fast enough," Alex said.

Aikman went to the closet and came back with a stack of files. "This is Sean McMahon," he said, dumping the papers on the floor next to Alex's chair. He returned to the closet and brought out a smaller stack. "Eileen Douglas," he said, placing the papers on the desk.

Alex put the single typewritten sheet down. "Everything?"

Aikman nooded. "Just follow that list. We start with numbers: take the date of birth and write it as one number, like 61544 for June 15, 1944. That goes on one card. Then *add* the numbers up and put the total, 20, on another card. Then add those digits, two plus zero equals two, on another card. Then take the numbers in their addresses and do the same thing . . . and height, weight, age, everything. When we're finished, we'll have complete numerical profiles of the victims, and the computer can tell us if anyone matches any of the others."

"And the other categories?" Alex said.

"Alphabet . . . letters in their name, letters in the names of the places where they were killed, street names where they lived. The computer can arrange those letters in a practically limitless number of ways, and if there's an anagram in there anywhere, we'll see it."

"Elements," Alex said.

"Exactly. Every fact, every detail in a victim's file reduced to an element, a possible reason why they were picked and killed. There's a system, something the killers are using . . ."

"Okay," Alex sighed. "I don't know if I buy it, but I'll go along for the ride."

"And don't be limited by that list," Aikman said. "If there's a category I left out, an element, a representation I didn't catch, put it down. It doesn't have to make any sense or follow any logic. All we have to know is if it matches with any other victim. Make jumps for me . . . whatever strikes your fancy."

Alex opened the first of the Sean McMahon files, grabbed a thick stack of file cards and a pencil and began reading. The hours dragged on as they worked silently, jotting the notations that would be transferred to an IBM card and fed into the electronic brain that would sort and sift and categorize. At dawn they stopped, ate breakfast, and brought a fresh pot of coffee to the study. They continued through the day. Alex went upstairs for a few hours' sleep while Aikman kept on. They worked out a pattern of shifts for eating and sleeping, and the days passed as Aikman brought file after file out of the closet and the box of completed index cards overflowed.

It took almost a week. It was a marathon of endurance, but Aikman's belief in the theory kept them going. They stopped only to sleep, answer the phone, or eat a quick meal. Near the end, Alex burst out laughing when she realized that Aikman was taking index cards and files with him to the bathroom.

They had over twenty thousand index cards when they closed the last of the files. Numbers, letters, places: every fact from every file reduced to single notations.

"Point me toward the stairs," Alex mumbled after making the final notation on D'Angelo. "What day is it, any-way?"

"Why does it matter?" Aikman answered. Alex got as far as the living room and collapsed on the sofa. Aikman put a pillow under her head, kissed her, and said, "I don't have to tell you what a help you are . . ."

"And I don't have to tell you what a pain you are," she mumbled.

After three days of searching, Brimingham, who'd drawn a hit the night of Marcus' explanation of the D'Angelo kill-ing, found the man he was looking for on West Third Street in Greenwich Village. Pasted to the grimy window of a nar-row storefront that housed the editorial offices of *Vil-lage/East*, a politically oriented underground newspaper, Birmingham stared at the photograph of the man he would kill . . .

. . . and enjoy killing.

On Tuesday afternoon, with Christmas five days away, Aikman took the index cards, bundled into shopping bags and cardboard boxes, to the FBI building on East Sixty-ninth Street. Phil Sarver, agent and computer expert, was waiting.

"Christmas cheer for the machine," Aikman said brightly, swinging a carton onto a Formica-topped table in the com-puter room. Behind a wall of glass, the tape transports pulled the reels around; flashing lights punctuated the passage of cards through the giant computer installation. In front of the glass, the input terminals were lined up.

Sarver flipped through a stack of cards. He would trans-fer each fact to punch cards by typing the information on one of the keyboards. From the cards, the bits of informa-tion would go to magnetic tape for a printout run. Sarver studied the cards. "Noah, I explained to you when you called that there's no way the computer can evaluate this information."

"I know that," Aikman said. "I'll do the evaluating. All I want the machine to do is make the comparisons. I want the elements in nice, neat categories."

"That we can do," Sarver said with a wide grin. He was a short man, just under five-eight, with short gray hair and a cropped gray mustache. Years of working in computer rooms under fluorescent lights had given him a gray pallor. All he needs. Aikman thought, is a gray flannel suit. But Aikman knew that Sarver was the best there was when it came to computers. He wouldn't trust anyone else to supervise the programming. "How long will it take, Phil?" he asked him.

"Three, four days," Sarver said, riffling the edges of a stack of index cards like a dealer in Las Vegas.

"Make it three," Aikman urged.

"I'll try," Sarver replied. Aikman nodded and turned to leave.

"Noah . . ." Sarver called.

"Yeah?"

"Don't call me . . . I'll call you."

"Computer comedy," Aikman mumbled.

He spent the evening cleaning and straightening the study. The leftover file cards were packed in a box and placed in the closet, forgotten coffee cups carried to the kitchen and washed, the typewriter returned to its table. He erased the scribblings on the blackboard, took one last look at the map, the red circles marking the locations of the killings standing out starkly amid the thick black lines, and turned off the light.

One way or another, that part of the case was over. The

answer wasn't going to come from the blackboard, the map, the huge files on the victims.

It had to come from the computer.

He called Leslie early the next morning. "Are you still in town?" she asked when she heard his voice.

Aikman laughed. "It's been rough . . . sorry I haven't called."

"Have you gotten anywhere?" she asked.

"Maybe. I'll let you know in three days."

"And what happens in three days?"

"The oracle spits forth its message," he said. There was a momentary silence.

"Oh sure," Leslie finally said, "I should have known."

"How about you?" Aikman asked. Any progress?"

"A lot," she said. "Raymond's back at Maplewood. He trusts me again, Noah, and he's coming out of his shell. I took him back to the hospital two days ago, and he lets the nurses play with him, accepts toys from them; it's amazing."

"No," Aikman said, "it was a lot of hard work and a lot of care. And you did it alone."

"It was worth it, every minute of it," Leslie said. "We'll be able to work with him again, teach him."

"Leslie," Aikman interrupted, "why don't you tell me about it over dinner . . . we'll celebrate."

"On one condition," she said.

"What?"

"You tell me about this oracle business."

Aikman ran down the procedure for programming the computer as Leslie sat at the kitchen table and watched him prepare their dinner.

". . . so the victims were never important *as people*," he

said, lowering the flame under a huge casserole dish. "The key is what they represented."

"And the computer will tell you that?" she asked.

"I hope so," he said softly.

"You don't sound hopeful."

"No, I'm hopeful," he smiled, "it's just that I don't like relying on a machine for the answer."

"But you said . . ."

"Oh, the computer will tell us what the common factor is," he said confidently, "but . . ."

" . . . you wanted to figure it out yourself."

Aikman grinned. "Something like that."

"No, I think exactly like that," Leslie insisted.

Aikman waved her toward the dining room. "Inside," he said. "You're bugging the chef and sending out hostile vibes to make my soufflé fall."

Leslie went into the dining room, and ten minutes later Aikman served a spectacular Brisbane prawn soufflé with boiled and buttered herb potatoes, a green salad, and a chilled bottle of dry white wine.

"I'm impressed," Leslie said, sampling the soufflé. "And I didn't make it fall . . ."

"The whole trick," Aikman said between bites, "is to gently fold the white sauce into the egg whites."

"Of course," Leslie smiled.

Over coffee in the living room, Leslie talked about Raymond. "He'll never be self-sufficient, but we're repairing the damage and bringing him back. There will be certain things we can teach him, things he can do for himself with diginity."

"Will he ever be able to talk about what happened?" Aikman asked.

"Not for a long time. We can't risk it, Noah. We've come too far with him to take a chance like that. He has to become comfortable back at the hospital. He has to learn to trust others, not just me and a few nurses."

Aikman nodded.

"You'll have to do it without him," she continued. "The computer run should tell you what you want to know."

"Not all of it," Aikman said. "It won't tell us who they are. Raymond saw one of them: No computer can give us that."

"I'm sorry . . ." she said, shaking her head.

It's frustrating to feel that you're close to them, that you have the means of identifying them, but can't use it," Aikman said ruefully. He caught her expression and smiled warmly. "Forget it. I'm just angry with myself because I couldn't put it together alone."

"You really didn't want to go to the machine, did you?"

"No. It's a last resort, and I hate last resorts. I know I've got all the pieces, but no matter how hard I've tried, I couldn't come up with anything."

Leslie frowned and started to say something.

"What?" Aikman prompted.

"I was just thinking about what you'd do if the computer run fails."

"I'll probably be forced to seek honest employment elsewhere," he smiled.

"Doing what?" she teased.

Aikman got up from his chair, went to the bookcase, and brought back a small leather case. He kicked off his shoes, sat facing her on the sofa, cross-legged, and opened the case. "Hustling backgammon," he grinned.

A half hour later, Leslie owed him $4.50. Aikman picked up the case and set it down on the coffee table. Then he put his arms around Leslie and kissed her.

"Hustler," she whispered.

The call came from Sarver at six-thirty on the night of the twenty-third. Aikman had spent the day in a mad rush of Christmas shopping, calling the FBI building three times, in case Sarver was trying to reach him.

"We're ready," the computer expert said.

"Be there in twenty minutes," Aikman snapped.

He made a call to Enders, grabbed his coat, and ran up the stairs for Alex.

"This is it," he said to himself, chain-smoking as he stared at the wall-long computer behind the glass.

"You look like a backer on opening night," Alex said, sitting on the Formica table.

"Huh?" Aikman mumbled.

"Broadway? Opening night? Get it?"

Aikman lit another cigarette and began pacing the room, unable to stand still any longer. He didn't turn around as Enders came into the room, threw his coat over the table, and stood by Alex.

"It's a correlation analysis study," Alex said to Enders.

"Oh?" he said.

"Right," Alex answered.

"Where did you get that from?" Enders frowned.

"From him," Alex said, pointing to Sarver, who stood at the console at the far end of the room, tapping the keys in a halting rhythm.

Aikman strode past them and left the room.

"The name doesn't matter," Sarver called to Enders, punching out the last digits. He walked toward Alex and the deputy chief. "What we're doing," he said, "is finding out what relationships exist among the victims, if any, and to what degree."

"How does that translate to English?" Enders asked.

"Well, if victim number one had a hamburger for lunch on the day he was killed, and so did victim number five, the computer will toss out that they were the only two ham-

231

burger lovers. And we'll have the percentage that that fact represents when compared to the whole." Sarver pointed to a blackboard on a rolling stand at the back of the room. "We've set up a matrix, a graph. We'll plot all the factors, and the graph will show us any and all overlaps. If one column on the graph under any factor fills up, we'll have the common element."

"If there is any," Enders commented, looking at Alex.

"Don't say that to my father," she cautioned.

"There are bound to be similarities," Sarver said. "We programmed in an incredible amount of information. There were ten thousand cards on that guy Witkin. We're going to get some matchups; we have to."

Aikman, coming back into the room with a paper cup of water, caught the last words of Sarver's explanation. "Some isn't good enough," he said.

"We're ready, Noah," Sarver said.

"Then do it," Aikman ordered.

Sarver punched a series of buttons on the first console, and the tapes began to whirl. Wide sheets of thick white paper, marked with fine green lines, began to chatter out of the top of the console. After five minutes, the paper stopped abruptly.

Aikman and Sarver leaned over the terminal. The computer had printed out the names of the victims, including the taxi, which Aikman had keyed "Checker Taxicab" on the input, and the categories of elements: numbers, letters, origins, travel, hobbies, religion . . . on and on through a hundred different classifications. The bottom line on the long sheet of paper read, "0 per cent." Nothing matched. Aikman crumpled the printout page and threw it on the floor.

"Don't panic," Sarver said quietly. "That's just the first run. Now we know that there is no single element common to all eleven—well, twelve, including the cab. We'll run for a percentage." Sarver punched another combination of buttons, and the machine came to life. Enders and Alex watched in fascination as the paper poured out of the terminal. Aikman glanced at the printout as it appeared, his body growing rigid, the pressure in his back building until he felt he was being squeezed in a vise. Sarver noted the percentages as they came out, plotting them on the blackboard.

Aikman stared at the computer with fierce concentration, as if he could force out the answer he knew was there. At the end of an hour he was exhausted. The percentages were meaningless.

Thirty-three per cent of the victims had brown hair and brown eyes; 25 per cent had common numerals in the numbers of their apartments; 30 per cent shared common astrological signs. The floor was littered with paper, piles of meaningless scrap. Aikman worked over the sheets that had printed the anagrams from the random letters in names and addresses and locations. The computer had played word games with street names, names of parks, buildings, and a bridge. Nothing.

He swept the pile to the floor. "It's there," he said evenly, a trace of menace in his voice. "We programmed it wrong; I know it's there."

"There's nothing there," Enders said. "It was a good try, but . . ." Alex put her hand on his arm and shook her head.

"No!" Aikman yelled, his patience gone. "We're staring right at it and we can't see it."

"If it was there, you'd see it," Alex said. "The computer would see it."

"We programmed it wrong," Aikman insisted. "Goddamnit, whatever the common factor is, we didn't feed it in. It wasn't on our cards. We missed it."

The door swung open and Peter Gregory, a cigar clamped in his teeth, came in. "They told me you were here," he said to Enders.

"They were wrong," Enders mumbled. Gregory carried a thin manila folder and handed it to Enders. "Jesus," Enders sighed, reading the report inside.

"What now?" Aikman asked, controlling his anger.

"We've got another one," Gregory answered. "The .45 this time, guy named Mark Lubin. They found him down on West Fourth Street about an hour ago."

"Lubin?" Aikman muttered. "I've heard that name somewhere."

"Very big in the middle and late sixties," Gregory nodded. "Organized the antiwar marches . . . arrested for burning his draft card in Washington Square Park."

"Washington . . ." Aikman mumbled.

"He finally got a conscientious-objector rating," Gregory said. "Fought the draft board through the courts and won."

Enders scanned the rest of the report as Aikman paced the room. Alex read the page over his shoulder.

"What was missing?" Aikman asked Gregory.

"His college ID. He was teaching political science at NYU. The radical turned professor," Gregory shrugged. "Two patrolmen found him in an alley a few doors away from the office of a Village newspaper. Lubin wrote a regular column for them. We figure he was leaving the office when the .45 got him."

"The same pattern of killing," Enders said.

"Not quite," Gregory said. "Lubin was on his back in the alley. The killer must have walked him in there at gunpoint. He shot him from the front, four slugs in the face."

"An execution," Enders said. Aikman glanced at the report, shook his head, and stalked out of the room.

At four in the morning he gave up trying to sleep and went into the kitchen, brewed coffee, and smoked. He changed into a heavy jogging suit and left the apartment at seven, ignoring the light snow and the biting cold. He crossed the street and entered Central Park, but his breath came in gasps, and his stride was labored. Too many goddamn cigarettes, he cursed to himself. He settled into an easy pace, synchronizing his thoughts with the slapping rhythm of the track shoes . . .

Nine months . . . four men . . . twelve dead . . .

Nine months . . . four men . . . twelve dead . . . McMahon, Douglas, Witkin, Loesser, Hayakimo, Rendelli, Gibbs, Cunningham, Krieg, cab, D'Angelo, Lubin . . .

Nine months . . .

Four men . . . Aikman pulled up, panting. His rhythm was off, his breathing was off . . .

He gave it up and went home.

At six o'clock he was still in the bathrobe he'd put on after his shower that morning. He sat at his desk in the study, pushing the eggs he'd made for dinner around his plate. When he looked up, he saw Alex watching him from the doorway, leaning against the frame. "Holding up the building?" he asked.

"Marx Brothers," she smiled. *"A Night at the Opera?"*

"A Day at the Aikmans'."

She walked into the room and sat on the sofa. "I'm ready," Alex announced cheerfully.

"For what?"

"To bounce this around," she replied.

Aikman smiled. "I've been bouncing for months."

"You've been bouncing off walls, is what you've been doing. How about we bounce off each other?"

"Forget it," he sighed. "I've hashed this thing to death."

"Nope," Alex said flatly. "Go get dressed."

"You taking me out to dinner?"

"We're going to do this like civilized people. You're going to get dressed and I'm going to fix something to drink, and we're going to figure it out."

"And for this I've got to get dressed?"

"Cases are not solved by detectives in bathrobes," she said smiling.

"Conan Doyle would not agree," Aikman muttered, but he got up and went into his bedroom. Five minutes later he came back wearing jeans, a T-shirt, worn tennis sneakers, and white sweat socks. "Civilized enough?" he asked.

"It'll have to do," Alex answered.

"I don't know why I humor you like this," he grumbled, falling into the swivel chair and picking up the cocktail glass she'd put on the desk.

"You've humored me ever since . . ."

"I've spoiled you," he said with a smile. He sipped the drink, made a face, and said, "You make rotten gimlets."

"Hire a bartender."

"Too much lime juice," he muttered, then stretched his legs and hooked them over the edge of the desk. "Okay, Sherlock, I'm ready."

"A lot of city employees have been killed," she began thoughtfully. "Someone's got it in for the city."

"Doesn't work and you know it: too many loose ends. How do you explain a singer, a hardhat? How do you explain a cab, for God's sake?"

"How do *you* explain it?"

"I don't," he answered, "in case you haven't noticed."

"The cab might represent the city . . ."

"You're groping."

"Well then, grope along," she smiled.

He stood up, set the glass down on the desk, and faced the map. "I've tried it every way I know . . . every way I could think of . . . by dates, weapons, locations . . . you know all the ways we tried. The computer came up with nothing . . . I came up with nothing."

"But you know it's there," Alex said.

"Yes, goddamnit . . . those men aren't crazy; they know exactly what they're doing. They pick and choose, they stalk their targets . . . Gibbs and Cunnungham proved that . . . but I can't see how they do it."

"That's the real puzzle for you, isn't it?" she said softly. "Not so much who they are, but how they're choosing who to kill."

"Once I find out *how*, I'll work on *who*," he answered shortly.

"Maybe you won't get the chance. Did you ever think of that?"

"Meaning?"

"Meaning one of them could make a mistake, get careless, and be seen. Maybe it'll all go down because some rookie cop spots our friend assembling his rifle in an alley one night and bingo . . . case closed."

Aikman didn't reply.

"But that's not the way it happens in Noah Aikman's cases, is it?" Alex asked, her voice rising. "No, that never happens to you, does it? You've got to solve it, don't you?"

"I don't have to do anything," he yelled, beginning to pace the room.

"Sure," she snapped. "You've got to do what the police can't do . . . you've got to see the patterns, see the logic . . . you've got to make the jumps because there's no one else who will."

"I've spent months looking for the key," he said, trying to control his mounting anger. "I've looked upside-down, inside-out, and cross-eyed and I can't see it."

"Then look harder, jump farther," she exploded. "Because if you don't, some beat cop is going to earn a gold shield when he stumbles over Dead-eye Dick and his sniper's rifle."

Aikman glared at her.

"If they could think up it up, you can figure it out," she prodded.

"Stop telling me that!" he shouted. "I don't need my ego massaged."

"You need anything you can get," she shot back.

"Yeah," he said, "and what I'm getting right now is a lot of crap about how great I am and how if I'm not greater this case is going to slip away from me through a fluke."

"Then this is it, right?" she needled, standing up. "Finish . . . the end. Noah Aikman can't outthink the bad guys anymore, right? So this is the one, finally . . . the one you've waited thirty years for."

"That's enough!" he yelled at her and stalked from the room.

In a rage he pulled the closet door open and grabbed an overcoat. He thrust his arms into the sleeves and clutched the coat around him as he stormed out of the apartment and into the street.

He walked blindly until the anger began to seep away, diminishing block by block until he stopped at the corner of Seventy-fourth Street and Fifth Avenue. He found a crumpled pack of cigarettes and a book of matches in his coat pocket. He turned his back to the wind, struck the match, and inhaled deeply.

She'd tried to push him past the boundary of frustration and tension, baiting him until his anger would turn to desperation and he would force his mind to see the answer. But it had failed. He buttoned the overcoat, tossed the cigarette away, and began walking back to his apartment.

"Once more, Aikman," he muttered to himself. "Where's the logic? Where's the jump?" He walked oblivious to the other people on the street. "I've made it complicated," he said out loud, and heads turned to stare at him. "It's got to be something so simple . . ."

He stepped from a curb and jumped back as a cab came around the corner, tires squealing. He took a step back glancing up at the red light. "He killed a cab," Aikman said flatly. "A yellow Checker . . . the yellow cab . . . what was that movie?" Aikman stood perfectly still as the light changed. *"The Yellow Cab Man* . . . one of Red Skelton's films . . ."

He started walking again, his mind roaming, playing with the words: "Red . . . sure, Red Witkin, the mayor's man . . . Red Witkin and the yellow cab . . ." He was at the next corner when he heard the wail of a police siren. Seconds later a patrol car flashed by, weaving in and out of lanes of traffic . . .

". . . and the boys in blue," Aikman breathed, the thoughts coming quickly now. His eyes shot up to the traffic light above him. Green . . .

"Oh my God," he whispered in amazement.

Noah Aikman made the jump.

Twenty minutes after Aikman returned home, the limousines started to pull up. Jerry Lawrence was first, then Ellison and Gregory at almost the same moment, then Sidney Holtzman and, finally, Carl Enders.

Harmon couldn't believe what he was seeing. He had followed Aikman up Fifth Avenue and had seen the sudden shock on Aikman's face as the criminologist stood on the corner of East Sixty-seventh Street. He trailed Aikman home, saw all the lights go on in the apartment, and took up his position in a doorway across the street. And now this: the deputy chief's parade.

It's more than just Cunningham, Harmon realized. More than Gibbs . . . it's Witkin, Loesser, those cops.

It's all of them.

Enders unbuttoned his coat and gave Alex a quick kiss as he walked into Aikman's living room.

"What is it?" he asked.

"We'll all find out together," she said and led him to the study.

Enders nodded to the others and took an empty chair at the end of a row facing Aikman's desk. To his right Gregory and Ellison sat stiffly, watching Aikman, who stood by the window, smoking a cigarette. Alex sat next to Holtzman on the sofa, and Jerry Lawrence stood on the other side of the doorway, leaning against the bookcase.

Enders looked up at the blackboard and frowned. Aikman had rearranged the grouping of the victims. There were four columns, with Sean McMahon and Billy Gibbs in the first; Eileen Douglas, Tony Rendelli, Billy Krieg, and Aldo D'Angelo in the second; the third column listed Charles Witkin and Jake Cunningham, and the last contained Aaron Loesser, Osea Hayakimo, the word "Taxi," and the name of the most recent victim, Mark Lubin. Aikman walked behind the desk and stood by the blackboard. Enders had the feeling that he was back in a classroom about to be called on by the teacher—and he didn't have the answer.

"It was there all the time," Aikman was saying. "We missed it when we programmed the computer." He glanced from Alex to Enders. "There are four elements," he went on, "but they're all part of the same thing." He paused and looked at each person in the room. "The killers are playing a game," he said softly. "They're playing against each other and against us. The victims were no more than parts of the game. They were never people . . . *who* they were didn't matter. They died because they stood for something in the game."

"What is it?" Enders asked sharply.

"Colors," Aikman answered. "Green, blue, red, and yellow."

Gregory stood up and took a step toward the blackboard.

"Where the hell do you get that from?" Enders demanded.

"Shut up, Carl," Gregory said in a low voice.

"Don't tell me to . . ." Enders began.

Aikman cut him off. "Hold it." He looked at Gregory. "Sit down, Pete."

Gregory backed up and eased himself into the chair, his eyes still on the blackboard and the four columns.

"Let's take them one by one," Aikman began. "Sean McMahon stood for green because he was Irish, and Gibbs wore the green jersey of the New York Jets. Eileen Douglas—she was an incredible choice—a singer, but a special kind of singer, a specific type . . ."

"Blues singer," Gregory muttered.

"Exactly," Aikman nodded, "and Rendelli and Krieg— blue uniforms."

"This is crazy," Lawrence snapped.

"No," Aikman said, "anything but crazy."

"Go on," Gregory urged. "How do you figure the rest of them?"

"D'Angelo," Aikman continued with a tight smile. "A very subtle, obscure choice, but once I figured out that the pattern was color, it wasn't hard at all. He was a blue-collar worker."

"Jesus Christ," Holtzman swore.

"And the reds," Aikman went on. "Charles Witkin, nick-named 'Red,' and Jake Cunningham, known as 'Indian.'"

"Aaron Loesser?" Gregory asked Aikman.

"A jeweler all his life," Aikman answered. "Working with diamonds and gold. It's the gold that killed him, the yellow metal."

"And Hayakimo," Alex said, "the oriental . . ."

"Yeah," Aikman nodded. "We all remember the yellow peril. And the one piece that never fit because it wasn't a person: the cab. But it was yellow, and that's all that ever mattered."

"How do you figure Lubin?" Ellison asked.

"The radical," Aikman said slowly, "the draft resister.

Our killers are military men. Wouldn't they consider Lubin a coward . . . chicken . . . yellow?"

Lawrence kept shaking his head. "No, it's not possible. There's no way . . ."

"Jerry," Aikman said evenly, "we're not dealing with psychopaths. The killers are ruthless, subtle, and egotistical. They've challenged us from the beginning, dared us to figure it out. And the killings have escalated, grown more spectacular as the game has gone on. This is the only possible explanation for the choice of victims and the pattern of what they're doing."

"What game are they playing?" Gregory asked.

"You don't really believe this crap," Lawrence shot at him.

"What's the game?" Gregory repeated, ignoring Lawrence.

Noah Aikman leaned on the desk and took a deep breath. "Parcheesi," he said, looking straight at Gregory. Before they could react, he went on. "They've twisted it to suit their purpose, but the basics of the game are all there: victims of particular colors, strategy, planning, and the element of chance that accounts for the scattering of the death sites." He moved to the map and swept his hand to encompass the circles that marked the locations of the killings. "You can think of it as a war game."

Alex smiled at Aikman. "I take back all the rotten things I thought about you."

"This is insane," Lawrence said.

"How does it work?" Gregory asked Aikman.

"Now, wait just a minute," Lawrence exploded. "I can't believe this. What the hell is the matter with all of you? Games . . . colors . . . it's ridiculous."

Gregory stood up and faced him, fists clenched. "Will you shut the hell up?"

Enders put his hand on Gregory's arm. "Take it easy, Pete."

Aikman went to the cabinet in the bookcase and tool out the cardboard box. He opened it on the desk, removed the board, and set up the pieces, four of each color—red, green, blue, yellow—on the four corners of the square surface. Lawrence cursed under his breath as the others crowded around the desk.

"At its most basic level, it's a chase," Aikman sighed. "Each of the four players controls one color and the four pieces of that color. From the corners, each piece enters the playing area one at a time and moves around the board according to rolls of the dice." Aikman turned one of the four dice cups upside down, tumbling cubes to the board. He traced the path of rectangles that angled around the surface. "There are sixty-eight spaces, and each player moves as many as the dice indicate. The object is to get around and up these paths," he said, pointing to the four vertical red sections of spaces, "to their 'home.' The first player to get all four men into his home wins."

"It's a kids' game," Enders snorted.

"On that level, yes," Aikman agreed. "But to those who know the implications, it takes on a different dimension."

Lawrence, who had been edging forward while Aikman spoke, said, "Translate that into English."

Aikman grinned. "You can advance your men by hitting your opponents, if the roll of the dice gives you the opportunity. So position is important: how you group your men or spread them out. You're always at the mercy of the dice, but the appeal of the game is that element of chance, and you make the most of it. You can blockade your opponents, you can sacrifice one of your men to pick up an opponent coming around behind you. It's very close to backgammon in complexity."

"And," Alex added, "you're playing against three others instead of one."

"How are they using the game?" Ellison asked.

"*If* they're using it," Lawrence said shortly. Gregory

flashed a glance at him, and Lawrence backed away from the desk.

"The first thing," Aikman explained, "is territory. The spaces on the board have to represent areas in New York. They may have numbered each space and somehow divided the city into the same number of sections. When one of them hits another player on the board, he has to make a corresponding hit in the city . . . match up the territory and the color he's hitting." Aikman moved to the map. "Take the wireman; he hit red on one of the spaces. The space corresponded to Harlem, and he found Jake Cunningham."

Aikman sat down behind the desk and leaned back in the chair. "It explains a lot of things," he said. "The killing of Krieg and shooting the taxi in one night. In the game you get a bonus when you hit another player. You get to move one of your men ahead twenty spaces. The sniper hit blue in the game, and saw that moving one of his men twenty would give him a hit on yellow. He took them both in the same night."

"How do you know? How can you be so sure?" Holtzman asked.

"Because once you have the color pattern, you have the game. And Sidney, I *know* this game . . . it all fits."

"It more than fits," Alex said. "It's perfect for our four friends. They're fighting each other, they're fighting us. They're military, and they've made it a war game."

"All right," Lawrence said with an edge in his voice. "Let's say you're right. I'm not saying I buy it, but if this is what's going on, why the hell are they doing it? What's the purpose?"

Gregory turned to him with a cold smile. "Don't you understand?"

"No," Lawrence said defiantly, "I don't."

"It's a game, for Chrissake!" Gregory roared.

"This is a game to them? Killing all those people . . . ?" Enders asked.

"Not *people*, Carl," Aikman emphasized again, "*colors*." He stood up. "There's no motive other than the game. They enjoy it, it's sport; we're dealing with incredible egos, men who are challenging us to stop them. They're doing it because they *like* it."

"That's what the identification is all about," Gregory breathed, looking at Aikman.

"Sure," Aikman nodded. "They're proving to each other that they fulfilled the requirement. And it explains the intervals between killings. There's no time limit in the game. A player has as long as he likes to make his move on the board, and they're doing the same thing when they hit on the street. You get as long as you want . . . or need."

"How the hell do we stop them?" Gregory asked, almost to himself.

"Congratulations, Pete," Lawrence said sarcastically. "You finally asked a relevant question."

Aikman glared at Lawrence. "You begin to stop them by understanding what they're doing."

"Well, I don't think this is it," Lawrence said flatly. "You can't convince me that four men are murdering people as part of a game."

"They're not *people*," Aikman said, a harder edge to his voice this time. "To the killers, they're just elements in a contest."

"You said that already," Lawrence snapped.

"Then why don't you listen?" Aikman demanded.

"You don't think men like that exist?" Gregory asked Lawrence in a low voice. "Men who could murder for thrill, for challenge? Men who could make death a sport? You don't think so, huh?"

Lawrence looked away. He had no answer.

"There's no other way to look at it, is there?" Ellison asked Aikman.

Aikman shook his head. "For the first time, it all fits; no stretching, no groping, no exceptions."

"What do we do now?" Holtzman asked.

"We keep it quiet," Enders sighed. "We can't let anyone know what we think . . . not yet."

"There's something else we can do," Aikman offered. "These men have to be into games. To play Parcheesi on the level we're talking about takes that kind of mind. They've got to be familiar with all kinds of games. We go after chess parlors, backgammon clubs, and bridge groups."

"I'll work on it," Gregory said, standing up. In silence they filed into the living room and put on their coats.

"There's one more question, Noah," Enders said, turning to Aikman.

"Just one?" Aikman asked.

"Yeah. You said that a player wins when he gets all of his men home. How do we know that one of them hasn't won the game? How do we know they're still playing?"

Part III

13

Reynolds stared at the Tramway, a thin smile on his lips as the dangling aerial car approached the midpoint of its journey over the East River to Roosevelt Island.

He thought of the back-slapping politicians and how they'd gloried in the Tram, the latest in a line of minor city accomplishments. Reynolds detested them all—the mayor, the City Council, all the assistants and paper-pushing bureaucrats who moved forward like frightened snails, second-guessing every inch and then wallowing in self-praise. But at this moment he was grateful for the Tramway: It would provide him with a victim.

He'd scouted for almost a week, getting a feel for the area: the buildings, the pedestrians, the traffic; the shadows and shelter on the island. It didn't particularly disturb him that there were only two ways on and off the island—the Tram and an access bridge into Queens. He'd come by the bridge and would leave the same way in a rented black Buick, courtesy of one of several drivers' licenses he held under assumed names.

Crouched behind a steel pillar, Reynolds assembled the rifle, his gloved hands easily setting the pieces into place. From the nights of observation, he knew his man would be getting off his shift at the end of this trip across the river. In the ground-level lean-to shelter which housed the Tram when it pulled in, the conductor who would be taking over the 3:00 A.M. to 9:00 A.M. shift walked back and forth, slapping his hands together, trying to warm them in the freezing January night. The Tram car glided along the cable, slowed as it approached the shelter, and then stopped. There were no passengers.

The on-coming conductor took a small black box from the off-duty man. They exchanged a bit of conversation as two people ran across the street directly behind them and hurried onto the Tram.

Leaving the fluorescent-lit area, the off-duty conductor walked behind the shelter toward the street. When he was directly in line with the steel pillar, Reynolds leaned in against the girder and brought the rifle up. The conductor had only a brief glimpse of a man in a blue overcoat pointing something at him when a bullet tore into his face.

The rifle in his right hand, Reynolds moved to the body. He knelt, and his left hand was reaching for the victim's back pocket when something caught the corner of his eye. He glanced up and saw the Tram, less than thirty feet away, moving back across the river. Through the Tram window, Reynolds saw the conductor staring down at him, a telephone receiver in his hand.

Reynolds acted without thinking: He was into his crouch and the rifle was up and he fired twice, the bullets shattering the glass and smashing the conductor to the floor. Screams burst from the car.

Reynolds found the wallet, ripped out the New York Transit Authority ID card, and ran back to the steel girder near the shelter. He had five minutes before the Tram reached the other side and the alarm went out—no time if the conductor's message got through or if one of the passengers picked up that phone.

He dismantled the rifle in seconds and ran forty feet to the Buick. He threw the briefcase into the car and started the engine.

For the first time, Reynolds felt the fear. The island could be sealed, he could be trapped. Gripping the steering wheel, he forced himself to drive slowly. He had to maintain control. There were police patrols on Roosevelt Island. It was 3:10 in the morning and he was the only car on the road.

The access bridge was less than a mile away.

García and his wife worked in the kitchen of Flower and Fifth Avenue Hospitals and had to be on the job by four o'clock in the morning, preparing breakfast for over one hundred patients in the hospital's opthalmic ward. They had just moved into an apartment on Roosevelt Island. It was a safe place to live, they'd heard, and convenient for traveling to their jobs.

But now this. The conductor was dead, horribly dead, and they were alone in the car, huddled on the floor, waiting for the next shot. There was a crazy man out there who would spray the car with bullets, and they would be torn apart like the conductor. But the bullets never came.

After an eternity, García opened his eyes and saw the phone dangling at the end of the car. He shook his wife and put his hand over her mouth to cut off the screams.

He could hear someone calling from the receiver: "Hello? What happened? Anybody there . . . ?"

García couldn't bring himself to move closer to the phone, closer to the dead conductor. He shouted across the car. "Someone shot the conductor; can you hear me?"

"What?" the voice answered.

"He's dead, someone shot the conductor."

At the other end of the line, John Sayers slammed a phone plug into the police emergency line.

"Police," the dispatcher said.

"Sayers, Transit Authority. Just got a call from the Roosevelt Island Tram. I think the conductor's been shot—

wait a minute." He looked up at the schedule on the wall and above it, the clock. "From the island side. If it's true, there's a guy with a gun on the Island."

"Where's the Tram?" the dispatcher asked.

Three minutes into the run. It's got another two to go before it hits the Manhattan side."

"We got it," the dispatcher said.

Hopkins and his partner considered Roosevelt Island a "nothing" duty, especially so at three in the morning. Then the radio crackled, ordering them to stop any car attempting to leave the Island, ordering them immediately to the access bridge leading to Queens. They had seen only one car the entire evening. Moments before, a black Buick passed them, heading in the direction of the bridge.

Reynolds saw the spinning red light slash at the rearview mirror and he slammed down on the accelerator. Where was the mistake? What had he done wrong? Then it came to him: The Tram was in the air, dangling on the cable, and anyone inside could see the ground below for a greater distance.

All right, he thought. It doesn't matter now. He pushed the accelerator harder and the Buick jumped forward. This was it, this was the test. The others had been easy, too easy. He'd proved he could kill someone on the street and walk away, but this time they were after him and he had a liability—the car. The cops were probably broadcasting a description right now.

He was fifty yards ahead of the patrol car as he came off the bridge and swung right onto Vernon Boulevard and raced along the river.

He felt the steering wheel through the thin gloves as a part of his body, like the rifle was a part of his body. He turned like off the boulevard and sped for the corner. He had to keep making the far corners before the cops could spot his tail lights. His thoughts were automatic, the reasoning process born of experience under extreme pressure. This was the test; *this* was what he had in mind for the game.

Another right turn, on the accelerator, right again, accelerator, left, another left. Keep making the corners, keep moving toward Jackson Avenue.

He had planned to leave the car in Queens and take the subway back to Manhattan. He could still do it, but he had to lose that patrol car before the reinforcements arrived.

Another left and he killed his headlights and glided the Buick in between two trucks on a side street near Jackson. He shut off the motor, turned his rear-view mirror out and down to pick up the street, and slumped, almost in a prone position on the front seat. He watched for a few minutes, waiting to see if headlight beams reflected on the street. Nothing. It was time to move.

He grabbed the briefcase and got out of the car, closing the door quietly like a shadow. It was quiet, too quiet. A cop trick, he thought, they've killed their sirens and lights, but they're out there somewhere, still looking.

The area of Queens was mostly factories; side streets with pockets of darkness, trucks huddled along the curbs, places to hide as he moved like a track runner from block to block until he saw the subway station directly in front of him on Jackson Avenue.

Reynolds made the run across the street, cutting in between the few cars waiting for the light to change.

He knew he still wasn't safe, even as he took the descending steps two at a time and jammed his token into the turnstile slot. He moved away from a couple on the platform and then leaned against a concrete pillar, holding the briefcase to his chest, catching his breath.

The IRT subway train pulled into the station and Reynolds got on as the doors opened. He walked in between the cars until he found one that was empty. The doors closed and the train began to move.

Reynolds walked to the far end of the car, set the briefcase down, pulled off his gloves, and wiped a thin film of sweat from his forehead. For a moment he stared at his hand: steady, not a tremor.

Reynolds smiled. He could still move through the jungle.

Police Commissioner Michael Forman was on Roosevelt Island forty-five minutes after the killings. He was escorted through the police lines and barricades by uniformed men and led to the body of the conductor on the street. He'd been briefed in the limousine and asked no questions. They'd missed the killer, perhaps by seconds, and that was all he needed to know. There would be time later for details.

At East Fifty-ninth Street and Second Avenue, Peter Gregory supervised the Forensic crew and the medical examiner's assistants. The photographs were taken, the measurements made, the floor of the Tram car chalked in the outline of the body. Behind the sawhorse barricades, a TV station mobile crew set up, floodlights turning night to day. The cameraman ducked around the people gathered at the perimeter, and the reporter reeled off details and speculation to an invisible audience; the broadcast would be served up with breakfast on the morning news.

Gregory scratched at the stubble on his cheek and pulled the woolen ski cap down over his ears. He dodged reporters on the way back to the squad car that had brought him to the scene. "There'll be a press conference this morning . . . no, I don't know what time . . ."

Inside the car he pulled off his hat and unbuttoned his

coat. The heat in the car made him sweat and, beneath a mismatched sport shirt and pair of slacks, his pajamas clung to his body.

The sniper's playing in my zone again, Gregory thought. He'd have to call Enders as soon as he got to his office . . . and Aikman . . .

. . . and Jerry Lawrence, he thought grimly. Let's see if this convinces him.

"You said the phone was off the hook, right?" Aikman asked, sitting up in bed.

"Yeah," Gregory said. "It was dangling on the end of the line, just hanging there."

"Then the conductor on the Tram doesn't count," Aikman said. "The blue target was the one getting off his shift. The man in the car saw the killing and was phoning for help. The sniper had to take him, too."

"That's what I figured," Gregory said, tonelessly. "There's no way to keep a lid on this one, Noah. There was a TV crew down there a half hour after the shooting. They got there before Forman, for Chrissake."

"That's not our problem," Aikman said. "It's going to scare the hell out of people, sure, but what we've got to worry about is anyone making a connection to the other killings."

"None of us is going to say anything," Gregory growled. "As far as we're concerned, it's an isolated incident, you know that."

"Yeah," Aikman said. "I'm not worried about that. I just hope Foreman doesn't let anything slip at the press conference."

"He knows better than that," Gregory assured him.

Aikman wasn't convinced. Forman would be getting pressure from the mayor to put more men on the case, to beef up patrols, to find witnesses, and to squeeze informants. If the police showed any sign of desperation, it was only a matter of time before the press would pick up the thread and throw the story on the front pages. Aikman thanked Gregory for the call and hung up.

Aikman got out of bed and dressed. It was only four-thirty in the morning, but he knew he wouldn't be able to get back to sleep.

At 6:00 A.M., Michael Forman met with the mayor at Gracie Mansion, and they called a press conference for nine. As Forman went over the details of the Roosevelt Island killings, Donahue nodded mechanically, his face pale, his mouth rigidly set. "It's the same guy . . . the one who hit the George Washington Bridge," Forman said.

There was no reaction from Donahue, and Forman felt a trace of pity for the mayor. Finally, Donahue scribbled some notes and walked stiffly to the conference room to face the reporters.

There weren't any speechwriters for Donahue to hide behind, but Forman, standing beside the mayor at the podium, knew that Donahue would pull it off. The mayor would find some way to express the outrage and anger in controlled, calm tones . . . some way to soothe the people and instill confidence in the police. But Forman saw beyond the mayor's outward appearance of control: He saw panic and fear in the man's eyes.

"Nothing yet, Noah," Fletcher sighed.

"Yeah, well, I've got something for you," Aikman said. He sat at his kitchen table, sipping coffee between sentences, gripping the phone tighter and tighter.

At the other end of the line, Warren Fletcher frowned as Aikman described what had happened in New York that morning. But the general turned pale when Aikman told him about the game. "I don't believe it," Fletcher said angrily. "You're wrong, Noah."

"Jesus, Fletch, c'mon: It's all there. All the pieces fit: the victims, the locations, the motive. You've got to believe it; you've got to help me find them.

"Whether I believe it or not has nothing to do with my helping you," Fletcher said.

"All right," Aikman said. "What've you got?"

"Lists and more lists."

"It's been three months, Fletch," Aikman complained.

"And I told you not to expect miracles," Fletcher said. "I've got people working their butts off. We're narrowing it down through the Veterans' Administration, checking off the deceased from a master list."

"How hard can it be to find the sniper?" Aikman demanded. "He's a specialist, right? He's got to stand out, right?"

"The classifications aren't set up like that," Fletcher drawled calmly. "We have to crosscheck with other files. You didn't give me a specific unit, of the time he was in the service . . ."

"I don't know that."

". . . so we have to take on the entire draft system. The sniper school list is inconclusive. Most of the men on it are dead, and the majority of the rest are handicapped. You're not even sure the guy was Army, are you?"

"No," Aikman said.

"Okay, so we may be looking for a Marine, a sailor, or a fly boy. That's what's taking time . . ."

"Where does that leave us?" Aikman asked without enthusiasm.

"With three other options," Fletcher said. "I think we should try for the pistol expert. You seem reasonably sure that he's Army. I'll keep a crew on the sniper, but I want to put some of my people on the pistol."

"Why not?" Aikman said.

Fletcher chuckled. "That's not like you, Noah. Don't go givin'up, y'hear?"

"Shit, no," Aikman said, pronouncing it, "shee-it," in his best southern accent. Fletcher laughed, and Aikman heard the doorbell. "Got to run, Fletch."

"I'll be talkin' to ya," Fletcher said, and hung up.

Aikman went to the front door and looked out the center glass panel. Through a light snowfall, he saw rumpled blond hair and a round, red-cheeked face. He'd seen that face somewhere. "Yes?" he said, opening the door a crack.

"Morning," the young man said. "John Harmon, New York *Times*."

"Too early for an interview," Aikman said.

"I'm here unofficially," Harmon replied quickly, as Aikman began to close the door.

"For what?" Aikman asked.

"I'm trying to build some bridges," Harmon said, looking straight at Aikman, "and I think you ought to talk to me." Aikman hesitated a moment and then opened the door. Harmon brushed snow from his coat and walked into the hallway, stamping his feet on the mat inside. Aikman hung up the coat and led him into the kitchen.

"Coffee?"

"Yes, thanks," Harmon said.

Aikman reheated the morning's coffee and poured two cups. On the kitchen counter a small television set played a news summary, and Mayor Donahue's face sweated in close-up. "Propaganda bullshit," Harmon muttered, watching Aikman's face carefully.

Aikman casually turned the set off. "What bridges were you talking about?"

"Big ones," Harmon said, relaxing and sipping his coffee. "Like from Billy Gibbs to Jake Cunningham, from Charles Witkin to the five top cops visiting you on Christmas Eve."

"We drink eggnog and sing carols," Aikman said. "It's a tradition."

Harmon smiled. "Won't work, Prof. I've been following you since Cunningham's murder. I'm the one who threw the curve at Jerry Lawrence at that press conference."

Aikman's jaw dropped. "Jesus, I must be getting old."

"Thank you," Harmon grinned.

"I recognize you from somewhere," Aikman said. "Not from tailing me, that's for sure . . . somewhere else . . ."

"I took one of your classes when you taught at NYU about two years ago."

"But you weren't with the *Times* then," Aikman said.

"You're not getting old," Harmon smiled. "I was just out of journalism school. I spoke to you about police work. I wanted to be a police reporter."

"And now you are," Aikman said.

"Well, not really," Harmon admitted. "I'm just a stringer with the *Times*."

"But you're not here for a story."

"No," Harmon said. "Not until I have it all. I'm still playing with the pieces, but I figured there was enough to bring to you. I want to know what's going on."

"What do you think is going on?" Aikman asked.

"I'm not a dummy, Professor. Donahue gets onstage this morning and gives us some crap about the conductors being killed as a part of someone's revenge . . . something in their personal or professional lives. That's bullshit. I read the paper I work for. There was no witness named Henderson to the Cunningham killing, but it didn't click in my mind until I remembered your lecture about that arson case. I knew you were involved somehow, and then I saw all the deputy chiefs show up and I figured it had to be bigger than just Cunningham." He reached into his jacket pocket and took out a worn notebook. He flipped it open and began to read from his notes: "Aaron Loesser and Mark Lubin, death by gunshot, still unsolved. Two cops killed: one stabbed, the other shot. Witkin, stabbed. An importer in the World Trade Center, death by strangulation. Cunningham, Ditto. Gibbs, shot. A tavern owner named McMahon, almost a year ago, shot. A teenager named Jim Forest, stabbed in Washington Square Park. A pimp in Harlem, shot down on the street . . ."

"Hold it," Aikman interrupted. "You're going too far."

"You'd like me to think so," Harmon said.

Aikman knew that there was no way he could get Harmon to keep quiet about what he knew if he tried to con him—the young reporter was too close. "All right," Aikman said, "You're right about some of it."

"I knew it," Harmon said. "Jesus . . ."

"You think you know," Aikman said mildly. "You've made some of the connections."

"So fill me in," Harmon prodded.

"I can't." Aikman shook his head.

"It's coming apart, Professor. If *I* could figure it out, there are other reporters who aren't far behind." Aikman didn't reply. He wondered how much he could hold back. "I want the story," Harmon insisted. "I'm not out to screw things up. I won't write anything that'll hurt what you're doing. I just want to know what's going on, and I want to be there at the end for an exclusive."

"And if I refuse, you'll go to the *Times* with what you've got?" Aikman asked.

"I don't want to do that," Harmon said quietly. Aikman studied the young, determined face and made up his mind. "It's bigger than you imagined," he said. "If you were to print anything, there'd be panic . . ."

"That bad?"

Aikman nooded. "We're looking for four men. They're acting together in these killings."

"Four different weapons," Harmon said, smacking the table with his palm.

Aikman nodded again. "We don't know who they are,

but I've figured out how they choose their victims, and I'm fairly certain I know why they're doing it." He stood up. "C'mon, let me show you my game room." He took Harmon into the study and filled in the details of the game and the motive, watching as the young man sat in rapt silence.

"What can I do to help?" Harmon asked when Aikman finished.

"Nothing right now," Aikman said, leading him toward the door. "But stay available."

"You've got to be kidding. I'll camp on your doorstep."

Aikman smiled. "Stay home, it's warmer. I give you my word, you've got the story when it breaks."

"Fair enough," Harmon agreed. "I'll sit on this, but I don't want to be part of the woodwork. Let me help you."

"If we need it," Aikman said.

"I'll call you," Harmon promised.

"Yeah," Aikman nodded, "but not too often."

Marcus called the others during the afternoon of the twelfth, two days after Reynolds killed the conductors. "I won't be having dinner with you," he said tersely. "I'll meet you at the club."

He arrived at Clarkson at seven-thirty, hoping to quell his rage before the others arrived. He would have to be calm. He had to convince them that Reynolds had lost control, that they were dealing with a psychopath who would get them all killed. Marcus paced the meeting room, fighting his temper. At five to eight Birmingham came in, placed his drink on the table, and sat down.

"How can you be so calm when the whole thing is falling apart around us?" Marcus asked tightly.

"What are you talking about?" Birmingham asked.

"I'm talking about Chris. What the hell do you think I'm talking about? He's gone too far this time."

"All right," Birmingham said, "maybe he was a bit extreme, but . . ."

"*A bit extreme?*" Marcus said, spitting the words. "A *bit?* Where've you been living, the salt flats? The city's going crazy. He's going to get us caught. I can't believe you're going to sit by and let this happen."

"Let what happen?" Reynolds asked, coming into the room.

Marcus gritted his teeth and slumped in a chair. "Where's Dick?" he asked after a long silence.

"Downstairs, getting a drink," Reynolds said. "Well? What's Birm going to let happen?"

Marcus gripped the arms of his chair and pushed himself up. "I asked you to take it easy. Did you listen? Did you even *hear* me? This one takes the prize, Chris; the whole city is screaming now. Did you see the mayor on TV?"

"I managed to miss it," Reynolds said.

"Well, I didn't," Marcus said. "The man looked like death warmed over. He's got to get results now. The cops are doing overtime on your stunts. They're not going to let up until they find you."

Reynolds laughed. "Is that what's worrying you? Jesus, I thought it was something serious."

"It *is* serious!" Marcus shouted.

"What are you getting upset about?" Reynolds asked calmly. "I got away, didn't I?"

"And that's all that's important, right?" Marcus thundered, slamming his fist on the table. "That's all you care about?"

Reynolds smiled. Yeah, he thought, that's what I care about . . . getting away. And I'll do it again . . . away from the cops, away from all of this.

". . . wonderful, just wonderful," Marcus was saying. "The man got away. Give him a Kewpie doll for getting out." He whirled on Reynolds and pointed his finger at him. "I asked you not to take it," Marcus said, trembling. "When you made that hit, I asked you to forget it because it was an island, didn't I? It was a death trap. Didn't I say that?"

"Yeah," Reynolds said, "you said that."

"And I was right, goddamn it! You almost got caught."

"Almost doesn't count in this game," Reynolds said. "Sure it was close. So what? And I was afraid; I'll admit it. But it was exhilarating—the fear, the instinct for survival, the chase—sure they were close, but I beat them."

"You're out of your mind, you know that?" Marcus said, forcing himself to calm down. "You're getting off on almost being caught."

"Jesus," Reynolds hissed, slashing the air with the side of his hand. "You still don't get it, do you? We've been at this almost a year, and you still don't see it, you stupid piece of shit! That's the whole point of what we're doing, idiot! To see if we can make it through, if we're good as we once were. The risk is part of it."

"Reasonable risk," Marcus said, taken back by the force of Reynold's outburst.

"There *is* no reasonable risk in this," Reynolds shot back. "Reasonable risk is playing the stock market with other people's money, you moron. Reasonable risk is Birm's insurance policies or Dick's loans of your investment in another goddamn machine to turn out your worthless calculators. That's reasonable risk. If that's all you need in your life, why the hell did you agree to play?"

"I didn't agree to let you jeopardize my life," Marcus said.

"And what do you think happens in war, shithead?"

"This is not war!" Marcus shouted.

"No, not for you, not the way you're going about it. But it's supposed to be."

"Don't give me that crap," Marcus said, his face flushed.

"I put myself on the line in Harlem. I played it out the way it's supposed to be."

"Big fucking deal," Reynolds answered. "You going to ride that one for the rest of your life? The challenges get bigger, the risks greater, you push harder and harder." Reynolds sat down and glared at Birmingham. "What do you say? You agree with this spineless wonder?"

Let me know when your tantrum is over," Birmingham said, staring at his glass.

The door swung open and Lyle strode in, two glasses in his hands. He held one out to Reynolds. "A drink for the Roosevelt Island Raider," he said, grinning.

Reynolds burst out laughing. "You see?" he said. "He understands."

"Understands what?" Lyle asked.

"They think I'm crazy," Reynolds said. "They think the risk was too high."

"Not this again," Lyle frowned at Marcus. "What's the matter with you guys?"

Marcus sighed. "It's impossible to get through to you, isn't it? He's going out of his way to entice the police, to tease them, to shove his ego in their faces. If you don't see how dangerous that is to all of us, then you belong in the same padded cell with the object of your affection." He jerked his thumb toward Reynolds.

But he got away with it," Lyle said flatly.

"*This* time!" Marcus screamed.

We're only talking about this time," Reynolds countered. "It's over. I got through it."

"And next time?" Marcus asked. "What will your ego demand of you then?"

"Whatever I want it to," Reynolds said. He stood up and faced Marcus. "You're afraid, aren't you? Not of me, not of what I'm doing. You're afraid to take bigger chances, to push yourself . . ."

"You miserable son-of-a-bitch!" Marcus exploded, leaping at Reynolds. Reynolds stood his ground and gripped Marcus' arms.

Lyle eased Marcus away from Reynolds. "That's enough, both of you," he said, holding onto Marcus. "Apologize, Chris . . . you know you're wrong."

"I don't know anything," Reynolds said.

"You know you're wrong," Lyle repeated. Reynolds caught the anger in Lyle's voice. The big man was staring at him, his face tight, menacing.

"If you say so," Reynolds mumbled.

"I say so!" Marcus shouted. "You're not the only one here with nerve. You're just the only egomaniac in the room. We don't have to prove as much to ourselves as you do. Who do you think you're impressing with your stunts? Not us. You're doing it for yourself."

"We're all doing it for ourselves," Lyle said, releasing Marcus. "This whole thing is out of hand. I'm not going to go on at the expense of our friendship. We've been together too long, gone through too much, and I'm not going to see it all thrown away."

"We're not throwing anything away," Reynolds said.

"Shut up," Lyle glared. "Where do you come off calling him a coward? If I didn't agree with you, would you call me a coward too?"

"No," Reynolds answered quietly.

"Look at us," Birmingham said softly, speaking for the first time. "We're starting to question each other's judgment, courage, even sanity. Sure, we all agreed to this, we all wanted to do it, but each one has his own way and his own feelings about what he has to prove . . . to himself and to all of us. You can't control that."

"I don't want to control it," Marcus said, turning to Reynolds. "I want you to consider all of us before you feed your ego."

265

"What about it, Chris?" Lyle asked. "We all know what you can do . . . and you know what we can do. We're in this together."

"All right," Reynolds sighed. "I'll just have to pass up shooting the mayor."

Birmingham and Lyle began to laugh, but Marcus shot Reynolds a quick glance. "You're not serious?" Marcus asked, half convinced that he was.

Reynolds flashed a dazzling smile. "You'll never know."

"Forget it, Ed," Birmingham said. "The mayor wouldn't fit any of the colors."

"Oh?" Reynolds said in surprise. "Isn't he Irish?"

"God almighty," Marcus moaned, "you weren't kidding."

"Don't get upset," Reynolds assured him. "Just a joke."

"You guys all right now? No more squabbling?" Lyle asked them.

"I'm okay," Marcus answered.

"I'll control myself," Reynolds said. "I don't want us to stop."

"Well, I do," Marcus sighed, holding up his hand as Reynolds' eyes flashed to him. "Let's let things settle down for a while," he said quietly. "We'll skip tonight and next week. Why don't we just have dinner on Thursday . . . four friends sharing a meal, okay?"

Reynolds nodded.

"I should have been a marriage counselor," Lyle said, relaxing back in the chair.

"With your track record?" Birmingham asked, smiling.

"Two isn't so bad," Lyle said.

"No," Reynolds agreed. "It's the alimony that hurts." He stood up and said to Marcus, "C'mon, have a drink with me."

Marcus considered for a moment and then nodded. "Sure," he said smiling. "If you don't mind drinking with a shithead, then neither do I."

As Marcus and Reynolds left the room, Birmingham asked Lyle, "Can your finances stand backgammon at fifty cents a point?"

"Can yours?" Lyle said with a wide grin.

Aikman waited impatiently for Leslie. She'd called about four in the afternoon, saying she had to talk to him and would come right over. It had to be about Raymond.

"Has he said anything?" Aikman asked as she came into the living room.

"He's talking about it . . . about Billy Gibbs and what happened," she said.

"Thank God," Aikman said. "Maybe now we can find out who they are."

"Don't get your hopes up," Leslie cautioned. "What he said doesn't make much sense to me."

"Tell me," Aikman prompted.

"I gave him some toys to play with. One of them was a small rubber football. He took it and looked at it for a long time and then said, 'Billy threw it.' I asked him if he remembered Billy, and he said he did. I didn't know how far to go, Noah, but he seemed to be able to talk about it."

"What else did he say?" Aikman asked, taking Leslie's hand. They sat down on the sofa.

"He said that Billy was gone . . . Billy was hurt. He seems to think that 'gone' and 'hurt' are the same thing. I asked him if he saw Billy hurt, and he said 'Yes.' We played with the football for a while, rolling it to each other on the floor, and then I asked him if he saw the man who hurt Billy. He didn't understand that. He said, 'Billy's gone.' I said that Billy was a good man, that Billy loved Raymond. I tried once more and asked him if he saw a man with Billy. He said, 'Not a man.' "

"Not a man?" Aikman repeated.

Leslie nodded. "I asked him if he could tell me what it was he saw, but I'd gone too far. He pushed the ball away. He was frightened, Noah. Whatever he saw, or thinks he saw, it was more than someone 'hurting' Billy."

"Not a man," Aikman said under his breath.

"It couldn't be . . . ?"

"No, it couldn't be a woman," Aikman smiled. "What else could he mean?"

Leslie shrugged. "Something about what happened, what he saw, left more of an impression on him than the actual killing. To him it's more important, more frightening than seeing Billy shot."

"Something about the man that makes him not a man," Aikman said. "What in hell . . ."

"I don't know, but I thought it might help you."

Aikman smiled. "Maybe, if I could figure out what it meant."

Leslie stood up. "I'll leave you to your figuring . . . call me." Aikman nodded absently and Leslie put on her coat and let herself out. Walking back to the study, Aikman said aloud, "Sooner or later, something in this miserable case is gonna be obvious."

It *was* obvious, and when it finally came to him at four in the morning, Aikman cursed himself for not seeing it sooner. He called Gregory at home, woke him up, and explained what he wanted.

"Say that again?" Gregory asked.

"I want the library opened . . . right now, and I want a car to pick me up. And I want the librarian there—not some flunky, but the head man."

Gregory squinted at his watch. "Noah, it's four o'clock in the morning."

"I have a watch, thank you," Aikman said shortly. "Have a car here in ten minutes."

"I don't think I can do it. Jesus, the New York Public Library . . . Noah . . ."

"Then hang up," Aikman said, "because I'm calling the mayor."

"All right, all right," Gregory groaned. "Don't get angry."

"And I'd like you to be there, too," Aikman said.

"I was afraid you were going to say that," Gregory said, but Aikman had hung up.

"Get dressed and c'mon down. We're going out."

"What time is it?" Alex asked, dropping the phone on the pillow. She heard Aikman's muffled voice and rolled over and picked up the receiver. "What?" she yawned.

". . . to the library. What's the matter with you?"

"Library? Did you say 'library'?"

"Everybody is hard of hearing this morning. Yeah, library."

"What've you got?" she asked him.

"We've got a way to find the man who killed Billy Gibbs," Aikman said.

"It was right in front of me," Aikman said as they sat in the back seat of the speeding squad car. "Why would Raymond say that the man was not a man? What could have frightened him more than Gibbs' death?"

"I'm not at my best at this hour," Alex mumbled. "You'll have to excuse my stupidity."

Aikman smiled. "*My* stupidity, you mean. It took so damn long to see it. Something about the man, something else that Raymond saw. And the only thing we had to work with on the Gibbs killing was the fact that the killer wore a uniform."

"The uniform frightened Raymond?"

"Not the uniform itself," Aikman said. "Something about the uniform . . . something *on* the uniform."

The squad car turned onto Forty-second Street, and Aikman saw a black sedan and a patrol car in front of the library. The driver pulled to the curb, and Aikman and Alex got out and hurried up the steps.

Inside, Gregory, two uniformed patrolmen, and a thin, middle-aged man in a heavy brown overcoat waited in the lobby. Henry Wentzel, chief librarian of the New York Public Library system, glared at Peter Gregory.

Aikman took Wentzel aside. They spoke in low tones for a few moments, and then Wentzel made his way to the bookstacks. Aikman and the others waited around a large table in the main reading room. Wentzel was back in five minutes, carrying a pile of books. Aikman took them, sat down at the table, and began to leaf through the first volume.

It went on for two hours. The uniformed officers brought coffee; Gregory and Alex wandered through the building, Alex explaining what Aikman had told her. "But what is he looking for?" Gregory asked. Alex shrugged.

Wentzel moved back and forth through the rooms, bringing more books, until, finally, he said, "That's the last one, Mr. Aikman." Aikman didn't reply. His coffee cup was untouched and his eyes didn't leave the pages.

Alex and Gregory came into the room and stared over Aikman's shoulder. Books on military insignia, World War II and Korea . . . photographs and drawings in black-and-white and in color . . . pages of heraldry flipped by. Aikman didn't read a word of text; only the photos and drawings held his attention: badges, patches, medals, wings, stars. The Seabees, the Signal Corps, Communications, helicopter squads.

When he saw it he gave no noticeable sign. He had known he was going to find it, and when it finally fell before his eyes, he felt no elation, only satisfaction. "All right," he said, closing the book, "let's get out of here."

"Not so fast," Gregory said and reached for the book. "I want to see what got me out of bed at this hour . . ." Aikman opened the book to the page he'd marked with the unused paper napkin. Gregory saw the patch, a half-page photograph in blazing color. "That's it, Pete," Aikman said. Alex came around the table and stared at the emblem over her father's shoulder. "That got to be it," Aikman repeated.

He led them out of the building and turned to Gregory, halfway down the steps. "I want a police artist to meet us in Central Park at the men's room where Gibbs was killed."

Gregory was on the car radio all the way to the park. They pulled up next to the lunch stand, closed and shuttered for the winter. Alex sat next to Aikman in the back seat and turned the pages of the book. "Are you sure?" she asked him.

"I will be," he said.

"What are you going to do?"

Aikman didn't answer.

"Aikman!" Alex demanded.

"I'm going to make sure," he replied evenly. "And once we're sure, we're going to put those bastards away." He turned his anger toward the killers, away from himself and what he had to do.

A squad car pulled up next to them, and a young man in a long black leather coat got out. He carried an artist's sketch pad and a narrow wooden box.

Aikman left the car and spoke with him, opening the book, pointing to the patch, and then gesturing toward the building where Billy Gibbs had been killed. Suddenly, Aikman spun around. "Jesus!" he cursed, then shouted, "Pete!" Gregory got out of the car. "The dumpster's gone," Aikman said.

"What do you need . . . ?" Gregory called.

"Pull the car up to the wall," Aikman cut him off.

"What?"

Aikman ran past him, got into the car, slammed it into gear, and drove up onto the grass. He slowed, easing the car around the building, inches from the side wall. When the car was directly under the window at the top of the wall he stopped, turned off the engine, slid across the seat, and got out. The police artist walked to the car, and while Aikman held the pad and the box of charcoals, he climbed up on the roof and peered through the window.

"Can you do it?" Aikman shouted.

"Yeah, I think so," the man answered.

Aikman handed up the materials and leaned against the car, watching. It took six tries before the shivering artist got what Aikman wanted: the perspective, the angle, the exact drawing.

Aikman tood the pad, tore the sheet off, and rolled it carefully, holding it tightly in his hand.

Gregory and Alex sat in the back of the car. Aikman got in the front, glancing for a second at Gregory. "Okay, Peter, we're on the last lap. Take me to Staten Island."

Alex stared for a moment at her father's profile as he looked out the window to his right, and suddenly she felt very cold.

Aikman instructed the driver to pull up a hundred yards from the building. "I don't want anyone to see the car. Wait here for me. I don't know how long it'll take, Pete." He glanced quickly at Alex huddled in the back seat, but she avoided his eyes and looked down at her gloved hands.

Gregory nodded, and Aikman left the car. He walked,

oblivious to the cold. He had to do it quickly, before he thought about it too much. There was no other way. He had the piece that would name the killers, but he had to be sure, and there was only one person who could give him that assurance. Someone has to pay the price, Aikman thought, as he passed through the doors of the Children's Rehabilitation Center.

"Dr. Hughes isn't in yet," the nurse at the reception desk said. "It's only eight-thirty. He never gets in before nine."

"Who's in charge?" Aikman asked.

"Dr. Miller."

"I'd like to see him."

She picked up a phone and dialed two digits. A minute later a young man in corduroy slacks and a turtleneck sweater came down the corridor. He shook hands with Aikman, and they sat down on one of the wooden benches along the wall.

"I've been consulting with the police on the Billy Gibbs case," Aikman began.

"Oh, yes," Miller said. "Raymond Brennan. Dr. Hutton has been making remarkable progress with him."

Aikman smiled. "Leslie suggested that I meet Raymond. I hope to be able to ask him some questions sometime in the future, and Leslie thought it would be best if I saw Raymond, talked to him, developed a rapport with him before trying to find out what he saw that day in the park."

"Get him used to you," Miller said, nodding.

"Exactly," Aikman agreed. "Leslie also thought that it would be good for Raymond to have some contact with a person from outside the hospital."

"Do you want to see Raymond today? Now?"

"I know it's a bit early, Doctor, but with the work I'm doing, the mornings are the only time I'm free. I thought if I could come by once or twice a week, at about this time, establish a pattern . . ."

"Fine," Miller said. "We can bring Raymond to the

playroom if you'd like. I think he'd be most comfortable there."

"That's the most important thing," Aikman said. "My visits shouldn't be anything unusual to him. Leslie suggested that a nurse be present, someone Raymond knows."

Miller went to the receptionist's desk and made a call. "I think we should make it a short visit the first time," Miller suggested, walking with Aikman through the maze of corridors. Aikman nodded. They passed through the double doors of a large, brightly painted room. Shelves lined an entire wall, and an array of toys was piled on each shelf. Small, round tables and wooden chairs were placed at the corners of the room, with the center area open. A few toys lay on the tile floor.

Raymond Brennan sat at one of the tables, a nurse at his side. The boy's eyes followed the up-and-down motion of tiny horses on a carousel on the table in front of him.

"Raymond," Dr. Miller said, "there's someone here to see you." Raymond looked at Dr. Miller and then at Aikman. "This man is a friend of Dr. Leslie's. Would you like to say 'Hello'?"

Aikman took off his overcoat and smiled at the boy. He held the coat over his left arm and moved forward slowly. "Hello, Raymond," he said softly.

The carousel slowed, and Raymond looked at the nurse. She turned the wind-up key, and the horses began to circle again. Aikman knelt by Raymond's side. "That's very pretty," he said, watching the carousel. "Did Dr. Leslie give it to you?"

"Dr. Leslie," Raymond said, nodding his head.

Aikman reached out and rewound the carousel. He stood up slowly, keeping his eyes on the toy and working his right hand into the folds of his coat. "I've never seen such colorful horses," he said.

As the carousel slowed, Raymond looked up at the tall man. "I'll make it go again," Aikman said.

In one smooth motion he pulled the sketch from the coat pocket and unrolled it before Raymond's eyes. A tall soldier in a tan uniform stood out starkly against the white paper. Soft pencil lines outlined the sinks and tile walls of the men's room. Raymond's eyes stared, frozen for a fraction of a second until they saw the bright colors on the sleeve of the soldier's jacket: Drawn deliberately oversized, the patch of the Screaming Eagles Squadron seemed to leap off the paper, the burning eyes and clutching claws of the garish eagle reaching for the boy . . .

Raymond's scream shredded the air. He threw his arms out, knocking the carousel to the floor, and scrambled to the nurse, clutching at her uniform. Aikman stepped away and turned toward the door and Dr. Miller.

The doctor's face was flushed in rage as he tore the sketch from Aikman's hand, looked at it, and hurled it away. "Get out, goddamn you, get out of here!" he screamed over the shrieks of the child.

Aikman walked quickly out of the room. Raymond's cries echoed in the hall and followed him as he left the building.

Gregory stood by the car as Aikman approached. He held the door, and Aikman slipped into the back seat next to Alex. "Did you get what you wanted?" Gregory asked as the car pulled away.

Aikman didn't answer. Alex put her hand gently on his arm.

"I got what I needed," Aikman said bitterly.

Exhausted, drained, he telephoned Fletcher from his apartment. "I've got a unit," Aikman said when the general picked up the receiver.

"Which one?" Fletcher asked.

"The Screaming Eagles. The pistol was in the Screaming Eagles Squadron."

"Now I've got something to work with," Fletcher said gratefully. "How'd you get it?"

"I got it. That's all that matters," Aikman said, his jaw set. "Now get me some names."

Aikman, Gregory, and Enders met the messenger from Washington two days later as he stepped from the plane at Kennedy Airport on the morning of the sixteenth. He carried a thin briefcase, which he handed to Aikman.

In Enders' car, Aikman opened the case. The lime-green computer printout sheets lay neatly inside. There were twenty-seven names.

They drove to Gracie Mansion and called the mayor out of a meeting with his budget director.

"We need your help," Aikman said, laying the sheets out on the table in the mayor's office. Aikman ran down what they had, concluding with, "The pistol expert is on this list."

"What do you need?" Donahus asked.

"Men," Enders said. "Special teams from all the boroughs, if need be. The men on this list have to be covered, twenty-four hours a day, until we find the one we're looking for. Then we cover him and everybody he meets, sees, or talks to for as long as it takes. It's more than Special Services can handle. We need a couple of hundred men."

Donahue pressed an intercom key. "Liz, get me Forman. I want him up here immediately."

As it started to move, Aikman had little to do. Reports came to him every hour. Policemen from all over the city made up the teams, with volunteers as backup. The men on stakeout and surveillance were told not to talk to anyone about what they were doing, not even their families. Gregory told Aikman that Parker was working twenty hours a day.

Twenty-seven names were chalked on Aikman's blackboard, the twenty-seven pulled from the files of ex-members of the Screaming Eagles, men who lived in or around New York City, men who qualified as expert with a .45. There would be no elimination: Every man on the list would be followed until the police isolated one.

Aikman was in his study on the second day of the surveillance when he heard the doorbell.

"I want to talk to you," Leslie said, brushing past him.

Aikman closed the door, followed her into the living room, and sat in the armchair next to the fireplace. "Sit down," he said.

Leslie shook her head. "You've been expecting me, of course," she said coldly. "The great detective would have figured out that I'd be coming to see him."

"Criminologist," Aikman corrected softly.

"What?"

"Criminologist, not detective. There's a difference."

"Oh, excuse me," Leslie said, her eyes narrowing in anger. "I should have known. Detectives don't terrorize children. That's the criminologist's job."

"Leslie," Aikman said, standing up, "I deal in theories, ideas . . . that's how I try to work out the cases I'm involved in. Sometimes it's not enough, and you have to do what your instincts tell you." He wanted her to understand. He cared for her, and he'd used her, used her name and the information she'd given him to lie to Miller, to get to Raymond. "It was necessary . . ."

"*You* decided that," she glared. "You elected yourself to make the decisions. Who the hell do you think you are?"

"I have the responsibility in this case."

"You have more than that," she said, taking a step closer to him. "Why don't you admit it to yourself? You've got your *interests* in the case. You've got to triumph, don't you? You have to come up with all the answers, all the brilliance. If there was another way of getting what you needed, a way that was out of your hands, you wouldn't take it, you wouldn't even suggest it. The answer has got to come from you, no matter how brutal or destructive the means."

"There was no other way," Aikman said. "It had to be done."

"I don't believe you," she said. "You get the answer, you solve the problems, no matter what you have to do. You're as ruthless as the men you're hunting. I think you'd do anything to win . . . use anybody, play any dirty game, manipulate any emotion." She backed away from him. "What you did was obscene. Who gave you the right to play God with other people's lives?"

The slam of the door was a rifle shot in the room.

Police surveillance on the scale called for by the case amounted to a small war: more than three hundred men, countless vehicles, tons of equipment. Each of the twenty-seven men had four police officers on him, around the clock. The men were photographed from cars, trucks, windows, and alleys, and everything was written down: whom they saw, where they ate, what work they did. Computer printouts from the FBI, the Army, and police departments around the country poured into New York. As the mountain of paper grew, the names became personalities, and everything funneled through to the deputy chiefs and Aikman.

Graham Parker, in a business suit and overcoat, worked the south side of Fiftieth Street on the third night of the surveillance. With his partner, who covered the north side of the street, they followed a tall, gray-haired man to a restaurant, and watched as another man approached and spoke with the first. Parker stopped a half block away, lit a cigarette, and shot glances toward the two. He stiffened as two other men came around the corner, joined the first two, and went into the restaurant. Parker walked past the restaurant and looked in through the window. A short, dark man in a tuxedo greeted the four and led them through the main dining room to a corner table.

Parker went to a pay phone a block away and called Enders. "I think I've got a live one," he said.

"Where are you?" Enders asked.

"Fiftieth Street, off Third Avenue. One of our boys just met three others at Lutece."

Fifteen minutes later an Econoline van drove up and parked across the street from the restaurant. Parker and his partner watched the front of Lutece from a doorway diagonally across the street.

Almost two hours later, the four men came out, and from the inside of the van they were followed and framed in 400-millimeter lenses. Infrared and high-speed film captured over fifty photographs. As the four split up at the next corner, each had a team of detectives behind him.

Aikman was at the police lab when the pictures were printed.

Harmon heard the insistent jangling of the phone as he stepped from the shower. He wrapped a towel around his body and raced to the living room. "Yeah," he said, "Harmon . . ."

"I need your help," Aikman said.

Harmon found a piece of paper and a pencil on the cluttered desk. "Shoot."

"Find out everything you can on a man named Andrew Birmingham. Newspaper clippings, *Social Register* . . . anything you can get your hands on. But keep it quiet; do it all yourself and don't talk to anyone."

"When do you need it?"

"Yesterday," Aikman said.

Harmon glanced at his watch. Eight-twenty. "I'll be at your house tonight." He hung up, threw on some clothes, and took a cab to the New York *Times* building.

Aikman sat at the dining room table, pages from the beginning file on Andrew Birmingham spread out around him.

The New York Police Department had no arrest record on the man. A parking ticket going back seven years was the only entry in their files. Birmingham had been followed to the offices of Allied Insurance on the first day of the surveillance. It was a medium-sized company, with branches up and down the East Coast. Birmingham's name was on the directory in the building on Fifty-fourth Street under the title "Vice President." Records from the Department of Motor Vehicles showed he had a driver's license, but had not had a car registered in his name for over ten years. The parking ticket had been issued on a rental in the upstate resort town of Saratoga.

"Not very much," Aikman said to Enders, who sat next to Alex at the table.

"Not yet," Enders said. "We'll have the FBI report tomorrow morning."

"We'll have Harmon's report tonight," Aikman smiled.

Alex leaned her elbows on the chair's armrests. "You can have my report right now," she said, frowning. "You've got a problem."

"What?" Enders asked.

"Suppose these guys are the ones we want, and suppose they move on another victim. You get the one trying to make the hit, but we lose the others."

"Because there's no evidence against them," Enders said.

"Right," Alex nodded. "You've got one guy on attempted murder, but without the weapons, without proof of the game, there's nothing to connect the other three."

"If one of them goes out to kill, we stop him," Enders said flatly. "We have to."

"We need time," Aikman sighed thoughtfully. "Time to make the other three, to find out where they're playing."

"We've got to put a man in the restaurant," Enders said. "Parker told me that the *maître d'* greeted those four like old friends, regulars. If they have dinner there again, we'll get their fingerprints, and Washington can give us the names and service records."

"I don't like it," Alex said, shaking her head. "If they get suspicious, we can lose them."

"We have no choice," Enders insisted. "We need someone in there to pick up their glasses, plates, forks . . . anything we can lift prints from."

"Then you'd better pick a good man, Carl," Alex warned.

"That's the easy part," Enders said. "We need an opening, a job that our man can fill. We're working on it now . . . getting a list of the restaurant employees from the IRS. We'll have to approach one of them, get him to cooperate—a waiter, a busboy."

"I think it stinks," Alex said. "What if this guy talks to someone?"

"No way," Enders said. "Once he agrees to help, we move him out of the city and babysit him."

The doorbell rang and Aikman went to answer it, coming back seconds later with Harmon. Aikman introduced the reporter to Alex and Enders and said, "What've you got?" as they all sat down.

Harmon flipped open his notebook. "I've got a pillar of society here. Vice President of Allied Insurance; with the firm for over twenty years. Big man in the charity sweepstakes; supports the Yale University Alumni Association and the Business School. Ex-Army major. Belongs to several associations, all connected with the insurance business. Member of a club here in the city: Clarkson Manor."

"What's that?" Enders asked.

"I did some fast checking," Harmon answered, turning to another page. "Ultraexclusive—got to have heavy credentials to get in. A gentlemen's club—a place for the rich and the powerful to unwind. Gym, sauna, library, bar, the works—got about sixty members." Harmon paused and reviewed more pages. "I checked up on the owner of the club: Lewis W-for-Wordsworth Clarkson, eighty-year-old son of the founder. A real character," Harmon grinned. "Every member has to be personally recommended to him, and he's very picky."

"Blacks need not apply," Enders mumbled.

"Oh no," Harmon said. "Clarkson's not a bigot; he may be a snob, though. You've got to have the money and the position and the manner of a gentleman to get in. His father founded the club in the 1860s, when he emigrated from England and brought his fortune with him. A 'touch of the old country' type of thing. The old man was tight with the Vanderbilts, the Morgans, and the Carnegies . . . and Lewis W. has been seen in the company of the Rockefellers and the Fords. Summers in Newport . . . has his own estate up there. Keeps a pretty low profile. The only time he made the papers was during Prohibition, when he issued a statement to the press, quote: 'I believe as the Prince of Wales does that a man has a right to drink if he wants to.' End quote." Harmon smiled, closing the notebook.

"We've got to know if the three men who had dinner with Birmingham are members," Aikman said.

"One more thing," Harmon interrupted. "The best for last: Clarkson Manor has for its members twenty private meeting rooms on the second floor."

"Bingo," Aikman said softly.

"We're depending on you," Enders said to Patrolman Luís Ortega.

Ortega smiled. "No problem."

Enders squirmed, wondering if the young man was too confident, too cocky. But Ortega had an excellent record on the force, and his file revealed that he had been a busboy before taking the police exam.

It had taken Enders a day to find the man they needed in Lutece. The IRS gave them a list of employees, and from it Enders picked Manuel Hernandez, twenty-two, single, a busboy at the restaurant for eight months. Enders talked to Hernandez for a half hour at the man's apartment, giving few details but stressing the importance of the case. "We want one of our men to take over your job for a week or so, that's all. The city will pay you your salary, and we'll see to it that the owners of the restaurant understand the situation once the investigation is concluded. We guarantee you will get your job back."

"This is a big case, huh?" Hernandez asked.

"Yes, and you'll know all the details as soon as it's over."

"All right, man. Why not?"

Enders breathed a sigh of relief. "And one more thing: When you call up to quit, you're to recommend a friend of yours for the job. Tell them you have family problems and have to leave town for a week or so, and your friend, Luís Ortega, will be happy to fill in for you. You tell them Ortega has experience and references."

"Sure, sure, I'll do it."

"Fine," Enders said, picking up the phone and handing it to Hernandez. The young man made the call. As he hung up, Enders opened the door, and three plainclothes detectives came in. "You're going on vacation," Enders said.

"Hey, wait a minute," Hernandez protested.

"This is a very important case," Enders stressed. "You wouldn't want to blow it."

The detectives hustled Hernandez out of his apartment and into an unmarked sedan. He would be a guest of the city in a motel upstate. He would not be permitted to talk to anyone or make any phone calls, but Enders knew that otherwise he would be treated royally.

Jean Léon, the *maître d'* at Lutece, seated the four men immediately on the night of January 22. Luís Ortega had been on the job only one day.

Jean Léon chatted with Marcus as the men sat down. His favorite customer, Marcus had long ago passed the test with his idiomatic French, impressing the *maître d'* with his correct phrasing and inflection. It was a pleasure to speak with one so cultured, Jean Léon often thought.

Ortega filled the water glasses as Jean Léon suggested the evening's menu, gesturing expansively as he described the delicacies. His arm brushed Ortega's hand, and the bus-boy spilled a few drops of water on the tablecloth. Jean Léon apologized, glaring at Ortega, but Lyle laughed and, in perfect Spanish, told Ortega that Jean Léon should look at himself if he wished to place the blame. Ortega smiled at the big man and said a few words in Spanish.

"What did you say to him?" Marcus asked Lyle when the *maître d'* left and Ortega moved to another table.

"I told him that Jean Léon was clumsy," Lyle said.

"What did he say?" Marcus asked.

Lyle grinned. "He put a curse on the restaurant. He said the Spanish would own it one day."

Reynolds burst out laughing. Marcus relaxed in his chair, congratulating himself for insisting that they skip last week's meeting at the club. The tension had slipped away during that dinner and now, a week later, they were behaving like the old friends they were.

Jean Léon brought a round of drinks and apologized

THE RANDOM FACTOR

again for the clumsiness of the busboy. "A new man," he said, shrugging. "What can one do?"

Marcus spoke to him in French, assuring him that they were not annoyed. "Your suggestions are good," Marcus said, then ordered the meal. *"Nous voudrions, pour commencer, consommé de volaille, ensuite des quenelles de brouchet, et puis des tournedos à la Rossini, salade d'endives, un plateau des fromages, et comme dessert, des gateaux assortis."*

Jean Léon smiled. *"Très bien, monsieur, comme d'habitude,"* he said and walked toward the kitchen.

"I feel left out," Reynolds said, looking at Marcus and Lyle across the table from him. "Maybe I should speak some Japanese."

"Next time we go to a Japanese restaurant," Birmingham said, "you do the ordering."

"What can you say in Japanese?" Lyle asked Reynolds.

"Surrender, you yellow dog," Reynolds deadpanned.

"That's sure to bring good service," Marcus smiled.

"It'll bring a karate chop to the throat," Birmingham grinned.

"If you're serious about a Japanese restaurant," Marcus said, "I'll bring Helen. She's nuts about oriental food."

"And she'll bring one of her eligible singles," Reynolds groaned. "She never stops trying to make matches."

"It's all in a good cause, Chris," Marcus said. "You need a woman in your life."

"Yeah, sure, that's just what he needs," Lyle growled.

"The alimony kid," Birmingham said. "Don't tell me you're beginning to sour on the institution of marriage."

"I think you should all leave the poor bastard alone," Lyle said. "Let him suffer . . . coming and going as he pleases, not having to account to anyone, fancy free."

"Listen to the voice of experience," Reynolds joked. "He's been there."

"Twice," Lyle said. "And if I can stay away from Helen," he looked at Marcus, "I won't make that mistake again."

Birmingham looked at Marcus. "Helen trying to match him up too?"

"Yeah," Marcus smiled. "Chris and Dick are personal crusades. She thinks it's sad that they're not married."

"Excruciating sadness," Lyle mocked, his eyes downcast.

"Are you talking about your alimony payments?" Reynolds said.

"You really know how to hurt a guy," Lyle said, shaking his head.

A silent waiter brought the first course, and Reynolds congratulated Marcus on getting the order straight. "You should speak English as well as I speak French," Marcus said.

Ortega appeared and took the soup bowls away and refilled the water glasses. Lyle smiled at him, and the young man returned the grin. An hour later, when they left the restaurant, Ortega carefully picked up the water glasses, forks, and knives and brought them to the back door of the kitchen. A detective waited outside with plastic bags.

Ortega closed the door, wiped the sweat from his forehead, and smiled.

After a few minutes, Reynolds noticed that Birmingham's mind wasn't on the game. "Your position's not that bad," he said.

"It's not that . . ." Birmingham said.

"Didn't sell any policies today?" Marcus asked.

"Something like that," Birmingham answered, his thoughts miles away.

"Okay, what is it?" Reynolds asked.

"We found out today that somebody in the company has been using the computer to write dummy policies— creating people, making it all up—then putting in claims and collecting the payments. It's complicated, but it's not too uncommon. A lot of companies have been hit pretty hard."

"Are you in any trouble?" Marcus asked.

"No, not me personally, but it's bad publicity for the company, and it can take weeks to unravel. The auditors started working this afternoon, going over everything."

"Claim executive privilege," Lyle suggested.

"Retire to San Clemente," Birmingham added.

"Stonewall it and burn the tapes," Reynolds smiled. "Let 'em twist in the wind."

"Okay, okay, give me a break, will you?" Birmingham pleaded.

"That serious?" Reynolds asked, the smile gone from his lips.

"Yeah, I'm afraid so. We'll work it out."

"Okay," Reynolds said, standing. "Let's pack it in for tonight. Your mind's not on it."

"Yeah," Birmingham agreed. "Thanks."

"No problem," Reynolds said. "C'mon, let's get a drink."

They cleared the table, putting everything away in the locked cabinet and went downstairs to the bar.

"You work the problem out, Birm," Reynolds said. "We'll wait until you're ready."

The records came in from Washington at six in the morning on the following Saturday, and by eight Aikman, Alex, and the deputy chiefs were in Enders' office. Aikman had called Harmon, and the young reporter was one of the first to arrive.

"He knows the whole story," Aikman said to Enders before the deputy chief could object to Harmon's presence. "Besides, he's already helped us, and I promised him that he'd be in on the whole thing."

"All right," Enders muttered, moving around his desk

and handing out photographs to everyone in the room. The eight-by-ten glossies pictured Andrew Birmingham and the three men he met for dinner. The blow-ups were grainy, and one or two a bit out of focus, but the features of the men were clear, and Aikman was convinced he was looking at the killers.

On Enders' desk were four files. "Photo number one," he said, opening the first folder and reading sections from the Army report. "Birmingham, Andrew Grayson, major, United States Army, retired. Attended Yale University, went to Officer Candidate School, attained the rank of captain during World War II . . . with the 101st at Bastogne; in the Battle of the Bulge; made the D-Day drop; made major at war's end. Co-ordinated Allied troop movements for the General Staff in Korea. A member of every pistol club in the Army since OCS, and was one of the best marksmen they had . . . set competition records, a few of which stand today." He closed the folder and picked up a yellow sheet of paper. "Our investigation so far," he said, reading the notes, "Vice President of Allied Insurance, married, two children in college."

Enders paused, put down the sheet, and opened the second file. "Photo number two: Marcus, Edmund Daniel, major, United States Army, retired. New York University . . . enlisted in the Army, assigned to 8th Airborne during World War II. Shot down over France, worked with the French Underground for the rest of the war. Awarded French Legion of Honor. His specialty in the underground was infiltration and assassination. His weapon was the garotte, and the French claim he took out over thirty high-level Nazis in a three-year period. By the time Korea came along, he was a major co-ordinating Allied Command air strikes." Again Enders read from the yellow sheet. "Married, two children in college, owner and President of Image Electronics. They make transistors and components."

He opened the third folder. "Lyle, Richard Handly, lieutenant, British Commandos, retired."

"What? British?" Harmon said.

Enders disregarded the interruption and went on. "At age sixteen joined the anti-Fascist forces after the outbreak of the Spanish Civil War. The background here is sketchy, but we know that during his time in Spain he specialized in taking out sentries for assault teams. Expert with any type of knife. When World War II broke out, he left Spain and joined the British Army, drawing a Commando unit. Reached the rank of corporal by the end of the war. He'd quit school in the States to go to Spain, and after the war he took an equivalency exam in Britain, passed, and was accepted at Oxford . . . courtesy of some gentle pressure from ranking officers in the British Army. Attended Officer Training School over there, made lieutenant. Attached to Allied Command sector in Korea, representing the British Army." Enders glanced at the sheet of paper on the desk and continued: "Vice President of Manhattan Mutual Savings and Loan . . . divorced . . . twice, we think . . . no children."

Enders lit a cigarette. "And finally, number four: Reynolds, Christopher Brian." He opened the file. "Master sergeant, United States Army, retired. With parental permission he joined at sixteen, was at Bataan and the fall of Corregidor. His unit hid on the island until MacArthur returned two years later. According to the reports of surviving members of the unit, Reynolds was a specialist at guerrilla and terrorist tactics. He supposedly saved the unit several times by circling and picking off the enemy, one by one, with his rifle. Master sergeant at the end of the war. Left the Army and went to Princeton on a scholarship; graduated *summa cum laude* in economics. Went back to the service after graduation . . . was offered officer's rank because of his education but refused it. In Korea, he was attached to Army Security Services as head of the

Courtier Division. Did not attend sniper school . . . there's a note here from Fletcher that says he was better than the instructors. He wasn't on file as a sniper and wasn't used in Korea in that capacity. Fletcher says there was no way of tracing him through sniper school." From the yellow sheet, Enders read, "Widower, no children. President of Marketing Consultants, a stock brokerage firm." Enders closed the file.

"And they're all members of Clarkson?" Lawrence asked him.

"Birmingham's the only one we're sure of, but after dinner on Thursday, they all went to the club. They were inside for a little over a half hour."

"It's a safe assumption," Ellison said.

"How old are they?" Harmon asked.

From the back of the yellow sheet, Enders read, "Reynolds is forty-eight, Marcus fifty one, Birmingham fifty-three, and Lyle fifty-five."

"What unit were they in?" Aikman asked.

"The Screaming Eagles," Enders said.

"All of them?" Alex asked. Enders nodded.

"I'm surprised it took them this long," Aikman said.

"What's that supposed to mean?" Enders asked sharply.

Aikman stretched out his legs. "Think about their personalities. They're intelligent, driven men. They've deliberately sought danger, met every challenge. Their achievements are remarkable. They meet in Korea, become friends, and they all wind up in New York, still friends, still feeding off each other." He shook his head in wonder. "But the wars are over, the real dangers are passed. Now they're at the top of their professions, they have nowhere else to go. Four elements: each one individually harmless, but put them together and let them stew for a while, and you're going to have an explosion."

"Like a chemical reaction," Gregory said.

"Exactly," Aikman agreed. "It was only a matter of time

before it all came together. Their social and business lives have to be incredibly boring if you think about what they went through in wartime. All they have is each other and their past accomplishments."

"So they bring back the good old days," Harmon said.

"I can't believe it," Lawrence snorted. "They've killed over fifty people."

"Other people's lives mean nothing to them," Aikman said. "They're only concerned with their own lives. They need the excitement, the challenge. And they think they're good enough, clever enough to get away with it."

"Well, they're not," Enders said, biting off the words. "Where do we stand?" he asked Alex.

"We need proof," Alex replied. "All you've got now are theories. We have to find the game and the weapons."

"The game's got to be at the club," Gregory said.

"Sure," Alex nodded. "But we don't have the probable cause needed for a search warrant."

"Plant a man at the club," Holtzman suggested.

"Forget it," Enders said flatly. "They've got to get suspicious if they see anything out of the ordinary. That club is their domain; they'll spot a newcomer in a second."

"Do you think the weapons are at the club?" Ellison asked Enders.

"Maybe . . . but that's not the problem. We've got all of them covered, twenty-four hours a day. If one of them makes a move, we'll have him. But it's not enough. Without the game, without all the weapons, we're going to lose three of them."

"I don't understand," Harmon said. "What do you need to pick these guys up?"

"A lot," Alex said. "The game itself, a map of the city, if they're using one, the weapons . . . and we have to catch one of them in the act. We book him for attempted homicide and get the others for conspiracy. Then, if we get the rifle or the .45, through Ballistics we can prove homicide—

any one of the gunshot victims—and we nail the others on conspiracy for that homicide."

"So get a search warrant and go into the club," Harmon said.

"A search warrant isn't a fishing license," Alex said impatiently. "I can't go to a judge and say we *think* the evidence is there: We've got to have proof."

"How about going right to Clarkson himself?" Gregory asked.

Alex smiled. "That's what I was thinking." She turned to Enders. "He owns the club, it's his property. If he gives us permission to look around, we don't need a warrant. And if we find anything, it's admissible evidence."

"All right," Enders said, "We'll talk to Clarkson."

"Let me call him," Aikman said. "It's going to be hard convincing him that four members of his club are mass murderers. I'll make the approach and set up a meeting."

Aikman alternated the calls throughout the afternoon: Clarkson's home, Leslie's office, back and forth. Clarkson's butler repeated the same message: "Mr. Clarkson will not be in before eight tonight," but Aikman's impatience kept him at the phone, checking and rechecking. Leslie was "unable to come to the phone," a secretary at Maplewood told him. Sooner or later he'd get through to her, he knew.

At eight-thirty Mr. Lewis Wordsworth Clarkson himself telephoned Aikman, and ten minutes later Aikman, Alex, and Enders were on their way to the man's home.

Like a Gainsborough portrait of royalty, Aikman thought as they were ushered into Clarkson's living room and the criminologist saw the eighty-year-old man sitting stiffly in a carved mahogany chair by a huge stone fireplace.

Alex and Carl Enders perched at the edge of their chairs while Aikman, unable to sit still, paced back and forth before the fireplace, telling the story.

"Impossible," the old man said, tapping an arthritic forefinger on the arm of the chair when Aikman finished. Wrapped in a smoking jacket, Clarkson had not moved during Aikman's recitation, his clear blue eyes fixed on Aikman's face. Senile, Enders thought hopelessly, as he watched the impassive face. But when Clarkson finally spoke, it was obvious that his mind was as sharp as the piercing eyes.

"I don't believe a word of it," he said. "I've known these men for over fifteen years, and they are not capable of such behavior."

"Under the right circumstances," Aikman said softly, "men are capable of the most extraordinary behavior; for example, who would believe that Lewis Wordsworth Clarkson would ever defy the law?"

A small smile creased the old man's features. "Prohibition was an abomination to men's rights."

"And women's," Alex muttered.

"Yes, and women's," Clarkson added. Alex jerked her head up in surprise. "My hearing is quite acute," Clarkson scolded. "But you haven't convinced me; I think you have reached the wrong conclusions in your search for a solution."

"No, sir," Aikman said, "we haven't. But if you're not convinced, will you at least give us the opportunity to prove that we're right?"

"I don't see why I should indulge your suspicions by violating the privacy of the members of my club."

"The city needs your help," Enders said. "Would you indulge us if the administration itself asked for your cooperation?"

Clarkson thought for a moment. "I wouldn't refuse a request from the government."

"Then call this number," Enders said, holding out a slip of paper. "It's the mayor's office. He's waiting for the call."

"You anticipated my reluctance," Clarkson said.

"Yes, sir, we did. And Mayor Donahue agreed to speak with you if it was necessary."

Clarkson reached for the phone, waving Enders' outstretched hand away, and dialed Information. "Gracie Mansion, please," he said to the operator. "Yes, thank you." He pressed the disconnect button and dialed.

Alex smiled at Aikman, and a silent message passed between them: There's nothing wrong with his mind—he remembered the number the operator gave him.

"Mayor Donahue, please. This is Lewis Wordsworth Clarkson," the man said into the phone. Clarkson greeted the mayor and listened intently for a minute, finally saying, "Yes, I will. Thank you, Mr. Mayor." He put the phone down.

"All right," he said. "I will take you to the club myself."

At Enders' urging, Clarkson agreed to wait until midnight, when they could be certain that the club was empty. Clarkson called the night watchman precisely at twelve and confirmed that all the members were gone for the evening.

They drove to the building in Clarkson's limousine. Enders said to Clarkson, "We're especially interested in the meeting rooms."

"Yes, young man," Clarkson interrupted, "I know."

Enders followed Clarkson into the building and called his office on the bar phone to make sure the four men were accounted for.

"They're home," Enders said, hanging up.

They followed Clarkson up the steps as the old man set a brisk pace despite his arthritis. He led them to a door, pulled a key from his pocket, and unlocked it. "This is their room," he said, flipping on the Tiffany lamp in the center of the room.

"Each cabinet," Clarkson said, pointing to the far wall, "contains members' personal possessions. If I remember correctly, they share this one." He walked to one of the cabinets and from his coat pocket took a huge key ring. He unlocked the first cabinet and stepped aside. Aikman and Enders knelt down and looked in. Several bottles of liquor, a rack of poker chips, and wrapped decks of cards filled the cabinet. "I don't think this is it," Enders said.

Clarkson shook his head. "I was sure . . . oh well, we'll try the next." The second compartment yielded a bottle of Vat 69 and a leather backgammon set. Clarkson mumbled and opened the third cabinet.

"Got it," Aikman exclaimed as he saw the cardboard box. On top of the box was a black notebook and a folded packet. Next to the game they saw cards, two bottles, and poker chips. Alex took a Polaroid SX-70 camera from her purse, snapped on a flash bar, and took three quick shots of the interior of the cabinet.

Aikman lifted the box and carried it to the table. The packet was a folded Hagstrom map of Manhattan, and Aikman spread it out. "Jesus Christ," he swore. "Look at this: They've taken the postal zones and divided the areas. Each section is numbered: sixty-eight sections." He opened the box and took out the game board. Each rectangle was numbered, one to sixty-eight.

"Noah," Enders said softly.

"Yeah?" Aikman said, staring at the map.

"I don't think I believed it until now," Enders said.

"Yeah," Aikman said.

Alex was turning the pages of the notebook. "You won't believe this, Carl. They've notated the game . . . their initials, the colors, the exact rolls, the spaces moved, the hits."

"There's a list of the victims," Enders said, peering over

her shoulder. Clarkson slumped into one of the chairs around the table. Alex shot picture after picture: the board, the map, the notebook.

"Mr. Clarkson, is there any place in the building that they might hide the weapons?" Enders asked. "Anything at all?"

Clarkson shook his head. "There are lockers in the gym, but the members bring their own locks and use the lockers only for the time they're in the gym. Nothing remains locked for any long period of time."

"We need the weapons, Carl," Alex said. "When one of them makes a move, we'll have enough to indict them all. We've got conspiracy, but without the weapons, it's a tough case."

"We'll get them," Enders promised.

Aikman started to put the items back in the cabinet, using the photographs Alex had taken before they emptied the compartment as a guide. He checked the positioning against the photos several times.

"We'll need a statement," Enders said gently to Clarkson, "verifying what you saw tonight. I'll have a stenographer at your house in the morning."

"All right," Clarkson agreed.

"And then," Enders added, "I'd like you to take a vacation, leave the city."

"Young man . . . " Clarkson began.

"Sir," Enders said firmly, "if you remain in the city, would you come to the club?"

"Yes, I drop in often, I . . . "

"And you might see one or more of these men, and without meaning to, you might give it away. You'll look at them differently, the tone of your voice will be different now that you know what they've done. They'll know something is wrong."

"I understand," Clarkson said. "I think warmer weather will help my arthritis, don't you?" Enders nodded.

Clarkson locked the cabinet, then the door as they left the room. He paused at the front door and said to Enders, "I'm ashamed of what they've done, ashamed that they played this game under my roof." He looked around at the huge entranceway. "Maybe it's time to close it up, to get out. Perhaps the club has outlived its usefulness . . . perhaps I have, too."

"Then who'll be left to defy the unjust laws?" Alex asked.

Clarkson smiled. "A younger man," he said, and led them out to the limousine.

The surveillance doubled.

As the week dragged on, Enders' office became a war room. A duplicate map was made, using the photographs taken at Clarkson Manor. Copy prints, negatives, and blow-ups of the game board, the notebook, and the map covered the walls.

Officers on stakeout called in every half hour, fresh teams were dispatched every four hours, cars and trucks were interchanged regularly so that no one vehicle was covering any of the men for longer than two hours. At Enders' suggestion, the police commissioner commandeered three cabs from one of the city's largest taxi fleets. Off-duty and volunteer patrolmen drove the cabs night and day past the apartments and offices of the four men.

On the following Thursday night, Lutece Restaurant and Clarkson Manor were ringed by police.

Reynolds checked his coat and joined the others at the table. Jean Léon brought a drink, greeted Reynolds, and left the ornate menus on the table. Birmingham was telling Lyle about the insurance-policy fraud, and it was obvious that he was still upset. Marcus signaled to Jean Léon and once again ordered the meal in French.

"Did you get to use your Spanish tonight?" Reynolds asked Lyle when Jean Léon left.

"No, there was a different boy tonight."

"Japanese, by any chance?" Reynolds smiled.

"No such luck," Marcus said. Reynolds grinned, but in the back of his mind a small doubt began to gnaw.

He ate silently, flicking his eyes over the room. After the main course, he said, "Be right back," and made his way to the men's room. On the way out, he stopped by Jean Léon's station at the entrance to the dining room. "My friend is disappointed that he didn't get a chance to show off his Spanish tonight," he said to the *maître d'*.

"Ah," Jean Léon said, frowning, "the busboy . . . he quit. Unreliable, all of them." He shook his head. "He was filling in for a friend . . . then, last Friday, or Saturday, I think, he calls in and quits."

"Did he say why?" Reynolds asked.

"They never say anything," Jean Léon snorted. "It's just as well. Totally incompetent. He didn't belong here."

Reynolds nodded and walked slowly back to the table. He didn't belong here . . . didn't belong . . .

"Wait till you see the dessert," Marcus said to him as he sat down.

"What?" Reynolds said, distracted.

"The dessert," Marcus repeated. "Wouldn't you like to know the delicacy I chose?"

"I trust you," Reynolds said. "Anything you say is fine with me."

As they walked to the club, Reynolds spotted the utility truck. No reason for it to be here at this hour, he thought.

All right, he said to himself: The busboy was a plant, undoubtedly a cop. Somehow, some way, the police were on to them. It didn't matter how they knew. . . . It was time to get out.

He played mechanicallly, blocking Lyle, moving one man slowly toward his home, far enough away from the others to stay out of reach. On a five-two roll he broke the block, moving a man to a safety. Lyle was forced to move ahead, and on Birmingham's roll, Lyle's man was hit.

"I'll take it," Birmingham said. "That's yellow, sector 21." Reynolds made the notation as Birmingham checked the map. "Shouldn't be too difficult," he said. "Riverside Drive area . . ."

Reynolds looked up at the map. Birmingham would be caught when he tried it, Reynolds thought. But I'll get away.

He walked slowly, aware of figures moving on the opposite sidewalk; a man getting into a taxi a block ahead of him; a dark sedan passing on the street. He turned onto Sixty-seventh Street and went into a bar, took a Johnny Walker Black to a rear table, and sat down. A minute later a man walked in, took a seat near the door, and ordered a beer.

It had to be Birmingham's uniform . . . that stupid, egotistical . . . all right, Reynolds thought, forget it . . . it doesn't matter how they found out. They wouldn't get him. He would have to duck the surveillance teams, that was the only problem. After that, everything was set up . . . identity, cash, a car . . . they'd never find him.

Suddenly an anger seized him, and his hand gripped the glass with tremendous force. Birmingham would pay for his mistake, and if the others didn't have escape plans, didn't notice the police tailing them, they'd pay for their stupidity. But the police win. Aikman wins.

No, Reynolds decided, they don't win: There was one

way he could beat them all—Birmingham, Lyle, Marcus, the cops, Aikman . . .

I win, Reynolds said to himself.

The next day was a nightmare for Birmingham. Auditors and investigators crawled all over his office, and the number of dummy policies grew. They still had no idea who was behind the whole scheme.

He found some escape in thinking about his hit. Nothing in the newspapers gave him a likely target, and he wondered if he could find an oriental in Sector 21, finally dismissing the idea. He'd never live down the razzing from the others.

He left his office at five.

The Con Ed truck had been parked across the street since early morning. Men in blue helmets worked in an open manhole, and the familiar sawhorses cordoned off the small area. Inside the truck, through one-way glass, three police officers watched for Birmingham. The men working in the street kept glancing at the entrance to the building.

When Birmingham came out, a radio call went to an unmarked sedan two blocks north, and the car discharged an officer in a business suit. Swinging his briefcase in a short arc, he walked a block ahead of Birmingham, checking window reflections for his man's position. After three blocks he turned off the street, and an officer from the other side crossed over and picked up Birmingham from behind.

Tired, without an idea for his target, Birmingham stayed in all night, numbing his mind with television. The men in the car across the street from his apartment drank coffee from huge Thermos bottles. Relief teams showed up every two hours.

Aikman stared at the telephone on the corner of his desk. Tapping a pen gently on the pad of paper in front of him, he decided to try one more time, another attempt in a series of last attempts to reach Leslie.

He began to write, explaining that his phone calls had gone unanswered, all carefully intercepted by a friendly-voiced secretary at the other end. He stopped for a moment, deciding to send this letter to her apartment, without return address on the envelope. Silly, he thought, a precaution a teen-ager would take, knowing he would do it anyway.

Continuing, he did more than apologize for using a confidence to his own end, for sacrificing a child and making the small boy pay such a heavy price. For the first time in a long time he tried to explain himself to someone else—not justifying his actions, no—but explain what happens to him during an investigation, explain what he felt in confronting Raymond. He wrote how a part of him, a section of his mind, had detested the action, and how the look on the child's face would haunt him, as it was doing now.

He liked her too much to let their relationship end on such a condemning note. Perhaps, he thought—but did not write—that he might even love her.

Sealing the envelope, he knew this letter would get a response. He'd written it in that manner. Some sort of response—a phone call, a letter, a visit maybe.

It would take a long time for Leslie to forgive him—if ever—or even feel a small amount of trust in him. He would be willing to settle now for just a touch of understanding.

Aikman buttoned his coat, walked to the corner, and pushed his hopes into the mail slot.

Reynolds slipped his tail the next afternoon. Years of listening to Marcus' tales of the French Underground gave him all he needed.

The most obvious and most important factor in getting away from anyone following you, Marcus had explained, is not to let the tail know that you're aware of him. He mustn't expect you to make a move. And then came the trick. You lose yourself in a crowd—a store, a market, at a train station—and you make a quick move away, around a corner, through a shop, anything . . . but you don't go all the way. You slow down, ease up, return to the street, let your man pick you up again. His momentary feeling of panic at losing you will turn to relief, and with relief comes carelessness; then you move.

Reynolds wore a hat and a gray topcoat and carried a package when he left his office. He took a cab uptown to Macy's Department Store, and made his way through the shoppers to the exchange desk. He stood on the line for half a minute and then turned, walking quickly around the exchange booth and up the aisle toward the escalator. He passed the moving stairway, headed toward the Sporting Goods Department, and ducked down an aisle crowded with shoppers looking at skis and ski poles.

The detective lost sight of him as he passed the escalator, and by the time he got through the crowd into the aisle, Reynolds was gone. The man pushed through the people, rushed down the aisle, glancing left and right until suddenly he saw Reynolds at the end of an aisle to his right, looking at a set of skis. With a sigh of relief, the detective passed the aisle, turned up the next one to his left, and waited. He had a clear view of Reynolds.

Placing the skis back in the rack, Reynolds turned the corner quickly. Ten feet away were the elevators, and Reynolds had timed it right. He slipped in as the doors closed, took off his hat, and rode up three floors. When he got out he took off the topcoat, left it with the hat and package on a bench near the elevator doors, and took the stairs to the main floor. To the right of the entrance to the store, a subway station tunnel led to the Seventh Avenue subway and, father on, a passageway connected to Penn Station. Reynolds raced down the passage. He was in Penn Station in less than a minute, moving to the opposite end and the Eighth Avenue downtown subway.

A block away from the West Fourth Street stop was the apartment he'd taken for his escape. With a disguise and new clothes, he'd be able to make the final preparations.

Aikman raged at Enders. "How in God's name could you lose him? What the hell is the matter with you? We've worked for a year on this."

Enders waited until the outburst subsided. "He knew we were there, Noah. Somehow he knew. . . . He put a perfect move on one of our men and was gone."

"It's no great mystery," Aikman snarled. "There's only one way he could have figured it out. He spotted your boy in the restaurant. Brilliant idea, Carl. I really have to hand it to you."

"And you had a better suggestion, right?" Enders shot back. "I didn't see you objecting . . . " Enders stopped short. "Jesus, Noah, we're tearing each other apart. What good does it do?"

"What about the other three?" Aikman asked, controlling his frustration.

"Still in sight," Enders said. "We added more men."

"I don't think they'll give you any problems," Aikman said slowly. "Reynolds may have spotted the busboy, but I don't think he'd tell the others. Not him."

"It doesn't matter," Enders said. "We're covering them as if we expected them to move. They won't make it."

"They won't try," Aikman said flatly and hung up.

The next day, Birmingham left his office at two in the afternoon and went uptown for a meeting with his attorneys. At four-thirty he came out and took a cab home. The driver was a police officer.

"Everything's covered," Enders repeated patiently. "Airports, bus terminals, trains, bridges, tunnels . . . everything."

"He won't leave," Aikman argued, leaning on Enders' desk and glaring down at the deputy chief. "He'll hide out, wait . . . "

"He can wait till hell freezes over," Enders snarled. "If it takes weeks, months, years, we'll find him."

"Sure," Aikman glared back. "Disguises . . . new identity . . . there are a dozen ways."

Enders clenched his fists. He knew Aikman was right. There was no foolproof way to stop Reynolds, short of checking every car, every person leaving the city. "We're doing everything we can," he finally said.

Aikman stormed out of the office.

Three cars covered Birmingham's apartment, and when he came out at seven-thirty, a moving tail went into operation. A car followed him for three blocks, dropped off, and another picked him up. When he got into a taxi, he had unmarked sedans front and back, with relief teams in radio contact with the following car. Twenty men would flood the area the minute Birmingham got out of the cab. At 108th Street, Birmingham paid the driver and got out of the taxi. A call went to Enders.

Alex and Aikman drove to Enders' office. Aikman mumbled an apology, and the three sat in silence. An open band on Enders' police radio brought constant reports.

Birmingham was walking around.

Old brownstones, small shops, garbage cans, a grocery . . . behind him the roar of cars on the West Side Highway. The streets were poorly lit and practically deserted. A few young men strolled from bar to bar; an old woman pulled a metal cart piled high with laundry. Steel grilles covered the windows of a pawn shop and a hardware store. A flash of brilliant red light from the neon sign at the corner: Food, Beer . . . Food, Beer.

An occasional car rolled past, windows shut tightly against the cold. Birmingham glanced left and right and dug his hands deeper into the pockets of his overcoat.

A blind beggar rattled a tin cup at him as he passed, and Birmingham smiled to himself.

Got it, he thought.

"He's heading back downtown," the voice in Enders' phone said.

"Call me the minute he gets to his apartment," Enders ordered. He put down the phone. "A scouting expedition," he said to Aikman. "Maybe tomorrow night . . . "

Alex stayed with Enders. Aikman went home.

Birmingham had the target, and the next night he left his apartment and walked downtown. He turned east on Fifty-third Street, continued to Second Avenue, and walked up the steps of a brownstone on the corner. He let himself into an apartment on the first floor.

A plainclothes cop walked past the doorway, glanced in, and moved on, finally stopping on the next corner.

From a radio car across the street, a detective called

Enders' office. "He just went into a building on Fifty-third Street on the corner of Second Avenue."

"He's going for the gun," Enders said to Gregory, who stood by the desk. "It's going to be tonight."

The surveillance team watched the front door, but when the man in the shabby overcoat walked out of the building, they paid little attention. He was halfway up the block, moving toward Third Avenue, when the plainclothesman on the street realized what had happened.

The walk was the same, the height, the build . . .

He dashed to the car and opened the door. "That's him, that's him," he said to the men inside. "He's changed clothes and he's got a beard, but it's him." The driver reached for the microphone.

A car on Second Avenue started up, turned onto Fifty-third, and passed Birmingham. At the end of the block, at Third Avenue, a detective watched as Birmingham walked down the steps of a subway station. The cop ran to the entrance.

He almost lost him in the subway. By the time he bought the token and reached the platform, Birmingham was on the train. The cop ran through the doors and moved forward through two cars as the subway rolled uptown. At every stop he darted out on the platform, then quickly back into the train when he didn't see the tall figure in the overcoat.

Birmingham changed trains at Columbus Circle and finally left the subway at the Cathedral Parkway stop. His left hand patted the overcoat, felt the bulk of the gun in his shoulder holster, the length of the silencer fitting through the special cutout he'd designed.

Enders had the area sealed. He couldn't sit still, and he wished he were on the street with his men, with Parker, who'd insisted on covering Birmingham tonight.

Birmingham had to have the gun . . . changing his appearance was proof that he was going to hit tonight, and the gun had to have come from that apartment on Fifty-third Street. The officer on the surveillance team had seen the door close on an apartment on the first-floor hallway, and Enders had phoned the information to Alex. When they were ready, they'd have their search warrant.

Birmingham stopped in front of the blind beggar, dropped a quarter in the man's tin cup, and took a pencil. The bent old man shook the cup and tapped his cane on the sidewalk. "Thank ya, thank ya," he mumbled. Matted gray hair stuck out from under his cap, and he wore a bright yellow slicker and torn woolen gloves.

Birmingham went into the bar on the corner. He ordered a drink and pocketed the yellow pencil, smiling. He had his trophy.

The cop behind the wheel of the surveillance car shut the engine off. They were diagonally across the street from the bar, a hundred yards away. The driver lit a cigarette and reached for the Thermos bottle. "If he's in there long, we'll freeze our butts off," he grumbled to the huddled figures in the back seat. "Have some coffee."

He passed the Thermos back and tossed two paper cups after it. He rubbed his sleeve along the fogged side window and settled back to wait.

The backup car pulled into the street, and three plain-clothesmen got out. One man separated from the others and moved through an alley to the rear entrance of the bar.

One man stood in the dark doorway of a building across the street, and the second went into the bar.

The driver of the surveillance car smiled. Tighter than the old drum.

Alex sat at Aikman's desk in his study, talking on the phone with an officer on duty at the DA's office. She watched Aikman get up from the couch and walk to the window. He stared out, puffing on his cigarette.

"Who's on the bench tonight?" Alex asked the officer. She smiled at the reply and said, "Good, he's reasonable when it comes to warrants . . . okay, thanks . . . I may be down later." She hung up and went back to the warrants spread out on the desk, carefully wording the requests to search the club and the apartment on Fifty-third Street.

"Why are you bothering with that now?" Aikman asked her.

"It's got to be done, sooner or later."

"You don't know he'll try it tonight."

"I'll fill in everything but the date," she smiled.

Aikman nodded, mumbling, "It'll probably be to-night . . ."

From the small table in the crowded bar, Birmingham watched through the window as the blind beggar began to tap his way down the street, moving west. The yellow slicker seemed to glow in the lights from the streetlamps.

Birmingham got up and left the bar.

He paced himself behind the beggar, studying the slow, labored walk. Ahead was an alley . . . Birmingham glanced around: a few parked cars, no one on the street . . . in the silence the tapping of the cane was a series of sharp, distinct clicks.

The blind man stepped off the curb and passed the entrance of the alley, but his cane missed the curb on the other side and he stumbled, the cup turning in his hand and spilling its coins and pencils on the street.

Birmingham moved up behind the man, shoved him into the alley, and drew the gun. He pushed the man again, throwing him deeper into darkness, and as the beggar opened his mouth to scream, Birmingham brought the gun up.

"Not one move," a voice exploded behind him, and Birmingham froze. "Put the gun down on the ground," the voice commanded. "Slowly . . . slowly . . . I'd just love to blow your fucking head off." Birmingham bent and laid the .45 on the pavement. He straightened and turned.

Graham Parker stood at the mouth of the alley, crouching, both hands on his .38.

The jangle of the phone broke the silence in the study, and Aikman snatched the receiver before the second ring.

Enders' voice seemed to come through a tunnel. "We got him, Noah. Just a few minutes ago, on 105th Street. He was going after a blind man."

"He didn't . . . ?"

"No, the guy's alive. Parker stopped him as he was going to fire."

"What color?"

"Has to be yellow. The blind guy's got a bright yellow raincoat on. Birmingham shoved him into an alley, but Parker was in the car down the block . . . it was close."

"Where are you?" Aikman asked.

"At my office. They're bringing him in here. Is Alex there?"

"Yeah," Aikman said. "You want to talk . . . ?"

"Tell her to move on the warrants. The apartment on Fifty-third is covered and we've got men at Clarkson Manor. Lyle and Marcus are at home. All we need are the warrants."

THE RANDOM FACTOR

"Okay, I'll tell her," Aikman said, nodding to Alex, who stood in the doorway of the study with her coat on. "Anything on Reynolds?"

"No," Enders said. "Everything's covered . . . "

"Yeah, just like the surveillance . . . "

"Noah, let's not go around on that again," Enders said.

"I'm sorry."

"Tell Alex there's a car on the way to your place. They'll take her to the DA's office for the warrants."

"Yeah, I know," Aikman said.

"Noah," Enders said, "we'll get Reynolds."

"I know," Aikman said without conviction. "Thanks for calling . . . " He hung up. "They're sending a car."

Alex nodded. "Anything on Reynolds?"

"They've got everything covered," Aikman said sarcastically.

"He's hiding out somewhere, waiting," Alex said.

"Maybe," Aikman said.

"What else could he do? Do you think he's out of the city?"

"I don't know . . . " Aikman shrugged.

"What would you do if you were Reynolds?"

"I'd get away," he said.

"We're back where we started."

"But there's more to it," Aikman said. "He knew we were on to him, but he didn't tell the others. He let Birmingham walk into a trap . . . and Lyle and Marcus are at home; they have no idea what's going on. He wanted them to be caught. His ego . . . he gets away and they get life in prison."

"He wins," Alex said.

"He wins," Aikman said, staring at her. "That's it: he has to win. Jesus . . . that's got to be it. It's not enough for him to run, to escape . . . not with his ego. He'd have to win. He'd have to have the last laugh."

310

They heard the screech of tires and the blast of a horn, and Alex kissed him lightly on the cheek. "Got to run," she said.

"Yeah," Aikman answered, staring after her as she left the apartment.

Enders edged away from the confusion in his office. Phones rang incessantly. At the DA's office, the other deputy chiefs waited for Alex and the warrants. Once they were signed by the judge, Clarkson Manor and the apartment on Fifty-third Street would be searched; Gregory and Ellison would pick up Marcus; Holtzman and Lawrence would take Lyle.

Down the hall, Birmingham was being booked for attempted murder and the pistol was on its way to Ballistics for tests.

Enders walked across the hall to the detective squad room, where Cross and McQuade were trying to calm the sniveling beggar so they could get a statement. Enders didn't know how they could stand being so close to him. He smelled like last week's garbage, and his face was covered with smears, smudges, and stubble.

Harmon hovered nearby, jotting down notes, filling in the details for his exclusive story. For the past week he had been Enders' shadow, practically living in the deputy chief's office.

"McQuade," Enders shouted. The squat detective stood up and came over to the doorway. "Get him out of here, will you? I can't stand that whining anymore. He can't identify Birmingham; he's useless. Tell him the sooner he gives a statement, the sooner he can go home."

Enders turned away in disgust. They didn't need the beggar. They had the gun, they had Birmingham on attempted murder. Within the hour, they'd have it all.

Except Reynolds.

At first, Aikman dismissed it. It was too outrageous, too nervy. But as he stood at the window and let it play in his mind, he became convinced.

There *was* a way for Reynolds to win the whole game . . .

Aikman grabbed the phone and dialed.

"Thirty-fourth precinct, Sergeant Roth . . . "

"This is Aikman. Give me Carl Enders . . . no, hold it." What if I'm wrong? he thought. And Enders is too involved, too emotional about Reynolds. Aikman grinned slightly, thinking: And I'm not? "Give me Graham Parker," he finally said to the sergeant.

It would have been easy for Aikman to tell Parker what he suspected and let the detective take it from there. But Aikman had to see it through. He had to be there. When Parker picked up the phone Aikman rattled off instructions. "I'll meet you in ten minutes," Aikman said; he hung up, grabbed his coat, and left the apartment.

Slowly, deliberately, Reynolds walked down Amsterdam Avenue. He slipped his free hand into the pocket of the loose-fitting coat and touched the butt of the .45. It had been close. A split-second's difference and he would've had to use it. Even now, he was prepared to shoot his way out.

He smiled to himself as he walked. His planning had carried him through again. He had anticipated and outmaneuvered the enemy. The Ninety-sixth Street subway station was only a few blocks away, and he would win.

Aikman hunched forward in the back seat of the cab as the driver took the curves of the Central Park Transverse, roared out of the park on 66th Street, and crossed to Amsterdam Avenue. The driver ran the red light and turned uptown. Aikman's twenty-dollar bill lay on the seat next to him.

The blocks rushed past as the cab swerved around cars. Into the seventies, the eighties . . . the cab slipped to the far left lane on Eighty-eighth Street and continued on, crossing Ninety-second moments later at forty miles an hour. The traffic light at Ninety-sixth turned red, and a truck crossed in front of them. Aikman's driver slammed on the brakes. The truck rumbled across the intersection, and as the driver started up, Aikman caught something from the corner of his eye. He glanced to his left. "Hold it," he shouted at the driver.

At the end of the block on Ninety-sixth Street, he saw Christopher Reynolds walking slowly to the subway station.

"Go up to the corner of 106th," Aikman said as he shoved the back door open. "There's a black cop waiting there; name's Parker. Tell him Aikman—you got that? Aikman—is following Reynolds into the Ninety-sixth Street subway." Aikman ripped another twenty from his wallet and shoved it into the driver's hand through the open window. "You've got to help me," Aikman said quickly. "My life's on the line."

"Yeah, sure," the driver answered uncertainly.

"Remember, Aikman is following Reynolds, Ninety-sixth Street station. Bring the cop back." Aikman loped halfway down Ninety-sixth, saw Reynolds was gone and ran the rest of the way to the south-side subway entrance.

The cab screeched to a stop at the corner. The driver rolled down the window and shouted at the black man. "Hey, you Parker?"

313

Parker moved toward the car. "Yeah . . . "

"This crazy guy sent me up here, told me to tell you that Aikman is following Reynolds into the subway at Ninety-sixth . . . "

Parker jerked the back door open. "Go," he said.

C'mon Parker, goddamnit, Aikman swore to himself, as he stood in the darkness at the far end of the subway station. Reynolds was standing at the center of the platform waiting for a train. Aikman had gambled, taken the downtown steps, and seen Reynolds moving along the platform. Aikman ran back up and sprinted to the opposite end of the station, taking the stairs slowly, silently, so that he'd be ahead of Reynolds, not behind him. If Parker gets here in time, we'll have him between us, he thought.

And if Parker doesn't? Aikman wondered. Could he chance following Reynolds onto the train?

On the uptown side of the station, a young couple waited for the subway, arms linked together, half leaning against the gum machine. On the downtown side, Reynolds stood alone, in the open, about five feet back from the edge. The station was cold, drafty, and Aikman rubbed his gloved hands together.

From the tunnel he heard the rumble of a train. He prayed it was the uptown subway . . .

The downtown express slowed to a rattling stop, and the doors slid open. Reynolds smiled to himself as he walked casually and without hurry toward the train. He'd won.

"Reynolds!" Aikman shouted.

It slipped out without conscious thought. He had to keep Reynolds in the station until Parker got there. If he followed him onto the train he'd be isolated, and Reynolds would be in control.

Aikman shouted again. "Turn around, Reynolds . . . "

Reynolds brought the gun out as he turned toward the tall figure ten yards away.

"Aikman? How in hell . . . ?"

He swung the gun up.

Parker heard Aikman's voice echo through the tunnel and pulled up at the top of the stairs. He opened his coat, took his gun out, and silently descended the steps, two at a time, peering ahead along the platform. Toward the far end, the blind beggar stood, and beyond him, Aikman.

Can't be . . . not the beggar . . .

But it had to be. With the gun gripped tightly in his hands, Parker moved forward.

"Reynolds . . . drop it," Parker shouted, sighting along the barrel at Reynolds' head.

Reynolds flashed a glance behind him.

The cop, the cop who got Birmingham . . . but one man, not the whole police force . . . not an army.

Control . . . I'm still in control here. "I'll kill him where he stands. Put your gun down on the platform." Reynolds' voice was icy, the words snapped off. "Put it down. I'll kill . . ."

The shots exploded in Aikman's ears. Parker's first bullet caught Reynolds in the side of the head and spun him around. Parker kept firing, emptying the gun into Reynolds' chest, neck, and shoulders. The body slammed back against the closed doors of the moving train, jerked convulsively forward, and collapsed to the platform.

Aikman stood frozen as Parker moved slowly to the body.

"Turkey," Parker hissed, staring down. The yellow slicker was blotched with red stains. The .45 lay near the edge of the platform. "It only happens that way on television, turkey." Aikman, pale and breathing too hard, stepped toward him, his legs shaky.

"You didn't think I'd let him take two hostages, did you?" Parker asked.

Aikman shook his head.

Softly, Parker asked, "You didn't think I'd let him kill you?"

"No," Aikman managed.

"But you weren't sure," Parker grinned.

"No," Aikman said.

"How'd you know it was him?"

Aikman took a deep breath. "It was the only way he could win," he said slowly, moving away from the body. "No one would ever suspect the last intended victim. He'd beat us all, right under our noses."

"He couldn't resist the challenge," Parker nodded. "I got to hand it to you, Professor."

"He almost made it," Aikman said, shaking his head.

"Almost doesn't count," Parker muttered. He heard sirens from the street. "The cavalry's always arriving after the fact."

Aikman started to walk toward the steps. He stopped, picked up the white cane, and tossed it to Parker.

The detective snatched it out of the air. "Stick around," he smiled.

Aikman shook his head. "The game's over."

Acknowledgments

The authors are grateful for the help, co-operation, and encouragement of:

> *Mary A. Barraco*, Engineer, AIL/CUTLER HAMMER
> *James Ceniglio*, a friend and military buff
> *Kevin Gilleece*, Bureau Chief, Homicide, Bronx County, New York
> *Mario Merola*, District Attorney, Bronx County, New York
> *Detective Thomas Mullins*, assigned to the DA's Squad, Bronx County, New York
> *Neil Solomon, Ph.D.*, Director of Family Therapy, Hempstead Consultation Service
> *Nathan Rosenblatt*, Senior Assistant District Attorney, Homicide Bureau, Bronx County, New York

The authors and publishers of THE RANDOM FACTOR acknowledge that PARCHEESI is a registered trademark of Selchow & Righter Company for its royal game of India and is used with permission.

Thanks also to:

Walter Bradbury, Don Congdon, Cheryl Diamond, Steve Feldman, Alan and Pat Fischler, Professor Paul S. Graziano, Ralph and Joan Hochberg, Miriam La-

Rosa, Jim Leggett, Bob Lehmann, Bob Lichtman, Bob Moskowitz, Bruce Stark, and Don Sutherland.

And, last but not least, appreciation of a very special sort to The Management.

THE VAN RHYNE HERITAGE

BY LOUISA BRONTE

The family that became a railroad dynasty, driven to greatness by daring dreams and bold desires...

THE VAN RHYNES—

They began on a humble dirt farm and became the millionaire titans of the industrial age. A family like no other, a law unto themselves, they would stop at nothing to win the golden prizes of ambition and desire.

With ruthless courage and pride, they built an unshakable dynasty and forged an American empire of passion and steel.

B12043105 $2.25

Available wherever paperbacks are sold

Second volume in
THE AMERICAN DYNASTY SERIES
launched by THE VALLETTE HERITAGE.

NT-35

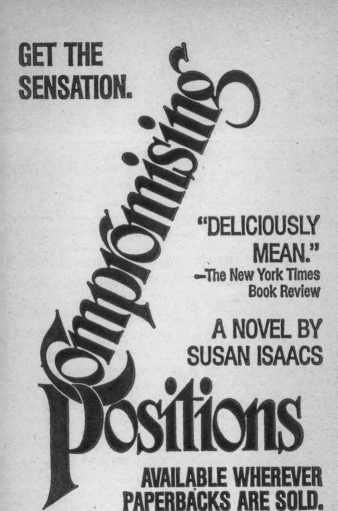